W9-CIN-390

THE APPRENTICESHIP
OF DUDDY KRAVITZ

"The work of an assured novelist . . .
a book of great originality and considerable stature."

—Penelope Mortimer

"There can be no doubt of Richler's
prodigal talent."
—Times Literary Supplement,
London

About the author . . .

Mordecai Richler was born in Montreal, the
child of a Jewish family from Russia and Poland. He published his first novel, **The Acrobats,** in 1954 at the age of 22. Now established
as one of the most brilliant writers of his generation, Richler's other novels are **Son of a
Smaller Hero** (1955), **A Choice of Enemies**
(1957), **The Apprenticeship of Duddy Kravitz**
(1959), **The Incomparable Atuk** (1963),
Cocksure (1968), and **St. Urbain's Horseman**
(1971). He has published two collections of
essays, **Hunting Tigers Under Glass** (1968)
and **Shovelling Trouble** (1972), as well as a
collection of stories, **The Street** (1969).

PARAMOUNT PICTURES PRESENTS
A Ted Kotcheff Film
THE APPRENTICESHIP OF DUDDY KRAVITZ
SCREENPLAY BY MORDECAI RICHLER
based on his novel

STARRING:
RICHARD DREYFUSS / MICHELINE LANCTOT
RANDY QUAID / JOSEPH WISEMAN
DENHOLM ELLIOTT / HENRY RAMER
JOE SILVER / and JACK WARDEN as MAX

Directed by: TED KOTCHEFF
Produced by: JOHN KEMENY
Executive Producer: GERALD SCHNEIDER
Adaptation by: LIONEL CHETWYND
Director of Photography: BRIAN WEST
Film Editor: THOM NOBLE
Casting: LYNN STALMASTER
Production Designer: ANNE PRITCHARD

The
Apprenticeship
of
Duddy Kravitz

Mordecai Richler

BALLANTINE BOOKS • NEW YORK

For Florence

Copyright, 1959, by Mordecai Richler

All rights reserved.

Library of Congress Catalog Card Number: 59-11885

SBN 345-24154-1-150

First Printing: July, 1974

Printed in the United States of America

BALLANTINE BOOKS
A Division of Random House, Inc.
201 East 50th Street, New York, N.Y. 10022

One

What with his wife so ill these past few weeks and the prospect of three more days of teaching before the weekend break, Mr. MacPherson felt unusually glum. He trudged along St. Dominique Street to within sight of the school. Because it was early and he wanted to avoid the Masters' Room, he paused for an instant in the snow. When he had first seen that building some twenty years ago, he had shut his eyes and asked that his work as a schoolmaster be blessed with charity and achievement. He had daydreamed about the potential heritage of his later years, former students—now lawyers or doctors or M.P.'s—gathering in his parlor on Sunday evenings to lament the lost hockey games of twenty years ago. But for some time now Mr. MacPherson had felt nothing about the building. He couldn't describe it or tell you how to get there any more than he could forget that Shelley's *Ode to the West Wind* was on page 89 of *Highroads to Reading*, the central idea being the poet's dedication to a free and natural spirit.

Since he had first come to the school in 1927—a tight-lipped young Scot with a red fussy face—many of Mr. MacPherson's earliest students had, indeed, gone on to make their reputations in medicine, politics, and business, but there were no nostalgic gatherings at his home. The sons of his first students would not attend Fletcher's Field High School, either. For making their way in the world his first students had also graduated from the streets of cold-water flats that surrounded F.F.H.S. to buy their own duplexes in the tree-lined streets of Outremont. In fact, that morning, as Mr. MacPherson hesitated on a scalp of glittering white ice, there were already three Gentiles in the school (that is to say, Anglo-Saxons; for Ukrainians, Poles, and Yugoslavs, with funny names and customs of their own, did not count as true Gentiles), and ten years hence F.F.H.S. would no longer be *the* Jewish high school. At the time, however, most Jewish boys in Montreal who had been to high school had gone to F.F.H.S. and, consequently, had studied history out of *The World's Progress (Revised)* with John Alexander MacPherson; and every old graduate had an anecdote to tell about him.

Mr. MacPherson's most celebrated former student—Jerry Dingleman, the Boy Wonder—liked to tell the one about the merit cards.

Once Mr. MacPherson tried giving out merit cards to his students for such virtues as exceptionally high examination results, good behavior, and neat writing. Each month he collected the cards and gave the boy who had earned the most of them the afternoon off from school. But at the end of the third month it was Jerry Dingleman who stood up to claim and, on demand, produce a suspiciously high stack of soiled merit cards. Now Mr. MacPherson knew that he had never awarded Dingleman, a most inattentive and badly behaved boy, one single card. On the threat of a week's suspension from school Dingleman confessed that he had won all the cards playing nearest-to-the-wall with the other boys in the toilet, and so the system ended.

Many of the other anecdotes, especially the more recent (and vastly exaggerated) ones, had to do with Mr. MacPherson's drinking habits. It was true that by 1947 he was a heavy drinker, though he was certainly not, as they say, a problem. He was still much slimmer than his first students, but his face seemed more bitingly angry and the curly black hair had grayed. Mr. MacPherson was more inclined to stoop, but, as on his first day at F.F.H.S., he still wore the brim of his battered little gray fedora turned down, rain or shine, spoke with a thick Scots accent, and had yet to strap a boy.

If Mr. MacPherson had altered somewhat with the years, the school building had remained exactly the same.

Fletcher's Field High School was five stories high, like the Style-Kraft building that flanked it on one side and the tenement on the other. Across the street at Stein's the bare-chested bakers worked with the door open even during the winter and, at school recess time, were fond of winking at the boys outside and wiping the sweat from under their armpits with an unbaked kimel bread before tossing it into the oven. Except for the cracked asphalt courtyard to the right of the school, separating it from the tenement, there was little to distinguish this building from the others.

There were, of course, the students.

At that moment several of the older boys leaned against Felder's frosted window. The biggest sign in Felder's tiny tenement store, DON'T BUY FROM THE GOYISHE CHIP MAN—FELDER IS YOUR FRIEND FOR LIFE, was no longer needed. The last time the chip man, an intrepid French-Canadian, had

8

passed with his horse and wagon the boys, led by Duddy Kravitz, had run him off the street.

Duddy Kravitz was a small, narrow-chested boy of fifteen with a thin face. His black eyes were ringed with dark circles and his pale, bony cheeks were crisscrossed with scratches, as he shaved twice daily in his attempt to encourage a beard. Duddy was president of Room 41.

"Hey, guess what," Samuels shouted, running up to the boys. "Mr. Horner's not coming back. He's got triple pneumonia or something. So we're getting a new class master. Mac, of all people."

"Mac'll be a breeze," Duddy said, lighting a cigarette. "He never straps or nothing. Mac believes in *per*-suasion."

Only Hersh failed to laugh. "We're lucky to get Mac," he said, "so let's not take advantage like."

Mr. MacPherson didn't want to cross the street in order to chastise the smokers, but the boys had clearly seen him.

"Weasel! Can the cigs. Here comes Mac himself."

"I should care," Duddy said.

"Kravitz! Put out that cigarette immediately."

"My father is aware that I smoke, sir."

"Then he's not fit to bring up a boy."

"He's my father, sir."

"Would you like to stay on in this school, Kravitz?"

"Yes, sir. But he's my father, sir."

"Then let's not have any more of your cheekiness. Put out that cigarette immediately."

"Yes, sir."

No sooner had Mr. MacPherson turned his back on them than Duddy began to hum "Coming Through the Rye." But, turning sharply into the boys' side of the courtyard, Mr. MacPherson guessed that he was far enough away to pretend that he hadn't heard.

"Boy, are you ever lucky," Hersh said. "Horner would've strapped you ten on each."

Mr. MacPherson began to climb the icy concrete steps that led into the school. When he was on the last step a high-pitched shriek rose among the students. He felt a plunk on the back of his neck as the snowball smashed to smithereens just above his coat collar. Particles of snow began to trace a chilling pattern down his back. Mr. MacPherson whirled about and turned on the students, knitting his eyebrows in an attempt at ferocity. An innocent bustle filled the courtyard. Nobody looked at him. Mr. MacPherson fled into the dark

9

stuffy school building. His horn-rimmed glasses fogged immediately. Ripping them off, he prepared to be vile in class all day.

Duddy Kravitz bobbed up in the middle of a group of boys. "How's that for pitching?" he asked.

"Oh, big hero. You didn't mean to hit him. You meant to hit me," Hersh said.

"Mighty neat, anyway," Samuels said.

The bell rang.

"Nobody gets away with insulting my old man," Duddy said.

When Mr. MacPherson entered Room 41 a few minutes later he was no stranger there. This was his first day as class master, but he already taught the boys history three times weekly and so knew them all by name and deed. Some, it should be said, stayed in Room 41 longer than others, par for the course being two years, grades ten and eleven.

The undisputed record-holding resident of Room 41 was, in 1947, still there. His name was Stanley Blatt, but everybody called him A.D. because, in flunking one among hundreds of oral exams, he had permanently endeared himself to the school inspector by insisting that A.D. stood for After the Depression. A.D., already sporting a mustache, had first entered Room 41 and found it was good in 1942, and there he had rested, but not nonstop, for he had served three years in the merchant marine during the war.

Room 41 had a reputation for being the toughest class in the school. There were those, Mr. MacPherson knew, who thought he was too soft a replacement for Horner. Only yesterday Mr. Jackson had said, "You shouldn't have put John at the mercy of Kravitz and Co. He's in no shape to cope these days."

"He's right, Leonard. Poor John hasn't stepped out of the house once since Jenny took ill."

"I've got a feeling he's usually up half the night with her, too."

"You should have given me Room 41," Mr. Coldwell had said with appetite. "I would have strapped plenty of respect into Kravitz."

The boys had been unusually quiet when Mr. MacPherson had entered Room 41 after the first bell. On the blackboard, drawn in a clumsy hand, was the chalk figure of a lean man being crushed by a snowball. Underneath was the inscription

10

OUR MAC. Mr. MacPherson contrived to appear calm. "Who did it? Whose filthy work is this?" Fully expecting the answering quiet, he smacked his copy of *The World's Progress (Revised)* against the desk and sat down. "We shall remain seated until the coward who has done this owns up."

Ten minutes passed in silence before somebody giggled in the back row. Mr. MacPherson whipped out his attendance book. "Hersh, erase the boards."

"But it wasn't me, sir. I should drop down dead it wasn't me."

Small, squinting Hersh was the butt of the class. His undoing had been a demonstration against the rise in the price of chocolate bars. A photograph on the back page of the *Telegram* had shown Hersh, his attempt to hide behind taller members of the Young Communist League unsuccessful, holding high a placard that read DOWN WITH THE 7¢ CHOCOLATE BAR.

"Erase the boards, Hersh."

Mr. MacPherson called out the names in his attendance book, asking each boy if he was responsible for the "outrage" on the board, and eventually he bit into Kravitz's name with special distaste.

"Present, sir."

"Kravitz, are you responsible for this?"

"For what, sir?"

"For the drawing on the board."

"Partly, sir."

"What do you mean, partly? Either you are responsible or you are not responsible."

"Sir, it's like—"

"Stand up when you talk to me. Impudent!"

"Yes, sir. If you want to know the truth we're all responsible like. But we only meant it for a joke, sir."

"Do you mean to insinuate that I haven't got a sense of humor?"

"Well, sir . . ."

"Answer my question."

"No, sir."

"All right, then, whose idea was this little prank?"

"I'm telling you we're all responsible."

"Was it your idea?"

No answer.

"This class will not go to the basketball game this afternoon, but will stay in for an hour after school is out. And you, Kravitz, will do the same tomorrow and the next day."

"That's not fair, sir."

"Are you telling me what's fair?"

"No, sir. But why am I different from everybody else?"

"I don't know, Kravitz. You tell me."

Mr. MacPherson smiled thinly. Everybody laughed.

"Aw, sir. Gee whiz."

"This class may do anything it likes for the next period. I absolutely refuse to teach the likes of you."

"Anything, sir?"

"Look here, Kravitz, you're a brat and an exhibitionist. I'm—"

"You said my father wasn't fit to bring me up. I've got witnesses. That's an insult to my family, sir."

"—not going to strap you, though. I won't give you that satisfaction. But—"

"You think it's a pleasure or something to be strapped? Jeez."

"—I know you're responsible for the drawing on the board and I think it cowardly of you not to have taken complete responsibility."

"*I'm* a coward. Who's afraid to strap who around here?"

"I'm not afraid to strap you, Kravitz. I don't believe in corporal punishment."

"Sure."

"*Sir.*"

"Sure, sir."

Outside, Duddy slapped Abrams on the back. "Mac is gonna wish he was never born," he said. "It's the treatment for him."

The treatment took more than one form. With Mr. Jackson, who wore a hearing aid, the boys spoke softer and softer in class until all they did was move their lips in a pretense of speech and Mr. Jackson raised his hearing aid to its fullest capacity. Then all thirty-eight boys shouted out at once and Mr. Jackson fled the physics lab holding his hands to his ears. The boys retaliated against Mr. Coldwell by sending movers, taxis, and ambulances to his door. Mr. Feeney was something else again. He would seize on each new boy and ask him, "Do you know what the Jewish national anthem is?"

"No, sir."

So Mr. Feeney would go to the board and write, "To the Bank, to the Bank."

"Do you know how the Jews make an *S?*"

"No, sir."

Mr. Feeney would go to the board, make an *S,* and draw two

strokes through it. Actually, he meant his jokes in a friendly spirit and the sour reactions he usually got puzzled him. Anyway, the boys got even with Mr. Feeney by filling out coupons for books that came in plain brown wrappers with his daughter's name and, with cruel accuracy, by writing away for bust developers for his wife.

Duddy pretended he was dialing a number on the telephone. "Hey! Hullo, hullo. Is Mac in? Hey, Mac? Em, this is the Avenger speaking. Yep, none other. Your days are numbered, Mac."

The boys split up. Those who had after-school jobs, like Hersh, went one way and the others, led by Duddy Kravitz, wandered up towards Park Avenue.

To a middle-class stranger, it's true, one street would have seemed as squalid as the next. On each corner a cigar store, a grocery, and a fruit man. Outside staircases everywhere. Winding ones, wooden ones, rusty and risky ones. Here a prized plot of grass splendidly barbered, there a spitefully weedy patch. An endless repetition of precious peeling balconies and waste lots making the occasional gap here and there. But, as the boys knew, each street between St. Dominique and Park Avenue represented subtle differences in income. No two cold-water flats were alike. Here was the house where the fabulous Jerry Dingleman was born. A few doors away lived Buddy Ash, who ran for alderman each election on a one-plank platform: provincial speed cops were anti-Semites. No two stores were the same, either. Best Fruit gypped on the scales, but Smiley's didn't give credit.

Duddy told the boys about his brother Bradley. "I got a letter from him only yesterday aft," he said. "As soon as I'm finished up at Fletcher's Field he wants me to come down to Arizona to help out on the ranch like."

Leaning into the wind, their nostrils sticking together each time they inhaled, Abrams and Samuels exchanged incredulous glances, but didn't dare smile. They were familiar with the exploits of Bradley. He had run away to the States at fifteen, lied about his age, joined the air force, and sunk three Jap battleships in the Pacific. They were going to make a movie about his life, maybe. After the war Bradley had rescued an Arizona millionaire's beautiful daughter from drowning, married her, and bought a ranch. Familiar with all of Bradley's exploits, the boys also suspected that he was a fictional character, but nobody dared accuse Duddy of lying. Duddy was kind of funny, that's all.

"Hey," Abrams shouted. "Look!"

Right there, on St. Joseph Boulevard, was a newly opened mission. The neon sign outside the little shop proclaimed JESUS SAVES in English and Yiddish. Another bilingual sign, this one in the window, announced THE MESSIAH HAS COME, over open copies of the Bible with the appropriate phrases underlined in red.

"Come on, guys," Duddy said.

Somewhat hesitant, the boys nevertheless followed Duddy inside. Trailing snow over the gleaming hardwood floor, they ripped off their stiff frozen gloves and began to examine the pamphlets and blotters that were stacked in piles on the long table. A door rasped behind them.

"Good afternoon." A small rosy-faced man stood before them, rubbing his hands together. "Something I can do for you?"

"We were just passing by," Duddy said. "Hey, are you a Hebe?"

"Of the Jewish faith?"

"Yeah. Are you?"

"I was," the man said, "until I embraced Jesus."

"No kidding! Hey, we guys would like to know all about Jesus. *Isn't that right, guys?*"

"Sure."

"How we could become *goyim*, Christians like."

"Aren't you a little young to—"

"Could we take some of these pamphlets? I mean we'd like to read up on it."

"Certainly."

"Blotters too?" A.D. asked quickly.

"*For keeps?*"

"Of course."

Duddy gave Samuels a nudge. "Hey, sir," he asked, "you ever heard of F.F.H.S.?"

"I'm afraid not."

Duddy told him about it. "I've got an idea for you, sir. Lots of guys there are dying to know about Jesus and stuff. Our parents never tell us anything, you know. So what I'm thinking is why don't you come round at lunchtime tomorrow and hand out some of these *free* pamphlets and stuff to the guys, eh?"

Racing down the street, A.D. goosed Samuels and Duddy pushed Abrams into a snowbank. The boys stopped short outside the Lubovitcher Yeshiva and began to arm themselves with snowballs. "They'll be coming out any minute," Duddy said

14

They had come to torment the rabbinical college students before. During another cold spell they had once given one of the smaller boys the alternative of having his faced washed with snow or licking the grill of the school fence. Stupidly, the boy had chosen to lick the grill. And there he had remained, his tongue adhering to the iron, until medical help had come.

"Here they come, guys!"

"Jesus saves. Read all about it!"

The alarmed students drew back into their school just as the F.F.H.S. boys began to pelt them with pamphlets and snowballs. Two bearded teachers, armed with brooms, charged down the steps and started after the boys. Duddy led the retreat across the street. There, joining arms, the boys marched along, stopping at the corner of Jeanne Mance Street to stuff a mailbox with snow. They sang:

> *Oh, Nellie, put your belly close to mine.*
> *Wiggle your bum.*

2

After he left the school that afternoon Mr. MacPherson decided that rather than getting right on a streetcar, instead of waiting in the cold and fighting for a place in the rush hour, he would go to the Laura Secord Shop to buy a box of chocolates for Jenny. Directly across the street from the shop was the Pines Tavern.

Once in the tavern, Mr. MacPherson was careful to seat himself two tables away from the nearest group of laborers. He decided that he had been morally right to call Kravitz a coward. But after he had delayed his trip to the Laura Secord Shop twice more he admitted to himself that there were more urgent reasons why it had been wrong to insult Kravitz. Tomorrow or the next day the bottle of ink on his desk would be mysteriously overturned. Pencils and sheets of foolscap paper would disappear from his drawers. The boys would be given to fits of coughing or, at a secret signal, would begin to hum "Coming Through the Rye." On his side Mr. MacPherson would bombard the boys with unannounced exams and cancel all athletics, assign at least two hours of homework nightly and suspend a few boys from school for a week, but he would not use the strap.

Long ago Mr. MacPherson had vowed never to strap a boy. The principle itself, like the dream of taking Jenny on a trip to Europe, keeping up with the latest educational books, or saving to buy a house, was dead. But his refusal to strap was still of the greatest consequence to Mr. MacPherson. "There," they'd say, "goes the only teacher in F.F.H.S. who has never strapped a boy." That he no longer believed in not strapping was beside the point. As long as he refused to do it Mr. MacPherson felt that he would always land safely. There would be no crack-up. He would survive.

Outside again, waiting for his streetcar, Mr. MacPherson kept kicking his feet together to keep them from freezing. Flattened against the window by the crush of people in the rear of the streetcar, anxious because the man next to him was sneezing violently, he thought, Another eight years. Eight years more, and he would retire.

Only when he hung his coat up on the hall rack did he realize that he had forgotten to buy that box of chocolates for Jenny. There were two strange coats on the rack. The woman's coat was gray Persian lamb. Briefly Mr. MacPherson considered slipping outside again.

"Is that you, John?"

"Yes."

"Surprise, John. We have visitors. Herbert and Clara Shields."

Ostensibly her voice was cheerfully confident, but Mr. MacPherson was familiar with the cautionary quality in it, and the fear also. Calling out to him, even before he got out of the hall, was a warning. Automatically Mr. MacPherson reached for the package of Sen-Sen he always carried with him. He also lit a cigarette before he entered the bedroom.

Jenny sat up in bed. Her mouth broke into a small, painful smile. Mr. MacPherson smiled back at her reassuringly and averted his eyes quickly. "Hello, Herbert, Clara," he said. "How nice to see you again."

Big, broad Herbert Shields charged out of his seat and grabbed Mr. MacPherson's hand. "You old son of a gun," he said.

"Herbert and Clara are in Montreal for the Pulp and Paper Convention. They're going abroad this summer. Herbert's been made an assistant to the vice-president. Isn't that lovely, John?"

16

"It is indeed. I'm very happy for you, Herbert. How nice of you to remember us. Really, I—"

"Look at him, Herbert," Clara said. "He hasn't changed one bit. He's still our John. I'll bet he thinks we're dreadful. Materialists, or philistines. John, are you still a what-do-you-call-it? A pacifist?"

"You old son of a gun," Herbert said.

The Shieldses had kept in touch with most of the old McGill crowd. Jim McLeod had his own law firm now and was going to stand for parliament. Chuck Adams—Hey, remember the time he sent out invitations to the Engineers' Costume Ball on pink toilet paper? Well, Chuck has finally married Mary. Walsh is Eastern Sales Manager for Atlantic Trucking and Wes Holt is buying up salmon canneries left and right on the West Coast.

Mr. MacPherson knew that Clara would write letters to all of them explaining why they never heard from John. "He's a failure, my dear, absolutely, and the Colby girl, the minister's daughter if you remember, well, she's turned out an invalid."

After the Shieldses had left, first making him promise that he would call them at the Mount Royal Hotel, Mr. MacPherson gave Jenny her medicines. He had meant to work on his history test papers, long overdue, but he was too tired. So, remembering to unhook the phone, he got into bed. He told Jenny about Kravitz.

"But what a rude thing for you to have said about the boy's father. I'm surprised at you, John."

"You ought to meet my boys one day." Mr. MacPherson laughed out loud. He reached over and touched Jenny's forehead. "Good night," he said.

Jenny awakened him around three in the morning, complaining of a nagging pain in her chest. He thought of calling Dr. Hanson. But Dr. Hanson would say that Jenny must get month's rest in the mountains or he wouldn't be held responsible for the consequences, and then he would shake his head, mildly exasperated, and prescribe the usual sedatives, so Mr. MacPherson administered the sedatives himself.

"Would you like me to read to you for a while?" he asked.

"Thanks, anyway, John. But I think I'll be able to sleep."

Mr. MacPherson sat down in his armchair and passed the night overlooking her difficult sleep, squeezing his hands together whenever she coughed.

Duddy didn't get home until after seven o'clock. His father was out, but he found Lennie in the bedroom.

"Hi!"

"Duddy," Lennie said, "how many times have I asked you not to barge in here when I'm studying?"

Duddy's face flushed.

"Look, Duddy, half the guys who flunk out do it in their second year. Anatomy's the big killer. Your supper's on the kitchen table."

Duddy ate his frankfurters and beans standing up, poured himself a glass of milk, and returned to the bedroom. "We got a new class master today," he said. "Mac, of all people."

No answer.

"Hey, guess what? I heard a rumor that a sort of mission's opened up on St Joseph Boulevard and the jerk who runs it is going to hand out pamphlets and stuff at F.F.H.S. Isn't that an insult to our religion like? I think somebody oughta complain."

"Look, Duddy, I really must get back to work."

Duddy jumped up. "You don't have to worry about your fees next year. I'm going to get a job as a waiter up north for the summer and you can have all my tips." Embarrassed, he fled.

"Duddy!"

"I know," Duddy said, half into his coat. "Uncle Benjy is gonna take care of your fees."

"I think I'm going to be free Saturday afternoon. You want to come to the movies with us?"

"Aw, Riva wouldn't like it. I'd be a fifth wheel like."

It's true, Lennie thought, and come Saturday morning he'd regret that he had asked Duddy to join them. "You're coming with us, that's definite."

"Sure."

"Hey, where are you going?"

"I'm invited to a musical evening at Mr. Cox's house. All the guys are."

Young Mr. Cox, the newest teacher in the school, was, in Duddy's opinion, the World's No. 1 Crap Artist. Once he had dropped into Irving's Poolroom after school to talk to the boys

—a terrifying intrusion. Another crazy thing he had done had been to come to the Students' Council tea dance in the gym ne day—not *so* crazy when you remember that he danced aree slow numbers with Birdie Lyman. But, wackiest of all, e invited the boys round regularly for musicales. Mr. Cox's ausic was a bore. But there were plenty of Cokes, hot dogs ometimes, and lots of laughs. Best, of course, was Mrs. Cox, ho was always chasing after you with questions like are you alous of your younger sister and how do you feel about re-ricted hotels, as if their parents could afford them.

After the second musicale Mrs. Cox tried to do something out the boys' language. "I know very well," she said, "that ou only use those words for their shock value and that's silly, ecause you can't shock me. You ought to know the *correct* ords, anyway. We can begin by naming the parts of the body. o you all know what a penis is?"

"Sure," Duddy said. "A pinus is a guy that plays the piano."

That ended the language lessons, but not the quarrels about ane Cox. One night the boys detected the shadowy shape of a unmistakably black lace brassiere under Jane's white cot-n blouse and this prompted Duddy to observe, "A broad ho wears a black brassiere means business."

"Maybe it wasn't black, smart guy. Maybe it was just a dirty nk one."

At this Duddy howled derisively.

"O.K.," Tannenbaum said, "it's black, let's say, but she uld wear it only for her husband's sake."

"She wouldn't need it for Cox, you jerk, because he can see er *completely* naked any times he feels like it."

This silenced everybody but Hersh. "You have to make erything dirty. Nothing's good for you unless you can make dirty."

That night, while the others were pretending to listen to a mphony, Duddy slipped out into the hall to examine the okcases. He did not notice Jane Cox hovering over his shoul-r until she coughed. Blushing, he shut the book quickly and treated. "I was reading a book, that's all. I wasn't stealing nything."

"But nobody accused you of stealing anything." She picked the book—*U.S.A.* by Dos Passos. "Do you usually read ch heavy stuff?" she asked with a faint smile.

"Why not, eh? You think I have to be a moron just because y old man is a taxi driver? My brother's studying to be a doc-r. I read lots of books."

"Are you sure," Jane asked, still smiling, "that you didn't

pick up this book simply because you were looking for . .
sexy passages?"

"Look, I'm not the kind of a shmo who has to get his se
secondhand."

Jane brought her hand to her mouth, suppressing a giggle
"Don't be alarmed. When I was your age I used to flip throug
modern novels for the same reason. It's normal. You're ju
at the age when a boy becomes aware of all the secret power
of his body."

"Oh, will you leave me alone? Will you please leave m
alone?"

Duddy rushed into the bedroom, grabbed his coat, and ra
down the stairs. Outside, it was snowing and he had to wait
long time for a streetcar. He sat down on the seat over th
heater and melting snow ran down his neck. Later, he thoug
Jane would tell Shmo-face Cox about catching him with tha
dirty book. Tomorrow Cox would repeat the story in the Ma
ters' Room and everybody would have a good laugh at his ex
pense. The hell with them, Duddy thought. He walked up t
Eddy's Cigar & Soda, across the street from the Triangle Ta
Stand, and there he found his father drinking coffee with som
of the other men. Josette was there, too.

"Duddy," Max said gruffly. "I thought you'd be home i
bed by this time." Turning to the others with a wide smile, h
added, "You all know my kid."

"That's Lennie?" Drapeau asked.

Max laughed expansively. "Ixnay. He's not gonna be a sav
bones. Duddy's a dope like me. Aren't you, kid?" He rumple
the boy's snow-caked hair. "Lennie's twenty-one. He's ha
scholarships all through school."

A big man, burly and balding, with soft brown eyes and a
adorable smile, Max Kravitz was inordinately proud of th
fact that he had, several years ago, been dubbed Max the Had
in *Mel West's What's What*, Moey Weinstein's column in th
Telegram, and that, as a consequence, he (along with West
most puerile Yiddishisms) had gone by that name ever sinc
Max was said to be on first-name terms with the Boy Wond
and, as Mel West would have put it, a host of others.

Max, in fact, delighted in telling tales about the legenda
Boy Wonder. His favorite, a story that Duddy had heard ov
and over again, was the one about the streetcar transfer. Ma
loved to tell this tale, one he believed to be beautiful, to ne
comers; and earlier that evening he had repeated it to Ma
Donald. Not just like that, mind you, because before he cou
begin Max required the right atmosphere. His customa

chair next to the Coke cooler, hot coffee with a supply of sugar cubes ready by his side, and a supporting body of old friends. Then, speaking slowly and evenly, he would begin, letting the story develop on its own, never allowing an interruption to nonplus him and not raising his voice until Baltimore.

"He was broke," Max began, "and he hadn't even made his name yet. He was just another bum at the time."

"And what is he now? The gangster."

"I'm warning you, MacDonald, if the Boy Wonder knocked off his mother, Max here is the guy who would find an excuse for him."

"I mean you could say that," Max continued. "We're like his, you know, and I'd say it to his face even. *The Boy Wonder was just another bum at the time.* Funny, isn't it? I mean his phone bill alone last year must have come to twenty G's (he's got lines open to all the tracks and ball parks all day long, you know), but only ten years ago he would have had to sweat blood before he coulda raised a lousy fin."

"No wonder."

"How that *goniff* manages to keep out of jail beats me."

"It's simple," Debrofsky said. "The whole police force is on his payroll."

Max waited. He sucked a sugar cube. "Anyway, he's broke, like I said. So he walks up to the corner of Park and St. Joseph and hangs around the streetcar stop for a couple of hours, and do you know what?"

"He trips over a hundred dollar bill and breaks his leg."

"He's pulled in for milking pay phones. Or stealing milk bottles, maybe."

"All that time," Max said, "he's collecting streetcar transfers off the street and selling them, see. Nerve? *Nerve.* At three cents apiece he's up a quarter in two hours, and then what? He walks right in that door, MacDonald, right past where you're standing, and into the back room. There, with only a quarter in his pocket, he sits in on the rummy game. Win? He's worked his stake up to ten bucks in no time. And what does he do next?"

"Buy a gun and shoot himself."

"I got it. He donates the ten to the Jewish National Fund."

Max smiled indulgently. He blew on his coffee. "Around the corner he goes to Moe's barbershop and plunk goes the whole ten-spot on a filly named Miss Sparks running in the fifth at Belmont. On the nose, but. And you guessed it, MacDonald, Miss Sparks comes in and pays eleven to one. The Boy Wonder picks up his loot and goes to find himself a barbotte game. Now you or me, MacDonald, we'd take that hundred and ten fish and buy ourselves a hat, or a present for the wife maybe, and consider ourselves lucky. We mere mortals, we'd right away put some of it in the bank. Right? *Right*. But not the Boy Wonder. No, sir."

Max dropped a sugar cube onto his tongue and took some time sucking the goodness out of it.

"Picture him, MacDonald, a twenty-nine-year-old boy from St. Urbain Street and he's not even made his name yet. All night he spends with those low-lifes, men who would slit their mother's throat for a lousy nickel. Gangsters. Graduates of St. Vincent de Paul. Anti-Semites, the lot. If he loses, O.K., but if he wins — *If he wins*, MacDonald? Will they let that little St. Urbain Street punk Jerry Dingleman leave with all their money? He's up and he's down, and when he's up a lot the looks he gets around the table are not so nice." Max cleared his throat. "Another coffee, please, Eddy."

But Eddy had already poured it. For, at this point in the transfer story, Max always ordered coffee.

"Imagine him, MacDonald. It's morning. Dawn, I mean, like at the end of a film. The city is awakening. Little tots in their little beds are dreaming pretty little dreams. Men are getting out of bed and catching shit from their wives. The exercise boys are taking the horses out. Somewhere, in the Jewish General Hospital let's say, a baby is born, and in the Catholic Hospital—no offense, MacDonald—some poor misguided nun has just died of an abortion. Morning, MacDonald, another day. And the Boy Wonder, his eyes ringed with black circles, steps out into God's sunlight—that was before his personal troubles, you know—and in his pocket, MacDonald, is almost one thousand de-is-ollers—and I should drop down dead if a word of this isn't true.

"But wait. That's not all. This is only the beginning. Because the Boy Wonder does not go home to sleep. No, sir. That morning he takes the train to Baltimore, see, and that's a tough horse town, you know, and they never heard of the Boy Wonder yet. He's only a St. Urbain Street boy, you know. I mean he wasn't born very far from where *I* live. Anyway, for six weeks there is no word. *Rien*. Not a postcard even. Imagine, MacDonald, try to visualize it. Has some dirty nigger killed him for his roll, God forbid? (There are lots of them in Baltimore, you know, and at night with those dim street lamps, you think you can even see those black bastards coming?) Is he a broken man, penniless again, wasting away in a hospital

22

maybe? *The public ward.* Six weeks and not a word. Nothing. Expect the worst, I said to myself. Good-by, old friend. *Au revoir.* Good night, sweet prince, as they say, something something something. Then one day, MacDonald, one fine day, back into town he comes, only not by foot and not by train and not by plane. He's driving a car a block long and sitting beside him is the greatest little piece you ever saw. Knockers? You've never seen such a pair. I mean just to look at that girl —And do you know what, MacDonald? He parks that bus right outside here and steps inside to have a smoked meat with the boys. By this time he owns his own stable already. So help me, MacDonald, in Baltimore he has eight horses running. O.K.; today it would be peanuts for an operator his size, but at the time, MacDonald, at the time. And from what? Streetcar transfers at three cents apiece. Streetcar transfers, that's all. I mean can you beat that?"

Whenever he told that story Max's face was suffused with such enthusiasm that the men, though they had heard it time and again, sure as they were that it would come out right in the end, unfailingly moved in closer, their fears and hopes riding with the Boy Wonder in Baltimore, who, as Max said, was only a St. Urbain Street boy.

But they were extremely fond of Max, anyway. He didn't push, he was always good for a fin, and though he never complained, it had been hard for him since his wife died.

Minnie had died eleven years ago and that, Max figured, was why Duddy was such a puzzle. A headache, even. All he ever wanted to do was play snooker. Max, of course, was anxious for Duddy to get started in life. About Lennie he had no worries, not one.

"Awright, Duddy, since you're here already, what'll you have?"

"A Scotch and soda."

Max shook with laughter. "Some B.T.O., my kid."

"Getting much?" MacDonald asked, winking at Duddy.

Drapeau guffawed and Debrofsky gave Josette a meaningful poke. But Max frowned. "You shouldn't talk like that, MacDonald. He's only a kid."

Small, sallow MacDonald smiled thinly. "Well, if he can drink Scotch . . ."

"Okey-doke, Eddy, give my boy a Grepsi and a lean on rye. I'll have the same." Max sat down beside Duddy at the counter. "Keep away from MacDonald," he said in a low voice. "He's new here and I don't like him."

Duddy told his father about Mr. MacPherson. "He said you weren't fit to bring me up, the bastard."

"If your teacher said that he had a good reason. What did you say first?"

"Do I always have to be in the wrong? Jeez. Why can't you stick up for me? Just once why can't you—"

"You're a real troublemaker, Duddy, that's why. Lennie never once got the strap in four years at Fletcher's."

Duddy repeated to his father about the missionary who was going to distribute pamphlets outside F.F.H.S. "Something oughta be done," he said. "The P.T.A. oughta complain."

"That's true," Max said. "It's not like we were Chinks or something."

But Duddy sensed that his father wasn't listening to him. He seemed edgy, and from time to time he glanced anxiously at Josette.

Josette was a handsome whore with splendid black hair and enormous breasts. "She wears a sign under her bra," Duddy had once overheard Max say, "and you know what it says? It says look out for the four-foot drop." She often came in to drink coffee with the drivers and occasionally, when there was no game going on in the back room, she went there with one or the other of them. In exchange, the men tried to be helpful. Josette was obviously drunk and seemed to be in a black mood.

"You finish your sandwich," Max said to Duddy, "and I'll drive you home. It's time to pack in, anyway."

"Hey, c'mere kid," MacDonald said. "Got something to show you."

"You put those cards right back in your pocket, MacDonald."

"You were glad enough to look through them, so why can't the kid . . . ?"

"Because he's a kid."

"Aw, come on, Daddy, lemme look at the cards."

"Your old man figures you still think it's got no other use but to piss with."

The phone rang and Debrofsky went to answer it.

"Don't needle me, MacDonald."

MacDonald flipped his deck of cards.

"When I lose my temper," Max said, "I lose my temper."

MacDonald looked closely at Max and retreated. Josette tittered. Max grabbed his boy firmly by the arm. "Let's go," he said. But Debrofsky blocked his way. "It's for you, Max."

Duddy, left alone, looked longingly at MacDonald. Mac-Donald smiled his thin, humorless smile, and walked towards the back of the store. Just as Duddy started after him Eddy called out, "You sit right down here and finish your sandwich. Come on, Duddy."

"I'm not a kid any more."

"You're a kid," Eddy said.

MacDonald began to lay out his cards face up on the pinball machine and the other drivers moved away from him.

"How're you doing at school?" Debrofsky asked.

"Aw."

Max stepped out of the phone booth and took Josette aside. They whispered together.

"I can't drive you home," Max said to Duddy.

"Why?"

"I've got to take Josette somewhere."

Josette began putting on more makeup.

"Where?"

"I can't take you home. You'll have to walk, that's all."

"I'll drive him home," MacDonald said.

"He'll walk."

"Why can't Debrofsky take Josette?"

"It's gotta be me. No more questions. O.K.?"

Duddy kicked an empty cigarette box with his toe.

"I can't explain," Max said. "Now will you go home, please."

Duddy hesitated.

"He gets it off the top," MacDonald said.

Max flushed. He took a deep breath, and the only sound was the click of Josette's compact. MacDonald slipped behind a chair, ready to pick it up, and Max started for him. He was stopped by the expression in Duddy's face.

Duddy smiled; he laughed.

"Jeez," he said proudly. "That's something. Jeez."

Max slapped his face so hard that Duddy lost his balance and fell against the counter.

"Get out of here. Go home."

Finger marks had been burned red into the boy's cheeks. Max buried his hands in his pockets.

"You're a pimp."

"Get out, Duddy."

Duddy got up and ran.

"I didn't mean to hit him so hard," Max said to the other drivers.

"He had it coming to him."

"Easy, Max. It wasn't your fault."

Max took Josette by the arm. "Awright," he said. "I haven't got all night. Let's go."

"You're hurting me," Josette said.

4

In the Masters' room of F.F.H.S. the next morning Mr MacPherson was interrupted when Mr. Coldwell burst angrily into the room. "If I ever find out which one of them phoned me last night," he said, "I'll fix it so that he can't get into any school in the city."

"So they've been calling you too," Mr. Jackson said.

"Are you sure it's the students?" Mr. MacPherson asked sleepily.

"Did you call me at one A.M., John? Shout obscenities into my ear and hang up?"

"I believe," Mr. Jackson began, applying his years of intimacy with the scientific method to the present banality, "I believe—now we must allow some margin for doubt—but I do believe I recognized Kravitz's voice last night."

Mr. MacPherson began to read his history test papers.

"Damn it, John," Mr. Coldwell said, "strap the little bastard and put an end to this nonsense."

"Strapping," Mr. MacPherson began in a small voice, "has never been a solution to . . ."

"Sure, sure," Mr. Coldwell said, "but until your socialist messiah comes along I'd like my sleep undisturbed by obscene phone calls. Strap him, John."

"I refuse to strap Kravitz."

Mr. Cox lowered his newspaper. "As a matter of fact," he said, "Kravitz and the rest of the Dead End Kids were at our place last night. I played some records for them."

"Young man, you'll hear more about this. I think we've had quite enough of your musical evenings."

"Why don't you try strapping me, Coldwell? You can make the same deal with me as you made with Kravitz. If I say nothing about my wrists bleeding you'll promise not to mark it in your book."

Even Mr. MacPherson joined in the ensuing laughter.

"Really, Cox," Mr. Feeney said, "you don't believe that story, do you?"

Mr. Cox's face turned white.

"What would you say," Mr. Coldwell said, his anger gone, "if Kravitz told you I beat him with chains?"

Luckily for Mr. Cox the first bell rang just then. He caught up with Mr. MacPherson just outside Room 41. "I want you to know," he said, "that I'm with you all the way in this. Strapping is the worst kind of reactionary measure. I'm a socialist too," he added warmly.

Mr. MacPherson saw Coldwell walking towards them. "Socialism is strictly for young men," he said loudly. "I hope you too will grow out of it in time."

A typed note was waiting for Mr. MacPherson on his desk in Room 41.

> KRAVITZ MAY BE A BRAT AND AN EXHIBI-
> TIONIST AND A COWARD, BUT THE GUY
> AFRAID TO STRAP HIM MUST BE A REAL
> CHICKEN.

Mr. MacPherson crumpled the note into a ball and tossed it into the wastebasket. "I'm warning you I won't stand for any nonsense today. If anyone so much as talks without raising his hand, he's as good as asking for a suspension."

When Mr. MacPherson got home that afternoon there was yet another note waiting for him.

> DEAR JOHN,
>   Dr. Hanson wants you to call him as soon as you get in. He gave me an injection and something to make me sleep.
>   JENNY

Mr. MacPherson phoned. Dr. Hanson was out on a call, Miss Floyd said, but Mr. MacPherson was to come to his office at nine A.M. tomorrow worning, without fail. Yes, he would have to miss school. This was urgent.

No sooner had he hung up than the telephone rang again. "Yes," he said tightly.

"Guess who?"

"Look here, Kravitz, I'm warning you—"

"Oh dear, do I sound Jewish, John?"

"I shall have you suspended for this. That's a promise."

"John, pet, it's me."

"Who's speaking, please?"

"Clara Shield-berg. Und vat's new vit you, Abie?"

"Oh, it's you, Clara. I'm sorry. You see, sometimes my students—"

"Never mind your students, pet. You get right into a taxi this minute and come over here and have a drink with us. We're in Room 341."

"Oh, I couldn't do that. Jenny isn't well and besides I—"

"If you don't come over here this minute Herbert says he'll report you to the police for having stolen his car."

The party, centered in Room 341, actually embraced the two adjoining rooms as well. Even the surrounding halls swarmed with merrymarkers. A lot of the men wore badges with their names and addresses typed on them and, underneath, the one word DELEGATE. All the women were smartly dressed. Embarrassed, Mr. MacPherson edged into a free corner and hastily lit a cigarette.

"It's great to see you again," Herbert said. "What brand of poison do you prefer, Mr. Chips?"

Clara kissed Mr. MacPherson on the cheek and it was a long time and lots of whiskies later when he next looked at his watch and discovered that it was three A.M. He had only meant to stay for an hour. Horrified, Mr. MacPherson rushed for his coat, ran outside, and hailed a taxi.

Once in the taxi, he recalled how Herbert had introduced him to a group of strangers. "I want you to shake the hand of the most brilliant student of our class at McGill. He could have been a success at anything he wanted. Instead he's devoted his life to teaching." It was clear that they still took him for the freshly scrubbed idealist who had left McGill twenty years ago. They had no idea that he was exhausted, bitter, and drained, and that given the chance to choose again he would never become a teacher.

Perhaps, he thought, there's still time. He hadn't strapped a boy yet, had he? Cox admired him. Next year, he remembered, two more young veterans would be joining the staff. Together, maybe, they could help the boys. A club could be formed, perhaps, as was usually done in movies about delinquents. *There might still be nostalgic reunions in his parlor.* Mr. MacPherson began to feel much better. Cheerful, even. There's still hope, he thought.

Mr. MacPherson tiptoed into the bedroom, but Jenny wasn't there. He found her crumpled up on the hall floor. The receiver dangled idiotically from the hook above her. Mr. MacPherson, who was still only vaguely conscious of what had happened, snatched it up immediately, but the party at the other end had hung up. So he stared accusingly at his wife or the floor, not knowing whether to rip his clothes into shreds or hold her dry hand in his or go out for another drink. After he had hovered over her dumbly for a time he knelt down and discovered that she was still alive. Quickly he telephoned for an ambulance.

5

Weidman and Samuels were playing o-x-o on the board.

"Hey, Duddy," Abrams shouted. "Guess who's coming back today?"

"Not my favorite Scotchman?"

"It's not so funny," Hersh said. "His wife died."

"Too bad it wasn't Mac," Abrams said.

"You know what," Cohen said. "My brother met Mac in the Pines Wednesday aft. And man oh man, was he ever shot! So anyways, my brother pats him on the shoulder. 'How's about a beer on me,' he says. So you know what? So Mac slaps him across the face."

Weidman and Samuels stopped their game on the board.

"So what did your brother do, jerkovitch?"

"What do you mean what did my brother do? He let him have it smack on the jaw. Bango!"

"Smack on the jaw. Yeah, I'll bet."

"O.K., ask Mac when he comes in, smart guy."

In the uproar that followed nobody noticed that Mr. Mac-Pherson had, indeed, entered the room, until he smacked his briefcase down on the class master's desk.

"Well, well, welcome back, sir."

Mr. MacPherson silenced Duddy with a scowl. The other boys scrambled for their seats.

"Glad to have you back, sir," Hersh offered timidly.

Clutching the class register tightly, Mr. MacPherson began to call out the boys' names in alphabetical order. "Abrams," he began.

"Present, sir."

He belched when he got to Waldman.

"He's drunk," Duddy howled. "Drunk as a lord."

The boys watched predatorily as Mr. MacPherson fiddled with the straps of his briefcase.

"Hey, sir. How's about a few pints after classes, eh?"

No reply.

"Is it true that Cohen's brother let you have it, sir?"

Hersh squeezed his hand together. "Cut it out," he said. "Leave him alone, please."

Duddy Kravitz shook a fist at Hersh. "We know how to deal with *tuchusleckers* here," he said. Then, turning to Mr. Mac-Pherson, he asked, "How's about a free period, sir?"

"All right."

Two minutes later Duddy shot up in his seat. "Sir, there's something I'd like to ask you. I've been looking at my hist'ry book and I see there's only one paragraph on the Spanish inquisition. You don't even mention it in class, so seeing we got lots of time now I thought you might like to tell us something about it."

"The trouble with you Jews," Mr. MacPherson said, "is that you're always walking around with a chip on your shoulder."

"Hey! Hey! there!"

"What exactly do you mean, *you Jews?*"

"This isn't Germany, you know."

"He's a nazi fascist!"

6

The man to avoid, as far as strappings went, was Mr. Coldwell. Mr. Coldwell strapped from an angle, so that the tongue curled around your hand and rebounded hard on the wrist. Usually he strapped a boy until he cried; then he'd say, "I'd hoped you'd take it like a man." Next came Mr. Feeney. Mr. Feeney took three steps backward with the strap resting lightly on his shoulder, charged, and struck. Mr. MacPherson, however, did not even know how to hold the strap properly. So when he led Duddy Kravitz into the Medical Room that afternoon, breaking with a practice of twenty years, the actual blows were feeble, and it was Duddy who emerged triumphant, racing outside to greet his classmates.

"Hey, look! Look, jerkos! Ten on each. Mac strapped me. Mac, of all people."

Mr. MacPherson strapped fifteen boys that week, and his method improved with practice. But the rowdiness in class and his own drinking, increased in proportion to the strappings. He began to sit around the house alone. He seldom went out any more. And then one night, a couple of weeks after he had returned to school, Mr. MacPherson sat down before his dead fireplace and broke open a new bottle of whisky. He sat there for hours, cherishing old and unlikely memories and trying to feel something more than a sense of liberation because Jenny, whom he had once loved truly, was dead. Half the bottle was finished before all of Mr. MacPherson's troubles crystallized into the hard, leering shape of Duddy Kravitz. Mr. MacPherson chuckled. Staggering into the hall, pulling the light cord so hard that it broke off in his hand, he rocked to and fro over the telephone. It did not take him long, considering his state, to find Kravitz's number, and he dialed it with care. The telephone must have rung and rung about fifteen times before somebody answered it.

"Hullo," a voice said gruffly.

Mr. MacPherson didn't reply.

"Hullo. Hullo! Who is that anyway? Hullo."

It wasn't Kravitz. He would have recognized Kravitz's voice. The room began to sway around Mr. MacPherson.

"Who's speaking?" the voice commanded.

"Mr. MacPhers—"

Mr. MacPherson slammed the receiver back on the hook and stumbled into the living room, knocking over a lamp on his way. The first thing he saw there were the history test papers. He ripped them apart, flung them into the fireplace, and lit them. Exhausted, he collapsed into his armchair to watch them burn.

7

Leonard Bush, the principal of F.F.H.S., was a man with many troubles. Only this morning a letter had come from the general manager of the Blue-top Milk Company to protest that Joseph Dollard, one of their drivers, had been innocently collecting empty milk bottles outside F.F.H.S. when somebody standing in a fourth floor window had urinated on him, which —Mr. Bush would certainly agree—could not have been accidental. Attached came a bill for cleaning charges. There was also a letter from the vice-president of the P.T.A. to ask about the man who had been handing out free copies of the New Testament outside F.F.H.S. For, with all due respects, Mr. Bush would certainly agree that this was an insult to people of the Jewish faith.

Leonard Bush was a capable, soft-spoken man in his early

fifties. His first visitor that morning, a Mrs. Yagid, wanted
know why her Herby, a remarkable boy—and I don't say th
because he's my own, we're not such common types—why h
Herby was not an officer in the F.F.H.S. Cadets, not a sergea
even, when that stinker Mrs. Cooperman's boy next door, th
one with the running nose, was a captain. His second visito
Glass the used-car dealer, told him it would be a shame, stup
even, to make his boy repeat grade ten again over a lousy tw
per cent, and besides, he had a little hunch that if Mr. Bus
dropped in to his lot tomorrow there might be a bargain, a re
steal, of a car there for him. Leonard Bush's third visitor w
Max Kravitz.

"I mean saying such a thing as 'you dirty Jews' to a bunc
of boys. I mean a phone call at three o'clock in the mornin
Mr. Bush. You know what I ask myself? What kind of men a
teaching my boy? How can they expect to make decent citize
of them when they themselves are like bad children? Tell me
I'm wrong, sir. You can be honest with me and I'll be hone
with you. That's what I'm like."

"We like honesty here too, Mr. Kravitz."

"You call me Max. I'm a simple man, Mr. Bush, a ta
driver. But a taxi driver, Mr. Bush, is a little like being a do
tor. Night and day, rain or shine, I am at the service of John
Public. You'd be surprised at the things that come up in m
life. Pregnant women to be rushed to the hospital, accident
fights, and older men with fine reputations, if you'll pard
me, trying to have sexual relations with young girls in the ba
of my taxi. No, thank you. But, like I said, it is nothing f
me to be called to an emergency in the middle of the nig
so, as you can well understand, I can't afford to have my sle
disturbed for nothing."

Mr. Bush assured Max Kravitz that Mr. MacPherson h
never called the boys dirty Jews. He also said that it was ce
tainly not Mr. MacPherson who had telephoned in the midd
of the night. It was, in his opinion, a student imitating M
MacPherson. But it was no use. Something, Mr. Bush kne
would have to be done. At first the staff had been symp
thetic about Mr. MacPherson's loss, but his drinking ha
since become the school joke. So the next morning Mr. Bu
suggested to Mr. MacPherson that he would like to have
quiet chat with him after school was out. That mornin
three weeks after Mr. MacPherson had returned to scho
he was confronted with the problem of history test pape

Duddy dashed out his cigarette. "My dear Mac," he sai
"the Room 41 gang doesn't care how many times a week y

32

go out to tie a load on. But if you don't mind, our parents work hard to keep us here. Our reports are supposed to come out next week. We want the results of our hist'ry test."

The boys applauded and Duddy bowed ceremoniously and sat down.

And it all came tumbling down on Mr. MacPherson—the drinking, the phone call, how Kravitz was master of the classroom and he was being ostracized in the Masters' Room. A quiet little chat after school was out, that's what Mr. Bush had said. My pension, he thought. They'll take away my job.

"C'mon! What about our marks?"

Mr. MacPherson pounced on the register. Abrams, he called. Abrams cupped his hand under his armpit and made a foul noise. Abromovitch, Bernstein. Nobody answered. He hadn't checked the attendance all week. But he kept on reading. "Kravitz!"

"Yes, your highness."

Something about him, the look in Mr. MacPherson's eyes maybe, made Weidman scramble back to his seat, sure that Mac had finally gone off his rocker. Cohen clutched a ruler in his hand, waiting. Mr. MacPherson walked slowly down the room towards Kravitz.

"It was you who phoned, wasn't it?"

"I don't know what you're talking about."

"It was you."

"So help me, sir, it wasn't."

"You killed my wife, Kravitz."

"Stay away from me. I'm warning you."

"You killed my wife."

Duddy put up his fists. "Why don't you have another drink, eh? You should be locked up, that's what. You have no right to be with children."

"You murdered her, you filthy street Arab."

"Leave him alone," Abrams whined.

"Please let him go, sir. We'll be good."

Mr. MacPherson mumbled something inarticulate and passed out. In falling, he banged his head against a desk.

"Duddy! Get the doctor. Hurry! I think Mac is dead!"

Hersh began to sob. "We killed him," he screamed.

Duddy stamped his foot on the floor. "What does he mean killed his goddam wife? I didn't mean nothing all the time. Nothing. We're all in this together, you understand?"

Once the doctor had assured him that Mr. MacPherson had revived completely, though he was still in a shocked state, Mr.

TEMPLE ISRAEL LIBRARY

Bush stepped into the Medical Room to speak to him. Mr
MacPherson, resting on the cot, immediately asked, "Have you
come to strap me, Leonard?"

"I'm glad to see you still haven't lost your sense of humor,
John." Mr. Bush laughed uneasily. He told Mr. MacPherson
that he thought it would be best if he took a few days off.
There would be plenty of time for their little chat another
day. Outside, a taxi was waiting.

"I don't want a taxi," Mr. MacPherson said. "I'd rather
walk."

Mr. MacPherson stopped short when he noticed Kravitz and
the others idling outside Felder's store. The boys seemed sub-
dued and unsure of themselves. Duddy started to walk toward
him, but then he apparently changed his mind, for he turned
around to rejoin the boys.

"Kravitz."

Duddy stopped.

"You'll go far, Kravitz. You're going to go very far."

Mr. MacPherson, smiling a little, walked away towards Pine
Avenue.

Lance Corporal Boxenbaum led with a bang bang bang on
his big white drum and Litvak tripped Cohen, Pinsky blew
on his bugle, and the Fletcher's Cadets wheeled left, reet, left,
reet, out of Fletcher's Field, led by their commander in chief,
that snappy five-footer W. E. James (that's 'Jew' spelled
backward, as he told each new gym class). Left, reet, left, reet,
powdery snow crunching underfoot, Ginsburg out of step once
more and Hornstein unable to beat his drum right because of
the ten on each Mr. Coldwell had applied before the parade.
Turning smartly right down Esplanade Avenue, they were at
once joined and embarrassed on either side by a following of
younger brothers on sleighs, little sisters with running noses,
and grinning delivery boys stopping to make snowballs.

"Hey, look out there, General Montgomery, here comes
your mother to blow your nose."

"Lefty! Hey, Lefty! Maw says you gotta come right home to
sift the ashes after the parade. No playing pool, she says. She's
afraid the pipes will burst."

Tara-boom, tara-*boom*, tara-BOOM–BOOM–BOOM, past
the Jewish Old People's Home, where on the balcony above,
bedecked with shawls and rugs, a stain of yellowing expressionless faces, women with little beards and men with sucked-in
mouths, fussy nurses with thick legs and grandfathers whose
sons had little time, a shrunken little woman who had survived a pogrom and two husbands and three strokes, and two

34

followers of Rabbi Brott the Miracle Maker watched squinting against the fierce wintry sun.

"Jewish children in uniform?"

"Why not?"

"It's not nice. For a Jewish boy a uniform is not so nice."

Skinny, lump-faced Boxenbaum took it out on the big white drum, and Sergeant Grepsy Segal, who could burp or break wind at will, sang:

> *Bullshit, that's all the band could play,*
> *Bullshit, it makes the grass grow green.*

Mendelsohn hopped to get back into step and Archie Rosen, the F.F.H.S. Cadet Corps quartermaster, who sold dyed uniforms at eight dollars each, told Naturman the one about the rabbi and the priest and the bunch of grapes. "Fun-*ny*," Naturman said. Commander in Chief W.E. James, straight as a ramrod, veteran of the Somme, a swagger stick held tight in his hand, his royal blue uniform pressed to a cutting edge and his brass buttons polished perfect, felt a lump in his throat as the corps, bugles blowing, approached the red brick armory of the Canadian Grenadier Guards. "Eyes . . . *Right,*" he called, saluting stiffly.

Duddy Kravitz, like the rest, turned to salute the Union Jack, and the pursuing gang of kid brothers and sisters took up the chant:

> *Here come the Fletcher's Cadets,*
> *Smoking cigarettes.*
> *The cigarettes are lousy*
> *And so are the Fletcher's Cadets.*

Crunch, crunch, crunch-crunch-crunch, over the powdery snow, ears near frozen stiff, the F.F.H.S. Cadets Corps marched past the Jewish Library, where a poster announced:

> *Wednesday Night*
> ON BEING A JEWISH POET
> IN MONTREAL WEST
> A Talk by H. I. Zimmerman, B.A.
> *Refreshments*

and smack over the spot where in 1933 a car with a Michigan license plate had machine-gunned to death the Boy Wonder's uncle. They stopped in front of the Y.M.H.A. to mark time while the driver of a Kik Kola truck that had slid into a No 97 streetcar began to fight with the conductor.

"Hip, hip," W. E. James called. *"Hip-hip-hip!"*

A bunch of Y.M.H.A. boys came out to watch.

"There's Arnie. Hey, Arnie! Where's your gun? Wha'?"

"Hey, sir! Mr. James! You know what you can do with tha stick?"

"Boxenbaum. *Hey!* You'll get a rupture if you carry tha drum any further."

"Hip, hip," W. E. James called. *"Hip-hip-hip!"*

Geiger blew on his bugle and Sivak goosed Kravitz. A snow ball knocked off Sergeant Heller's cap, Pinsky caught a frozen horse-bun on the cheek, and Mel Brucker lowered his eye when they passed his father's store. Monstrous icicles ran from the broken second floor windows of his home into the muck o stiff burned dry goods and charred wood below. The fire had happened last night. Mel had expected it because that after noon his father had said cheerfully, "You're sleeping at Grand maw's tonight," and each time Mel and his brother were asked to sleep at Grandmaw's it meant another fire, another store.

"Hip, hip. Hip-hip-hip."

To the right Boxenbaum's father and another pickete walked up and down blowing on their hands before the Nu Oxford shoe factory, and to the left there was Harry's Wa Assets Store with a sign outside that read:

IF YOU HAVEN'T GOT TIME TO DROP IN
—SMILE WHEN YOU WALK PAST

Tara-boom, tara-*boom*, tara-BOOM–BOOM–BOOM, pas the Hollywood Barbershop where they removed blackhead for fifty cents, around the corner of Clark where Charna Felde lived, the F.F.H.S. Cadet Corps came crunch-crunch-crunch Tansky started on his drum, Rubin dropped an icicle dow Mort Heimer's back, and the cadets wheeled left, reet, lef reet, into St. Urbain Street. A gathering of old grads and slack ers stepped out of the Laurier Billiard Hall, attracted by th martial music.

"Hey, sir. Mr. James! Is it true you were a pastrycook in th first war?"

"We hear you were wounded grating *latkas*."

"There's Stanley. Hey, Stan! Jeez, he's an officer or some thing. *Stan!* It's O.K. about Friday night but Rita says Irv too short for her. Can you bring Syd instead? Stan! *Stan?*"

Over the intersection where Gordie Wiser had burned th

Union Jack after many others had trampled and spit on it the day Ernest Bevin announced his Palestine policy, past the house where the Boy Wonder had been born, stopping to mark time at the corner where their fathers and elder brothers, armed with baseball bats, had fought the Frogs during the conscription riots, the boys came marching. A little slower, though, Boxenbaum puffing as he pounded his drum and thirteen or thirty-five others feeling the frost in their toes. The sun went, darkness came quick as a traffic light change, and the snow began to gleam purple. Tansky felt an ache in his stomach as they slogged past his house and Captain Bercovitch remembered there'd be boiled beef and potatoes for supper but he'd have to pick up the laundry first.

"Hip, *hip.* Hip-hip-hip."

To the right the A.Z.A. clubhouse and to the left the poky Polish synagogue where Old Man Zabitsky searched the black windy street and saw the cadets coming towards him.

"Label. Label, come here."

"I can't, *Zeyda,* it's a parade."

"A parade. *Narishkeit.* We're short one man for prayers."

"But *Zeyda,* please."

"No buts, no please. Rosenberg has to say *Kaddish.*"

Led by the arm, drum and all, Lionel Zabitsky was pulled from the parade.

"Hey, sir. A casualty."

"Chick-en!"

Past Moe's warmly lit cigar store where you could get a lean on rye for fifteen cents and three more cadets defected. Pinsky blew his bugle faint-heartedly and Moxenbaum gave the drum a little bang. Wheeling right and back again up Clark Street, five more cadets disappeared into the darkness.

"Hip, hip. *Hip-hip-hip.*"

One of the deserters ran into his father, who was on his way home from work.

"Would you like a hot dog and a Coke before we go home?"

"Sure."

"O.K., but you mustn't say anything to Maw."

Together they watched the out-of-step F.F.H.S. Cadet Corps fade under the just starting fall of big lazy snowflakes.

"It's too cold for a parade. You kids could catch pneumonia out in this weather without scarves or rubbers."

"Mr. James says that in the First World War sometimes they'd march for thirty miles without stop through rain and mud that was knee-deep."

"Is that what I pay school fees for?"

37

Where Duddy Kravitz sprung from the boys grew up dirty and sad, spiky also, like grass beside the railroad tracks. He could have been born in Lodz, but forty-eight years earlier his grandfather had bought a steerage passage to Halifax. Duddy could have been born in Toronto, where his grandfather was bound for, but Simcha Kravitz's C.P.R. ticket took him only as far as the Bonaventure Station in Montreal, and he never did get to Toronto. Simach was a shoemaker, and two years after his arrival he was able to send for his wife and two sons. A year later he had his own shop on a corner of St. Dominique Street. His family lived upstairs, and outside in the gritty hostile soil of his back yard, Simcha planted corn and radishes, peas, carrots and cucumbers. Each year the corn came up scrawnier and the cucumbers yellowed before they ripened, but Simcha persisted with his planting.

Simcha's hard thin dark figure was a familiar one in the neighborhood. Among the other immigrants he was trusted, he was regarded as a man of singular honesty and some wisdom, but he was not loved. He would lend a man money to help him bring over his wife, grudgingly he would agree to settle a dispute or advise a man in trouble, he never repeated a confidence, but about the conditions of his own life he remained silent. His wife was a shrew with warts on her face and she spoke to him sharply when others were present, but Simcha did not complain.

"He's only a shoemaker," Adler said, "so why does he act so superior?"

Once Moishe Katansky, a newcomer, dared to sympathize with Simcha Kravitz about his marriage, and Simcha raised his head from the last and looked at him so severely that Katansky understood and did not return to the shop for many months. Simcha's shop was a meeting place. Here the round shouldered immigrants gathered to sip lemon tea and to talk of their fear of failure in the new country. Some came to idolize Simcha. "You could," they said, "trust Simcha Kravitz with your wife—your money—anything." But others came to resent their need to go to his shop. They began to search him for a fault. "Nobody's perfect," Katansky said.

Simcha's stature increased immensely when it became

known that he was respected even among the Gentiles in the district. That came about after Blondin the blacksmith had been kicked by a horse. Simcha, not the first man on the scene, forced Blondin to drink some brandy and set the broken bone in his leg before the doctor came. After that whenever there was an accident as far as the lead foundry eight blocks away on one side and the sawmill nine blocks away on the other, Simcha was sent for.

The old grizzled man would not talk about his private life, but there was one thing that even he couldn't hide. His first-born son, Benjy, was a delight to him. The others would often see Simcha Kravitz coming out of the synagogue and walking down St. Dominique Street holding the boy's hand, and that, if you knew that man, seemed such a proud and difficult display of intimacy that the others would turn away embarrassed. Those who liked him, the majority, and knew about his bad life with his wife hoped that Benjy would justify his love. But some of the others, men who had broken down in the shop and still more who owed him money they couldn't repay, sensed that here at last Simcha was vulnerable and they wished bad luck on Benjy.

"He's got his mother's dirty mouth."

"He's fat and feminine. Poor Simcha. He doesn't see."

But fat, caustic tongue, and other failures too, Benjy prospered. And more. He revered his father and did not once abuse the old man's love. He was a shrewd boy, intelligent and quick and without fear of the new country, and he undoubtedly had, as Katansky put it, the golden touch. The fat teen-age boy who ventured into the country to sell the farmers reams of cloth and boots and cutlery was, at twenty-six, the owner of a basement blouse factory. From the beginning he paid the highest wages and like his father lent money and, though he was loquacious, he never repeated a confidence. On Saturday mornings father and son could be seen standing side by side in the synagogue, and when Benjy began to read Mencken and Dreiser and no longer came to pray his father said:

"Benjy does what he believes. That's his right."

Nobody, not even Katansky, could have accused Benjy of marrying for money. The bride was a pants presser's daughter. A beauty. Ida was a slender girl with curly red hair and a long delicate neck and white skin. She went everywhere with Benjy and everywhere she went with him she could not stop looking at him. The old man adored her too. He often brought her vegetables from his garden and on Sunday afternoons the three of them had a habit of going for a drive, leaving Mrs. Kravitz and Max and Minnie and their children to wait at home. A year later, when Simcha's wife died, he refused to go and live with Benjy and Ida; he said it would not be wise, and he continued to live alone. Then the trouble started.

"I went to see Benjy in his office yesterday," Adler said, "and I'd swear he was drunk."

Ida began to take trips alone and the round-shouldered men in the shoe repair shop began to ask questions.

"When are they going to have children?"

"These modern marriages. Oi."

Simcha never replied and the questions stopped for a time. Simcha was hurt because Benjy did not visit very often these days and when he did come to the house it was only after he had had a lot to drink. Then one day Adler came into the shop and patted Simcha tenderly on the back. "I'm sorry," he said.

"I hear your daughter-in-law's off in Miami again," Katansky said.

At the synagogue the other old men became sad and gentle with him. Simcha never asked why. He took his regular seat every Saturday morning and acknowledged the others' sympathetic looks with the stiffest of nods. But he began to look at the rest of his family with more curiosity and, without any preamble, he took Duddy into the back yard one Sunday morning to teach him how to plant and fertilize and pull out the killing weeds. Then, one day soon after Ida had left on another trip, he sent for Benjy. This was the first time he had ever actually asked his son to come to see him.

"If there's something the matter with her I'm your father and you can tell me."

Benjy turned to go.

"Strangers know something I don't know."

"It's Max. He talks too much."

"Max is a fool."

When Benjy came again about six months later Duddy was working with his grandfather in the back yard. He watched his uncle follow his grandfather into the kitchen. Duddy couldn't hear what was said, but only two minutes later Uncle Benjy came out of the house carrying what looked like a little jar of preserves. Seeing Duddy, he stopped and gave the boy a frightening look. "If you hurt him . . ."

"Wha'?"

But he didn't finish or explain. He walked off, staggering a little, and Duddy went back to pulling weeds. Simcha joined him about a half hour later. "Your grandfather was a failure in this country," he said.

40

"Why?"

"Your Uncle Benjy with all his money is nothing too. Of your father I won't even speak."

The old man squashed a mosquito against his cheek with a surprisingly quick hand.

"A man without land is nobody. Remember that, Duddel."

Duddy was seven at the time, and a year earlier his mother had enrolled him in the Talmud Torah parochial school. Uncle Benjy was going through his Zionist phase at the time, and he paid the tuition. Uncle Benjy also knew that his father, whom he hardly ever saw these days, walked hand in hand with Duddy on St. Dominique Street. But the round-shouldered men did not wonder or turn away when they saw Simcha walking with his grandson. The old man had no more enemies —even Katansky pitied him. The round-shouldered old men looked at Duddy and decided he was mean, a crafty boy, and they hoped he would not hurt Simcha too hard.

9

At the parochial school until he was thirteen years old Duddy met many boys who came from families that were much better off than his own and on the least pretext he fought with them. Those who were too big to beat up he tried to become friendly with. He taught them how to steal at Kresge's and split streetcar tickets so that one could be used twice, how to smoke with bubble pipes, and the way babies were made. After he had been at the school for three years mothers warned their children not to play with that Kravitz boy. But boys and girls alike were drawn to dark, skinny Duddy, and those who were excluded from his gang, the Warriors, felt the snub deeply.

Such a boy was blond, curly-haired Milty Halperin, the real estate agent's son. Milty's mother drove him to school every day. He was an only child and he was not allowed to ride a bicycle or eat crabapples. Duddy delighted in tormenting him, while Milty, on his side, yearned to join the Warriors. So one day Duddy said it would be O.K. if only Milty agreed to drink the secret initiation potion first. The potion, made up of water, red ink, baking soda, pepper, ketchup, a glob of chicken fat and, at the last minute, a squirt of Aqua Velva, went down with surprising ease. Afterwards, however, Duddy feigned hysteria.

"Jeez. This is terrible. I made a terrible mistake."

"What is it?"

"The wrong recipe. Jeez."

"But I drank it. You said if I drank it I could become a Warrior. You swore to God, Duddy."

"It's terrible," Duddy said, "but this means your beezer is a cinch to fall off and you'll never grow a bush. And Milty, if a guy doesn't grow a bush . . ."

Milty ran off crying and that night he was violently ill.

"What is it, pussy-lamb?"

"I'm never going to grow a bush, Mummy."

"*What?*"

"Duddy Kravitz says . . ."

Max Kravitz was called in once more by the principal and Duddy became the first boy ever to be suspended from the parochial school: he was sent home for a week. Milty was terrified. He lived in an enormous house alongside the mountain and it was he who answered the door when Duddy showed up with three other Warriors the following Saturday afternoon.

"What do you want?" he asked in a small voice.

"Why Milty, boy, we've come to play with you."

"Hiya, Milty old pal."

Milty hesitated. The maid had gone out for a walk; he was all alone.

"You never came to play with me before."

"Jeez. Aren't you going to let us in, Milty?"

"No."

"Wouldn't you still like to become a Warrior like?"

"You mustn't touch anything," Milty said, opening the door. "You promise?"

Duddy crossed his heart. So did the others.

"Some dump, eh, guys? Where does your old man keep his cigs?"

"You can't stay. You have to go."

"Gee whiz, Milty."

"You want to play monopoly?" Milty asked.

"Monopoly! Jeez. Where do your mother and father sleep? Have they got the same bed like?"

Milty bit his thumb.

"He's going to cwy, guys."

"I thought you wanted to play with me."

"Sure. Sure we do."

Milty watched, terrified, as Duddy wandered about the living room examining china figurines here and there. A rubber plant stood before the glass door that led into the garden. It reached almost to the ceiling. Duddy stopped to stare at it.

"Why don't we sit in the garden, Milty?"

"We mustn't."

Mrs. Halpirin, an amateur horticulturist, was strict about the garden.

"I thought we were pals, Milty."

Milty led the boys into the garden. The five of them sat down on the swing and Duddy told them a story about his brother Bradley. "The poor jerk. Jeez. I got a letter from him only yesterday aft and he's going to try and escape. Otherwise he'd have to stay in the Foreign Legion for another two years, you know."

"No kidding?"

"If he makes it he's going to come back here for me. He's going to take me to South America. We're going to get a yacht. I mean all he has to do once he's out is dig up that buried money and—"

"How could he write you he's going to try and escape?" Milty asked. "Don't they read his mail? My father told me that in the army letters—"

"You poor stupid jerkhead. Haven't you ever heard of invisible ink? Hey," Duddy said, jumping up, "what's wrong with the tulips?"

"What do you mean what's wrong with the tulips?"

"Why, they're closed." Duddy looked horrified.

"So what?"

"Tulips should be opened," Duddy said.

"Should they?"

"Hey, what kind of a stupid jerk are you anyway? Ask Bobby."

"Sure they should be opened."

Duddy bent down to pluck a tulip.

"Don't touch anything."

"I just wanted to show you."

Milty hesitated. "All right," he said. "But only one. Promise?"

"On my word of honor." Duddy picked up a tulip and opened it carefully. "There," he said, "doesn't that look better?"

"Wow."

"How beautiful."

Even Milty had to admit that the tulip looked better opened and, as a nice surprise for his mother, he helped Duddy and the others open every tulip in the garden.

"My mommy will be home soon," Milty said. "She'll give us milk and apple pie."

"Naw," Duddy said. "I think we'd better go. See you."

Duddy Kravitz's Warriors operated in wartime and many of their activities were colored by the conflagration in Europe. Take their tussle with the CPC, for instance.

What with so many able-bodied young men already stationed overseas in 1943, Montreal, the world's largest inland seaport, seemed to invite enemy attack. The Nips and even the hated Huns, it's true, were some distance away, but remembering Pearl Harbor, the city played it safe. Older citizens, those who couldn't fight in the regular army, joined the Canadian Provost Corps, a sort of civil defense organization. Members of the CPC were issued steel helmets and dark blue zipper suits of the type that Churchill had made popular. The officer in charge of Duddy's neighborhood—tubby, middle-aged Benny Feinberg—was seldom without his helmet, his suit, or an enormous flashlight that he wore strapped to his belt. Feinberg's zeal did not go down well on St. Urbain Street, and the first time he marched past Moe's Cigar Store the dangling flashlight inspired some rather obvious jokes. To these Feinberg was too dignified to make a reply, but when Moe observed, "No wonder we haven't opened a second front yet. With Montgomery tied down in Libya and Feinberg looking after things here, who have they got left to take command?" Feinberg felt that he had been pushed too far.

"A bunch of slackers," he said, "the whole lousy lot of you."

The Warriors, to begin with, were on the side of the CPC to the man. Feinberg had assured them that in the event of an air raid they would all be evacuated to the mountains. Some of them, he said, might even be orphaned before the war was done, and this they took to be a promise. Feinberg and a few other CPC enthusiasts aside, the Warriors probably longed for the devastation of Montreal more than anyone. A direct hit Feinberg warned them, might kill and maim "untold" hundreds of people. They were left with only one worry. The bombers might miss their chosen targets. Long into the night they once debated whether or not it would be sabotage— could a boy be hanged, for instance—if he painted a bull's-eye on the roof of the Talmud Torah.

Then the tide, so to speak, turned. The Warriors discovered that behind their backs Feinberg had given instructions and issued a real first aid kit to a Y.M.H.A. club, and Duddy decided to fix him. His first chance came the night of the lackout. It was, to be sure, only a practice blackout, but real sirens were to sound the alert. The streets were to be cleared and all blinds were to be drawn. The CPC was to be out in force checking for offenders and, according to Feinberg, saboteurs and dirty spies.

Five minutes after the sirens wailed, leaving the city in darkness, the Warriors, faces smeared with mud, commando style, crept two by two down St. Urbain Street, spilling kerosene on the street here and there; and then they dispersed to the balconies and rooftops. After Feinberg and his men had passed, searching windows for telltale strips of yellow, Duddy slipped two fingers into his mouth and whistled as loud as he could. All along the street clothespin guns came out and matches were slipped into place. Duddy counted to ten and whistled again. The guns were fired simultaneously. As the matches struck the pavement most of them ignited immediately and in an instant St. Urbain Street was ablaze with light. As it so happened an airplane, probably New York bound, was flying overhead at the time. Feinberg, they said, was the first to take cover, but there were those who insisted that Lance Corporal Lerner beat him to it. Others, like Shubin, did not dishonor the blue zipper suit. Shubin rushed quickly to the scene of the enemy action, and but for the fact that he had put on his gas mask in some haste—an impediment to movement and vision —he would have caught Duddy Kravitz anyway. As it was, all the Warriors escaped.

When the all-clear sounded several theories were hotly disputed at Moe's Cigar Store. During the blackout OPEN UP A SECOND FRONT NOW stickers had been pasted on many windows and it was Debrofsky's theory that the communists were responsible for the street fires too. Lyman didn't agree. He believed that Adrien Arcand's boys, the local fascist group, were responsible for the fires. Moe muttered something about the newly arrived refugee who had moved in around the corner and was rumored to have a short-wave radio set. But when the incident was mentioned in the *Gazette* the next morning it was clearly stated that a group of juvenile delinquents had been responsible for the outrage.

"Of course. What else do you want them to say?" Feinberg demanded when cornered. "You expect them to admit we got spies in Montreal?"

But a week later Feinberg stopped wearing his blue zipper suit and the St. Urbain Street section of the CPC could no longer be considered an effective fighting force.

Duddy Kravitz's other parochial school activities were de
cidedly more commercial. He got his start in stamps, like s
many other boys, by answering an advertisement for salesme
in Tip Top Comics. The company, one of many, sent yo
stamps on approval sheets to be sold. In payment, you go
some free stamps, catalogues, and sometimes even a com
mission. Unlike the other boys, however, Duddy soon estab
lished two fascinating facts about the companies in question
Once you had sold successfully two or three times, makin
a prompt return of money to the company, you were sent
truly expensive kit of approvals to handle. The other fac
was that a minor couldn't be sued—certainly not by an Amer
ican company. So, dealing with seven companies under a var
ety of pseudonyms, he eventually worked each one of them u
to the truly expensive approval kit point, and then he wa
never heard from again.

Some of his stamp business profits Duddy invested in th
comic book market when, during the war, American one
were hard to come by due to dollar restrictions. (Canadia
comics, not even printed in color, were unreadable.) H
bought, at twenty cents apiece, a considerable quantity of co
traband American comics, and these he rented out for thre
cents a day until glue and Scotch tape would no longer hol
them together. This led him into another and more question
able channel of distribution. One of Duddy's comic book su
pliers, a Park Avenue newsstand proprietor named Barne
showed him one day a sixteen-page comic-book-like produc
tion titled *Dick Tracy's Night Out*. The drawings, crude blac
and white copies of the original, were obviously the work of
local artist and printer. The books looked shoddy. In the ve:
first frame, however, Dick Tracy, sporting an enormous ere
tion with the words "drip, drip, drip" and an arrow pointing
it from underneath, looked ravenously at Tess Trueheart. Mi
Trueheart was clad only in black panties. The adventure, b
gun there, continued for fifteen more action-packed pages, a
the whole book sold for seventy-five cents retail. There we
many other volumes available in the same series: *L'il Abn
Gets Daisy Mae, Terry and the Dragon Lady, Blondie Pla
Strip Poker, Gasoline Alley Gang Bang,* and more.

The Talmud Torah boys were getting older, American comic books were beginning to trickle into the city again, and so Duddy was attracted by this new line. After some haggling he agreed to order by the dozen if, in exchange, he was given exclusive rights to a territory that, after even more bargaining, included three Protestant schools, two parochials, the B'nai B'rith Youth House, a yeshiva, and at least four poolrooms and a bowling alley. This venture was the first of Duddy's to end in disaster. Three weeks later, when the going was really good, Barney was picked up by the police and fined. Duddy, unfortunately, was caught with a large stock on hand. He took fright and threw them in the furnace.

Other projects, like the hockey stick sideline, were more profitable.

At the age of twelve Duddy discovered that smiling boys with autograph books could get in to hockey practices at the Forum. Getting in to see minor league teams like the Royals was a cinch, and if you were quick or smart enough to hide in the toilet after the Royals had left the ice you could also get to see the Canadiens practice, and those were the years of Lach, Blake, and the great Maurice Richard. While they were on the ice the players' spare sticks, kept in a rack against the wall in a gangway leading into the passages out, were guarded by a thirteen-year-old stick boy. Duddy guessed that these sticks, each with a star player's name crayoned on it, would be treasured by many a fan. So he worked out a system. Getting another boy, usually A.D., to come along with him and talk to the stick boy, leading him gently away from the rack, Duddy would then emerge from under a seat, grab as many sticks as he could manage, and run like hell. The sticks netted him a tidy profit. But even though the stick boy was changed from time to time, making further forays possible, the business was a risky one. It was only seasonal too.

Duddy took his first regular job at the age of thirteen in the summer of 1945. He went to work in his Uncle Benjy's dress factory for sixteen dollars a week, and there he sat at the end of a long table where twelve French-Canadian girls, wearing lowered housecoats over their dresses, sewed belts in the heat and dust. The belts were passed along to Duddy, who turned them right side out with a poker and dumped them in a cardboard carton. It was tedious work and Duddy took to reversing the black and red and orange belts in an altogether absentminded manner. Supporting the poker against his crotch, he'd roll the belts over it one by one. The girls began to make jokes about his technique, but Duddy did not understand at first

47

what the fuss and giggles and slow burning looks were a
about.

The girls, however, seemed agreeable enough. Funny-look
ing and thin mostly, that was true; one with a squint and thre
with crucifixes, five with black hair worn pompadour style an
two with wedding rings and another, without a ring, who wa
pregnant. Gabrielle had a bad rumbling cough and when th
one with the squint lowered to thread a needle you could se
something of her bosom. She had the biggest breasts of th
twelve. Her name was Theresa and there was always a Pep
beside her machine. She usually consumed at least four b
noon and as they day wore on big wet patches spread under he
armpits and she began to smell bad. The girls punched in eac
morning at five to nine, and by nine A.M. they had all a
sumed their places by the machines: a tense crouch. At on
minute past nine there was a bell, a whir, the machines bega
and the girls, taking deep breaths, bent their heads lower ove
their work. One of them, Jacqueline, was a chain-smoker, an
by ten-thirty her smock and everything around her were li
tered with ashes.

Around the time when Duddy began to understand the joke
about his method of rolling belts, he also noticed that on
two men worked on the third floor. Malloy, who duste
coats on manikins at the far end of the floor, was an old ma
with a fierce tattoo on his chest. Herby, the sweeper, was
colored boy, and Duddy always watched him for the pink flas
of his tongue and the palms of his hands. Other men—eve
Uncle Benjy himself—occasionally passed through the thir
floor. Manny Kaplan, the (as he put it) personnel manag
and a nephew on the other side of the family, came in once
the morning and again in the afternoon. He swept in with
big frenzied smile and shouted, "Atta boy," at the girls, "at
boy," and leaning and looking he counted how many belts the
still had to do, making a note of who was behind and who wa
absent. Much more popular was little Epstein, the silver-hair
cutter who came once a day with chocolate cookies, a poun
of Bing cherries maybe, or two dozen plums for the girls, a
ways stopping to pinch or kiss them, rolling his eyes and sa
ing, "Mn-mn" in a way that made the girls laugh and feel goo

Duddy noticed that there were only two other men on th
floor and that when he supported the poker against his crotc
Adele, the youngest girl at the table, watched him out of th
corner of her eye. She was a nervous girl, too, forever gettin
up to go to the toilet. One hot afternoon, after Duddy had g
up to let her pass, Theresa indicated with a jerk of her hea

48

that Duddy ought to follow her. He waited a moment, coughed, and excused himself. The other girls giggled when he went off.

Unfortunately for Duddy, his Uncle Benjy passed by a half hour later and saw that Adele and Duddy were gone and guessed where they were. Uncle Benjy had Duddy transferred to the cutting room.

Uncle Benjy was a wealthy man. A disappointed one too. His wife, Ida, went to Florida every winter. And when they were together for an important wedding or an old friend's funeral or the summer they both had a lot to drink before going to bed.

"They say there's a new doctor in Los Angeles who can work miracles."

"Benjy, please."

"What harm could it do to give him a try?"

"You ought to leave me, Benjy. I'd understand."

"Got yourself lined up good in Miami, eh? Some ritzy bachelor who can make his ears wiggle."

"Benjy."

"Or maybe that physio-what's-it you told me about. You know, the blond exerciser with the Ph.D."

"Gil?"

"That's the one. Come clean, Ida. I can take it."

She would pass out at last and Benjy would get out of bed and gather up her dress and girdle and stockings where they had fallen on her way to bed. Afterwards he would usually sit up in the kitchen for hours. A short fat man in enormous blue shorts with a golf ball pattern, he might fry himself a couple of eggs and read the socialist magazines he subscribed to that came from England and the United States. These bored him even more than Miami. Foolishness, romance about what the workers were, and advertisements for family planning and summer camps where solemn Negroes sang progressive songs.

Always, before going to sleep, he kissed Ida on the forehead. Sometimes, more drunken times, he would hold her close, his head squeezed against her breasts, and she would waken dizzy and afraid. He never knew that. She made sure he never realized that her sleep had been disturbed. But come morning Ida would be gone again.

Finally Benjy's father called him to the house. "Why are there no children?" he asked.

"I'm impotent."

The old man gave Benjy a bottle. "It's made from herbs. An old country recipe."

At home Benjy flushed the bottle's contents down the toilet, and he and his father never discussed the matter again. Meanwhile, Benjy made more money and enemies. He refused to contribute to the synagogue building fund. "Praying went out with the spears, Sam. You can quote me." A known supporter of communist causes, he was always good for a touch when there was a strike or a defense fund or the *Tribune* was in trouble. He enjoyed bragging about these contributions in the company of other manufacturers.

"Comrade Peltier—he drops in from time to time, you know —told me the other day that when we get round to nationalizing the needle trade I'm likely to be in charge."

"Another season like this and you can take charge tomorrow."

"That means that in your sweatshop, Sam, you'd have to allow a union."

"Over my dead body."

"All right. Over your dead body, then. And Harry here is going to have to put paper and soap in those filthy toilets of his."

Uncle Benjy got along no better with the communists who came to him for money. He couldn't forgive them their abuse of Trotsky and they were unhappy about his little irreverences, like making an ostentatious sign of the cross when Peltier mentioned Stalin. Books, probably, gave him the most enjoyment, and Benjy was a prodigious reader. But here too there was more disappointment than pleasure. Tolstoi, yes, and Balzac. Gorki, too. But where among the modern belly-achers was there a writer to teach him about a fat factory owner hopelessly in love with a woman who dyed her hair, wore too much rouge, and preferred contract bridge to Bach. A foolish woman. Ida. "Even if we could have a son," he often thought, "Ida would be no fit companion for my old age, so why . . ." He didn't understand why and nobody could tell him. Meanwhile, he helped keep the family together and drank alone.

When Max had come to tell him he was getting married, Benjy said, "Bring her around, sure. I can hardly wait. The girls who would marry the likes of you I have to see to believe." His wedding gift was to set Max up with a taxicab. "I'd give you a job in the factory but I happen to be in business to make a profit." And Max, familiar with his older brother's acid tongue, had smiled affably and made no reply. "Imagine," he once told Debrofsky, "not being able to get it up. Ever, I mean."

"No wonder he's such a lush," Debrofsky had said.

"Once," Max had said, dropping a sugar cube on his tongue, "just after he began to make his name but before his personal trouble, the Boy Wonder won a bet by spending a night in the Ford Hotel banging three different broads. He's got a whang that could choke a horse. *I* know, we had a leak together once . . . But to get back to poor Benjy, he's got his good points, you know. For my Lennie he'd do anything."

It was true.

Benjy was in the hospital the night Lennie was born and he held him and bloodied his knuckles the day he was circumcised. He had a specialist flown in from Toronto when Lennie developed an unusually severe case of rheumatic fever and he picked the boy's school, the books he ought to read, and took him to every circus that came to town.

"It's not right, Max," Minnie said. "You're the father."

"I'm the father. Sure I'm the father. But Benjy can't—well, you know."

Uncle Benjy took pride in all of Lennie's achievements. The medals, the scholarships, and ultimately his acceptance by the McGill University Faculty of Medicine. He paid the boy's fees, gave him a weekly allowance, and was certainly prepared to set him up in practice when the time came.

* * *

Uncle Benjy felt differently about Duddy, but it did not come out until the boy went to work for him. He did not like Duddy on sight, it's true. The thin crafty face, the quick black eyes and the restlessness, the blackheads and the oily skin, the perpetual fidgeting, the grin so shrewd and knowing, all made a bad impression on Uncle Benjy. He was prepared to give Duddy a chance, however, but Duddy went and loused it up. Two weeks after he had been transferred to the cutting room he charged into Uncle Benjy's office and told him, "That old geezer in the cutting room, Laroche, is swiping lengths of cloth. I saw him."

But Uncle Benjy looked at him with displeasure.

"What'sa matter?"

"I'm not interested."

"He's stealing from you. Jeez, aren't you gonna fire him?"

"Next time you come in here with a story like that I'll fire you."

Duddy leaped to his feet.

"Wait." Uncle Benjy could see that the boy's eyes were full, but he could not stop himself. "In all my years in the trade I've never hired anyone to spy on the workers here."

"Why?"

"What?"

Duddy smiled thinly and his voice quieted. "Are you afraid that there are even more of them stealing?"

"What?"

"That maybe with all your loans and favors to them they still think you're the boss like?"

"Some kid. Some kid you are."

"Not like Lennie?"

"You're only here a week and already you may have got a girl in trouble. Two weeks in the cutting room and you come to me with this story about Laroche Manny tells me you've been selling the girls underwear and stuff you get from some mail order house. Is that true?"

"How did you make all your money, Uncle Benjy? Tell me that."

"Some kid."

"Sure. Why not?"

"I don't like squealers. Try to remember that."

"Why don't you fire me, Uncle Benjy?"

"I'm not going to fire you because it would hurt your grandfather."

"Is that so?"

"You're some kid, Duddy, some kid, but this much you ought to know. If you ever do anything to hurt your grandfather I'll break every bone in your body beginning with the little fingers."

"How come you care so much? You never even go to visit him any more."

Uncle Benjy pushed his chair back from his desk. "I think you'd better get back to work," he said.

Uncle Benjy, Duddy figured, had humiliated him, and he would remember that.

"When the Boy Wonder," Max had once told him, "loses his temper he could eat bread and it would come out toasted. That's the size of it."

Duddy liked to think that his anger was made of the same hot stuff. He liked to think, in fact, that point for point he was a lot like the Boy Wonder before he had made his name. Duddy had seen him stepping outside the synagogue on Yom Kippur once, before his personal trouble, and left and right men had waved heartily or turned pale and the women had followed him with their eyes. The Boy Wonder was no atheist, like Uncle Benjy. Even, as Max had once explained to him, if

Yom Kippur fell on the same day as the Kentucky Derby and a heavyweight champion fight together the Boy Wonder would place no bets. Max knew because, even though he was a taxi driver, he was an intimate of the Boy Wonder and one day he would introduce Duddy to him.

"Not yet. Next year maybe. When you're ready."

But it was a promise all the same.

Meanwhile Duddy worked on the weekends and each summer (though never for Uncle Benjy again), and he continued to put money in the bank. For Duddy had never forgotten that his grandfather had said, "A man without land is nobody."

Duddy wanted to be a somebody. Another Boy Wonder maybe. Not a loser, certainly.

COMMENCEMENT

They arrived by fives and eights and threes. A surge of mothers and fathers and brothers and sisters and grandparents to a hot sticky gym. They came with smiles and jokes and embarrassment, the men pulling at their ties and the women choked by their girdles, walking through the halls of learning to see their sons and daughters, the class of '48, graduate classes one, two, and three from Fletcher's Field High School to—as Leonard Bush, M.A. (McGill), said each year—the wide world. Here, Max Kravitz said, was the door to the sub-basement where the Boy Wonder had organized a lunchtime crap game. There with the red face goes Feeney, an enemy of our people. Here comes Mendelsohn's boy, the scholarship winner. There was the exact spot, Benny Rabinovitch pointed out, where Mickey "The Mauler" Shub had KO'd the sometime principal of F.F.H.S., Dr. Ross McEwen.

The men mopped their necks with handkerchiefs and the women, wearing too much make-up, fanned themselves with programs that announced GREETING, GRADS, *from* MORRIE THE TAILOR, and scholarships for a hundred dollars donated by Steinberg's Groceterias and for fifty dollars in everlasting memory of Mrs. Ida Berg.

"It goes off the income tax," Sam Fine said.

They arrived too soon and thirsty and proud and immediately shamed their sons and daughters by waving and whistling at them.

"Yoo-hoo."

High over the platform loomed the mighty black and green crest with the inscription WORK AND HONOR.

53

"Well, well, if it isn't Tannenbaum in the flesh. You got son here?"

"Why not?"

"Is yours going to a night club afterwards? I gave mine a ten-spot. Aw, what the hell I said to myself. Next week he goes to work in the store."

"Mine's going to McGill to be a lawyer."

"The way you operate, Tannenbaum, you'll need him."

Fanning themselves, they watched as the staff filed in silent and severe and took their places on the platform at last.

"White men," Panofsky said sourly.

"What'sa matter with women teachers that they never have no watermelons?"

"Sam, please, people can hear you."

One chair was empty. Mr. MacPherson wasn't there.

"That's Coldwell, the torturer. Yeah, that one."

Mr. Feeney sat next to Mr. Cox. Mr. Gyle, who had failed engineering and decided to become a teacher, sat next to Miss Bradshaw. Mr. Jackson adjusted his hearing aid.

"Becky! Be-cky! No, over here. Why does she turn away Louis?"

The choir of two hundred boys and girls came marching in according to height, the boys in white shirts and black bow ties and the girls in school tunics.

"Listen, with the speeches and everything we'll be lucky to get out of here by two o'clock."

"Sh."

> Ten men went to mow,
> Went to mow a meadow,
> Ten men, nine men, eight men,
> Seven men, six men, five men,
> Four men, three men, two men,
> One man and his dog
> Went to mow a meadow.

"A Yiddish song they couldn't sing? It would be against the law?"

Martin Abromovitch, his Adam's apple making his black bow tie bobble, strode across the platform to play the *Polonaise* by Chopin.

"I know that. It was in *A Song to Remember*."

"Sh."

"Oh sh-sh yourself. Pain in the neck!"

There was some mistaken applause at the end of the first

section, more at the end of the second and still more, these decidedly resentful, at the end of the third. When Martin Abromovitch finally finished playing, the wary ones among the audience waited until he stood up and bowed twice before joining in the ovation with warm charitable looks for the uncultured early applauders among their neighbors.

"So, Abromovitch, are you proud of your grandson?"

"He played without a hat."

"Paw. For Christ's sake!"

"It would hurt him to wear a hat?"

"Have you ever heard of the wheel, Paw? Some damn fool invented this thing you attach to a wagon and it turns. We've got this business called electricity too now. You press a button, see, and . . . *this is modern times.*"

"He doesn't wear a hat and he can't speak Yiddish."

"Neither could Chopin."

"Who?"

"Skip it. Never mind. Look, there's the speaker."

Captain John Edgar Tate, author (*Canada, Land of Contrasts*), famous broadcaster and lecturer, journalist, explorer (first white man to paddle and chart all the tributaries of the Peace River), world traveler and proud descendant of a family of United Empire Loyalists, clutched the speaker's rostrum like a ship's prow, cleared his throat fiercely and looked down from under graying beetle brows at his audience of small skeptical round-shouldered men, women with too much rouge, and children, some restless and yawning and others inclined to pick their noses—looked down and stroked a puffy red cheek and measured and realized too late that he had brought the wrong speech with him. But he did not falter. He spoke feelingly of the Red Indian and the first British and French-Canadian settlers who came to the country; and he talked about Jacques Cartier, La Salle, and General Wolfe.

"You see that red nose he's got? That comes from too much Johnnie Walker."

"Louder. *Louder, please.*"

"Why couldn't they have invited one of our own to speak?"

"Who, for instance?"

"Dr. Rosen, there's a speaker for you. To hear him talk about cancer . . ."

Captain John Edgar Tate shifted his attention to the present age, the wide world today's graduates would have to contend with, and after some dark warnings about the communist threat, he concluded, "Don't drop the ball. Because if you drop the ball you're passing it to Uncle Joe."

There was some mild applause.

"In Japan when a man gets up to speak he has to hold ice cubes in his hands, and he can only speak for as long as he can hold them. That's for me."

"I'll tell you, Sydney, this speaker—"

"Don't tell me. *I know,* Paw. He doesn't wear a hat."

"Oh, am I ever dying for a cold drink."

"How's about some watermelon instead, Harry? Ice-cold."

"Hoo-haw. Don't speak."

At last the graduates were called up to get their diplomas. First came small squinting Hersh (he had come second in the province and won a scholarship to McGill), and behind him came Mendelsohn's boy, another scholarship winner, and Rita Bloom, who had come fifth in the province.

"My boy's in the minors," Brown said. "He probably doesn't get his diploma until three in the morning."

Shmul Berger was awarded the Ida Berg Scholarship.

"It's a gyp. He should have been disqualified."

Shmul's father, Rabbi Isaac Berger, was supposed to have a photographic memory. They said he could stick a pin through any volume of the Talmud and, given the number of the page it had come out on, tell you the exact word it had punctured.

"That's the last of the prize winners. Main event now."

"About time."

One by one to milder and milder applause the boys and girls stepped up to shake the hand of Leonard Bush, M.A., and take their diplomas.

"There he is!"

Duddy Kravitz was the four-hundred-and-tenth boy to be handed his diploma. He had graduated third class with failures in history and Algebra 11. He accepted his diploma with a thin smile, turned sharply away from Mr. MacPherson's empty seat on the platform, and walked away on squeaky black shoes.

Max Kravitz clapped loudly. "Atta boy, Duddy. Atta boy."

"Sh," Lennie said.

Uncle Benjy turned to his father and the old man looked at the floor.

"Atta boy," Max said.

11

Duddy found the land he wanted quite by accident.

That summer, the year he graduated from F.F.H.S., he went to work as a waiter in a hotel in the Laurentian mountains. Rubin's Hotel Lac des Sables was in Ste. Agathe des Monts, and of all the waiters taken on for the summer, only Duddy was not a college boy. The others were first and second year McGill boys, none had ever been to F.F.H.S.—they came from more prosperous families—and Duddy found it difficult. Some of the other employees, like Cuckoo Kaplan, the recreation director, and the boys in Artie Bloom's band, had their own rooms, but all the waiters slept in the same dormitory over the recreation hall that extended above the lake. After a long day's work they often shared a bottle of rye and sang songs like:

> We're poor little lambs who've lost our way,
>   Baa! Baa! Baa!
> We're little black sheep who've gone astray,
>   Baa-aa-aa! . . .

Duddy, leaping into a lapse in the harmonizing, tried to introduce items like:

> Oh, the captain had a one-eyed mate,
> He loved him like a brother,
> And every night at half-past eight
> They buggered one another.

But the boys, though they never actually asked him to shettup, would not join in and gradually Duddy's voice died. On other nights, when the boys went on midnight swims or to drink beer in Val Morin, Duddy was not invited.

Duddy, alone among the boys, was not rattled by the heat and the hurry, the quarrels and the sometimes spiteful squalor of the kitchen. The gift of a bottle of rum insured the cook's goodwill—Duddy had no trouble getting his orders. In fact he was so quick in the dining room that after two weeks Mr. Rubin gave him three extra tables. This seemed to antagonize the other boys even more and, provoked by Irwin Shubert, they began to ride Duddy hard.

"It's the cretinous little money-grubbers like Kravitz that cause anti-Semitism," Irwin told the boys.

Irwin Shubert was nineteen, a tall bronzed boy with curly black hair, sleepy black eyes, and a mouth too lavish for his face. Persistently bored and with a tendency to smile knowledgeably, an insider sworn to silence, he seldom lifted his voice above a liquid whisper. His father was one of the most famous criminal lawyers in the province and it was said that Irwin promised to be even more brilliant. He kept his books locked in a suitcase. He owned a marriage manual and a copy of Krafft-Ebing, but his prize was an enormous, profusely illustrated medical volume that was supposed to be restricted to members of the profession. All these books Irwin feigned to approach with scientific disinterest, but Duddy was not fooled. He recognized the hoard as a creep's equivalent of his own library, beginning with *Gasoline Alley Gang Bang,* through *Kitty* to Tiffany Thayer's *Three Musketeers,* and he recommended some reading to Irwin.

"God's Little Acre," he said, "that's the horniest."

He made this suggestion on his second day at the hotel and thereby also alienated Irwin. Duddy couldn't understand this. For, at the beginning, Irwin fascinated him. He claimed to be able to hypnotize people and he told dandy stories about women and whips and boy scout masters. Duddy didn't believe any of the stories; he always laughed, in fact, and that infuriated Irwin still more. "You're great," he'd tell Irwin. "Jeez you know more hot stuff . . ."

Irwin began to bait Duddy when the other boys were there.

"Next time you intend to practice self-abuse, David, would you be good enough to lock the toilet door?"

Another time it was, "Tell me, David, is it true that you and Yvette are cohabiting?" Yvette was the second floor chamber-maid. "I'm told she's wild about *soixante-neuf.* But take care child. She's got gonorrhea."

"Don't worry. I wouldn't touch her with a ten-foot pole."

Yet another day it was, "Would you do us all a favor," Irwin asked, flicking Duddy hard enough with a towel to make him wince, "and take a bath? You stink."

"How would you like to hold this for a while?"

The splash of laughter that followed then and at other times Duddy at first mistook for approval of his wit. Some of the other boys, like Donald Levitt, seemed fond of him. Bernie Altman had once invited Duddy to join him for a beer and

58

said that when he graduated from McGill he was going to go to Israel. Then one morning Bernie discovered ten dollars missing from his wallet.

"*I'm* missing fifteen," Irwin said.

"But we all went to Val Morin last night," Donald said. "It must be an outsider."

"David didn't come with us," Irwin said.

"I'd better check again," Bernie said. "Maybe I'm mistaken."

"Sh," Irwin said, "here it comes. The Judas."

For the first two weeks of the season Duddy and Irwin were separated in the dormitory by an empty bed, that's all. Irwin often stayed up late and read with a pocket flashlight. Around three o'clock one morning, when all the other boys were asleep, Duddy woke to see Irwin sitting up in bed with the flashlight and the enormous medical book. He took one look at Irwin's agonized face, saw the book and the other hand under the covers, and quickly guessed what was happening.

"Jeez."

Irwin looked up, startled and pale. Duddy grinned, he winked, and gesturing enthusiastically, he said, "Atta boy, Irwin. Whew! Pull!"

Irwin dropped his flashlight, he trembled. It seemed that he had begun to cry, but Duddy was not sure. The next morning, however, Irwin would not talk to him and the troubles that were to last all summer began.

Irwin spoke to Rubin's only daughter.

"Look, Linda, I don't want to cause any trouble. Don't say a word to your father either, because I don't want to get the Kravitz kid fired, but somebody's been stealing money from the boys in the dorm and I want to know if any guests are missing things."

Sunday, with so many people checking out and new guests constantly arriving, was the most nerve-wracking day of the week. At ten P.M., his work finally finished, Duddy went to collapse on his cot. He found a bottle of Scotch lying there with a note. The bottle, it seemed, was a gift from Mr. Holstein, who had left that morning without tipping him.

"Aren't you going to offer us a drink?" Irwin asked.

The other boys sat on their cots, heads drooping.

"I'd like to send the bottle to my grandfather. A gift like."

"Oh, *it* has a grandfather," Irwin said, getting glasses. "Come on, child."

"Let him keep it," Donald said.

"Naw. Irwin's right. Let's all have a drink on me."

Irwin quickly brought Duddy the glasses and he filled them one by one.

"Linda Rubin's got a crush on you," Irwin said. "Did you know that?"

"Aw."

"Never mind. Hotel owners' daughters have fallen for poor boys before. Well, *à la vôt*—" Irwin lifted the glass to his mouth, made a horrible face, and spilled its contents on Duddy. "You filthy little swine," he said, "is this your idea of a joke?"

"Wha'?"

"Don't any of you touch your glasses. Do you know what this is?"

Duddy sniffed his glass and his face went white.

"I know we haven't exactly been friendly," Irwin said, "but if this is your idea of how to pay us back—Let's make him drink his, guys. He deserves it."

The other boys, too whacked to fight or decide, began to file out.

"I came in and I found the bottle on the bed," Duddy shouted. "So help me God. You all saw. I came in and the bottle was on my bed."

Irwin started after the others. "You're lucky, Kravitz. They should have made you drink it. What a disgusting stunt."

Shunned by the college boy waiters, Duddy began to investigate Ste. Agathe on his own when he had time off.

Some sixty miles from Montreal, set high in the Laurentian hills on the shore of a splendid blue lake, Ste. Agathe des Monts had been made the middle-class Jewish community's own resort town many years ago. Here, as they prospered, the Jews came from Outremont to build summer cottages and hotels and children's camps. Here, as in the winter in Montreal, they lived largely with their neighbors. Friends and relatives bought plots of land and built their cottages and boathouses competitively, but side by side. There were still some pockets of Gentile resistance, it's true. Neither of the two hotels that were still in their hands admitted Jews, but that, like the British raj who still lingered on the Malabar Coast, was not so discomforting as it was touchingly defiant. For even as they played croquet and sipped their gin and tonics behind protecting pines, they could not miss the loud, swarthy parade outside. The short husbands with their outrageously patterned sports shirts arm in arm with purring wives too obviously full for slacks, the bawling kids with triple-decker ice cream cones

60

he squealing teen-agers, and the trailing grandfather with his beard and black hat. They could not step out of their enclaves and avoid the speeding cars with wolf-call horns. The lake was out of the question. Sailboats and canoes had no chance against speedboats, spilling over with relatives and leaving behind a wash of empty Pepsi bottles. Even the most secluded part of the lake was not proof against the floating Popsicle wrapper, and the moonlight canoe trip ran the risk of being run down by a Cuckoo Kaplan-led expedition to the island. Boatloads full of honeymooners and office girls and haberdashery salesmen singing, to the tune of "Onward, Christian Soldiers":

> *Onward, Rubin's boarders,*
> *Onward, to the shore,*
> *With sour cream and latkas,*
> *We're staying two weeks more.*

Rubin's was not the only Jewish resort in Ste. Agathe, either. There were many others. But Rubin had, in the shape of Cuckoo Kaplan, Ste. Agathe's undisputed number one comic. "Cuckoo may be a Montreal boy," Rubin said, "but he's no shnook. He's played night clubs in the States."

Cuckoo was billed as Montreal's Own Danny Kaye and his name and jokes often figured in *Mel West's What's What.* Short and wiry, with a frantic, itchy face, Cuckoo was ubiquitous. At breakfast he'd pop up from under a table to crack an egg on a bald man's head and at midnight he'd suddenly race through the dance hall in a Gay Nineties bathing suit and dive through a window into the lake. He always had a surprise for lunch too. Once he might chase the cook through the dining room with a meat cleaver and later in the week chances were he'd hold up two falsies, saying he had found them on the beach, and ask the owner to claim them. Aside from organizing games when it rained and his regular nightly act—his Romeo and Juliet Capelovitch skit was a knockout—Cuckoo had some special routines for the winter season and was good at getting publicity. He got his picture in the paper on the first subzero day of winter by sawing a hole in the ice and taking a dip. For his annual picture, with Rubin's Hotel Lac des Sables prominent in the background, Cuckoo wore a hilarious wig, blackened two front teeth, and put on a long black woolen bathing suit. Once, after his annual dip, he was in bed with a fever for two weeks.

Cuckoo's father couldn't understand him. "What is it with

you, Chaim? For a lousy ninety dollars a week," he said, "t make a fool of yourself in front of all those strangers."

But Cuckoo was not without hope. He had once been hel over for three weeks in a night club in Buffalo and anothe time he had stopped the show at the Pink Elephant in Nev Jersey. Each year on his vacation he went to New York an walked from one agent's office to another with a large foli under his arm. Meanwhile, he was adored in Ste. Agathe Guests from all the other hotels came to Rubin's on Saturda night to catch his act.

Duddy, too, was most impressed with Cuckoo, and he use to bring him breakfast in bed. Cuckoo, who was familiar wit Max the Hack by name, gave Duddy bit parts in two of hi skits. He could see that the boy was lonely and he didn't min when he came to his room late at night to talk.

The bed in the hot, smoke-filled little room was always ur made. Usually the breakfast tray was still on the floor and ther were cigarette butts and soiled laundry and empty rye bottle everywhere. Duddy usually cleared a space for himself on th floor and Cuckoo, reduced to his underwear, curled like coiled spring on a corner of the bed with a glass in his han mindless of the cigarette ashes he dropped on the sheets.

Duddy told Cuckoo about some of his business ideas.

Next summer, he thought, he might try to set up in the movi rental business. All he needed was a truck, a projector, and goy to run the camera, and with a good movie, playing a di ferent resort each night, he would rake in no fortune, but . . Another idea he had was to make color movies of wedding and bar-mitzvahs. There might be a goldmine in this, he tol Cuckoo, and he was thinking of calling himself Dudley Kar Productions. Who knows, but if the idea caught on, five-si years from now he might be able to make a feature-lengt comedy right here in Montreal, starring Cuckoo Kaplan. B to begin with, he needed that truck and projector and a go to operate it. Maybe the Boy Wonder, who was an intimate his father's, would stake him. Duddy said that he would se about that in the autumn.

The rye helped to calm Cuckoo. Gradually he stoppe scratching his head and, if Duddy stayed long enough, l sometimes tried out one of his new routines on him. But fir he'd say, "You've got to be honest with me. I want to kno exactly what you think. I can take it."

Duddy was flattered by the tryouts in the small bedroo and every one of Cuckoo's routines made him howl.

"You kill me, Cuckoo. My sides hurt me, honest."

When Cuckoo was depressed after playing to a hostile house on a Saturday night, Duddy would hurry to his bedroom with sandwiches and a pitcher of ice cubes. "Look," he'd say, "you think it was always such a breeze for Danny Kaye when he was playing the borscht circuit?" On and on Duddy would talk while Cuckoo consumed rye with alarming haste. When Cuckoo replied at last, he'd say in a slurred voice, "That's how biz, I guess. That's show biz." It was his favorite expression.

"You know something, kid, my trouble is I've got the wrong face for a comic. People take one look at Danny Kaye or Lou Costello and right off they howl. I have to work too hard. They take one look at my kisser and they want to buy me a sandwich or help me find a girl."

Cuckoo took lots of vitamin pills and he ate sparingly. Many times after a show that only went over so-so he was sick to his stomach. Then, perched on his bed ready for instant flight, wiping his thin chest with a towel, he would wait until he felt sufficiently settled inside to start drinking again. On one night like that he told Duddy, "I'm going to be famous one day. I'm going to be very famous. And I'll never forget you."

Something else about Cuckoo was that he too hated Irwin Shubert.

One night after the show Irwin phoned Cuckoo to say he was in the bar at Le Coq d'Or twelve miles away with a Broadway producer on vacation who was looking for fresh faces for his latest musical. Irwin's manner was so urgent, so sincere, that Cuckoo hurried right over there. While Irwin and the producer went through a couple of bottles of champagne he did his Romeo and Juliet Capelovitch act twice and his James Cagney bar-mitzvah speech. "Can you dance?" the producer asked. Cuckoo danced. "Let's hear you sing something?" Cuckoo sang. The producer ordered more champagne. "Let's see the Capelovitch routine again. If you're not too tired, I mean?" Cuckoo obliged. "Thanks a million," the producer said, and he got up and left the bar.

"Where's he going?" Cuckoo asked, out of breath.

"He wants to talk to me privately," Irwin said. "You wait here."

Cuckoo waited an hour, he waited two hours, he waited until closing time, and then he was given a bill for two dinners and whole evening's drinking. It came to nearly thirty dollars. Only a couple of afternoons later he overheard Irwin say to one of the guests, "Not only is he the most puerile comedian I've ever seen, he's also the most gullible. The other night

Jerry and I were stuck with a big bill at the Coq d'Or so phoned Cuckoo and . . ."

The story spread. People smiled at Cuckoo and slapped him on the back. "Hey, how'd you like to meet a producer to night?" So Cuckoo took to waiting for Irwin on the beach. Then, once Irwin's back was turned, Cuckoo would wink at the others, lick his index finger and wet his eyebrows with it and walk off saucily. That was usually good for a laugh, but Duddy warned him against it one night. "They say he and Rubin's daughter are going to get hitched. They go riding to gether a lot. So watch it, eh?"

Yet another business idea Duddy told Cuckoo about was his plan for a Ste. Agathe newspaper. There were nine hotels in town, he said, and each one must have a list as long as your arm of addresses for all over the States. Wouldn't it be smart publicity for them to keep Americans in touch, to remind them out of season about Ste. Agathe and the swell times they had had there? And think, too, of the possible advertisers who would want to reach American tourists passing through Mon real. Night clubs, department stores, hotels, restaurants. Jee everybody. The newspaper could organize beauty contests and regattas and fight racial prejudice. This was an idea that could work. Duddy was convinced of it and he told Cuckoo that he would like him to write a funny column for the newspaper. He thought he might call it the *Laurentian Liner*, because it would travel everywhere, and Cuckoo agreed the name was a catchy one. Duddy said he would speak to the Boy Wonder about it in the autumn.

Duddy had been putting money in the bank since he was eleven and in his first month at Rubin's he had earned nearly three hundred dollars in tips, but what he needed was a re stake.

At night, lying exhausted on his cot, Duddy realized how little money he had in big business terms and he dreamed about his future. He knew what he wanted, and that was to own his own land and to be rich, a somebody, but he was not sure of the smartest way to go about it. He was confident. But there had been other comers before him. South America, for instance, could no longer be discovered. It had been found. Toni Home Permanent had been invented. Another guy had already thought up Kleenex. But there was something out there, like let's say the atom bomb formula before it had been discovered, and Duddy dreamed that he would find it and make his fortune. He had his heroes. There was the strange no had walked into the Coca-Cola Company before it had made its name and said, "I'll write down two words on a piece of paper, and if you use my idea I want a partnership in the company." The two words were "Bottle it." Don't forget, either, the man who saved that salmon company from bankruptcy with the slogan *This salmon is guaranteed not to turn pink in the can.* There was the founder of the *Reader's Digest* —he'd made his pile too. The man who thought up the supermarket must have been another shnook of a small grocer once. There was a day when even the Boy Wonder gathered and sold streetcar transfers. Sure, everyone had to make a start, but it was getting late. Duddy was already seventeen and a half and sure as hell he didn't want to wait on tables for the rest of his life. He needed a stake. When he got back to Montreal in the autumn he would speak to his father and go to see the Boy Wonder.

"I'm not," he once told Cuckoo, "the kind of a jerk who walks around deaf and dumb. I keep my eyes peeled." And already Duddy had plenty of ideas. He had even had letterheads printed—Dudley Kane, Sales Agent—and every week he marked the advertising section of the Sunday edition of the New York *Times* for novelties, bargains, and possible agencies. That was a hint he had picked up from Mr. Cohen, whose family was staying at Rubin's for the entire summer. Duddy replied to several advertisements in the *Times*. He was, at one time, interested in a new soap that was guaranteed not to sting the eyes.

Duddy watched all the businessmen who came to the hotel. He made sure they got to know him, too, and that they made no mistake about his being a waiter. That was temporary. He watched the way they avoided their wives and the sun and sat around playing poker and talking about the market and the boom in real estate. Most of them ate too much and took pills. One, a Mr. Farber, had summoned Duddy to his table on his first day at the hotel and torn a hundred-dollar bill in two and given Duddy half of it. "We're here for the season," he had said, "and we want snappy service. You give it to us and the other half of this note is yours. O.K., kid?"

Duddy dreamed, he planned, he lay awake nights smoking, and meanwhile Irwin continued to torment him. One night a bottle of ketchup was emptied on his sheets and once he discovered a dead mouse in his serving jacket pocket.

The other waiters began to feel badly. "Aw, lay off," Bernie Altman said. Another night Donald Levitt said, "Take it easy, Irwin. I'm warning you. He's had enough."

But Irwin couldn't stop and Duddy began to retaliate. When Irwin started to mock him in the dormitory with the others there, Duddy would begin to improvise songs.

> *Hauling away,*
> *There I lay,*
> *Hauling away.*

Another went:

> *Take yourself in hand,*
> *Said the sailor to his mate,*
> *Because in this world*
> *A guy's gotta learn to hold his own.*

12

With the coming of July, the hottest and most grueling month of the season, the waiters were soon too drained for midnight jaunts to Val Morin. They rose listlessly at seven to set their tables and squeeze fruit juices for breakfast, and once the last breakfast had been served, say ten-thirty, it was necessary to set the tables again for lunch. The brawls in the kitchen quickened and the competition for tips got fiercer. After lunch, if the boys had no cutlery to polish, they were usually off duty for two hours and all of them slept, either on the beach or in the darkened dormitory. Not Duddy, however. He hung around the card tables and picked up additional tips running errands for the players.

"There's nothing that little fiend wouldn't do for a dollar," Irwin told Linda, "and that's how I'm going to teach him a lesson. I've got it all figured out."

It was a long hot summer and soon a misplaced toothpaste tube or a borrowed towel was enough to set one boy violently against another. The dormitory over the dance hall had a corrugated tin roof and there were nights when it was too stuffy to sleep. Bernie Altman lost seven pounds and circles swelled under Donald Levitt's eyes, but Duddy showed no signs of fatigue. One afternoon, however, he felt faint, and instead of waiting on the card players he searched for a place to rest. He didn't dare go to the beach because he was a lousy swimmer and Irwin was certainly there, anyway, and he would ridicul his thin white body again, making the girls laugh. The garden was no use because he would surely be asked to fetch a handbag from a third floor bedroom or search for a misplaced pair of sunglasses. So Duddy wandered round the back of the hotel and sat down on a rock. It was so different here from the beach or the main entrance with its flower beds and multicolored umbrellas and manicured lawns. Flies buzzed round a heap of garbage pails, and sheets and towels flapped on a dozen different lines that ran from the fire escapes to numerous poles. A group of chambermaids and kitchen helpers, permanent staff, sat on the fire escape. Dull, motionless, their eyelids heavy, they smoked in silence. Yvette waved, another girl smiled wearily, and Duddy waved back, but he didn't join them. He returned the next afternoon, however, and the afternoon after that, and each time he sat nearer to the drained, expressionless group on the fire escape. On Sunday afternoon he brought six bottles of ice-cold beer with him, laid them on the steps, shrugged his shoulders, and walked off to his rock again. Yvette went over to him.

"Is the beer for us?"

"Let's not make a fuss, eh? I got some big tips today, that's all."

"You're very nice. Thanks."

"Aw."

"Won't you join us?"

"I've got to get back," he said, "see you," and he hurried off, embarrassed, to the dormitory. He found Irwin going through his suitcase there. "Hey!"

"Somebody stole my watch."

"Keep away from my stuff or you'll get this," Duddy said, making a fist. "You'll get this right in the kisser."

A couple of afternoons later Irwin rushed into the dormitory. "Do you know what Duddy told Linda this afternoon?" he asked the boys. "Some fantastic story about a brother Bradley who owns a ranch in Arizona."

"So?"

"I happen to know he only has one brother. He's in med, I think."

"All right. He lied. Big deal."

"He's taking Linda out tonight," Irwin said in his liquid whisper.

When Duddy entered the dormitory a half hour later, the boys watched apprehensively as he shaved and shined his shoes. Bernie Altman would have liked to warn him that something was up, but Irwin was there and it was impossible.

Duddy was pleased, but he felt jumpy too. He didn't know much about broads, though there had naturally been lots of rumors and reports. Of Flora Lubin, for instance, he had heard it said, "That one likes it the Greek way," but watching Flora walk down the street with her schoolbooks held to her breast Duddy couldn't imagine it. Neither could he credit another report, this one about Grepsy Segal's big sister, that, as A.D. put it, she jerks away for dear life every night. (A girl couldn't, anyway, she didn't have a tool.)

Through the years Duddy had collected lots of injunctions about broads and the handling thereof. War Assets safes are not safe. Tell them anything but never put it in writing. "Talk, talk, talk, but no matter what they say there's only one thing they really want." Don't give your correct name and address unless it's really necessary. The hottest are redheads and the easiest single ones over twenty-seven. "A good thing is to start with tickling the back of the neck. That kills them. It's a scientific fact." Gin excites them. Horseback riding gives them hot pants too. Cherries are trouble, but married ones miss it something terrible. "Jewish girls like it just as much as *shiksas*. More, maybe. *I* know."

Sure, Duddy thought, sure, sure, maybe it was all on the legit, but applying it was another thing. A guy could get his face slapped, or worse.

There were various approaches, of course. He had learned some at the hotel. Paddy Schwartz, the bachelor who came to Rubin's every summer for a two-month stay, had a crack at all the goods under forty-five. "If nine say no," he told Duddy, "then maybe the tenth will be agreeable. The thing is to keep in there pitching." Paddy was tall and dark with graying curly hair, but Duddy was disheartened to discover that his private approaches were never nearly so dashing as his public style. After filling his filly of the night—that's what he called them —with drink, he'd say he had a bum ticker and had been given only six months to live. Then, his eyes filled with tears, he'd add that the filly was the most beautiful he had ever met, and was she going to send him to his maker without a night of love? Ed Planter, the furrier in 408, pursued the single ones, the office girls, but only after it had become clear to them that the vacation was ending with no marriage candidate around. He'd take them out, spending lavishly, and then, back outside the single room at the hotel, he'd say, "I had a little dream about you last night, honey. I dreamt that you were nice to me, *very* nice to me, and I made you a gift of a little fur jacket to keep you warm in winter here . . . and here . . . and here." Rubin onfined himself to the chambermaids. "Why not?" he'd say. "To them it's nothing." But actually all he ever did was pinch hem. He pinched hard.

Duddy knew that there were many techniques and he had ad some experience himself. There had been that afternoon e had got Birdie Lyman's brassiere half off when the goddam novie had suddenly ended, and once with a Belmont Park ick-up he'd had everything but. Still, he was scared.

"Yvette's got a real lust for you," Cuckoo told him one night. Why don't you do something about it? You could bring her ere if you wanted . . ."

"Aw. Yvette. Those are a dime a dozen."

But Linda was something else. Soft, curvy, and nifty enough or one of those snazzy fashion magazines, she seemed just bout the most assured girl Duddy had ever met. She had been o Mexico and New York and sometimes she used words that nade Duddy blush. Her cigarette holder, acquired on a trip o Europe, was made of real elephant tusk. At night in the ecreation hall she seldom danced but usually sat at the bar oking with Irwin and Paddy and other favorites. Every after-oon she went riding and Duddy had often seen her starting own the dirt road to the stables, beating her whip against her oot. Linda was nineteen and the daughter of a hotel owner— he was maybe an inch and some taller than he was too—and Duddy couldn't understand why she wanted to go out with im. He'd been leading Thunder back to the stables when he ad run into her.

"Day off today?"

"Yeah."

"Buy me a drink?"

"Wha'?"

"I'm thirsty."

"Sure. Sure thing."

He took her to the Laurentide Ice Cream Bar.

"No," she said. "A *drink.*"

It was not even dark yet.

"Let's go to the Châlet," she said.

The bartender there greeted her warmly. Luckily Duddy had ots of money on him because she drank quickly. Not beer, ither.

"Well, Duddy, how do you like shoveling food into the reedy mouths of the *nouveaux-riches?*"

"Your father is a very decent man to work for," Duddy said arnestly. He couldn't understand why she looked so amused.

"Why?"

"Jeez. I dunno. I mean . . ."

"Did you know that he pinches all the chambermaids' little bums?"

"Maybe we oughta go?"

"No. Let's have another. Hey, Jerry. Two more on the rocks." Turning to Duddy again, she laughed. "You shouldn't let Irwin pick on you like that. You ought to talk back to him."

"I'm not scared. I keep quiet, but I've got my reasons."

"Is that so?"

There was that amused smile again. He didn't like it.

"Yeah."

"Like what?"

"Well," he said, feeling a little dizzy, "I don't really have to work as a waiter, you know. My father's in the transport business. But I'm making a study of the hotel business like."

"Shouldn't I warn my father that he's harboring a future competitor in the dormitory?"

Duddy laughed. He was pleased. "Hey, have you ever read *God's Little Acre?*"

Duddy figured if she had, and admitted it, there might be something doing. But she didn't reply.

"I'm not much of a reader, really, but my Uncle Benjy has read millions of books. Hard-covered ones. My brother Lennie is gonna be a doctor."

"What are you going to be?"

Without thinking, he said, "I'm gonna get me some land one of these days. A man without land is nothing."

He told her about his brother Bradley and that the Boy Wonder, an intimate of his father's, was willing to back him in any line he chose.

"Why don't you take me dancing tonight?"

Duddy drank three cups of black coffee and took a swim to clear his head before he returned to the dormitory. Irwin, lying on the bed, made him nervous—Linda was supposed to be *his* girl—and Duddy couldn't understand why the other watched him so apprehensively while he dressed. Duddy took half an hour combing his hair into a pompadour with the help of lots of brilliantine. He selected from among his shirts a new one with red and black checks and the tie he chose was white with a black and blue pattern of golf balls and clubs. His green sports jacket had wide shoulders, a one-button roll, and brown checks. A crease had been sewn into his gray flannel trousers. He wore two-tone shoes.

Bernie Altman looked hard at Irwin and stopped Duddy a

was going out. "Listen," he said, "I'll lend you my suit if ou like."

"Jeez, that's nice of you. Bernie. I'm going dancing tonight. ut this is the first chance I ___ to wear this jacket. A heavy ate, you know. Thanks anyway."

Irwin choked his laughter with his pillow.

"Look, Duddy, I—Oh, what's the use? Have a good time."

Outside, Linda leaned on the horn of her father's station agon. Duddy ran.

"You're a son of a bitch, Irwin. A real son of a bitch."

"Did I pick those clothes for him?"

"Why is she going out with Duddy?"

"Yeah, what have you two cooked up?" Donald asked.

Duddy and Linda drove to Hilltop Lodge, the resort with e best band, and ordered Scotch on the rocks. Many of the right young people there waved. Two or three raised their yebrows when they saw that Linda was with Duddy. "We're gaged," Linda said. "He uses Ponds."

Duddy danced with her three or four times. She was O.K. the slow ones, but when the band played something hot, a oogie-woogie, for instance, Duddy switched to his free-swing-g F.F.H.S. Tea Dance style and all at once the floor was eared and everyone stood around watching. At first this emed to delight Linda, she laughed a lot, but the second time und she quit on Duddy in the middle of a dance. Once, dur-g a slow number, he held her too close.

"Please," she said.

"This is called a 'Y' dance," Duddy said. But she didn't get e joke.

Linda invited three others to their table and Duddy ordered rinks for them. Melvin Lerner, a dentistry student, held hands ith Jewel Freed. They were both working at Camp Forest and. The other man was bearded and somewhat older than e others; he was thirty maybe. Peter Butler lived in Ste. gathe all year round, he had built his own house on a se-uded part of the lake.

"Peter's a painter," Linda said to Duddy.

"Inside or outside?"

"That's good," Peter said. "That's very good." He slapped s knees again and again.

Duddy looked puzzled.

"He's not joking," Linda said. "Peter's not a house painter, uddy. He paints pictures. Peter is a nonfigurative painter."

"Like Norman Rockwell," Peter said, laughing some more.

"*Touché*," Linda said, and she ordered another round drinks.

"What do you do?" Melvin asked Duddy.

"He's making a study of the hotel business like," Linda said

Peter and Linda danced two slow numbers together and when Duddy looked up again they were gone. An hour late Linda returned alone, her face flushed and bits of dead leave stuck to her dress. "I need a drink," she said. "A big one."

"Maybe we oughta go. I've got to be up at seven tomorrow."

"One for the road."

So Duddy ordered another round. Maybe it was the liquo —he was certainly not used to it—but all at once it seeme to him that Linda had changed. Her voice softened and sh began to ask him lots of questions about his plans for the fu ture. She was not ridiculing him any more, he was sure of that and he was no longer afraid of her. From time to time the room swayed around him and he was glad he wasn't the one wh would have to drive home. But dizzy as he was he felt fine. H no longer heard all her remarks, however, because he wa thinking that hotel owners' daughters had fallen for poor boy before and, given a shot at it, there were lots of improvement he could make at Rubin's. There was the *Laurentian Line* too.

"Well, Duddy, are you game?"

The room rocked.

"Tell me if you don't want to. I won't be angry. Mayb Irwin would . . ."

"No, no. I'll do it."

"It'll give you a good start on your stake."

She helped him outside and into the station wagon. H head rolling and jerking loose each time they hit a bum Duddy tried, he tried hard, to remember what he had agree to. He had told some lies about himself and the Boy Wonde they had talked about the gambling house he ran, and th conversation had come round to roulette. Duddy pretende to be an expert and Linda just happened to own a wheel. The what? He told her he had already earned more than four hu dred dollars in tips and Linda said that was plenty. Plenty Plenty for him to act as banker for the roulette game they wer going to run in the recreation hall beginning at one A.M. Su day night. Wouldn't her father object? No, not if ten per ce of each win went into a box for the Jewish National Fun He couldn't lose—there was that too. She told him so. H might even come out a few hundred dollars ahead.

"Can you make it upstairs yourself?"

"Sure."

"Aren't you going to kiss Linda before you go?"

"Mn."

13

That was Wednesday, and in the three days to go before the game Duddy began to fear for his money. "Sure you could win," Cuckoo said, "but you could lose too. If I were you I wouldn't do it." But if he was afraid for his money, neither did he want Linda to think that he'd welsh on a promise. She was so sweet to him these days. At night in the recreation hall she sometimes called him over to join her for a drink. Still, he thought, maybe I ought to speak to her. I work hard for my money and I need it. Then people began to stop him in the lobby or on the beach.

"I'll be there, kid," Paddy said.

Farber slapped him on the back and winked. "Count me in," he said.

Mr. Cohen stopped him outside the gym. "Is it O.K. if I bring along a couple of pals?"

The Boy Wonder, Duddy thought, would not chicken out in a situation like this. He would be cool. But Duddy couldn't sleep Friday night and he was ashamed to go and tell Cuckoo again that he was scared. He wouldn't want Linda or Irwin to know that, either. It was so nice, too. Suddenly people looking at him and smiling. He no longer had to go round to the back of the hotel to sit with the kitchen help and chambermaids for companionship. Aw, the hell, Duddy figured out that if the bank ever dropped below one hundred dollars he would stop the game, but he withdrew three hundred just in case. Linda took him aside on Saturday afternoon. "Maybe we'd better call it off," she said. "You might lose."

"You said I couldn't lose."

"I said, I said. How do I know?"

"I'm not calling it off. I can't. All those people. Jeez."

Cuckoo pleaded with him once more. "But what if you lose, Duddy?"

"Simple," Duddy said. "If I lose I drown myself. That's show biz."

On Sunday night the boys in Artie Bloom's band, who were

in on the story, broke up early and everyone pretended to be going off to bed or somewhere else. The lights in the recreation hall were turned out and the front door was locked. Fifteen minutes later some of the lights were turned on again and a side door was opened. The players began to arrive. Duddy set up the table and announced the odds in a failing voice. He would pay thirty to one on a full number and the top bet allowed was fifty cents. That would pay fifteen dollars, one-fifty of which would go into the J.N.F. box. Linda, who was helping him, began to sell change. Farber bought five dollars' worth and Mr. Cohen asked for ten. Once Duddy had counted forty players in the hall he asked for the door to be shut.

"Don't worry," Linda said. "The more players, the more money on the board, the better it is for the bank."

But Duddy insisted.

"I'll only take ten dollars' worth for a start," Irwin said.

Duddy looked sharply at Linda and it seemed to him that she was even more frightened than he was. "O.K.," he said. "Place your bets."

Duddy counted at least thirty dollars on the first run. Jeez, he thought. His hands shaky, he was just about to spin the wheel when a voice in the darkness shouted, "Nobody leave. This is a raid."

"Wha'?"

"My men have got the place surrounded. No funny stuff, please."

A spotlight was turned on and revealed was Cuckoo Kaplan in a Keystone Cop costume. His nightstick was made of rubber and the height he shook it at made all the women laugh.

"You're a dirty pig, Cuckoo."

"Some cop."

Duddy shut his eyes and spun the wheel and number thirty-two came up. Nobody was on it. He paid off even money on two blacks, that's all.

Cuckoo took off his shoe, reached into an outlandishly patched sock, and pulled out a dollar bill. "Rubin just gave me an advance on next year's salary. He's crying in the kitchen right now."

"Cuckoo!"

"Put the works on number six for me, but I can't look."

After an hour of play Duddy was ahead more than two hundred dollars. "I'll tell you what," he said. "Lots of you seem to be losing. I'm no chiseler. From now on you can bet a dollar on a number if you want."

That's when Irwin changed another twenty-five dollars and

74

sat down at the table and began to play in earnest. His bets seemed to follow no apparent pattern. On each spin of the wheel he placed a dollar on numbers fifteen, six, thirty-two, three, and twelve, and it was only the next morning when he looked closely at the wheel that Duddy realized these numbers ran together there. Irwin won; he didn't win on each spin, but whenever one of his numbers came up he collected thirty dollars and twice if his number repeated. Others, riding his streak of luck, began to bet with him, and once Duddy had to pay off three different people on number three. That cost him ninety dollars, not counting the side and corner bets.

"Don't worry," Irwin said. "David's father is in the transport business. He doesn't *really* have to work as a waiter."

Duddy turned to Linda, his look astonished.

"His brother Bradley is a big rancher in Arizona," Irwin said. "All David has to do is wire him for more money."

"It's getting late," Mrs. Farber said.

Ed Planter yawned and stretched.

"Don't go," Duddy said. "Not yet, please. Give me a chance to win some of my money back."

Farber saw that Duddy was extremely pale.

"Don't worry, kid," Mr. Cohen said. "Your luck will change."

But Duddy's luck didn't change, it got worse, and nobody at the table joked any more. The men could see that the boy's cheeks were burning hot, his eyes were red, and his shirt adhered to his back. When Duddy paid out on a number his hands shook.

Cuckoo pulled Irwin aside. "It's your wheel, you bastard. I found out."

"Really?"

"Do you know how hard that kid works for his money?"

Irwin tried to turn away, but Cuckoo seized him by the arm. "I'm going to speak to Rubin," he said. "First thing tomorrow morning I'm going to talk to him."

"Linda and I are going to be engaged," Irwin said. "Rubin is very pleased about that. I thought maybe you'd like to know."

"Come on," Duddy said. "Place your bets. Let's not waste time."

The men at the table were tired and wanted to go to bed, but they were also ashamed of winning so much money from a seventeen-year-old boy and they began to play recklessly, trying to lose. It was no use.

"We want to see you upstairs later, Irwin," Bernie Altman said.

On the next spin Duddy went broke and he had to close the game.

"That's show biz," Irwin said. "Right, Cuckoo?"

The men filed out without looking at Duddy, but Linda stayed on after the others had gone.

"Thanks," Duddy said. "Thanks a lot."

"How much did you lose?"

"Everything. Three hundred dollars." Duddy began to scream. "You said I couldn't lose. You told me it was impossible for me to lose."

"I'm sorry, Duddy. I had no idea that—"

"Aw, go to hell. Just go to hell please." He gave the wheel a shove, knocking it over, and rushed outside. Once on the beach he could no longer quell his stomach. Duddy was sick. He sat on a rock, holding his head in his hands, and he began to sob bitterly.

"Hey," Cuckoo shouted, entering the lobby, "has anybody here seen Duddy?"

"No."

"He still hasn't shown up at the dorm," Bernie said. "It's more than an hour now . . ."

"What's going on?" Rubin demanded. "I'm the boss here."

Duddy clenched his teeth and pulled his hair until it hurt. "Goddam it to hell," he said. Some stake. Six weeks of hard work and not a cent to show for it. He was back where he'd started from. Worse. He was probably a laughingstock too. Jeez, he thought. "Goddam you."

Some scraping on the sand disturbed him and Duddy hid behind a rock. He recognized Cuckoo's voice.

"Somebody saw him run towards the beach. There's no telling what he might do."

Linda said something he couldn't make out and Cuckoo's reply was lost in the wind. Then he heard Linda say, "I knew it was his wheel, but I never thought . . ."

Footsteps approached from another direction. Somebody had a flashlight.

"Duddy!"

Let them think I've drowned, he thought. It would serve them right. He had seen a drowned woman once at Shaw-bridge, and the thought of his own face bloated like that— Irwin hanging for it, the bastard, and his father maybe feel-

76

ing sorry he hadn't treated him as well as Lennie—made a hot lump in Duddy's throat. He began to sob again.

"*Duddy!*"

There was a dip of oars and a rippling in the water. A boat had started out.

"*Hal-lo! Duddy!*"

Scampering barefooted across the sand, Duddy broke for the protecting woods. He heard Rubin's gruff voice, "That little bastard, I'll kill him. There was a drowning at the Hilltop Lodge once and the next day there weren't two guests left at the hotel. If this got into the papers it could ruin . . ."

Duddy was seized by an uncontrollable fit of laughter. He rolled over in the grass, biting his arm to muffle the noise.

". . . send for the cops?"

Next came Rubin's voice. "Oh, no you don't. No cops. That little bastard I'll choke him to death."

Duddy came out on a dirt road on the other side of the woods and started back into Ste. Agathe. Three times he stopped, his laughter immense. The thought of them searching for him all through the night and Irwin certainly catching shit galore almost made him forget the three hundred dollars. Almost, but not quite.

Pajama-clad guests drifted down into the lobby one by one.

"I wouldn't like to be in your shoes, Rubin."

"How could you let a seventeen-year-old kid lose all his tips in a roulette game?"

"I knew nothing about it. I swear I—"

"Save it for the reporters tomorrow. When they drag the kid out of the lake—"

"Bite your tongue," Rubin shouted.

"The poor kid."

"Next season it's Hilltop Lodge for me," Mrs. Dunsky said.

"Me too," Mrs. Farber said.

Rubin reminded his guests that there had been a case of ptomaine poisoning at the Hilltop Lodge last year.

"You think your food goes down so good, Rubin? Around the corner at the drugstore bicarbonate sales are booming."

"We're doing everything humanly possible," Rubin said. "All the boys are out searching."

"The bottom of the lake?"

The guests stared accusingly at Rubin. "Why don't you all go to sleep," he said.

"In a hotel where tragedy has just struck?"

"Tomorrow," Paddy said, "you can change the name from the Hotel Lac des Sables to Rubin's Haunted Hotel."

"Already it's beginning to feel spooky in here. Hey, open up the bar, Rubin."

"Yeah, we could do with some salami sandwiches too. This is going to be a long night."

"All right," Rubin said. "All right."

Circling back over the highway, Duddy re-entered Ste. Agathe through those streets, remote from the lake, where the French-Canadians lived. His legs ached from the long hike; he was starved and searched for an open restaurant. He found a French-Canadian chip place open on the edge of town. Yvette was there.

"Duddy!"

Duddy didn't realize it, but his clothing was muddy and he had ripped his shirt in the bushes.

"Were you in a fight?"

He sat down and told her, between explosions of laughter, what had happened. Yvette felt rotten about the three hundred dollars, but when he got to the part about Rubin she began to laugh too.

"Have something else?"

Duddy had already consumed three hot dogs and two orders of chips.

"I think they want to close," he said. "Why don't we go for a walk?"

Avoiding the main streets and the lake shore, or anywhere he might run into a searching party, they started out together holding hands. She led him towards the railroad tracks as the stars started to fade out and light began to spread across the sky. Duddy saw for the first time the part of Ste. Agathe where the poorer French-Canadians lived and the summer residents and tourists never came. The unpainted houses had been washed gray by the wind and the rain. Roosters crowed in yards littered with junk and small hopeless vegetable patches and Duddy was reminded of his grandfather and St. Dominique Street, and he promised himself to send the old man a postcard tomorrow. There were faded Robin Hood Flour signs on some walls and here and there a barn roof or window had been healed with a tin Sweet Caporal sign.

"This way," Yvette said.

Crossing the tracks, they came out on a rocky slope on the edge of the mountain. The dew soon soaked through Duddy's shoes and trouser bottoms. His body ached. The excitement of the game and search past, he longed for his bed, but Yvette led him deeper into the field. Down a bumpy hill and up the other side onto a flat table of a rock. There she made him rest.

"It's so nice to see you lie still for once," she said.

"Wha'?"

"You're always running or jumping or scratching . . ."

Duddy was surprised and flattered to discover that anyone cared enough to watch him so closely. "I like you," he said.

"Do you think I'm pretty?"

"Sure. Sure thing."

He edged closer to her and, to his surprise, she didn't withdraw. Duddy fondled a breast tentatively. She kissed him, forcing his mouth open.

"Listen, Yvette, I haven't got a . . ."

But she didn't care. Jeez, he thought, if the guys could see me now.

"You're my speed, Yvette. You're for me."

Duddy and Yvette returned to Ste. Agathe by another route, separating before they reached the laskeshore. Yvette kissed him on the cheek. "You work too hard," she said. "There's nothing but bones . . ."

"Aw."

She told him that she was off on Wednesday afternoon.

"Let's go swimming," he said.

It was almost nine when Duddy entered the lobby of the Hotel Lac des Sables and the guests were beginning to come down for breakfast.

"Duddy!"

"It's the Kravitz boy. He's back."

Guests came rushing out of the dining room and smiled, still clutching orange juice or slices of toast. Linda embraced Duddy in front of everybody. "Boy," she said, "am I ever glad to see you!"

Rubin slapped him on the back. "You little bastard," he said. "You lousy little bastard." But even he smiled and Duddy could see that he hadn't shaved yet. Probably he'd been up all night.

"Are you O.K.?" Bernie asked.

The guests cheered when he entered the dining room.

"Don't worry," Mr. Cohen said with a meaningful wink. "Everything's going to work out fine."

Duddy looked puzzled.

"He can take the next two days off," Rubin announced in a booming voice. There was some applause. "But no complaints please if the service is slow. Duddy's my top man in the dining room."

"*If* the service is slow. Is that what the man said?"

After breakfast Duddy went to the dormitory. He had only

79

just sat down on the bed to rest when Bernie and Donald came in. They had brought Irwin with them. "He has something for you," Bernie said severely.

Irwin smiled.

"Give it to him."

"I want to tell you how thrilled I am," Irwin said, "that you didn't drown. I was so worried."

"Give it to him right now, please."

Irwin handed over his winnings. It was just short of three hundred. "I intended to return the money anyway," he said.

"Nobody's going to know about this, Duddy," Bernie said, "so don't worry."

"They were afraid you might be too proud to take the money," Irwin said. "Isn't that amusing?"

"Shettup, Irwin."

"You cheated me. You arranged it all with Linda and the wheel was crooked. I hope you had a good laugh."

"The wheel wasn't crooked."

"Cheaters never prosper," Duddy said. "I hope this'll be a good lesson for you. I hope you'll profit from it in the future."

That night a delegation comprised of Farber, Mr. Cohen, and Paddy invited Duddy to have a drink with them in the recreation hall. Mr. Cohen, ever since he had winked meaningfully at Duddy, had been an awfully busy man. All morning and most of the afternoon he had waylaid guests in the lobby and on the beach and even—once the word had got out—in their rooms. "Think of what the poor kid must be going through," he'd say for a starter.

"It's my fault maybe."

"Look," he'd say, "if you can afford a month here you can afford this. Would it be better to spend the money on doctors?"

Everyone smiled at the delegation when they sat down at the bar with Duddy. Mr. Cohen held out a large envelope. "We want a promise from you first," he said.

"Wha'?"

"How much did you lose last night?"

"Three hundred bucks, but—"

"No buts, Duddy. You've got to promise us no more roulette. Finished."

"Sure."

He handed Duddy the envelope. "It's from all the guests together. A hundred and forty-two contributors."

"I don't get it."

"I may have given more than Farber but we're not saying

Twenty dollars is the same as five," Mr. Cohen said, looking hard at Farber. "It's the spirit that counts."

"I don't know what to say. I mean . . ." Duddy pressed the envelope, testing it for thickness and substance. ". . . Well, thanks . . ."

"You'd better go to sleep now. You must be tired."

Duddy rushed upstairs, emptied the envelope on his bed, and started to count the money. There was close to five hundred dollars in the envelope. Duddy laughed, he shouted. He rolled over on the floor and did a couple of somersaults.

"Hi."

It was Linda.

"I had no idea Irwin was going to bet that much. Honestly, I didn't."

With all your college education, he thought, what are you? A couple of crooks. "Sure," he said tightly.

"Do you really think we were after your money?"

Will you go, please, he thought. I work for your father but that doesn't mean I have to talk to you.

"I've broken with Irwin."

"Congratulations."

"It was a bad joke. I'm sorry. But I had no idea—"

"—that the wheel was crooked?"

"The wheel wasn't crooked. But it's only a toy and it's an old one. It has certain tendencies. Irwin knew them."

Duddy shrugged. *Ver gerharget,* he thought.

"I thought you went out with me because you liked me. Boy, was I ever a sucker. That night at the Hilltop Lodge must have cost me twenty bucks."

"You want the money back?"

"You think I'm dirt," he said, "don't you?"

Look at me, he thought, take a good look because maybe I'm dirt now. Maybe I've never been to Paris and I don't know a painter from a horse's ass. I can't play tennis like the other guys here, but I don't go around spilling ketchup in other guys' beds either. I don't trick guys into crazy promises when they're drunk. I don't speak dirty like you either. You make fun of your father. You don't like him. Tough shit. But he sends you to Europe and Mexico and who pays for those drinks in the afternoon? You're sorry for making a fool out of me. Gee whiz; my heart bleeds. Take a good look, you dirty bitch. Maybe I'm dirt today. That bastard of a black marketeer Cohen can give me twenty bucks and a lecture about gambling and feel good for a whole week. But you listen here, kiddo. It's not always going to be like this. If you want to bet on something bet on me. I'm going to be a somebody and that's for sure.

"Did you laugh," he shouted, "tell me, did you laugh when I told you about my plans for the future? I'll bet you and Irwin split your sides."

She flushed.

"Thank you," he said. "Thanks a lot."

"You have no right to be angry. I kept my promise," Linda said, indicating the money on the bed. "I said you couldn't lose and you didn't."

"And something else," Duddy screamed, stepping between her and the money. "He's not in the transport business."

"What?"

"My father."

She looked puzzled.

"He's a hack and he picks up extra money pimping. My father's a pimp. Now beat it. Scram." He ran after her. "Go tell Irwin. Hurry. That ought to be good for a laugh. My old man's a lousy pimp."

Duddy slammed the door after Linda and the next morning he gave Rubin his notice. Since it was the height of the season, however, he agreed to stay on for another week if he was given a room of his own—any room—and did not have to eat with the other waiters. Duddy was the quickest boy in the dining room and Rubin agreed. He hoped Duddy would stay the season.

14

On Wednesday afternoon Duddy met Yvette at one of the rear entrances to the hotel.

"Wow."

Yvette had black hair and large black eyes. A pretty girl even in her maid's uniform, today she wore a straw hat with a wide brim and a white linen dress and little white shoes.

"C'mon," Duddy said. "I'll get one of the boats."

"No. We're going somewhere special. Another lake."

Duddy looked pained and he wondered if she realized that he was ashamed of being seen with her on the lake.

"Do you like my dress?"

"You're a knockout."

Yvette took his arm. "I don't have to be back until nine," she said. "What about you?"

"I'm off until tomorrow breakfast. What's in the basket?"

"You'll see."

Yvette led him across the railroad tracks again and up the rocky slope. They started up a narrow path over the mountain.

"Jeez. I thought we were going swimming."

"You'll see."

On top of the mountain she took a bottle of beer out of the basket and shared it with Duddy. He tried to pull her to him. "No," she said. "Not yet."

They came down on the other side of the mountain and walked through a field of corn and a wide, hilly cow pasture. They crossed some disused tracks, hopped from rock to rock over a swirling creek, climbed a wooden fence and crawled under a barbed wire one, and entered a thick wood. An hour later they emerged from the woods and started up a gentle green rise. On a shelf of level land near the hilltop Yvette stopped and pulled Duddy down on the grass with her. "You close your eyes and rest," she said.

When he woke he saw a roast chicken and bread and beer and pickles spread on a white tablecloth on the grass. They were both famished and ate quickly. Yvette rolled over into his arms and Duddy eagerly began to undo the buttons down the back of her dress.

"Have you got your suit on?" she asked.

"No."

"Me neither. We don't need it here."

Swimming in the nude, he thought, may be O.K. at night, but—"Are we going to walk naked to the lake?".

Yvette laughed. He kissed her and began to pull tensely at her dress.

"The lake's right here," she said.

"Wha'?"

Duddy jumped up impatiently, abandoning her on the grass with her dress half off. "Where?"

"Go to the top of the hill."

Duddy climbed the rest of the rise. "For Christ's sake," he said. "God."

Yvette embraced him from behind, pulling out his shirt and loosening his belt.

"This is really—For Christ's sake!"

Duddy's heart began to pound. Yvette was undressing him, she bit his neck, but Duddy hardly noticed. He stepped absently out of his trousers. Before him spread a still blue lake

83

and on the other side a forest of pine trees. There was not one.
house on the lake. Some cows gazed on the meadow near the
shore and over the next hill there were a cornfield and a silo.
There were no other signs of life or ownership or construction.
Duddy cracked his knuckles, he beat his fist into the palm of
his open hand again and again.

"It's beautiful, isn't it?"

Her voice startled him. He had come to think he was alone.

"What's wrong?" she asked quickly.

"Beautiful?" Duddy laughed wildly. He broke rudely free of
her embrace and raced down the hill and plunged into the
lake.

"Wait. I'm coming."

But he ignored her. She watched as he swam out and dived
down to the bottom time after time. Once or twice he stayed
down long enough to worry her.

"Duddy, that's all. Come back."

Once more he plunged to the bottom, nearer the shore this
time. When he broke to the surface again there were scratches
on his forehead and chest.

"The bottom's fine. There are rocks here and there that'll
have to be cleared, that's all," he said, stepping out of the
water.

Yvette failed to understand. "You stayed in too long," she
said. He trembled. His lips were purple, his teeth were chatter-
ing. Yvette began to rub him fiercely with a towel. "Will you
stand still for just *one* minute, please," she said.

"Have you ever brought anyone else here before?"

His expression alarmed her.

"Answer me!"

"You're jealous," she said.

He stiffened against her embrace.

"That's nice," she said softly. "I'm glad."

Duddy realized that they were both nude and for the first
time he was embarrassed.

"You fool," he shouted. "You little fool. I'm not jealous.
But you've got to tell me. I want the truth. Have you ever been
here with anyone from the hotel?"

"No."

"But you've come here before?"

"Yes."

"Many times?"

"Yes."

"God damn it."

84

"You don't understand. Not with . . . men. We used to come here to swim when we were kids."

"Oh. Oh, I see."

He began to walk up and down, scratching his arms.

"What's wrong, Duddy?"

"How far is it to the road?"

"About half a mile, maybe more."

"Can you see the lake from there?"

"No."

He started to pace again.

"Are you angry with me?"

"Listen," he said, "you mustn't tell anyone—absolutely no-body—that we came here today."

"But we haven't done anything wrong?"

"Jeez. What can I do to make you understand?"

Yvette waited.

"Just promise me that, will you? You'll tell nobody we came here and you will never bring anybody else here."

"Why?"

Duddy took a deep breath. He shook his head. "If you prom-ise me that I'll give you fifty dollars."

Yvette turned and ran up the hill. Duddy took off after her. He watched sullen and afraid as she hurried into her clothes. "Are you cold?" he asked hopefully.

"I'm going."

"Why? It's still early."

"I don't like you any more. I don't want your stinking money."

He tried to take her in his arms but she pushed him away. "Jeez, Yvette, I'm sorry. I'm—I'm just so excited, that's all. Don't go. Please don't go. I need your help."

Yvette hesitated.

"Please . . ."

"You wouldn't be ashamed if you had come here with Linda. You'd never offer her money, either."

"Oh, Yvette. Yvette. You don't understand. Let's go back and look at the lake again."

The lowering sun blazed behind the mountain. He's all skin and bones, she thought, and she picked up his shirt and trou-sers. "Take these," she said. "You mustn't catch a chill."

Duddy made love quickly to Yvette by the shore.

"I feel so good," she said. "Do you feel good?"

He could watch the lake over her shoulder and in his mind's eye it was not only already his but the children's camp and the

85

hotel were already going up. On the far side there was a farm reserved for his grandfather.

"I've never felt better."

"Do you like me? A little, even."

"Sure. Sure thing."

He would have to buy up the surrounding fields with infinite care. Guile was required. Otherwise prices would surely skyrocket overnight. Yvette lit a cigarette for him and Duddy decided where he would put the camp play field. The land there is as flat as a pool table, he thought. It's a natural. His heart began to pound again and he laughed happier than he had ever laughed before.

"What's so funny?"

"Wha'?"

"You were laughing."

Once the land was his, and he would get it if it took him twenty years, he could raise money for construction by incorporating the project and selling shares. He would never surrender control, of course.

"Do you trust me, Yvette?"

"Yes."

"I want to buy this lake."

She didn't laugh.

"I'm going to build a children's camp and a hotel here. I want to make a town. Ste. Agathe is getting very crowded and five years from now people will be looking for other places to go."

"That's true."

"A man without land is nobody," he said.

Yvette felt that his forehead was hot and she made a pillow for him out of a towel.

"If the wrong person saw this place he might get the same idea. That's why you mustn't tell anyone we came here or bring anybody else here. Who owns the land, Yvette?"

Brault owned a third of it, maybe. She wasn't sure about the rest. Brault was a hard man to deal with.

"So am I," Duddy said. "And this land is mine."

He told her about the Boy Wonder, and how he would have to ask him for a stake. He explained that he did not have more than two thousand dollars saved and it might take him several years to buy up all the land surrounding the lake and she must help him. The farmers would be wary of a young Jew—they might jack up prices or even refuse to sell, but another French-Canadian would not be suspect. He was too young to marry, he explained calmly, and in any event he might have to marry

86

a rich woman if he could get one, but if she helped him he would always look after her and she would get a share in the profits. He had to return to Montreal tomorrow and get started but before he left he would leave her money to cover the preliminary costs of inquiries, notaries, and anything else that might come up. He said he'd keep in close touch with her and come to Ste. Agathe whenever he could manage it.

"I've got nearly three hundred dollars in the bank," Yvette said, "if it's of any help."

They talked a lot longer and had to return by the road—it was too dark to attempt the woods or climb the mountain—and they did not get back to the hotel until two A.M. Yvette went right to bed, but Duddy saw a light in Cuckoo's room and he went to see him.

"Gevalt! What's happened to you?"

Duddy's trousers were caked with mud. He felt hot and sweaty, but he didn't realize that his eyes were swollen and his cheeks were burning red.

"You're sick," Cuckoo said.

"Gwan."

"Where in the hell have you been all night?"

Feverish but happy, Duddy could not hold back his fantastic find. He told Cuckoo about the lake, though not where it was, and pledging him to secrecy, he swore that there would be a job for him.

"Sure, sure. But I think you'd better take a couple of aspirins and get right into bed."

Duddy fainted and had to be carried into his room, but the next morning he was gone before anyone was up.

"Somebody saw Yvette with him at the station," Cuckoo told Linda at the bar the same night.

"Were he and Yvette—?"

"She's crazy about him."

"Obviously I underestimated him."

"He didn't even say good-by to me."

"Me neither. Let's face it, Cuckoo, he's a twisty one and a little liar too." Linda chuckled. "Among other things he pretended to me that he was an intimate of Jerry Dingleman's."

Cuckoo was surprised. He thought everyone knew that when she was in Montreal Linda went to all of the Boy Wonder's parties.

"He's probably knocked up Yvette," Linda said, "and that's why he's skipped town like that."

"Well, that's show biz," Cuckoo said. "But you couldn't beat Duddy for a dreamer."

"Don't I know it? He thinks he's going to make millions.

"I'm worried, though. He seemed so sick like last night. I don't mean the fever. I mean sick in the head. He went on and on about some lake he'd found and how he was going to build a whole town on it."

"No kidding?"

"Isn't that terrible? I mean isn't it awful that a bright kid like that should have to live on pipedreams?"

"Listen, Cuckoo, are you sure about Duddy and Yvette? I couldn't care less, but . . ."

"I'm telling you. She was crazy about him from the start."

Linda got up. "I wonder if he left his address with my father."

"You want to see him again?"

"Don't be absurd," she said sharply. "But if he got Yvette into a jam I'm not going to let him get away with it."

Cuckoo remained at the bar.

"The same poison again?"

"Reet you are," Cuckoo said. Maybe, he thought, I shouldn't have mentioned the lake. He had promised Duddy—Aw, it was all too crazy. Cuckoo turned around on his stool. The guests looked bored. Maybe a quiz game, he thought, or a dance contest. Here comes Rubin.

"I was just going to get the show on the road," Cuckoo said.

Two

Max always had his breakfast at Eddy's Cigar & Soda. His usual fare was a salami sandwich and a Pepsi.

"Kee-rist," Debrofsky said. "According to Parsley's column the Dodgers are going to draft Bridges."

"What's that got to do with the Jewish problem?" Max asked, hoping for a laugh and not getting one.

"Hey, look who's here!"

"Duddy!"

Duddy dropped his kitbag and ran to his father and embraced him.

"Hey, easy there," Max said, breaking free. "Take care for my *kishkas*."

"Where's your sunburn, for Christ's sake? Two months in the mountains and you're still as white as a sheet."

"Aw."

"He's taller," Eddy said, placing a coffee before Duddy. "He musta shot up at least three inches."

Max ruffled his boy's hair. "You're right, Eddy. I have to reach up now. It seems only a week ago I had to bend down to . . . Hey, what are you doing here, anyway? Were you fired?"

"I quit."

"You're sure there was no trouble? You're not holding anything back."

"Jeez."

"You don't look too hot. Are you sick?"

"I've got a fever."

"Come on," Max said, getting up, "I'll take you home."

Duddy leaned back in the car with his eyes closed. There were beads of sweat on his forehead. "Why didn't you answer any of my letters?" he asked.

"Oh, you know me. I'm not one for the letters."

But Duddy remembered that when Lennie had worked as a camp counselor one summer his father had written every week. He had driven out to visit him twice. "How's Lennie?"

"Plugging away as usual. Anatomy's the big killer, you know."

"Yeah."

"His nerves are all shot. Lennie's not like you or me, you

know. Those bright guys are never physically strong. Your Uncle Benjy is sending him to Cape Cod for a couple of weeks' rest."

"That's nice. How's the *zeyda?*"

"The same. Still strong as a horse and digging away in that back yard. He brought me round some radishes last week and they were so bitter you could die. I had to eat them but. The old bastard sat there with me all the time, and do you know what? Afterwards he says to me, 'Those are terrible radishes, Max. How could you eat them? I tried one and had to spit it out.'"

Duddy laughed. "Did he ask about me?"

"He sure did. The old man's crazy about you. I swear it."

Lennie was home. He was in the bedroom, dressing to go out. "Duddy," he shouted, "how are you?"

"Can't complain."

"Look at him, Daddy. He'll soon be taller than me."

Duddy punched Lennie lightly on the shoulder. His brother replied with a left to the belly and Duddy, suddenly pale, had to sit down.

"What's wrong?" Lennie asked.

"Nothing. A cold, that's all."

"He's getting right into bed," Max said.

"Where are you off to so early, Lennie?"

"Tennis."

"He's got a new girl. Style? *Style.*"

"Hell," Lennie said quickly, "I forgot to get some money from Benjy yesterday. Listen, Duddy, can you lend me ten bucks until tomorrow?"

Duddy handed him three tens. "I was going to get you a gift, but I didn't have the time. So you get it yourself now. O.K.?"

"Well, thanks a lot!"

"Skip it."

"Have a good time, Lennie." Max waited until he heard the front door shut. "I'm so glad when he takes his nose out of those books and gets some fresh air for once."

"He looks pretty sunburnt to me," Duddy said. "What's happened to Riva?"

"Gone with the wind, I guess. He hangs out with a new bunch now. Most of them aren't Jewish and maybe they drink more than they should, but what the hell. They're all college kids and they come from good families."

"And the girl?" Duddy asked, taking his clothes off.

"A knockout from Westmount. A blondie too."

"Is it serious?"

92

"Serious? She's a *shiksa*."

"I think I'll try and sleep now. But wake me up when you come in. I've got some important things I want to talk over with you. Oh, I almost forgot," he said, rising, "I bought you half a dozen sports shirts in Ste. Agathe. One of them is hand-woven." Duddy started for his kitbag.

"Never mind. Get into bed. You can give them to me to-night."

"Sure. Sure thing."

Max had only been gone a moment when Duddy began to cry. Maybe it was the fever, maybe it was his bed and the room he shared with Lennie again, but Duddy wept long and bro-kenly before he finally fell asleep. He woke the next after-noon with a foul taste in his mouth, but the fever was gone. There wasn't much to eat in the kitchen. Duddy heated a tin of chicken soup and broke an egg into it. Afterwards he felt better, a little woozy, perhaps, but good enough to go out. Duddy found his grandfather bent over the last in the shoe repair shop. "*Zeyda*, it's me."

The old man rose and stroked Duddy's cheek. "You've been home two days," he said.

"I was sick. I was in bed, *Zeyda*," he said, "I've found some land. It's in the country."

Simcha smiled, he made a deprecating gesture with his hand. "Lie to an old man," he said.

"No. I'm serious." He told his grandfather about the lake. "The greenest field is reserved for you. For a farm like."

Simcha looked shrewdly at Duddy. He nodded his head. "You're bigger," he said, "and the pimples are gone. My grand-son is going to be handsome."

"A somebody," Duddy said.

"I'll make tea," Simcha said, and he looked Duddy up and down again, his delight undisguised. "What a change in you. My God."

The little baby-fat there had been in Duddy's face was gone. He was taller, more broad, and he had no more need to encour-age a beard. The boyish craftiness in his eyes had been dis-placed by tough adult resolution. He was able to sit still longer and he seemed calm and confident. Like his grandfather he now gave the appearance of a man who held plenty in reserve. Duddy didn't chew his nails any more, either. Unknowingly emulating his grandfather, he had taken to sitting with his big broad-palmed hands gripping his knees. He held his head high, if a little to one side. But not quite eighteen years old yet, he

93

was practically a chain-smoker. His fingers were dark wi
nicotine.

"I brought you something," Duddy said, placing a package
on the counter.

"You don't have to bring me gifts."

"I want to."

Simcha undid the brown package, carefully rolling up the
string again and putting it in a drawer. There were a pair of
blue overalls, a couple of dozen seed packages, and a pair of
gardening shears.

"For the farm."

Simcha folded the brown wrapping paper in four and put it
in another drawer.

"If you don't like it I can take it back. I kept the bills."

"Let's have a drink," Simcha said, and from under the
counter he brought out a bottle of cognac. "You pour it in
your tea. That makes you warm here, Duddel. Watch me."

That night Duddy waited up for his father. He was alone in
the house; Lennie had gone out in the afternoon to play tennis
and still hadn't come home. When Max came in Duddy made
him some scrambled eggs and coffee.

"About a half hour ago," Max said, "two guys stop me and
ask to be driven out to Dorval. I keep a lead pipe behind me
under the seat special for such jokers. Last week they rolled
one of the Diamond drivers. The damn fool tried to fight with
them and got fifteen stitches in the head for his trouble.
Where's Lennie?"

"He's not home yet."

"It's almost two o'clock." Max took off his shirt and got his
backscratcher out of the kitchen drawer. "Hey, did I tell you
about last week? The cops caught this young punk from
Griffintown trying to steal the radio out of Debrofsky's new
Dodge. That would have made the fifth one swiped in a month.
Anyway, the cops took the kid into the can and broke his arm.
Boy, did he ever yell."

"Why didn't they just pull him in?"

They said that's no use. They get off too easy. This way
they said he won't be swiping radios for another few months
at least. Listen, they oughta know what they're doing . . . Aw,
that's the spot. You want to borrow it for a minute?" he asked,
offering Duddy the scratcher.

"No."

"Where in the hell's Lennie? I don't like this."

"Daddy, I want you to take me to the Boy Wonder tomorrow. I have to speak to him."

"Pardon me while I clean the wax out of my ears."

"What's wrong?"

"What do you mean you want to speak to him? You're a kid."

"You always promised you'd take me to him."

"When you were ready. Don't forget. I always said when you were ready. Max the Hack is no welsher."

"I'm ready, Daddy."

"Ask around. Go ahead. Never in my life have I welshed on a promise."

"I have to see him important."

"Oh, there's trouble coming. I can smell it."

"No trouble. There's a deal I want to speak to him about."

"A deal! Do you think the Wonder waits to hear from *pishers* of eighteen for deals?"

"I want you to take me there tomorrow."

"Impossible. He's in Florida."

"When does he get back?"

"In two weeks, they say. But with him you never know. I remember once," Max began, "when the Boy Wonder flew to Paris, France, just for the weekend. It was a Friday afternoon and—"

"I know that story."

Max looked hurt.

"As soon as he gets back I want you to take me to him."

"What about? A job."

"I can't say."

"I'll take you to him under two conditions. One, you must be ready. Two, you have to tell me why first."

"If you don't take me I'll go myself."

"And embarrass me?"

"Why are you always afraid I'm going to embarrass you?"

"Don't shout at me," Max said, making a fist. "When I lose my temper I lose my temper."

"I remember," Duddy said acidly.

"You shouldn't have said that. You have no right to bring that up again."

Duddy glared at him. He started to say something, but the doorbell rang and rang. Somebody was leaning against the bell. "I'll go," Duddy said. It was Lennie, and he was dead drunk. "Daddy's sitting up in the kitchen. He mustn't see you like this."

"Gotta get t'bed."

"Listen," Duddy said, shaking him, "you wait here. I'll be right out. Jeez."

95

In the kitchen Duddy said, "It was the wrong address. It wa a lush. Go to bed, Daddy."

"Where are you going?"

"For a walk."

"I'm going to wait up for Lennie."

"If I were you I'd go to bed."

Duddy found Lennie sitting outside on the next door steps, his head hanging between his shoulders. "It's terrible," Lennie said. "Terrible."

"Gwan. You're drunk, that's all. Here. Grab on. I'll take you round through the lane and we'll climb in the window."

"It could ruin me for life."

"What?"

"So there wouldn't be a doctor in the family. Who cares?"

What did you say?

Lennie grinned. He rocked to and fro.

"What did you say about no doctor in the family?"

"Why, it's Duddy Kravitz, the kid who once cornered the comic book market on St. Urbain Street."

"Awright. *Very* funny. Now tell me what's going to ruin your life."

"I'm gonna be sick."

Duddy supported him. He held his forehead. "Better?" he asked.

"Bed."

"Lennie, listen to me. Lennie! Listen. Are you listening? I want you to tell me if you're in trouble. This is no joke."

Lennie burped. "Whoops," he said.

"I'm going to keep you standing here. No bed. Until you tell me—"

Lennie squinted, he swayed, and he brought Duddy into focus once more. "I've fallen behind in my studies," he said. "Too much tennis. Anatomy's the big killer, you know."

"Is that all?" Duddy asked, releasing him. "You sure?"

"Sure I'm sure." Lennie pretended to be conducting an orchestra. He sang, "We are little black sheep—"

"Shettup," Duddy said quickly.

"What?"

"I don't care for that song, that's all. C'mon We're going home."

Duddy got him in the back window and into bed withou much trouble. His father was no longer in the kitchen, but th light was on in his bedroom.

"Daddy?"

"Lennie?"

96

"He just got in. He's in bed asleep already. I thought I'd tell you."

Lennie woke when Duddy entered the room. "Thanks," he said. "Thanks a lot."

"Aw."

"Want to know something? I think Uncle Benjy is a pain in the ass."

Duddy laughed.

"He stinks. *Uncle Benjy is a big stinker!*"

"Quiet," Duddy said warmly, "you'll wake Daddy."

"Did you know he was impotent?"

"Wha'?"

"He can't have babies. He can't even—"

"You oughtn't to say that. He's been very good to you."

"He'll kill me. If he finds out he'll . . ."

"What did you say?"

"Nothing. Thanks, Duddy. Thanks a lot."

"Let's go to sleep, eh?"

"I just want to say thanks."

"O.K."

"Thanks a lot."

"Jeez."

"Thank *you* very much. *Merci.*"

"For Christ's sake, let's go to sleep."

" 'Night."

"Good night."

"And thanks. Thanks a lot."

Duddy pulled the blankets over his head.

He waited two weeks before he approached Max again about the Boy Wonder. "He's back," Duddy said. "I know that for a fact."

"Listen, Duddy, he dropped a fortune in Florida. They say he's in a black mood."

"I'll take my chances. Speak to him for me tomorrow."

"Tomorrow's Friday."

"Yeah, and the day after that's Saturday. So what?"

"First thing next week I'm going to speak to him. That's a promise."

Duddy was not idle while he waited for his father to introduce him to the Boy Wonder. The morning his fever had gone he began to size things up. He figured he would need at least fifteen thousand dollars down for the land he wanted (he'd have to sign mortgages for the balance) and no job advertised in the *Star* would bring him in that kind of dough, not in twenty years. He had to make a killing. A real killing. But these things just don't fall into a guy's lap, he thought, and meanwhile it would be wise to bring in as much money as he could whatever way possible. You've got to start operating, he told himself. It's getting late.

But where does a guy start, he thought. Where and how?

He read enviously about the real estate boom in Toronto and of men who had bought land as farms and sold it at twenty to thirty cents a square foot two months later. Other guys had gone prospecting for uranium in Labrador and come back with a mint. Television, he had heard, was the coming thing. Dealers had already made a fortune in the States. Duddy got an appointment with the representative of a big American firm and tried to get an agency, but the man, obviously amused, asked Duddy how much selling experience he had had, what his education was, did he own a car and how much capital was he willing to invest in stock. He told Duddy that he was too young and advised him to try for something smaller. "You can't run before you learn how to walk," he said. So Duddy grew a mustache and began to take the *Reader's Digest* and work hard on How To Increase Your Word Power. He also came to an arrangement with his father about the taxi. While Max slept Duddy drove.

Duddy drove at night and during the day he got a job selling liquid soap and toilet supplies to factories. For this work he had to have a car of his own and here Debrofsky helped out. He took Duddy to his son-in-law's used car lot and got him a '46 Chevvie cheap and on excellent terms. While Debrofsky was bargaining Duddy visited the clothing factory next door and got a medium-sized order for soap and paper towels. He usually slept from four to six and at a quarter to seven he drove down to Wellington College, where he was taking a course in business administration. He joined the cine club at ellington and that's where he met Peter John Friar, the distinguished director of documentary film. Mr. Friar had come to Wellington to speak on "Italian Neo-Realism, What Next?" He had a lot to say against Hollywood (it was a soul-killing place, he said) and he seemed to be against something called the witchhunt, but Duddy wasn't sure. Mr. Friar had a difficult British accent and he spoke softly. There was a question period after he was finished and Mr. Friar was asked point-blank did he think Huston had gone permanently commercial and what had become of Sir Arthur Elton? Afterwards Duddy pulled him aside. "I'm going into the film business here myself soon and there's something I'd like to talk over with you," he said.

Mr. Friar checked his smile. Irving Thalberg, he remembered, had been only twenty-two when he took over MGM, and besides, the most surprising people had money in Canada. "Why don't we have a drink together," he said.

They went to a bar around the corner and Mr. Friar immediately ordered a double gin and tonic.

"Your talk was a pleasure," Duddy said. "It was very educational."

"Jolly decent of you to say so."

Duddy hesitated. The palms of his hands began to sweat. "I hope you like it here. Montreal," he said, "is the world's largest inland seaport."

Mr. Friar lifted his glass and gave Duddy an encouraging smile. "Cheers."

Peter John Friar was a small, pear-shaped man with a massive head and a fidgety red face. His graying hair was thin but disheveled and there were little deposits of dandruff on his coat collar. He seemed especially fond of stroking his graying Vandyke beard, knitting his fierce eyebrows, and—squinting against the smoke of a cigarette burnt perilously close to his lips—nodding as he said, "Mm. Mm-hmm." He wore a green tweed suit and a shirt with a stiff collar. Duddy figured him for forty-forty-five and something of a lush maybe. He had those kind of jerky hands and the heavily veined nose.

"Have another on me," Mr. Friar said.

"No, thanks. But you go right ahead."

Duddy wanted to ask Mr. Friar for advice, but lots of drinks were consumed before he got a chance to say anything. Mr. Friar, stammering a little, told him about the documentary he made for an oil company in Venezuela. It had been shown at the Edinburgh Festival and had won a prize in Turkey, but even though he had directed it his name was not actually

on the picture for a dark reason he only hinted at. Mr. Fr
had come to Canada from Mexico to work for the National
Film Board, actually, but he was having trouble again because
he was a left-winger. An outspoken one. Temporarily, he said
he was at liberty. "Grierson," he said, "is madly determined for
me to come to Ottawa, but . . ."

"Jeez," Duddy said, "I feel a bit embarrassed now to bother
such a B.T.O. with my plans."

"Dear me. Why?"

"Naw. You wouldn't like it. They're what you called . . .
commercial."

"Let's have another. But this one's on me, old chap."

Duddy said there was plenty of money around these days.
He told him about his idea to make films of weddings and bar-
mitzvahs.

"A splendid notion."

But that, Duddy said, would only be a beginning. He wanted
to investigate the whole field of industrial films and one day
he hoped to make real features. He had under contract, in fact,
Canada's leading comedian, and next week he was going to
meet a potential big backer. "Listen," Duddy said, "I'm no
shnook. I can see you're a very sensitive man. I know you
couldn't care less about making films of weddings and bar-
mitzvahs but if you could help me with advice about equipment and costs I would certainly appreciate it. I'd be willing
to show my appreciation too."

Mr. Friar waved his hands in protest. "Have you any interested clients?" he asked.

"I have two orders in hand," he said, "and a long list of
weddings and bar-mitzvahs that are coming up soon. I spent
some time in the hotel business and I know lots of people in
Outremont. All I need is to get started," Duddy said, leaning
back in his chair with his hands resting on his knees.

"I just might be interested. You see," Mr. Friar said, "it
so happens that for years I have been absorbed in folklore and
tribal customs in every shape and form. I'm not unfamiliar
with Hebraic rituals, you know. Your people have suffered so
much. The lore is rich."

"Wha'?"

"The record of a wedding or bar-mitzvah needn't be crassly
commercial. We could concentrate on the symbolism inherent
to the ceremony."

"They'd have to be in color. That would be a big selling
point."

"I say," Mr. Friar said, "there's one thing I like to warn

every producer about before I start on a project. I demand a completely free hand. I will tolerate no interference with my artistic integrity."

"I don't know a camera lens from a horse's ass, so stop worrying. But look. Mr. Friar, I've got a feeling that the important thing about this kind of movie is not the symbolism like, but to get as many relatives and friends into it as humanly poss—"

"That," Mr. Friar said, "is exactly what I mean," and he leaped up and started out of the bar.

"Hey, wait a minute," Duddy shouted, starting after him. The waiter stepped in front of Duddy. *"You* wait a minute, buster."

The bill came to eight dollars. Duddy paid it and hurried outside.

"Have you ever got a temper. Jeez."

"In my day, Kravitz, I've thrown more than one bloody producer off a set."

"No kidding?"

"If I could only learn to be as obsequious as Hitchcock I wouldn't be where I am today."

Duddy could see that Mr. Friar's eyes were red. He took his arm.

"I have no home," Mr. Friar said. "I'm a vagabond."

"Listen, I'm starved. Why don't we go in here and grab a smoked meat? My treat."

"I'm going back to my flat."

"Where is it? I'll walk you."

"You are tenacious, Kravitz, aren't you?"

"Aw."

"I'd really like to be alone now. Sorry, old chap."

"Aren't you interested in my project any more?"

Mr. Friar hesitated. He swayed a little. "Tell you what, Kravitz. You come to my flat tomorrow at four. We can talk some more then." He gave Duddy his address and shook hands with him. *"Hasta mañana,"* he said.

"Sure thing."

Mr. Friar lived in an apartment on Stanley Street and Duddy was there promptly at four the next afternoon. He had brought a bottle of Booth's Dry Gin with him. There was no bell on the door and Duddy had to knock again and again.

"Avante."

Mr. Friar was in the nude, his fallen belly thick with curly gray hair.

"Hiya!"

Every drawer in the living-room-cum-bedroom was open and dripping underwear or shirtsleeves. One wall was completely covered with bull-fighting posters.

"It's not my flat, actually. It belongs to Gilchrist. He was my fag at Winchester. A proper bastard. Well, Kravitz, sit down."

Mr. Friar freed a couple of glasses from the pile of pots and pans in the sink, wiped the lipstick off one with the corner of his sheet, and poured two drinks. He knocked all the magazines off the coffee table with a scythelike sweep of hairy leg and set down a tray of icecubes beside the bottle.

"Cheers," Duddy said quickly.

"Prosit."

But Duddy continued to stare. Mr. Friar sighed, retrieved an old *New Yorker* from the floor, and covered his genitals with it.

Duddy began to talk quickly, before Mr. Friar could begin on his reminiscences once more. He told him that he had no equipment and not the vaguest notion of the production costs of a bar-mitzvah picture. Mr. Friar, speaking frankly, could be of invaluable service to him. Duddy explained that he was the one with the connections and it was he who would risk his capital on equipment. "But you're the guy with the know-how," he said, and he offered Mr. Friar one-third of all the profits. "We can help each other," he said. "And if you don't trust me the books will be open to you any time you like."

"Your glass is empty." Mr. Friar poured two stiff drinks.

"Prosit," Duddy said quickly.

"Chin-chin."

Mr. Friar told Duddy that he was not interested in money. All he wanted was enough to keep him and a guarantee of non-interference.

"You've got a deal," Duddy said.

"One moment, please. There's another stipulation. I won't be bound by any contract. I'm a vagabond, Kravitz. I've got the mark of Cain on my forehead. I must be free to get up and go at any time."

And then Mr. Friar became very businesslike. He told Duddy that to begin with they ought to buy their own camera but rent everything else they needed. He said that he knew lots of people at the Film Board in Ottawa and he was sure that they would let him edit and process the film there. That, he said, would be a substantial saving. He told Duddy he'd need five hundred dollars down towards equipment and he asked for an advance of one hundred dollars against personal expenses.

"Agreed."

"Let me refresh your drink."

Duddy told Friar that he had his eye on an office in the Empire Building. First thing tomorrow morning he would put down a deposit on it. He would have DUDLEY KANE ENTERPRISES printed on the glazed glass door and, since the Empire Building was in the Monarch exchange area anyway, he would pay a little, if necessary, to get a phone number that spelt MOVIES and then he could advertise "Dial MOVIES" in all the newspapers.

"Brilliant."

Another thing, Duddy added, was that he wanted Mr. Friar to give him a write-up on his past work and stuff. He hoped to get a story in the *Star* and maybe a paragraph in *Mel West's What's What*.

After a few more drinks Duddy could see that Mr. Friar's eyes were red again and he began to worry.

"I should have followed my brother into the FO," Mr. Frair said. "Winchester and King's did me no good in Hollywood. I couldn't speak *Yiddish*."

"Jeez."

Mr. Friar wiped his eyes and poured himself another drink, straight gin this time. "It's no good, Kravitz. I can't do this to you. You're young. I have no right to ruin what promises to be a brilliant career even before it's begun."

Duddy looked puzzled.

"I'm afraid I've been concealing something from you, old chap. I'm a communist."

"So?"

"I believe in the brotherhood of man."

"Me too," Duddy said forcefully. "Do unto your neighbor . . . Aw, you know."

"I am a card-holder," Mr. Friar said in a booming voice. He stood up and the *New Yorker* dropped to the floor. "I tell you that here but no committee could drag it out of me with wild horses. Do you realize what that means?" Mr. Friar touched Duddy's knee. He lowered his voice. "I fled the United States one step ahead of the F.B.I. I'm on the blacklist."

"No kidding!"

"I *must* be. I've never attempted to conceal my beliefs."

"So?"

"Don't you see, Kravitz? I will not direct again without a credit. But if you hire me it's likely that you'll never be able to work in Hollywood. Don't hesitate. I'll understand perfectly if you want to call the deal off."

"We're partners, Mr. Friar. Shake."

Duddy saw Mr. Friar daily after that, but the next time he came he only brought a half bottle of gin. On Monday he moved into his office. He took out a subscription to *Variety* and, quickly adapting himself to the idiom of the trade, learned to think of himself as an "indie." Duddy waited until the paragraph he wanted had appeared in Mel West's column before he went to see Mr. Cohen about his son's bar-mitzvah. He had kept putting the visit off because if Mr. Cohen was not interested he was in trouble. Mr. Friar was anxious to get started. "You told me you had two orders," he said.

"Sure. Sure thing."

If Mr. Cohen didn't bite Duddy would be in bad trouble. The office cost him a hundred dollars a month and, added to that, there was the price of standard office equipment. He had to give up driving the taxi when Max was off. One night he had just avoided getting Farber for a fare. He could not approach people as a budding businessman by day and take their tips by night. Duddy carried on selling liquid soap and other factory supplies, but that didn't bring in a hell of a lot. He continued to pursue his father about the Boy Wonder, and soothing Mr. Friar consumed lots of his time. He kept in close touch with Yvette, too. A week after he had returned to Montreal she sent him a large envelope by registered mail. It was a map of Lac St. Pierre with all the bordering fields subdivided into farms and listing the landowners. Duddy was relieved to find that they were all French-Canadians. Farmers, probably. The largest landowner was a man named Cote and Brault, the man Yvette had spoken of, owned a good-sized pasture round the bend of the lake. Duddy hid the map under his mattress. Later he transferred it to his office, where he kept it locked in a desk drawer. A week after it had arrived the map was already greasy from too much handling. Sometimes Duddy would wake at two in the morning, drive down to his office, and study the map until he could no longer keep his eyes open.

Yvette had sent a letter with the map. A notary she trusted had estimated that the land had a market value of four to five hundred dollars an arpent and if Duddy wanted all of it and could pay the price he needed twenty thousand dollars cash. He would have to assume mortgages for the balance—probably another thirty thousand dollars. He could pay these mortgages off over the next five to ten years, at five per cent interest, if he were lucky. But the notary also said that the land was good for nothing better than a pasture. If somebody was foolhardy enough to want to invest in a development of summer cottages there then he'd better count on buttering up more than one member of the town council to get them to bring in electricity and sewers. The half-owner of one large farm was in an insane asylum. Her brother couldn't sell until she died. Two other farms were owned by a fierce nationalist who would sell to nobody but another French-Canadian. Yvette also wrote that the notary said it would cost thousands of dollars to build on the land. In a postscript she added that Duddy, in any event, was still a minor and that made for other difficulties. It's true that he could legally own land. But a minor couldn't enter into most contracts without being assisted by his tutor, unless the purchase and sale of land was his business. So it would be best to have somebody act for him. His father, perhaps.

Two days later another large envelope came. Maybe Yvette felt she had been too discouraging. Anyway, this one contained sixteen photographs of the lake that Yvette had taken herself. Duddy drove up to Ste. Agathe that Friday night and took Yvette to a bar where they would not be seen. "I think I'm going to be fired," she said. "Linda's taken a dislike to me. She finds fault with everything I do."

Duddy tried to change the subject, but Yvette persisted. "She asked me a lot of questions about us one afternoon. I pretended not to understand what she was talking about and that made her angry."

"About us?"

"She likes you. You needn't look so pleased."

"Who gives a damn?" Duddy told Yvette about Mr. Friar. He said that he wanted her to quit the hotel, anyway, and learn to type and take shorthand because any day now he was going to need her in Montreal. He had to have somebody he could trust in the office. He had thought that would please Yvette and he could not understand why it only made her angrier.

"What makes you think I want to go to Montreal to work for you?"

"Why not?" he said. "Jeez," and he made a mental note to bring her a gift next time he drove out.

"You're too sure of yourself," Yvette said.

"Aw."

A day before Duddy was supposed to see Mr. Cohen about the bar-mitzvah picture Yvette phoned. She called early in the morning and he was startled when she told him she was actually waiting for him in a drugstore around the corner. Duddy hurried down there.

"Brault wants to sell right away."

"Wha'?"

She told him that Brault's wife had died and he was going to move to Nova Scotia to live with his son. He wanted to sell out for cash and just as quickly as possible. Yvette had gone out with the notary and offered him four hundred and fifty dollars an arpent; half cash. That came to thirty-two hundred dollars down. He had accepted, and Yvette had put down a deposit of two hundred and fifty dollars. "If you can give me a check for the rest," she said, "I can be back in Ste. Agathe before the banks close."

Duddy began to bite his nails.

"What's wrong? I thought you'd be pleased. Look," she said, "there were two other people interested. I had to act quickly. Maybe we could have got it for less, but—"

"No. The price is O.K."

"The land will have to go on my name. You're still a minor. Is that what's bothering you?"

"How long have we got to pay the balance?"

"Three weeks. Haven't you got the money, Duddy? You told me you had nearly three thousand dollars in the bank. You mustn't lie to me."

He told her what the camera and other equipment had cost and that he had rented an office. He had six hundred dollars left in the bank, maybe less. He would need money for film too.

"Sell the car," she said.

Duddy laughed. "The car isn't even paid for. Look, don't worry. We've got three weeks and I'll raise the rest of the money even if I have to kill somebody for it."

But Duddy was obviously worried himself. He drove her back to Ste. Agathe and all the way there he hardly spoke.

"Stay the night with me," she said.

"I can't. I have to see that bastard Cohen at nine tomorrow morning."

"You don't have to make excuses."

"Oh, for Christ's sake."

Duddy couldn't sleep. He smoked one cigarette after another. Lennie hadn't come again, he had told Max he was spending the night at a friend's house. Duddy knew better, but he didn't care. All he could think of was that if he was Lennie and needed three thousand dollars he'd only have to say pretty please Uncle Benjy. Son of a bitch, Duddy thought. If he was Lennie he'd probably even be able to get the money from the old man. But for him there was not a hope. Max would say he was too young and too dumb to buy land. He wasn't even proud that Duddy had an office. "Go ahead," he had said. "Throw your money away. It'll teach you a good lesson." His grandfather might have that much money. He'd lend it to him too. But Duddy had promised him a farm and he wasn't going to go crawling to Simcha for the money to buy it with no matter what.

Duddy didn't fall asleep until shortly after seven and he was late for his appointment with Mr. Cohen.

"Sure. That's right, Duddy. My Bernie's going to be barmitzvah in three weeks' time. I'm sorry I couldn't ask you to the dinner, but . . . well, you know. At second cousins we put a stop to it. Listen, come to the ceremony anyway and have a schnapps."

Duddy showed him the write-up in the *Star* and the paragraph from Mel West's column. He told him that when Farber's daughter got married he was making a movie of it. He went on and on hopefully about Mr. Friar, and how lucky he was to have such a talented director. "All my productions will be in color. A lasting record like," he said. "For your grandchildren and their grandchildren after them."

"It's O.K. for Farber. His girl's marrying into the Gordons. They can afford it."

"You say that without even asking me a price. I'll bet you think it would cost you something like three thousand dollars for the movie."

"What? Are you crazy? Do you know how much it's costing me just for the catering?"

"You see. But it wouldn't cost that much. I can make you a top-notch movie for two thousand dollars."

"The boy's mad."

"But on one condition only. You mustn't say a word to Farber about the price we made. It's a special."

"Look, when I want to see a movie I can go to the Loew's for ninety cents. My Bernie's a fine kid, but he's no Gary Cooper. I'm sorry, Duddy."

"All right. No hard feelings. I just felt that since Bernie is such a good friend of the Seigal boy and I'm doing that barmitzvah in December—"

"That cheapskate Seigal is paying you two thousand dollars for a movie?"

"He should live so long I'd make him such a price. Well, I'd better go. I've got another appointment at eleven."

"All right, smart guy. Sit down. Come on. Sit down. You're

trembling like a leaf anyway. There, that's better. I oughta slap your face."

"Wha'?"

"I happen to know that you're not making a movie for Seigal. O.K.?"

"Are you calling me a liar?" Duddy demanded in his boldest voice.

"Sit down. Stop jumping around. Boy, some kid you are. Now, for a starter, how do I even know that a kid who's still wet . . . wet? . . . *soaking* behind the ears can make a movie?"

"Mr. Friar is a very experienced director."

"Sure. He's Louis B. Mayer himself. Duddy, Duddy, what's he doing here making bar-mitzvah pictures with . . . with a boy?"

Duddy flushed.

"Have you got lots of money invested?"

"Enough."

"Oi."

"It's going to work. It's a great idea."

Mr. Cohen sent out for coffee. "O.K., Duddy, we'll see. I want you to tell me straight how much it would cost you to make a color movie of the bar-mitzvah."

Duddy asked for a pencil and paper. "About nine hundred to a thousand," he said at last.

"Lies. You lie through your ears, Duddy. O.K., your costs are six hundred dollars let's say."

"But—"

"Shettup! I'd like to see you get a start and I'll make you a deal. You go ahead and make me a film of Bernie's bar-mitzvah. If I like it I'll give you a thousand dollars for it. If not you can go and burn it."

Duddy took a deep breath.

"Before you answer remember I should have thrown you out of the office for lying to me. Think too of the prestige you'd get. The first production for Cohen. I could bring you in a lot of trade. But it's a gamble, Duddy. I'm a harsh critic. There are many academy award winners I didn't like and if I don't care for the picture . . ."

"I can make you a black-and-white for twelve hundred dollars."

"Get out of here."

"Look, Mr. Cohen, this is a real production. I have to pay for the editing and the script and—"

"All right. Twelve hundred. But color, Duddy. And only if I like it. Come here. We'll shake on it. What a liar you are.

Wow!" Mr. Cohen pinched his cheek. "If you're going to see Seigal now about his boy's bar-mitzvah you have my permission to say you're making one for me. Tell him I'm paying you two thousand. He can phone me if he wants. But listen, Duddy, he's not like me. Don't trust him. Get five hundred down and the rest in writing. Such a liar. Wow!"

Duddy drove for fifteen minutes before he figured out that he had no advance and nothing in writing from Mr. Cohen. The film would cost him at least five hundred dollars—more, when you considered the work and time it would take—and there was no guarantee of a return on his investment. That lousy bastard, Duddy thought, and he makes it sound like he was doing me a favor. He went to see Seigal at home and his wife talked him into letting Duddy make the picture. Seigal paid an advance of two hundred and fifty dollars and signed an agreement to pay fifteen hundred in all if he liked the film and another six hundred even if he didn't want it. It was a mistake to see Cohen at the office, Duddy thought afterwards. You've got to get them at home with the wife and boy there.

He phoned Yvette and told her he was sending her a check for three hundred dollars in the morning. He said he was making the movie for Mr. Cohen, but he didn't tell her that if Mr. Cohen didn't like it there was no deal. He was so happy about Seigal, too, that he didn't realize until he got home that the Seigal bar-mitzvah was six weeks off and even if he got paid right away it would be too late. He still had to raise twenty-five hundred dollars to pay Brault and twenty days was all the time he had. In the next three days Duddy visited eight potential clients. They were interested. Nobody showed him the door exactly, but first they wanted to see one of his productions.

"You can't blame them," Duddy told Mr. Friar. "We'll have to rent a screening room or something for the Cohen picture. I want to send out lots of tickets."

"When's the bar-mitzvah?" Mr. Friar asked.

"Two weeks from Saturday," Duddy said, rubbing his face with his hands.

"I'd like to start looking at some of the locations tomorrow."

"Wha'?"

"Can you take me to the synagogue?"

"Yeah, sure."

"I say, old chap, you do look down in the mouth. Haven't you been eating?"

"Sure. Sure I have." Jeez, he thought, even if Cohen likes the picture that money will be too late too.

"We've got to hit them with something unusual right in the first frame. Have you ever seen Franju's *Sang des Bêtes?*"

"I don't think so."

"It was a documentary, old chap. A great one. We could do worse than to use it for our model."

"It's got to be good, Mr. Friar. Better than good, or I'm dead."

Mr. Friar could see that Duddy was depressed. He gave him his most genial smile. "Come on, old chap, I'm going to take you out for a drink. But this time it's definitely on me." In the bar Mr. Friar tried to amuse him with scandalous stories about celebrities, but Duddy didn't even smile once.

"I want you to think about that picture, Mr. Friar. I want you to think about it night and day. It's got to be great."

Mr. Friar assured him that he kept a notebook by his bed and marked down all his creative ideas, even if he had to get up at three A.M. to do it. "I'm thinking of the part when the boy is up there reading his chapter from the Torah. I see a slow dissolve into the boy's racial memory. We could begin with the pain of the baby's circumcision and—"

Duddy jerked awake. "Hey, you can't show a kid's pecker in this picture. There are going to be women and children there."

"Remember," Mr. Friar said severely. "No artistic interference."

"Right now I can see myself waiting on tables again."

"Let's have another," Mr. Friar said.

They had one more and then Duddy called for the waiter and paid the bill. Outside, Mr. Friar was not as loquacious as usual. He seemed self-absorbed.

"Thanks a lot for the drinks, Mr. Friar."

"Don't mention it. *À demain.*"

3

Duddy was exhausted. I'll sleep in tomorrow morning, he thought. I need the rest. But he woke with a scream at three A.M. from a dream that was to become a recurrent nightmare. Bulldozers, somebody else's surveyors, carpenters and plumbers roared and hammered and shouted over the land round Lac St. Pierre. Irwin Shubert held an enormous plan in his hands. He smiled thinly.

"Waaa . . ."

Somebody shook him. "Duddy, wake up! Duddy! It's me. Lennie."

Max rushed into the room. "What's going on here?"

"It's Duddy. He had a nightmare."

"You O.K.? You want a Coke or something? Tea?"

"Listen, Duddy. Listen closely. I want you to try to remember everything about your dream." Lennie grabbed a pencil and paper. "Anything that comes into your head you tell me. I'll analyze it for you."

"Jeez."

"Go ahead. Tell him."

"I dreamt I was screwing this broad," Duddy said.

"That's my boy."

"Were there any doors? Did you have to go through passages to get to her? What made you—"

"There was a bed like. Her cans were something out of this world . . ."

"Oh, for Christ's sake," Lennie said, putting his pencil and paper away.

"What'sa matter?" Max asked. "Aren't you interested in that kind of dream? Go ahead, Duddy. I'm listening."

"Are you making tea?"

They couldn't get to sleep again. Max and Lennie sat at the kitchen table and Duddy made one of his huge and intricate omelets.

"I don't get it," Max said, getting out his backscratcher. "If you were in bed with this broad why did you scream?"

"She bit my toe."

"Even if you didn't dream that," Lennie said, "it's a very significant remark."

"Hey," Max said, "what did you put in this omelet?"

"It's great," Lennie said. "Duddy makes the best omelet this side of the Rio Grande."

Lennie said that yesterday in the operating theater he had seen a baby delivered for the first time He described it for them and said that three students had fainted. Max made both his boys laugh with his story of the drunken American who had got into his taxi and asked to be taken to where the king lived. He wanted to see the palace. "Can you beat that?" Max asked.

Duddy's imitation of Mr. Friar brought tears to Lennie's eyes.

"You know what," Max said, thumping the table. "I'm taking Sunday off. We're going out for a drive and a first-class feed. The three of us."

"Atta boy."

"I'm sorry," Lennie said, "but I've got a date."

"Can't you break it?"

"Not a chance."

"Well," Max said, "maybe next Sunday. We don't see enough of each other. I'm your father. You're supposed to come to me with your problems."

Lennie frowned. "I'd better turn in," he said. "I've got an early class tomorrow."

"You go to bed too, Duddy. I'm going to sit up for a bit."

"I'll sit with you. 'Night, Lennie." Duddy made more tea.

"Do you know anything about Lennie that I should know?"

"No. Why?"

"There's something funny going on."

"Aw. It's your imagination." Duddy started to tell him about his adventures as an "indie," but Max wasn't interested. "Daddy, have you ever thought of getting married again?"

"*What?*"

"Jeez. Don't get angry. I thought maybe you were lonely like."

"Nobody could ever replace your mother for me," Max said sternly. "You're a funny kid. I can't figure you. Out of left field you come running with the craziest questions."

"I don't remember her very well. I was only six when she . . ."

"You missed out on plenty, brother. Plenty. Minnie was some wife."

There was a picture in the living room of Max and Minnie on their wedding day. He wore a top hat and her face was in the shadow of a white veil. But her smile was tender, forgiving. It looked to Duddy as if she had probably used to laugh a lot. He could remember her laugh, come to think of it. Something rolling, turning over dark and deep and endless, and with it hugs and gooey kisses and a whiff of onions. He remembered too that Max had held him pinned down to the bed once, saying over and over again, "Easy, kid. Easy," while Minnie had applied Argyrol drops to his nose. Once more Duddy was tempted to ask his father if Minnie had liked him, but he couldn't bring himself to risk it.

"Omelets weren't coming out of our ears in those days," Max said. "I used to come home after work and for a starter there'd usually be chopped liver and what gefilte fish she made! Ask Debrofsky. Ask your Uncle Benjy even. He was

112

crazy about Minnie. You'd be surprised how often he used to come here in the old days. We used to sit around the dining room table after dinner on a Friday night cracking nuts and waiting for the eleven o'clock news. Your mother used to keep up with all the radio programs. On Monday night we'd sit together in the living room, me with my books on electrical studies and Minnie making cookies with one ear open in case you should start bawling your head off, and together we'd listen to the Lux Radio Theater. That's still an excellent program, but without Minnie—We used to play parchesi a lot, too, and Chinese checkers, and if I had the boys round for a poker game they loved it. Minnie would make us *latkas* or open up some herring she'd pickled herself and the boys were so happy that when she came round to collect for a raffle for the new synagogue or something nobody ever made a smart remark. The boys," he said, his voice filled with marvel, "would even buy up a whole book just because it was Minnie, and a dollar was a dollar in those days.

"Montreal wasn't what it is now, you know. For kids these days everything's a breeze. I remember when the snow in winter was often piled higher than a man on the streets. There was a time back there when they had horses to pull the streetcars. (That's why even today they say horsepower and measure an engine's strength by it.) Hell, they tell me that new rabbi in Outremont, Goldstone I think his name is, runs a sort of marriage clinic where he gives sex talks. In my day all you had to do was mention the word sex to a rabbi and you'd get a clap on the ear that would last you a week. Look at you," he said, his anger rising, "eighteen years old and driving a car of your own already. My father never even bought me a bicycle. O.K., I didn't pay for your car, but I could have, you know." Max paused, searching Duddy's face for skepticism. But Duddy merely grinned. "Boy, if I got into half as much trouble at school as you did the *zeyda* would have taken off his belt to me. Aw, kids these days. Softies." Max replaced his backscratcher in the kitchen drawer and got up and yawned. "Why don't we turn in?"

"Tell me more about Maw."

"Some other night."

"O.K., I'll just do the dishes and then—"

"The noise'd wake Lennie. They'll keep. C'mon to bed. Hey," Max said, "I almost forgot. The Boy Wonder will see you at eleven-thirty tomorrow."

"Jeez. No kidding."

"A promise is a promise."

113

Duddy embraced Max. He punched him softly on the shoulder.

"Just be punctual," Max said, "and don't make trouble," and he started for his bedroom.

"One minute. That means I'm ready, doesn't it, Daddy? That means you think I'm like O.K. now."

"Don't make trouble. That's all I ask. This is a special favor the Wonder is doing me."

"I won't make trouble, Daddy. You'll be proud."

4

Jerry Dingleman, known to many as the Boy Wonder since Mel West had done a complete column on him, was a man with many offices. His most impressive office was on the top floor of his gambling establishment on the other side of the river, but on Wednesday mornings he did business in a poky little office off the Tico-Tico dance floor. The Boy Wonder was only a St. Urbain Street boy to begin with, he remembered well his own early hardships, and he liked to lend a helping hand. Time was precious, however, and so he limited his consideration of favors to Wednesdays. Wednesday was known to his inner circle as Schnorrer's Day and from ten to four the supplicants came and went. Third cousins once removed and just off the train from Winnipeg came. Chorines too old even for the streets tried him and crackpot inventors who claimed to have been at F.F.H.S. with him came at least once a month. Cops who wanted to borrow against the pay-off and side men too far hooked to ever play again were among the Schnorrer's Day regulars. The collector from the Liberal Party and aged lushes with lice crawling over their faces sat in the same stiff-backed chair opposite the Wonder's maplewood desk. When the Jewish General Hospital went out on a building campaign it sent a representative too.

The Boy Wonder was a God-fearing man and he didn't smoke or drive his car or place bets on the Sabbath. His father had spent ten years in prison and his Uncle Joe had been shot down on the street during the bad days, but Jerry Dingleman had never been involved even indirectly in any bloodshed or spent a day behind bars. Not before the time of his personal trouble, anyway.

His legs were twisted and useless. At the age of twenty

114

ight the Boy Wonder had been struck by polio and when he got out of bed many months later he could walk only with the help of crutches. He never once spoke about his illness but there were lots of stories about it. Mel West had printed the one about the insurance policy. The Wonder, it seems, had carried a polio policy worth fifty thousand dollars and, according to West, when the doctors told him he would never walk again the Wonder had replied with a tough smile, "Yeah, but I beat Lloyd's. I never lose a bet." This led West to compare Dingleman with F.D.R. and the Boy Wonder barred him from his clubs for two years.

The story nobody ever mentioned to his face had to do with the girl. There were many versions. But about several facts there could be no question. Before his illness Jerry Dingleman had been engaged to Olive Brucker and two weeks afterwards she had sailed for Europe alone. There was some dispute about who had broken the engagement, but there was no argument over whether or not the two young people had been in love.

"You must never repeat this. Not a word of it," was how Max always began the Wonder-Olive story, "but you should have seen the Wonder in those days. Handsome? *Handsome.* He had a smile that melted the rubber bands in the girls' panties left, right, and center. For good looks he could have wiped the floor with Clark Gable or any other star. You take your pick. And Olive? A knockout! If old man Brucker wasn't so stinking with cash, if it wasn't that she needed money like I need a headache, she could have raked in plenty as a model. When she walked down St. Catherine Street it was enough to stop the traffic . . . Only the Wonder was always by her side and the guys stepped on the gas quick again, let me tell you. They were inseparable. Not only that but they looked so right together that complete strangers would take one look and smile, they felt so good inside.

"That son of a bitch Brucker should only live long enough to choke to death on razor blades. They say it was the Wonder who called it off because he didn't want her stuck with a cripple. But that's a dirty lie. The old scum-bag, may his stocks all through the bottom of a graph tomorrow and his balls float in sulphuric acid the day after, he was the one. He packed her off to Europe before she could say Jack Robinson."

Some other facts were beyond dispute too. Polio wrought immense physical changes in Jerry Dingleman. At thirty he was no longer a handsome man. His shoulders and chest developed enormously and his legs dwindled to thin bony sticks.

He put on lots of weight. Everywhere he went the Boy Wonder huffed and puffed and had to wipe the sweat from the back of his rolled hairy neck with a handkerchief. The bony head suddenly seemed massive. The gray inquisitor's eyes whether hidden behind dark glasses—an affectation he abhorred—or flashing under rimless ones unfailingly led people to look over his shoulder or down at the floor. His curly black hair had dried. The mouth began to turn down sharply at the corners. But the most noticeable and unexplained change was in the flesh of his face. After his illness it turned red and wet and shiny. His teeth, however, remained as white as ever and his smile was still unnervingly fresh.

The smile that somehow retained an aura of innocence made those who feared or disliked the Boy Wonder resent him all the more. A man, they said, after a certain age is responsible for his face, and following that they always brought up in a whisper the riddle of the Wonder's sex life since his personal trouble. He was still capable. But some insisted he was now indefatigable and others said that he had picked up some dirty specialties. There was the question of the girls in and out of his apartment three-four at a time, a rumor of incredible films imported from Europe, books of photographs, and amazing statues. Nobody really knew. It was intriguing, that's all.

But people did know what had happened to Olive—and it was a dirty shame. She had gone through three husbands; two she had divorced and one had committed suicide. All of them had been handsome and, they said, had looked a lot like the Wonder before his personal trouble. Olive darted to and fro between Montreal, New York, Paris, and the Riviera. She usually looked potted and there were some who said you don't get like that on booze: it was something else. Olive never stayed in Montreal for more than three weeks at a time but each visit spawned a multitude of scandalous stories. Murray Gold swore that he had seen her come running out of the Wonder's apartment building one wintry night with a bloody nose and no shoes. She was not allowed into the gambling house on the other side of the river or any of his restaurants or night spots. Olive, they said, had a head-shrinker in New York that cost fifty bucks a crack. The same people said that although he wouldn't see her in Montreal the Wonder visited her in New York. It was Dingleman, they said, who got her out of Bellevue that time.

But little was known for certain about the Boy Wonder's activities. Only a favored few, not counting the girls, ever actually got inside his apartment, and even on Schnorrer's Day he

116

visitors had to pass Mickey "The Mauler" Shub before they were allowed inside the poky little office.

Shub, another F.F.H.S. graduate, had in his prime been rated number one challenger for the welterweight crown in *Ring Magazine*. He had fought lots of bouts in Madison Square Garden in the days before television when a fight there drew maybe twenty thousand fans. People in the know said that had he been handled right, if he hadn't got mixed up with gamblers, Shub could have been world champion. He had the stuff. He also fought too long and his two comeback attempts were disastrous. The last time out Ike Williams had knocked him silly in three rounds. So naturally Shub came to see Jerry Dingleman. He said he wanted to cash in while he still had a name and open up a fancy tailor shop right in the downtown area. His father and his younger brother would do the cutting for him. The Boy Wonder backed him, but the tailor shop developed into more of a hangout than a business. Shub's father, for instance, seldom got a chance to use the cutting table because it was generally in use for poker. The occasions when it was free he just had enough time to scrub it clean of smoked meat fat and pickle juice before another game got started or some friend in a hurry came in with a girl and the old man was sent on a long message. After the tailor shop failed, Dingleman hired Shub to be his chauffeur and all-round personal assistant.

Shub was a pale, shuffle-shouldered man with little puzzled eyes and a huge spread of shapeless nose. From time to time he was fuzzy in the head and had to stay home. There were some guys who liked to suddenly bang a fist on the table when Shub wasn't looking. This unfailingly made Shub leap to his feet, assuming his famous stance, and the guys would look at each other and laugh. Bang, bang, bang, the fist would come crashing down again. Then, while they still had him on the go, some guy was sure to shout in his ear, "Ike Williams!"

"Yeah, how long did you last against Williams?"

". . . Fifteen rounds . . ."

"Three, you bastard. *Three*."

But nobody ever got funny with him when the Boy Wonder was around and there were times when Shub got his own back too. "On Schnorrer's Day," Murray Gold once said, "Dingleman sits like God in that office and this one, a regular St. Peter, stands outside with the keys." When one of his tormentors showed up for a loan Shub always kept him waiting.

Shub, however, had no grudge against Duddy and he did not keep him waiting. "What's your name, kid?"

"Kravitz."

Duddy sat down beside an embarrassed man with a briefcase on his lap and watched as Shub slipped inside the office.

"The Kravitz boy is here," Shub said.

"Who?"

"Don't you remember, Mr. Dingleman? The taxi driver's kid. He was here to ask you about him a few days ago."

"Oh, I remember. Listen, take him to see Charlie. Say I said he should start him as a busboy and see how he does. Will you send Kennedy in, please?"

Shub told Mr. Kennedy to step inside and turned to Duddy. "You've made it, kid. We're going to take you on as a busboy right here at the Tico-Tico. Isn't that something?"

"There must be some mistake. Did you tell him it was Kravitz? Duddy Kravitz."

"Look, you've got to start somewhere. If you're O.K. Charlie'll be giving you some tables of your own in no time. C'mon."

"Isn't Mr. Dingleman even going to see me?"

"He's a very busy man, you know."

"But I'm no waiter. Didn't you tell him that I was Max Kravitz's boy?"

"Sure I did. Let's go, kid. Come on."

Duddy turned pale. "I'm not moving," he said. "I'm staying right here until he comes out."

The office door opened and Mr. Kennedy stepped out. He looked shaken. "By this afternoon," Dingleman shouted after him.

"I'll try my best, Jerry. That's all I can do."

Duddy slipped past Shub into the office. "I'm Max's boy," he began. "Duddy Kravitz. There must be some mistake. I—"

"What's this?"

Shub grabbed Duddy quickly from behind. "I'm sorry, Mr. Dingleman."

"I'm no shnook," Duddy shouted. "I don't need your help to become a lousy waiter."

"Let him go."

Duddy rubbed his shoulder where Shub had held him.

"Are you in the habit of barging into other people's offices, sonny?"

"My father said we had an appointment." Duddy whipped out his newspaper clippings. "I'd like you to look at these, please, sir."

Dingleman grimaced.

"We can help each other," Duddy said.

He laughed. "Another time, sonny."

The phone rang. "Get it, Mickey. If it's New York I'm here."

"Won't you even look at them? One's from Mel West's column."

"Are you still here?"

"It's New York, Mr. Dingleman."

Dingleman wiped his face with a handkerchief and held the receiver to his breast. "I'll see you next Wednesday, sonny."

"Oh, sonny yourself, you big fat lump of—"

Shub gripped Duddy's collar with one hand and the seat of his pants with the other and lifted him out of the office.

"He's still got my clippings," Duddy said.

"Are you looking for real trouble?"

Duddy picked up his coat and ran to the door. "Tell him he can go and kiss my ass," he shouted on the run.

Shub started after him.

"Mickey! *Mickey!*"

"I'm coming. I'm here."

Dingleman wiped his neck and spit into his handkerchief. "Where's that boy gone to?"

"He beat it."

"Get the car. I want to see him right away. Wait. Tell Shirley to book two sleepers on tonight's train to New York. Tell her to phone Kennedy's office and remind him that I said *this* afternoon."

5

Duddy had to wait a half hour before Max turned up at Eddy's, but he was no calmer when his father entered the store with a smile.

"Hi, Duddy. How'd you make out?"

"You lousy liar. Afraid I'd embarrass *you*, were you?"

The other taxi drivers began to file out. Only Walsh stayed. He had three free games coming to him on the pinball machine.

"An intimate of the Boy Wonder? Hah! He doesn't know you from a hole in the ground."

"Duddy, please. Not here. The other guys—"

"All those stories. Ever since I was a kid. How could you let me build on it when I need a stake so badly right now?"

"Easy. Easy, kid."

"Couldn't you have told me the truth? Do you think I would have cared? It's the time wasted and the hopes. It's— How could you do this to me?"

"Do what? You talk so fast I can't keep up with you. You ask me to get an appointment and you got one. Right? *Right.* You think any *shtunk* can walk in off the street and see the Wonder just like that?"

"Aw, forget it. Skip it."

"Oh, no. No sir. Not just like that. You said some dirty things to me."

"Yeah," Duddy said in a small voice.

"Take them back."

"I take them back."

"There. Isn't that better than yelling at the old man?"

But Duddy stiffened when Max tried to ruffle his hair. "I'm a big boy now," he said.

"O.K. Sure."

A car stopped outside and Shub opened the door for Jerry Dingleman. "Max Kravitz," Dingleman said, smiling his freshest smile, "how are you?"

"Mr. Dingleman!" Max grinned broadly and gave Duddy a poke. "Hey, Eddy. Eddy quick! Would you like a drink?"

"No thanks. Hullo, Duddy."

"A sandwich maybe?"

"I'm on a diet."

"A coffee?"

"Stop begging him."

"You shettup. I'm your father and you shettup. Mr. Dingleman and I are old pals. Isn't that right?"

Dingleman nodded. "Here," he said, handing Duddy his clippings. "That's an intriguing idea you have there. I'd like to talk to you about it."

"You don't say?"

"Be polite," Max said, gritting his teeth. "Talk nice."

"I have to go to New York tonight. We can talk on the train."

"Wha'?"

"You heard what the man said."

"We'll only be gone three days. I'll handle your fare and expenses and something more. Mr. Shub can't come with me. Can you drive a car?"

"Sure he can, Mr. Dingleman."

"I don't get it."

120

Max stepped in front of Duddy. "What time do you want him at the station, Mr. Dingleman?"

"Ten."

"He'll be there."

"One minute." That would mean leaving Mr. Friar on his own for a few days. He could do plenty of damage.

"He'll be there with bells on," Max said.

Dingleman left and the other taxi drivers hurried back into the store.

"No questions," Max said, making a sweeping gesture with his arm. "I'm not free to talk."

Debrofsky ordered a lean on rye.

"Jerry's taking Duddy to New York tonight. More I can't say."

Shub missed two traffic lights running.

"What's wrong, Mickey?"

"Nuttin'."

But Shub was concerned. It was true that Mr. Dingleman's hunches had always worked out right before, but—

"Don't worry," Dingleman said. "The boy is innocent. He's perfect."

Dingleman didn't turn up at Central Station until a minute before departure time. He smiled absently at Duddy and led him into the club car. "Here," he said, handing him a one-hundred-dollar bill. "Order anything you want. I'm going to sleep. We can talk tomorrow." But the next morning at breakfast in the hotel Dingleman did not say a word to Duddy. He read the market reports in the *Times*.

"It's nice here," Duddy said. "I've never been to New York before like."

Dingleman lowered his newspaper. "I'm going to be tied up all day," he said. "Why don't you see the sights?"

"Didn't you want me to drive you around or something?"

"Not today."

Duddy bit his lip. "What do you want me here for?" he asked.

"Meet me in the lobby at seven-thirty. We're going to a play together tonight. Afterwards I'd like to talk to you about your film company. It sounds fascinating."

Duddy went to see the Rockettes at Radio City Music Hall. He visited the planetarium, he sent postcards to his father, Lennie, and Yvette, and he wandered up and down Broadway until his legs ached. He got back to the hotel on time but

Dingleman was more than three quarters of an hour late. "Did you enjoy yourself today?" he asked.

"Yes. Thank you."

"Good."

There were some new books lying on the taxi seat beside Dingleman. One was by somebody called Waugh and two others, Duddy observed gleefully, were in French with plain covers.

"Have you ever read *God's Little Acre?*" Duddy asked.

Dingleman laughed. He squeezed Duddy's knee. "Here we are," he said. "I hope you'll like the play. It was very difficult for me to get tickets."

There were no movie stars in it. Some bit players. Duddy recognized Lee J. Cobb from the movie with William Holden about the boxer and the violin. He thought he had seen the Kennedy guy before too, but he couldn't remember in what movie. The play went on and on with people shouting and using dirty language. The jokes were from hunger and there was only one sexy scene, but the broad in it was old and not much to look at. A big deal, he thought.

"Did you like it?"

"It had a lot to say about life," Duddy said.

At supper Duddy began to talk uneasily about his film company, and gathering courage with the wine, he gave away more than he had intended. Dingleman asked him more and more questions, and at first Duddy took this for genuine interest, but each reply made the Wonder laugh harder, and when Duddy told him about Mr. Friar, Dingleman slapped the table again and again and said, "That's too much. Too much."

"What I'm really looking for is a silent partner. An investor."

"I'm sure you'll find one. Let's get out of here. We're invited to a party."

The party started off to be a bore for Duddy. There was lots to drink, it's true, the view of the river from the window was A-1, and three or four of the broads there he wouldn't have tossed out of bed on a cold night, but for a long time nobody spoke to him. He could have been a piece of wood for all they seemed to care. Two o'clock came, soon it was after three, and nobody even bothered to turn the lights out. New guests were still arriving, in fact. Then, all at once, Dingleman summoned Duddy to his crowded corner and he became the center of attention. "Tell them what you thought of the play," Dingleman said.

He did.

"Isn't he the end," a girl said.

She was, Duddy noticed, as flat as a board. The jerk with her was introduced to him as a painter and Duddy, winking at Dingleman, asked, "Inside or outside?"

Dingleman explained that Duddy was a movie producer. A vital new Canadian talent. "Tell them about Mr. Friar," he said.

Duddy's imitation of Mr. Friar went over bigger than anything Cuckoo Kaplan had ever done. Dingleman laughed so hard he had to keep wiping his neck.

"Jerry," a woman said, approaching timidly. "Don't be angry. They told me you'd be here, Jerry."

Dingleman's smile shut like a purse. "Get me my coat, Duddy."

"Jerry, I've got to have some. Please."

An embarrassed man tried to lead the woman away but she wouldn't be pushed. "Jerry," she said. "I'll go crazy. Please, Jerry."

"You're a tramp," he said so that nobody else could hear. And puffing, his face red and shiny, he started for the door where Duddy waited with his coat. From behind he heard her empty, foolish laughter. "It's like a scissors," he heard her tell somebody. "When he walks on those four legs it's just like a scissors."

Duddy hailed a taxi.

"We're not going to the hotel," Dingleman said. "Tell him to take us to Harry's on Seventh Avenue."

Dingleman consumed one cup of coffee after another.

"Shouldn't we get back to the hotel? Aren't you sleepy?"

"Why are you so crazy to make money?"

Duddy was startled. He stiffened. "I want to get me some land," he said. "A man without land is nobody."

Dingleman grasped that the boy was repeating somebody else's platitude, and he laughed in his face.

"I wish you'd stop laughing at me. I'm not that stupid. And while we're at it, why did you lug me all the way down to New York? For a joke?"

"I know your uncle. Benjamin Kravitz. He's a childish man. I don't like him."

"Maybe he doesn't like you either."

"Maybe. But you like me."

"What makes you so sure?"

"There's something wrong. A mistake somewhere when a boy your age is already pursuing money like he had a hot poker up his ass."

123

"Look, do I stick my nose into your business?"

"Come. Let's go for a walk."

"Wha'?"

"I can walk further than most men. Don't worry. Come on."

He could not only walk further but he walked faster. Duddy was half asleep. He yawned again and again. "How's about a little rest?" he asked.

"This bench here?"

Duddy slumped on the bench, holding his head in his hands. "Couldn't we go back to the hotel now?"

"Quiet."

When Duddy looked up again he caught Dingleman unaware. Something had happened to him. His neck had contracted. The massive head had rolled uselessly to one side and the piercing eyes were shut. I don't have to stay here with him, Duddy thought. There's no law that says I can't go back to the hotel.

"Sit down."

"I wasn't going anywhere," Duddy said.

"Come. We're going to sleep."

But in the taxi Dingleman had some instructions for Duddy. "Remember that woman at the party? I want you to go into the lobby and see if she's there."

She wasn't there. Duddy also walked ahead to Dingleman's room, but she wasn't waiting outside there either.

"Come in and have a drink with me."

"I'm tired."

"You can sleep in tomorrow."

Duddy accepted a straight Scotch. The phone rang. It rang and rang. "Aren't you going to answer it?"

"You're right for once. If not I'll never get any sleep." He picked up the receiver and without waiting to hear who was on the other end said, "I'm sorry. I'm not giving you any more." There was a pause. "That's right. I brought him down from Montreal with me. I've picked up with boys now . . No. Absolutely no more." Dingleman turned to Duddy, intending to ask for his drink, but Duddy was already by his side with it. "My," Dingleman said, "aren't you ambitious?"

Duddy retreated.

"Look," Dingleman said into the phone, "no more. And don't try to phone me here again because I'm telling them not to put any more calls through. Good night." He hung up.

"O.K. You can go to sleep now."

By morning Dingleman's mood had altered again. He was

very businesslike. "Be packed and ready by eight. We're leaving tonight."

"I thought we were staying three days?"

"There's been a change in plans. Look, I'm sorry, I thought I'd really need you down here, but things didn't work out that way. I'm going to pay you for the trip anyway. Oh, one minute. There *is* something you can do for me. I want you to take this suitcase with your luggage."

Duddy wandered in and out of Broadway restaurants all afternoon and shortly after four he made a business contact. He met a young man who had been in the pinball machine business. Recently, however, the mayor had come down hard on machines—they were illegal, in fact—and he was stuck with ten of them in his basement. They cost three-fifty each new, he said. Duddy was in a giddy mood. He'd wasted two days on a crazy trip. Probably Dingleman would give him fifty bucks for his trouble. No more. "I'll tell you what," Duddy told the young man, "if you can get those machines across the border, I don't care how and I don't care when, I'll give you a hundred bucks apiece for them." The smiling young man's name was Virgil. Duddy left him his card.

Dingleman was waiting for him at the station. "I'm not going to sit with you on the train, Duddy. As a matter of fact when I leave you here you don't know me until we get to Montreal. I may have to get off at the border on some business. If that's the case don't worry. You don't even know me. Understand?" Dingleman dug into his pocket. "Here's five hundred and fifty dollars. The fifty is for all the little things you did for me here and the five is a loan. I wish it could be more, but . . . Oh, I almost forgot. Here are the keys to the suitcase and a list of what's in it. Just in case they ask you to open it at Customs. If I'm not on the train when we get to Montreal, Mr. Shub will be waiting for you at the station. You can give him the case."

Duddy counted the money, put it away, and read the list for the suitcase. "Two shirts, two boxes of chocolate, a tin of imported cookies, and a pound of coffee. There are no other items to declare."

Jeez, Duddy thought. What in the hell's going on here?

He was scared, but it was too late. He couldn't return the suitcase to Dingleman now. I could throw it out of the window, he thought as the train started. I can pretend it's not mine. Aw, he thought, there's probably nothing in it. He's a funny guy and this is his idea of a joke. Duddy closed his eyes and tried to think about his land. He'd saved fifty of the first hundred Dingleman had given him and so that made six altogether for two days' work. Another fourteen and he'd own Brault's land. Another fourteen, Jeez. There was less than three weeks left. Maybe he could squeeze two-fifty out of Cohen? A fat chance.

"Anything to declare, son?"

"A couple of shirts, that's all. Oh, and a tin of imported cookies for my Auntie Ida and a carton of cigarettes."

The inspector didn't even bother to look inside the suitcase. Duddy, relieved, looked outside and saw Dingleman standing on the platform. Two men were talking to him. One of them wore a policeman's uniform. The train started up again, but Duddy didn't wave. He waited another ten minutes and locked himself in the toilet with the suitcase. But Dingleman had told the truth. Aside from the items mentioned on the list there was nothing in the suitcase but soiled laundry. Duddy felt in all the side pockets, he tried the case for a false bottom, he slipped his hand between all the shirts and shook out each soiled sock carefully. Jeez, he thought, and he went through the suitcase again. This time he noticed that although the cookie and chocolate boxes were all secured with gift wrappings the coffee tin was not sealed. He opened it. But what he was looking for—"hot" gems—he didn't find. There was no coffee in the tin, but the white sweet-smelling dust inside meant nothing to him. He salted away some of it in an envelope, though, just in case. Probably, he thought, the jewels or diamonds are individually wrapped inside each chocolate. Boy, he thought, that would be something. But he didn't dare open either of the boxes for fear he'd never get the wrappings on right again.

Shub met him at the station.

"Jerry got off at the border. He told me to give you this suitcase."

"Thanks. You're a good kid."

When Dingleman got into town that night Shub was waiting for him in his apartment. "The coffee tin was open," he said.

"It's O.K. I opened it."

"I thought you weren't going to let her have any more?"

"Get me Kennedy on the phone, please. I want to speak to him right away."

6

The Cohen boy's bar-mitzvah was a big affair in a modern synagogue. The synagogue in fact was so modern that it was not called a synagogue any more. It was called a temple. Duddy had never seen anything like it in his life. There were a choir and an organ and a parking lot next door. The men not only did not wear hats but they sat together with the women. All these things were forbidden by traditional Jewish law, but those who attended the temple were so-called Reform Jews and they had modernized the law to suit life in America. The temple prayer services were conducted in English by Rabbi Harvey Goldstone, M.A., and Cantor "Sonny" Brown. Aside from his weekly sermon, the marriage clinic, the Sunday school, and so on, the rabbi, a most energetic man, was very active in the community at large. He was a fervent supporter of Jewish and Gentile Brotherhood, and a man who unfailingly offered his time to radio stations as a spokesman for the Jewish point of view on subjects that ranged from "Does Israel Mean Divided Loyalties?" to "The Jewish Attitude to Household Pets." He also wrote articles for magazines and a weekly column of religious comfort for the *Tely*. There was a big demand for Rabbi Goldstone as a public speaker and he always made sure to send copies of his speeches to all the newspapers and radio stations.

Mr. Cohen, who was on the temple executive, was one of the rabbi's most enthusiastic supporters, but there were some who did not approve. He was, as one magazine writer had put it, a controversial figure.

"The few times I stepped inside there," Dingleman once said, "I felt like a Jesuit in a whorehouse."

But Mr. Cohen, Farber, and other leaders of the community all took seats at the temple for the High Holidays on, as Mr. Cohen said, the forty-yard line. The rabbi was extremely popular with the young-marrieds and that, their parents felt, was important. Otherwise, some said with justice, the children would never learn about their Jewish heritage.

Another dissenter was Uncle Benjy. "There used to be," he said, "some dignity in being against the synagogue. With a severe Orthodox rabbi there were things to quarrel about. There was some pleasure. But this cream puff of a synagogue, this religious drugstore, you might as well spend your life being against the *Reader's Digest*. They've taken all the mystery out of religion."

At the bar-mitzvah Mr. Cohen had trouble with his father. The old rag peddler was, he feared, stumbling on the edge of senility. He still clung to his cold-water flat on St. Dominique Street and was a fierce follower of a Chassidic rabbi there. He had never been to the temple before. Naturally he would not drive on the Sabbath and so that morning he had got up at six and walked more than five miles to make sure to be on time for the first prayers. As Mr. Friar stood by with his camera to get the three generations together, Mr. Cohen and his son came down the outside steps to greet the old man. The old man stumbled. "Where's the synagogue?" he asked.

"This is it, Paw. This is the temple."

The old man looked up at the oak doors and the magnificent stained glass windows. "It's a church," he said, retreating.

"It's the temple, Paw. This is where Bernie is going to be bar-mitzvah."

"Would the old chap lead him by the steps by the hand?" Mr. Friar asked.

"Shettup," Duddy said.

The old man retreated down another step.

"This is the *shul*, Paw. Come on."

"It's a church."

Mr. Cohen laughed nervously. "Paw, for Christ's sake!" And he led the old man forcefully up the steps. "Stop sniffling. This isn't a funeral."

Inside, the services began. "Turn to page forty-one in your prayerbooks, please," Rabbi Goldstone said. "Blessed is the Lord, Our Father . . ."

The elder Cohen began to sniffle again.

"Isn't he sweet," somebody said.

"Bernie's the only grandchild."

Following the bar-mitzvah ceremony Rabbi Goldstone began his sermon. "This," he said, "is National Sports Week." He spoke on "Jewish Athletes—From Bar Kochva to Hank Greenberg." Afterwards he had some announcements to make. He reminded the congregation that if they took a look at the racehorse chart displayed in the hall they would see that "Jewish History" was trailing "Dramatics Night" by five lengths. He hoped that more people would attend the next lecture. The concealed organ began to play and the rabbi, his voice quivering, read off an anniversary list of members of the congregation who over the years had departed for the great beyond. He began to read the Mourner's ⟨...⟩ as Mr. Friar, his camera held to his eye, tiptoed closer for a medium close shot.

The elder Cohen had begun to weep again when the first chord had been struck on the organ and Mr. Cohen had had to take him outside. "You lied to me," he said to his son. "It is a church."

Duddy approached with a glass of water. "You go inside," he said to Mr. Cohen. Mr. Cohen hesitated. "Go ahead," Duddy said. "I'll stay with him."

"Thanks."

Duddy spoke Yiddish to the old man. "I'm Simcha Kravitz's grandson," he said.

"Simcha's grandson and you come here?"

"Some circus, isn't it? Come," he said, "we'll go and sit in the sun for a bit."

Linda Rubin came to the bar-mitzvah. So did Irwin. "Well," he said, "look who's here. Sammy Glick."

"All right," Linda said sharply.

Duddy introduced Cuckoo Kaplan to Mr. Friar and Cuckoo did some clowning for the camera. "You've got a natural talent," Mr. Friar said.

Duddy apologized to Cuckoo because he couldn't pay him for being in the movie.

"That's show biz," Cuckoo said.

At the reception that night Duddy danced with Linda once. "If Yvette knew she'd be jealous," Linda said.

"Aw."

"Am I going to be invited to see your movie?"

"Sure."

But in the days that followed, Duddy began to doubt that there ever would be a movie. Mr. Friar was depressed. His best roll of film had been overexposed. It was useless. The light in the temple was, he said, a disaster. "I say, old chap, couldn't we restage the *haftorah* sequence?" he asked.

"You're crazy," Duddy said.

Mr. Friar went to Ottawa to develop the film at the National Film Board, and when Duddy met him at the station three days later Mr. Friar was very happy indeed. "John thinks this is my greatest film," he said. "You ought to see the rushes, Kravitz. Splendid!" But Duddy was not allowed to see the rushes. Night and day Mr. Friar worked in secret on the cutting and editing. Duddy pleaded with him. "Can't I see something? One reel. A half of a reel, even." But Mr. Friar was adamant. "If I were Eisenstein you wouldn't talk to me like that. You'd have confidence. You must be fair to me Kravitz. Wait for the finished product."

Meanwhile Mr. Cohen phoned every morning. "Well?" he asked.

"Soon, Mr. Cohen. Very soon."

Duddy, still trying to meet the Brault property deadline, was out early every day pushing liquid soap and toilet supplies. He began to drive his father's taxi during off hours again. Then he had a stroke of luck. Brault accepted a further payment of a thousand dollars and agreed to wait one more month for the final payment. "Everything," Duddy told Yvette, "depends on Mr. Friar. If the movie's O.K. we're in. If not . . ."

"Duddy, you look terrible. Look at the circles under your eyes. You've got to stop driving that taxi and get some sleep at night."

Three weeks after the bar-mitzvah Mr. Friar was ready. He arranged a private screening for Duddy and Yvette. "I'm beginning to think we'd be making a grave error if we sold this film to Mr. Cohen. It's a prize winner, Kravitz. I'm sure we could get distribution for it."

"Will you turn out the goddam lights and let me see it, please?"

Duddy didn't say a word all through the screening, but afterwards he was sick to his stomach.

"It's not that bad," Yvette said. "Things could be done to it."

"You think we'd be making a mistake?" Duddy said. "Jeez I could sell Mr. Cohen a dead horse easier than this pile of—"

"If you so much as cut it by one single frame," Mr. Friar said, "then my name goes off the film."

Duddy began to laugh. So did Yvette.

"Timothy suggested we try it at Cannes."

"Jeez," Duddy said. "Everyone's going to be there. But everyone. The invitations are all out."

Duddy took to his bed for two days. He refused to see anyone.

"I'm so worried," Yvette said.

Mr. Friar kissed her hand. "You have a Renaissance profile," he said.

"He won't even answer the phone. Oh, Mr. Friar, please!" she said, removing his hand.

"If there were only world enough and time, my love . . ."

"I'm going to try his number once more," Yvette said.

But Duddy was out. On the third day he had decided that

he could no longer put off seeing Mr. Cohen. He went to his house this time. "Ah," Mr. Cohen said, "the producer is here."

"Have you got the movie with you?" Bernie asked.

Mrs. Cohen poured him a glass of plum brandy. "If you don't mind," she said, "there are a few more names I'd like to add to the guest list."

"I've got some bad news for you. I'm canceling the screening. Tomorrow morning my secretary will call everyone to tell them the show's off."

"Aw, gee whiz."

"Is it that bad?" Mr. Cohen asked.

"It's great. We're going to enter it in the Cannes Festival."

"I don't understand," Mrs. Cohen said.

"You won't like it. It's what we call *avant-garde*."

"Watch it," Mr. Cohen said. "This is where he begins to lie. Right before your eyes the price is going up."

Duddy smiled at Mrs. Cohen. "I suppose what you expected was an ordinary movie with shots of all the relatives and friends . . . well, you know what I mean. But Mr. Friar is an artist. His creation is something else entirely."

"Can't we see it, Maw?"

"Aren't you taking a lot for granted, young man? Don't you think my husband and I can appreciate artistic quality when we see it?"

"Don't fall into his trap," Mr. Cohen said.

Duddy turned to Mr. Cohen. "I'll let you in on a secret," he said. He told him that Mr. Friar had been a big director, but he had had to leave Hollywood because of the witch-hunt. That was the only reason why he was in Montreal fiddling with small films. He wanted to make his name and get in on the ground floor of the Canadian film industry, so to speak. Turning to Mrs. Cohen, he added, "Please don't repeat this, but if not for Senator McCarthy I wouldn't have been able to hire a man as big as Friar for less than five thousand dollars. Not that he isn't costing me plenty as it is."

Mr. Cohen started to say something, but his wife glared at him. She smiled at Duddy. "But why can't we see the movie? I don't understand."

"It's different. It's shocking."

"Oh, really now!"

"Mr. Friar has produced a small screen gem in the tradition of *Citizen Kane* and Franju's *Sang des Bêtes*."

"How can we cancel all the invitations at this late date? We insist on seeing it."

131

Duddy hesitated. He stared reflectively at the floor. "All right," he said, "but don't say I didn't warn you first."

Mr. Cohen laughed. "Don't believe a word he says, Gertie. It's good. It must be very good. Otherwise he wouldn't be here talking it down. But listen here, Kravitz, not a penny more than I promised. Wow! What a liar!"

Duddy gulped down his plum brandy. "I'm not selling," he said. "That's something else. You can see it, but . . ."

"Hey," Mr. Cohen said, "hey there. Are you getting tough with an old friend?"

"I want it, Daddy. I want the movie! Gee whiz, Maw."

"You outsmarted yourself, Mr. Cohen. You wouldn't give me an advance or put anything in writing."

"Sam, what's the boy saying?"

"You gave me your word, Kravitz. A gentleman doesn't go back on his word."

Bernie began to cry.

"You can't blame him, Mrs. Cohen. He didn't want to take too big a chance on a young boy just starting out."

"All right," Mr. Cohen said hoarsely, "just how much do you want for the film?"

"Money isn't the question."

"Such a liar! My God, never in my life—Will you stop crying, please. Take him out of here, Gertie."

"I'm not going."

"Well, Kravitz, I'm waiting to hear your price. Gangster!"

Duddy hesitated.

"Please," Mrs. Cohen said.

"I can't sell outright. I'd still want to enter it in the festival."

"Of course," Mrs. Cohen said warmly.

"We can't talk here," Mr. Cohen said. "Come up to my bedroom."

But Duddy wouldn't budge. "For fifteen hundred dollars," he said, "I'll give you an excellent color print. But you'd have to sign away all rights to a percentage of the profits on Canadian theater distribution."

"What's that? Come again, please?"

"We're going to distribute it as a short to Canadian theaters."

"Gee whiz."

"For twenty-five hundred dollars in all I'll make you a silent partner. I'd cut you in for twenty per cent of the net theater profits. My lawyers could draw up the agreement. But remember, it's a gamble. This is an art film, not one of those crassly commercial items."

"Would my husband's name appear anywhere?"

"We could list him in the credits as a co-producer with Dudley Kane Enterprises."

Mr. Cohen smiled for the first time. "A boy from the boys," he said, "that's what you are."

"Maybe you'd like to think it over first."

"Moe."

"All right. O.K., I'll write him a check right now." Mr. Cohen looked at Duddy and laughed. "Look at him. He's shaking."

After Duddy had left with the check Mr. Cohen said, "I could have got it for less if you and Bernie hadn't been here."

"Then why are you smiling?"

"Because yesterday I spoke to Dave in Toronto. He's with Columbia of Canada now and he told me a screen short is worth up to twenty thousand dollars. I could have got it for less, it's true, but in the end it still won't have cost me a cent for the color print. And think of the publicity. It must be terrific, you know. Otherwise he wouldn't have talked it down like that. He's still got a lot to learn, that boy."

Duddy met Yvette at a quarter to ten the next morning. He told her what had happened while they waited for the bank to open. "But that's wonderful," she said.

"Yeah, sure, until they see the damn thing. Then the lawsuits start. And nobody in town will ever want me to make a movie for them again."

"Maybe they'll like it."

"Are you kidding? Listen, I'm taking cash for this check. Pay Brault and put the rest in your account. If they sue I'll go into bankruptcy."

"All right."

"I hope the check's still good. Maybe he's stopped payment on it."

THE SCREENING

DUDLEY KANE ENTERPRISES

with M. Cohen, Inc., Metal Merchants
Presents

A Peter John Friar Production

"HAPPY BAR-MITZVAH, BERNIE!"
executive producer d. kravitz

directed, written, and narrated by
p. j. friar

additional dialogue by
rabbi harvey goldstone, m.a.

"So far so good."
"Would you mind taking off your hat please, Elsie?"
"Sh."

1. A close shot of an aged finger leading a thirteen-year-old boy's hand over the Hebrew letters of a prayerbook.

2. Grandfather Cohen is seated at the dining room table with Bernard, teaching him the tunes of the Torah.

NARRATOR: Older than the banks of the Nile, not so cruel as the circumcision rite of the Zulus, and even more intricate than a snowflake is the bar-mitzvah . . .

"Hey, what's that he said about niggers being clipped? I thought—"
"—Comparative religion. I take it at McGill."
"Comparative *what*? I'll give you such a *schoss*."

3. In the synagogue Bernard stands looking at the Holy Ark. His reaction.

CHOIR: Hear, O Israel, the Lord is Our God, the Lord is One.

4. Grandfather Cohen, wearing a prayer shawl, hands the Torah to Mr. Cohen, who passes it to his son.

NARRATOR: From generation to generation, for years before the birth of Christ . . .

"Hsssssss . . ."
"O.K., smart guy. Shettup!"

NARRATOR: . . . the rule of law has been passed from hand to hand among the Chosen People. Something priceless, something cherished . . .

"Like a chinchilla."

"One more crack out of you, Arnie," Mr. Cohen said, "and out you go."

In the darkness Duddy smiled, relieved.

NARRATOR: . . . a thing of beauty and a joy forever.

    5. The wrappings come off and Mr. Cohen holds the Torah aloft.

CHOIR: *(recites in Hebrew)*: In the beginning God created heaven and earth . . .

    6. Camera closes in on Torah.

NARRATOR: . . . In the beginning there was the Word . . . There was Abraham, Isaac, and Jacob . . . There was Moses . . .

As choir hums in background

King David . . . Judas Maccabee . . .

Choir to climax

. . . . and, in our own time, Leon Trotsky . . .

"What's that?"

"His bar-mitzvah I would have liked to have seen. Trotsky!"

NARRATOR: . . . in all those years, the Hebrews, whipped like sand by the cruel winds of oppression, have survived by the word . . . the law . . .

    7. A close shot of a baby being circumcized.

"Lock the doors. Here comes the dirty part."

"Shame on you."

"Awright, Sarah. O.K. You've seen one before. You don't have to pretend you're not looking."

NARRATOR: . . . and through the centuries the eight-day-old Hebrew babe has been welcomed into the race with blood.

Tomtoms beat in background. Heightening.

8. *(Montage)* Lightning. African tribal dance. Jungle fire. Stukas diving. A jitterbug contest speeded up. Slaughtering of a cow. Fireworks against a night sky. More African dancing. Torrents of rain. An advertisement for Maidenform Bras upside down. Blood splashing against glass. A lion roars.

"Wow!"
"Are you all right, *Zeyda?*"

Drums to climax. Out.

9. A slow dissolve to close-up of Bernard Cohen's shining morning face.

NARRATOR: This is the story of one such Hebrew babe, and how at the age of thirteen he was at last accepted as an adult member of his tribe.

"If you don't feel well, *Zeyda,* I'll get you a glass of water."

NARRATOR: This is the story of the bar-mitzvah of Bernard, son of Moses . . .

10. A smiling Rabbi Goldstone leads Bernard up the aisle of the temple. In the background second cousins and schoolmates wave and smile at the camera.

"Good," Duddy said. "Excellent." He had asked Mr. Friar to work Rabbi Goldstone into every possible shot.
"Look, there I am! Did you see me, Mommy?"
"You see Harry there picking his nose? If he'd known the camera—"
"A big joke!"

11. As Bernard and Rabbi Goldstone reach the prayer stand.

NARRATOR: As solemn as the Aztec sacrifice, more mysterious than Helen's face, is the pregnant moment, the meeting of time past and time present, when the priest and his initiate reach the *ho'mat.*

Rabbi Goldstone coughed. "That means priest in the figurative sense."

"He's gone too far," Duddy whispered to Yvette. "Jeez."

CHOIR: *(singing in Hebrew)*: Blessed is the Lord our God, Father of Abraham, Isaac, and Jacob . . .

"There, *Zeyda,* isn't that nice?"
"Oh, leave him alone, Henry."
"Leave him alone? I think he's had another stroke."

12. As Bernard says his blessings over the Torah the camera pans around the temple. Aunt Sadie giggles shyly. Ten-year-old Manny Schwartz crosses his eyes and sticks out his tongue. Grandfather Cohen looks severe. Mr. Cohen wipes what just might be a tear from his eye. Uncle Arnie whispers into a man's ear. The man grins widely.

13. A close shot of Bernard saying his blessings. The camera moves in slowly on his eyes.

Bring in tomtoms again.

14. Cut to a close shot of circumcision again.

"It's not me," Bernie shouted. "Honest, guys."
"Atta boy."
"Do you think this'll have a bad effect on the children?"
"Never mind the children. I've got such a pain there now you'd think it was me up there."

15. Resume shot of Bernard saying his *haftorah.*

NARRATOR: The young Hebrew, now a fully accepted member of his tribe, is instructed in the ways of the world by his religious adviser.

16. A two-shot of Rabbi Goldstone and Bernard.

NARRATOR: "Beginning today," the Rabbi tells him, "you are old enough to be responsible for your own sins. Your father no longer takes them on his shoulders."

As choir hums Elgar's "Pomp and Circumstance"

137

17. Camera pans round temple again. Cutting back again and again to Bernard and the rabbi.

Superimpose Kipling's "IF" over the above

NARRATOR: Today you are a man, Bernard son of Moses.

18. (*Montage*) Lightning. Close shot of head of Michelangelo's statue of David. Cartoon of a Thurber husband. African tribal dance. Close shot of a venereal disease warning in a public urinal.

"*Zeyda*, one minute."
"You'd better go with him, Henry."

Soldiers marching speeded up. Circumcision closeup again. Upside-down shot of a hand on a woman's breast.

"Hey," Arnie shouted, "can you use a new casting director, Kravitz?"
"Haven't you any appreciation for the finer things?"
"Hoo-haw."
Duddy bit his hand. The sweat rolled down his forehead. "This is meant to be serious, Arnie. Ah, he's such a fool."

A lion roars. Close shot of Bernard's left eye. A pair of black panties catch fire. Lightning. African tribal dance.

NARRATOR: Today you are a man and your family and friends have come to celebrate.

Giuseppe di Stefano sings drinking song from "La Traviata."

19. Close shot of hands pouring a large Scotch.

20. Cut to general shots of guests at temple *kiddush*.

"There I am!"
"Look at Sammy, stuffing his big fat face as usual."
"There I am *again!*"
"What took you so long, Henry?"
"Did I miss anything?"

"Aw. Where's the *zeyda?*"

"He's sitting outside in the car. Hey, was that me?"

"I'd like to see this part again later, please."

"Second the motion."

NARRATOR: Those who couldn't come sent telegrams.

    21. Hold a shot of telegrams pinned against green
        background.

As choir hums "Auld Lang Syne"

NARRATOR: Happy bar-mitzvah, Bernie. Best Uncle Herby . . .
May your life be happy and successful. The Shapiro
Brothers and Myrna . . . Best wishes for health, happiness,
and success from the Winnipeg branch of the Cohens.
Surprise parcel follows . . . My heart goes out to you
and yours today. Myer . . .

"You notice Lou sent only a Greetings Telegram? You get a
special rate."

"He's had a bad year, that's all. Lay off, Molly."

"A bad year! He comes from your side of the family, you
mean."

NARRATOR: Those who came did not come empty-handed.

"Try it some time."

    They came with tributes for the boy who had come
    of age.

    22. Camera pans over a table laden with gifts. Re-
        vealed are four Parker 51 sets, an electric razor, a
        portable record player . . .

"Murray got the player wholesale through his brother-in-
law."

    . . . three toilet sets, two copies of *Tom Sawyer*, five
    subscriptions to the *National Geographic Magazine*,
    a movie projector, a fishing rod and other angling
    equipment, three cameras, a season's ticket to hockey
    games at the Forum, a set of phylacteries and a prayer
    shawl, a rubber dinghy, a saving account book open at

a first deposit of five hundred dollars, six sport shirts, an elaborate chemistry set, a pile of fifty silver dollars in a velvet-lined box, at least ten credit slips (worth from twenty to a hundred dollars each) for Eaton's and Morgan's, two set of H. G. Wells's *Outline of History* . . .

As choir sings "Happy Birthday, Bernie!"

23. Hold a shot of numerous checks pinned to a board. Spin it.

"Dave's check is only for twenty-five bucks. Do you know how much business he gets out of Cohen every year?"

"If it had been Lou you would have said he had a bad year. Admit it."

"Hey, Bernie," Arnie yelled, "how many of those checks bounced? You can tell us."

"I was grateful for all of them," Bernie said, "large or small. It's the thought that counts with me."

"Isn't he sweet?"

"Sure," Arnie said, "but he could have told me that before."

24. A shot of Rabbi Goldstone's study. Bernard sits in a enormous leather chair and the rabbi paces up and down, talking to him.

NARRATOR: But that afternoon, in the good rabbi's study, the young Hebrew learns that there are more exalted things in this world than material possessions. He is told something of the tragic history of his race, how they were exploited by the ancient Egyptian imperialists, how reactionary dictators from Nehru to Hitler persecuted them in order to divert the working classes from the true cause of their sorrows. He learns—like Candide—that all is not for the best in the best of all possible worlds.

As Al Jolson sings "Eli, Eli"

25. Rabbi Goldstone leads Bernard to the window and stands behind him, his hands resting on the lad's shoulders.

"Five'll get you ten that right now he's asking Bernie to remind his father that the temple building campaign is lagging behind schedule."

Rabbi Goldstone coughed loudly.

NARRATOR: (*recites*): I am a Jew: hath not a Jew eyes? Hath not a Jew hands, organs, dimensions, senses, affections, passions, fed with the same food, hurt with the same weapons, subject to the same diseases, healed by the same oils, warmed and cooled by the same winter and summer as a Christian is? If you prick him does he not bleed?

> 26. Rabbi Goldstone autographs a copy of his book, *Why I'm Glad To Be a Jew,* and hands it to Bernard.

> 27. Hold a close shot of the book.

From there the movie went on to record the merrymaking and odd touching interlude at the dinner and dance. Relatives and friends saw themselves eating, drinking, and dancing. Uncles and aunts at the tables waved at the camera, the kids made funny faces, and the old people sat stonily. Cuckoo Kaplan did a soft-shoe dance on the head table. As the camera closed in on the dancers Henry pretended to be seducing Morrie Applebaum's wife. Mr. Cohen had a word with the band leader and the first *kazatchka* was played. Timidly the old people joined hands and began to dance around in a circle. Mr. Cohen and some spirited others joined in the second one. Duddy noticed some intruders at the sandwich table. He did not know them by name or sight, but remembering, he recognized that they were F.F.H.S. boys and he smiled a little. The camera panned lovingly about fish and jugs and animals modeled out of ice. It closed in and swallowed the bursting trumpeter. Guests were picked up again, some reeling and others bad-tempered, waiting for taxis and husbands to come round with the car outside the temple.

And Mr. Cohen, sitting in the first row with his legs open like an inverted nutcracker to accommodate his sunken belly, thought, it's worth it, every last cent or what's money for, it's cheap at any price to have captured my family and friends and foolish rabbi. He reached for Gertie's hand and thought, I'd better not kiss Bernie. It would embarrass him.

As choir sings Hallelujah Chorus

74. Rear view long shot. Mr. Cohen and Bernard
    standing before the offices of M. Cohen, Inc.,
    Metal Merchants.

Fade out

Nobody spoke. Duddy began to bite his fingernails and
Yvette pulled his hand away and held it.

"A most edifying experience," Rabbi Goldstone said. "A
work of art."

Everybody began to speak at once.

"Thank you very much indeed," Mr. Friar said. "Unfortunately the best parts were left on the cutting room floor."

"Play it again."

"Yeah!"

7

When Duddy came home he found out about Lennie.

"What do you mean he's gone?" Duddy asked.

Max could hardly speak. He paced up and down the
kitchen. "His clothes are gone. Every drawer in the bedroom
is empty. Here's the note. Read it yourself."

> I'll get in touch with you as soon as I can,
> but I'm not going back to Medical School.
> I'm sorry. Please forgive me.
>   LEONARD

"That explains a lot," Duddy said. "What do you think,
Uncle Benjy?"

Uncle Benjy poured himself another drink. Standing behind his older brother, Max gestured urgently to tell Duddy
not to question him; he's looped.

"I can't understand it," Uncle Benjy said. "You'd think he
would have got in touch with me whatever it was."

"*I'm* the father."

"Jeez. Are we going to have a family quarrel at a time like
this?"

Uncle Benjy looked sharply at Duddy. "I haven't seen you
in a long time," he said. "You've changed."

"He's in business for himself. An operator."

"I heard."

"You wait. He'll burn his fingers."

Duddy lit a cigarette off his butt. "How's Auntie Ida?" he asked.

Max made more urgent gestures. He grimaced.

"She left for Florida this morning. I'm your uncle, you know. You shouldn't hold a grudge. Bygones are bygones."

"Sure thing."

"O.K." Uncle Benjy emptied his glass. "If that's how you feel."

"What's between you?" Max asked. "How come I never know what goes on around here?"

Duddy sighed.

"Don't look at me like that," Max said. "I'll brain you."

"Easy, Daddy. Easy. What's the name of Lennie's girl?"

"We phoned," Uncle Benjy said. "She sick in bed. I spoke to the father."

"Have you tried his friends?"

"Nobody knows from nothing."

"I think you both ought to go to bed," Duddy said. "We can't do anything at this hour. I'll get up early tomorrow and start seeing his friends. Somebody will know something."

"Look who's in charge," Uncle Benjy said.

"Do you expect me to sleep at a time like this?"

"I sure do. Would you like me to drive you home, Uncle Benjy?"

"I'll call a taxi. He's right, Max. We ought to get some sleep."

"It's easy for you to talk. He's my son but. His blood is my blood."

"Daddy, for Christ's sake!"

"Maybe I never had lots of money to give him. I don't talk very fine either. But he's my son and maybe he's lying dead in a ditch right now."

"Daddy. Easy, Daddy." Duddy held his father close. "He's been studying too hard, that's all. I'm sure he's all right."

"I never tried to take him away from you, Max. I was only trying to help out."

"I've got feelings. You'd be surprised."

Uncle Benjy phoned for a taxi.

"Come on, Daddy. You get into bed and I'll bring you some tea."

"You think it's easy to bring up two boys without a wife?"

"We'll find him tomorrow," Duddy said, pulling back the bedspread. "I'm sure."

"Good night," Uncle Benjy said. "Let's keep in close touch."

"I'm sorry," Max said, "but you know me. When I lose my temper I lose my temper."

Uncle Benjy nodded. Duddy touched his father's head.

"Good night, Duddel."

"I'll call you as soon as there's any news."

Duddy made tea. But when he was ready to serve it his father had fallen asleep, so Duddy shut the bedroom door softly and sat down at the kitchen table. "At a time like this," he said aloud, "just when everything is beginning to move. That's what you call luck."

After the screening of *Happy Bar-Mitzvah, Bernie!* Duddy had felt so marvelous that he had invited Mr. Friar and Yvette out. "We'll go to Ruby Foo's," he said.

Some of the people who had been at the screening were already there. "There's young Kravitz himself," somebody said.

"That's the director. He's English. I'll tell you something Gertie told me about him, but you must promise not to repeat it."

Duddy waved.

"Congratulations, kid."

"A fine job."

Duddy couldn't see Linda anywhere. She hadn't even come up to him after the screening. The hell with her, he thought. He introduced Mr. Friar to people here and there. Yvette waited to one side.

"We've got a table for you now, sir."

"A bottle of champagne," Duddy said. "The best."

He told Yvette that after the screening he had been offered enough wedding and bar-mitzvah contracts to carry them through into January with an estimated gross of eight, maybe ten thousand dollars. Not only that, he added when Mr. Friar went to spend a penny, but he had had a long chat with Grossman, the owner of Camp Forest Land, and next summer Duddy was going to make a film there. He had offered Grossman such a cut-rate price that the poor bastard couldn't afford to turn him down. That meant, Duddy said, that he would have an opportunity to see the camp from the inside. The information he'd gather about costs, prices, staff, and the handling of kids would be invaluable to him. He'd also get an address list of all the kids there so that they could be invited to the screening. Grossman was a crap artist. He didn't suspect a thing. "What's wrong?" Duddy asked. "You're in a bad mood."

Yvette didn't reply.

144

"Tonight of all nights. Jeez. Hey, *garçon*. More champagne." Yvette laughed. "That's my girl. Here's Mr. Friar."

Duddy filled all the glasses. *"Prosit."*

"Here's looking at you."

"Hey, Mr. Friar, remember that first night? You know, after the lecture. You weren't angry when you walked out of the bar. You just didn't want to get stuck with the bill."

"It seems to me I paid for the drinks that night."

"And every other night. Aw, you're a great guy. I don't know what I'd do without you. Or you too, Yvette."

"Thanks."

"Order anything you want. The sky's the limit. Jeez, does this stuff ever make you wanna piss. Excuse me a minute."

"It's the first door to the left, old chap."

"Thanks, old chap."

"Not the most delicate boy in the world, is he, Yvette?"

"Maybe not."

"But not without his charms, I'm sure."

"Let's order. I'm starved."

"He'll never marry you."

"Let's not start on that again, please."

"A Hebrew never marries outside his own race. I'd marry you. I'm mad for you."

"He's your friend. He admires you. And I'm supposed to be his girl."

"He didn't even introduce you to anyone here."

"You don't miss a thing," Yvette said coldly.

"He's callow. His manners are unbelievably gauche. Why, he hasn't the first notion of how to treat a woman. What on earth do you see in him?"

"Plenty. Here he comes. Please be sweet, Peter. He's so happy tonight."

"Yvette," Duddy said, "I've just made an important decision. I've decided to get an apartment of my own."

"Earth-shaking."

"What's eating him?"

"He's teasing. Sit down, Duddy."

"Did I say anything wrong, Mr. Friar? Are you angry because I kidded you about that first night before? Jeez. You're my best friend. You can have as much to drink as you want."

"Merci mille fois."

"Where would I be without him?"

"That's enough, Duddy," Yvette said.

Duddy gulped down another glass of champagne. "Know something, Yvette? We ought to find a dame for Mr. Friar.

We're supposed to be his friends like. I'm sure it's no fun for him always tagging along like this."

"I think we'd better order," Yvette said.

At a time like this, Duddy thought, just when I need every minute I can spare for the business, I have to start chasing around after Lennie. Jeez, he thought, what if he *is* in trouble? Maybe it's something serious. Duddy was kept awake considering all the catastrophes that could have happened to his brother. Yvette will help me, he thought. We'll find him all right.

Lennie was nervy, it was true—sensitive—even as a kid the smallest things used to upset him. He was only six years older than Duddy and there had been a time when they had been real pals. There had been that summer when Duddy had still been at the Talmud Torah and Max had taken a cottage with the Debrofskys. Shawbridge with that river like coffee that had been left standing was no paradise, but Duddy had had fun there. Together he and Lennie had built shacks on the mountain and made field telephones out of empty oil cans and yards of carefully waxed string. When the other guys complained about Duddy always coming with them, saying things like what do we need the kid with us for, Lennie always stuck up for him. "Duddy's my kid brother," he'd say. "Where I go he goes."

It had changed, of course. When Lennie was in the tenth grade at F.F.H.S. the brothers no longer saw so much of each other. But Duddy still took pride in all of Lennie's achievements.

"Rank one again," he'd say. "You're a genius, Lennie. Congrats."

They still shared the same bedroom. Duddy's side was thick with pennants and airplane models he had made and Lennie's side was laden with gifts from Uncle Benjy, the Book of Knowledge and the Harvard Classics. Lennie used to tell him about his talks with Uncle Benjy. "He wants me to be the kind of doctor that's a helper to the poor. He says I shouldn't worry if I can't get into Medical School at McGill because of the anti-Semitism there. Because he'll send me to Queens or Switzerland. Anywhere. He's becoming a boozer, you know. After he'd had a lot he held me so tight I got scared. You're going to have to be my *kaddish,* he said. I don't get it. Half the time he talks against religion and then when he's drunk he goes and says a thing like that."

Once Lennie entered McGill he was no longer amused when

Duddy reported things like, "Boy, have I ever got a bone on tonight."

He still told Duddy about Uncle Benjy, but his tone had changed. "You mustn't tell him I've joined Hillel. He says it's a reactionary organization with a ghetto mentality."

"What did you say to that?"

"Nothing. You think I'm crazy?"

Occasionally Lennie would revert to the intimacy of their younger days together. "Boy," he told Duddy once, "did I ever have a time at the Oneg Shabbat tonight! That Riva Kaplan. I mean I never thought a Jewish girl . . ."

"It's going up," Duddy said.

Lennie laughed. "Her house in Outremont has about six telephones. I'm taking her to the Arts Ball. Uncle Benjy is lending me his car."

"Let's stay up and talk all night. I'll make us an omelet."

Then when Duddy bragged about his brother one night it turned out that one of the girls at the dance was a cousin of Riva's. She knew all about Lennie and he had never mentioned that he had a brother. He wasn't a St. Urbain Street boy either. He lived on Côte St. Catherine Road. That was Uncle Benjy's address. But there were still things that Lennie liked to share with him. There had been, for instance, a brief but burning conversion to socialism. A time when he had begun to see a lot of Uncle Benjy again and had tried to make a convert of Duddy.

"Are you aware that during the depression tons of oranges were being dumped into the Pacific to keep prices up while people in New York were starving?"

But once he had entered medical school Lennie had no more time for politics. He studied continuously, his headaches worsened, and he became very short-tempered.

I've got to find him, Duddy thought. After all those years of study he can't throw in the sponge just like that.

He woke when he heard Max drop the frying pan on the kitchen floor. "I thought you were getting up early this morning," Max said, "to start looking for him."

Duddy stretched. His eyes were puffed.

"Did I ever have a night," Max said.

"Don't worry. I'll phone you at Eddy's the minute I find out anything."

8

Duddy phoned Yvette to tell her about Lennie. "That means I won't be in today," he said.

Yvette said she'd like to go to Ste. Agathe for a couple of days. The notary wanted to see her and it was her brother's birthday tomorrow.

"Sure thing. Just call the telephone answering service before you go. If you're short there must be at least thirty bucks in the petty cash."

"I can live on my salary," Yvette said in that special cold voice.

Those dames, Duddy thought, there's no need for them to tell you when they've got the curse. "Have a nice trip," he said, and hanging up he added, *"Ver gerharget."*

College kids, Duddy discovered, do not get up too early. He loitered longer than an hour in Hillel House before he saw a familiar face. It was nice there, but he couldn't relax: he was worried that he was sitting in somebody else's chair or that his fly might be undone. Some girls in cashmere sweaters drifted in and there was a sweet-looking boy with a pipe. Duddy began to whistle and one of the girls raised an eyebrow. "It's from *Carmen,*" Duddy said, clearing his throat. Then he saw Riva. She wore a McGill blazer. "Riva," he said, "I've got to speak to you for a minute."

Riva looked surprised.

"I'm Lennie Kravitz's kid brother. Remember?" Duddy explained that Lennie was home sick in bed. Nothing serious, mind you, but his father was worried, and Duddy wanted to know if she had noticed anything odd about him recently. "Bothering him like."

"We move in different circles these days."

Riva, he gathered, was going to Tel Aviv to teach school once she graduated from McGill. "That's a fine ambition," he said, "but what about Lennie?"

"He's become an assimilationist."

"Wha'?"

"You never see him at Hillel any more. Jewish boys and girls aren't good enough for him. It's a disgrace, honestly. Every time they take him into one of their frat houses he practically licks their boots."

148

Riva was late for Eng. 1 and had to run. She couldn't meet him later, either. She was busy.

"Duddy! Duddy Kravitz!"

"Bernie!"

"Boy, is it ever good to see you."

"Yeah," Duddy said. "No kidding?"

"You're a big business success. I've heard all about you. Congratulations."

"Aw."

"Never mind. One day I'll be saying I knew him when."

"*You'll* be saying that? Gwan. You're getting a real education. You're going to be an architect."

"What are you doing here?"

Duddy repeated the story he had told Riva. He said he was anxious to find out anything he could about Lennie's life at McGill.

"Well," Bernie said, "I knew I'd never get to that sociology class. Come around the corner with me. We'll have a coffee."

They joked for a while about the old days at the hotel before Bernie got serious. "Look," he said, "I don't want to interfere. Lennie minds his own business and he's entitled to choose his own friends."

"Give," Duddy said.

Bernie told Duddy that Lennie had a rep for being a plugger. He had never been very popular but nobody had really disliked him either. He had hardly been noticed, in fact, until he began to take out Riva. She was a popular number, a bit flighty, and soon Lennie was seen at parties with her everywhere. "He was crazy about her," Bernie said. "Unfortunately Riva liked to dance close with all the boys and she wasn't beyond a little friendly necking, if you caught her in the right mood. Lennie didn't go for that. He began to cut in on all of Riva's dances. Once, at a party I was at, he caught her fooling around with one of the guys in the upstairs hall and later I found him sitting on the steps outside. He'd been crying. His nerves were all shot. I really think that guy studies too hard."

"Anatomy's the big killer," Duddy said.

"Anyway things went from bad to worse and one night they had a fight at a party. He was hysterical. I think it was just after the mid-terms and he looked like he hadn't slept for weeks . . . Well, he called her lots of ugly names. Everybody was there and he yelled things at her he shouldn't have."

"Like what?"

"Maybe I shouldn't be telling you all this, Duddy . . . Well, you know . . ."

"He isn't sick in bed. He's run away from home." Duddy told him about the note. "Like what?" he asked.

"Like Outremont whore. Daughter of a war profiteer. Well, you know. The works. Up to that point everyone was on his side. But you know it wasn't Riva's fault that he was so serious about her. She's flighty. I told you that. But she's got a good sense of humor and everybody likes her. You want the gory details?"

"Yeah."

"She slapped his face. Then Lennie began to call everyone in the room dirty names. Well, you know. We weren't such big shots just because we had cars and he was as good as any of us . . . He tried to pick a fight with Shelby Horne and then he took a poke at me. Christ, he's even skinnier than you are. I could have laid him flat with one whack. Anyway we got him home—What are you going to do, Duddy? Have you any idea where he's gone to?"

"Not yet."

"Only three Jewish kids got into med in his year. A lot of people are expecting him to get the medal. Christ."

"Tell me the rest, Bernie. I'm sure there's more."

"Well, you know, he dropped out of sight for a while. Then the next thing I'd heard he'd picked up with the Joe College bunch. The football crowd. Well, you know, drink chug-a-lug and all that. Listen, everyone's entitled to enjoy themselves the way they want. It's not for me, that's all. They're mostly rich kids, Duddy. *Goys.* Some of them live in Westmount but most come from out of town and have rooms in the frat houses. They run sports cars and get the prettiest girls. Well, you know, the campus beauty queens. I don't know how Lennie ever got mixed up with them. I can understand about Irwin Shubert, but—"

"Irwin! That bastard."

"He's the only other Jew in their crowd. It costs plenty to keep up with them and I don't know where Lennie got the money."

"There was a broad, wasn't there? A blonde."

"Sandra Calder? That's something else that used to puzzle me. I've seen her around a lot with Lennie recently, but she's really Andy Simpson's girl. Everybody knows that. Andy's made the Olympic hockey team."

Duddy got up.

"What are you going to do?" Bernie asked.

"First I'm going to see the girl. She's sick at home. What

150

want to find out is if she's sick like I said Lennie was sick. Maybe they eloped?"

Bernie whistled. "If they eloped you can stop worrying. Old Man Calder is a millionaire. He's on the Board of Governors at McGill."

Westmount was where the truly rich lived in stone mansions driven like stakes into the shoulder of the mountain. The higher you climbed up splendid tree-lined streets the thicker the ivy, the more massive the mansion, and the more important the man inside. Mr. Calder's place was almost at the top. "Jeez," Duddy said aloud, getting out of his car. He had been in Westmount before in the taxi but usually at night and never this high up. Below, the city and the river hummed obligingly under a still cloud of factory fumes. What a site for a restaurant, Duddy thought. Looking up at the Calder house again, he wondered what the bastard did with all those rooms. Maybe he's got eighteen kids, he thought. A Catholic like.

"Yes."

The butler was a British movie sprung to life.

"I'd like to see Sandra."

The butler told him that she was indisposed.

"It's important. I'm one of her best friends."

"I'm so sorry, but the doctor's with her right now. If you'd like to leave a message . . ."

Duddy thought of slipping the butler a fin. That, he thought, is what the Falcon would have done.

"Is there any message?" the butler asked sharply.

Duddy retreated a step. "Naw. Thanks anyway. I'll call again."

As the door closed gently on him Duddy began to curse himself. What's the matter with me, he thought. I should have insisted. There was a Bentley parked in the driveway. An Austin Healey too. The third car had a doctor's license plate on it. Well, that proves something anyway, Duddy thought, and he drove off.

The office was lonely without Yvette. Duddy locked the door and got out the map of Lac St. Pierre. Twice already he had filled in with red crayon the land that used to belong to Brault. His land. He started to go over it with crayon again when the phone rang.

"I thought you were out looking for Lennie?"

"I just got in this minute, Daddy. There's no news yet. I'm seeing more people tonight but."

Seigal phoned. "About the movie," he said, "the *goy* was

151

here again today to look over the house. Not only did he drink up all my Johnnie Walker, but he tried to get my Selma to sit on his lap. She's only seventeen."

"Artists are like children," Duddy said.

"It was Black Label. The best. He wrote a dirty poem to her too. It's called, quote, Advice to Virgins to Make Much of Time, unquote. It—"

"That verse might be worth a lot of money some day," Duddy said. "If I were you I'd hold on to it." But he promised to be there next time Mr. Friar came.

Duddy met Bernie at nine and they went to the bar where the students gathered. At one table boys and girls drank beer and sang and at another a long thin Negro sat with a girl who wore slacks. The girl had dirty fingernails.

"Steve," Bernie said, "this is Duddy Kravitz. He's Lennie's brother. Steve takes a lot of classes with Lennie."

"What happened to Lennie today?"

"He's at home sick. Nothing serious, mind you."

"Just a nervous breakdown," Steve said.

"That's a joke, Duddy," Bernie said.

"A joke? We've had two already this term. Three others have dropped out."

"He's teasing you," Bernie said.

"Is it Leonard *Kravitz* you're talking about?" the girl asked.

"Yeah. Why?"

"He's a suicidal type, isn't he, Steve?"

"Oh, you're a pair," Bernie said. "A real pair."

"Did he say we're a pair?"

"I think so. One minute I'll ask him. Did you say we're a pair?"

"His brother's sick. Can't you see he's worried?"

"I think what he's trying to say is that this guy's brother is sick."

"The pair type?"

"I'm not sure. One minute. Bernard, you were saying—"

"Oh, *that's* Bernard. I thought Bernard had committed suicide."

"Come on, Duddy," Bernie said, and he hurried him outside. They got into the car and drove off. Duddy didn't speak. He chain-smoked.

"You're driving very fast," Bernie said.

"I think I'd better take you home, Bernie." What a time for Yvette to be away, he thought. The bitch. "I'm going home too. My father must be worried sick by this time." Duddy thanked Bernie for all he'd done and promised to ring him as soon as he had any news. "Good or bad," he said morosely.

"Maybe he's home right now," Bernie said.

But Lennie wasn't there.

"Where in the hell have you been all this time?" Max asked.

"At the movies. O.K.?"

"Oh, you're in that kind of mood. That's all I need." Max pulled his backscratcher out of the drawer. "How the *zeyda* found out about all this I'll never know. But he wants you to call him tomorrow. My word he won't take."

"I need some coffee."

"O.K. Sit down before you fall down. You're white as a sheet. Boy, have you ever got a lousy build. Why don't you ever use my weight lifts any more?"

"Tomorrow."

"A guy's got to keep in shape, you know. This world is full of shits. When you meet one and he gives you a shove you want to be strong enough to shove him back. Right?"

"Right."

"O.K.," Max said, "now tell me what you found out today."

Duddy omitted the part about suicide. He didn't say anything about Lennie's fight with Riva, either.

"That Altman sounds like a prince of a fella," Max said.

"He sure is. Oh, another thing. They expect Lennie to win the medal. A lot of people think he'll come first."

"Wouldn't that be something?"

"Don't worry, Daddy. We'll find him and he'll go back to school."

"Maybe Lennie'll turn out to be the guy who finds the cure for cancer?"

"Another Pasteur."

"Bigger. Wow, the cure for cancer."

Duddy rose and rubbed his eyes. "Tomorrow I'm going to try to see the Calder girl again. There's also this Andy Simpson guy."

"That would be a big thing for the Jews. One of ours finding the cancer cure. Aw, they'd still make us trouble."

"I'd better call Uncle Benjy before I go to sleep. I promised."

"Don't waste your time. He's asleep on the sofa in the living room. Benjy's going to be a real catch for the A.A. one of these days. He can go through a bottle of Scotch quicker than I can drink a Pepsi."

"What kind of signals were you trying to give me last night?"

153

"One minute." Max tiptoed into the hall and shut the living room door. "It would be a good idea if you didn't mention Auntie Ida to him for a while."

"Why?"

"She was supposed to stay here for two months. She only got here yesterday afternoon, you know. They had a big row right off and, wham, she left for Florida again the same night."

"You think she asked him for a divorce?"

"Maybe. I dunno. Imagine not being able to get it up. Even I mean."

"I'm dead, Daddy. I'm going to sleep."

"He can't even get into the States any more. That's what l gets for being such a smart guy."

"Wha'?"

"Listen, there wasn't a petition invented that Uncle Ben didn't sign in triplicate. They don't want commies there the days. You blame them?"

"Good night. Go to sleep, Daddy."

Duddy lay on his bed with his eyes open. The police would have reported it, he thought. *What if he jumped in the cana* A body could stay under for two-three days. Oh, no, Dudd thought, please. You're crazy.

"Do you mind if I come in?"

"Naw. sit down, Uncle Benjy."

Duddy repeated the story he had told his father. "I'm go ing to try to see the girl tomorrow," he said.

"You're holding something back. I'm not your father. I wa to know all the facts."

Duddy jerked awake. "Why don't you lay off my father f a change? It hasn't been easy for him all alone since my moth died."

"He told you that?" Uncle Benjy asked, smiling a little.

"Never mind."

A car slowed down outside. Duddy rushed to the windo but it passed.

"Do you think he's committed suicide?"

"Shettup," Duddy said.

"I see. It's been eating you too."

"Lennie hasn't committed suicide. He's not the type."

"There's no such thing as the type. You'd be surprised the people . . ."

Aunt Ida, Duddy thought. She's tried it, I'm sure. Dud searched his uncle's fat funny face in the darkness. The hea

154

bloodshot eyes returned the look coldly. "You were saying?" he asked.

"It's a possibility. Let's face it."

"He took all his clothes," Duddy said.

"That's true."

Duddy yawned.

"You want to sleep. I'll go."

"What were you trying to tell me about my mother before?"

"Nothing. Good night."

"He couldn't have killed himself. It's impossible."

"I hope so, Duddele."

"Good night."

"When I was a boy in your *zeyda's* house," Uncle Benjy said, "I used to say my prayers before I went to sleep. He used to come in and listen and then he'd kiss me. That was a long time ago."

"Why are you such a boozer, Uncle Benjy?"

"Good night and God bless."

Uncle Benjy lurched towards the door. Outside, he belched.

9

At ten the next morning Duddy came charging out of a bottomless sleep, unsure of his surroundings but prepared for instant struggle, the alibi for a crime unremembered already half-born, panting, scratching, and ready to bolt if necessary. He shook his head, recognized his own room, and sighed gratefully. Staggering out of his bedroom, he tripped over a set of dumbbells that had been left before his door and stubbed his toe badly. His father had left a note for him on the kitchen table.

> Remember, the world is full of shits.
> *Exercise!* Soon as you hear something
> phone me at Eddy's.
>
> POP

Duddy ate breakfast around the corner at Moe's and read Dink Carroll in the *Gazette*. Next he turned to the financial page.

"Look what's worried about the market," Moe said. "Only last year if he came in here it was to steal cigarettes."

155

Duddy ignored the remark and turned to the *Apartment to Let* column.

"One year the nose is running," Moe said, "and the nex they buy a jockstrap for eighty-nine cents and you can't say word to them any more."

Duddy marked off some of the more interesting ads. H graded the apartments available like movies in the *Tely*, giv ing one place on Tupper Street three stars. "Another coffe please, sonny," he said to Moe.

"It talks," Moe said.

Duddy turned to Fitz's column. It's no use, he thought, can't stall here all morning. I've got to get in to see that gi somehow. Duddy tossed a quarter on the counter. "There yo are, old chap," he said.

Duddy took the longest route to Westmount, just as if h were driving the Dodge and had an out-of-town fare in th back. He blessed every red light, too, but eventually he go there. A maid answered the door.

"I've got an urgent message for Miss Sandra Calder," h said.

"I'm sorry, but—"

Duddy forced his way into the hall.

"Edgar," the maid called. "Edgar."

A blonde girl in a kimono came through a glass door. "Is for me, Doris?"

The butler came through another door wiping his chin wit a napkin.

"I'm Lennie's brother."

The blonde girl lifted a hand to her cheek. "Let him in, she said.

"Your father said you were to have no visitors," Edgar sai

"He won't be back for hours. Come inside."

" 'Scuse me, Ed," Duddy said, stepping past the butler, an he followed Sandra through an enormous dining room wit paneled walls into the breakfast room. Sandra poured hi coffee, but she didn't speak until the maid had gone. "How Leonard?"

"Oh, fine. Just fine."

"You have the same mouth. Otherwise there's not much a resemblance."

"So they tell me."

"Did he send you?"

"Sure thing."

"Tell him Daddy doesn't know. Dr. Westcott promised n to tell him."

"Is that so?"

"But he's going to try his best to find out who did it and when he does, brother, he's threatened everything but a lynching. Look, tell Leonard not to worry, because now that I'm all right I think I can talk Dr. Westcott into keeping his mouth shut. Why don't you say anything?"

"Aw."

"You think I'm not being fair to Leonard. You think I'm using him."

She's going to cry, Duddy thought. "Easy," he said.

"Everything's going to work out. Tell him that, please. Dr. Westcott's furious right now, but I can handle him. He adores me. What's wrong?"

Duddy bit his fingernail.

What is it?

"Lennie didn't send me. I don't even know where he is."

"What?"

"Give me his address. I've got to see him."

"No!"

"Listen here—"

"Oh, God, what did I tell you? How could you lie to me like that?"

Duddy grabbed her by the wrist. "I want his address," he said.

"I can't give it to you. I promised."

"You promised," he shouted. "You think I care what you promised?"

"I can't do it."

"He left a note saying he was going to quit medical school. Do you know how much sweat and struggle has gone into making Lennie—"

"But he needn't quit. I'll handle Dr. Westcott."

"Give me his address. Come on."

She shook her head violently and tried to break free of him.

"You see this fist," he said. "Honest to God . . ."

"Edgar!"

Duddy let her go. "O.K.," he said, "I'm sitting here until Daddy-waddy comes. I'm going to tell him Dr. Westcott knows something he doesn't know. O.K.?"

"You're terrible."

Ver gerharget, he thought. *Platz.*

"That would just about ruin Leonard."

"Give me his address."

Edgar came. "It's all right," Sandra said. "I found what I wanted."

Duddy waited until he'd gone again. "Look," he said, "all I want is to see him. Why should I do Lennie harm? He's my brother."

"No. I can't."

"Will you stop the waterworks please?"

"I can't give you his address."

"I'm not a busy man. I'll just wait here until your father comes."

Ten minutes passed. Sandra lit a cigarette. "The coffee' cold," she said. "I'm not going to talk to you any more," she said. "I'm going to ignore you."

"Don't make *me* cry," Duddy said.

"I'm going up to my room."

There was a pause. "Well," Duddy asked, "what's keeping you?"

"Aren't you going?"

"I'm waiting here for your father. I told you that."

"If I gave you his address would you promise not to make any trouble?"

"Give me his address. Come on."

Sandra wrote out the address and led him through the dining room again.

"You could fit a bowling alley into here. Jeez."

"I don't even know your name. All you told me is that you're his brother."

"Dudley. I'm in the film business. An indie."

"I beg your pardon?"

"An independent producer," he said, handing her his card. "Hey, you must know a lot of debutantes like . . ."

Sandra was still absorbed by his card.

"Listen," Duddy said, "have you ever heard of Peter John Friar?" He told her about him. "We could do a top-notch picture on a coming-out party. A record for your grand kiddies and their grandkiddies after them."

Sandra smiled.

"Don't lose that card. You get us a job in Westmount and there'll be something in it for you. I'm no piker, you know."

"Do I look as if I need the money?"

"I never met a pretty girl yet who couldn't use a few extra bucks for a nice dress."

"Tell Leonard not to worry."

"Can do," Duddy said. "Cheerio."

Max was out. Duddy phoned Yvette and his grandfather and Uncle Benjy and when he returned to the office he called his father again. "He's in Toronto."

"What in the hell's he doing there?"

"A fling. He's been studying too hard, that's all. I'm leaving on the four o'clock train. I'm too tired to drive."

"Maybe I oughta go with you?"

"Ixnay."

"He's awright? You're not kidding me?"

"I'll bring him home tomorrow as good as new."

"You're a good kid."

"Sure."

Max phoned back two minutes later. "Listen, is Uncle Benjy going with you?"

"No. Certainly not."

"Awright. Hey, one minute. Has Lennie got a broad with him there?"

"A dozen maybe. If they're any good I'll bring one home for you."

"Hey, I'm your father. Don't forget that. There should be respect."

Duddy laughed.

"I mean that," Max said.

"That's not why I'm laughing. I'm laughing because I feel good. Cheerio."

Duddy phoned Bernie and then he rang Mr. Friar. He told him he had to go to Toronto for a couple of days. There were some things he wanted to discuss with him first, however, and they arranged to meet for a drink.

"First off," Duddy said, "keep your hands off Seigal's girl. He's on to you. Here's a list of suggestions for the movie."

"I told you when I started, Kravitz, that I will tolerate no artistic interference."

"They're only suggestions. You can throw them out if you want to. Do you need any money?"

Mr. Friar began to stammer. "Here." Duddy gave him a hundred dollars. "Oh, before I forget. Yvette will be back at seven. Take her out for a good dinner, Mr. Friar. I'd really appreciate that."

"Doesn't the competition worry you?"

Duddy's face brightened. "Gwan." He clapped Mr. Friar on the back. "You're old enough to be her father."

"What a charming boy you are!"

"I'm going to miss my train," Duddy said.

"Wait. There's something I want to ask you. In some ways you're just about the shrewdest bastard I've ever met, yet I happen to know that you're buying land under Yvette's name."

Duddy set down his bag.

"Don't worry. She didn't tell me. I couldn't help overhearing."

"So?"

"Doesn't it worry you having the deeds under her name?"

"A friend is a friend. You've got to trust somebody . . . Jeez, I've gotta run." But Duddy stopped short at the door. "Hey," he shouted, "I've got a seat in the club car. *Style?* Style."

Mr. Friar lifted his glass to him. "Cheers," he said.

"I'd trust you too," Duddy shouted. *"Prosit."* And he ran off.

Duddy got into Toronto at ten-thirty. He had never been there before and he had no hotel reservation. Imagine, he thought, if my grandfather had had another ten bucks in his pocket when he came to Canada I would have been born here. I would never have gone to F.F.H.S. or found Lac St. Pierre. He took the address Sandra had given him out of his pocket again. A number on Church Street. That tells me a lot, he thought. But Duddy was in an excellent mood. He had never traveled so far on his own before and the excitement of the club car was still with him. At least eight guys had exchanged cards with him. I'm good at making contacts, he thought. One of the men who had sat with him in the diner, the gray-haired one, was going all the way to Chicago. He was with Massey-Harris. "The market is hard this year," he told Duddy. Another guy in the diner, this one very nice, had told him, "I like doing business with the people of your race. I've never had any trouble with them."

"Good of you to say so."

The last man to make up their dinner party was a jovial Westerner. Ed Brody was stopping off in Toronto for the Grey Cup Finals. "Are we ever going to give those Argos a licking," he said. "Christ Almighty."

They discussed the communist menace.

"If I were Truman," the gray-haired one said, "I'd pull out of the U. N. It's just a glorified debating society."

"You've got a point there," Duddy said.

Duddy had no trouble getting a taxi outside the station. The address was a door over a Chinese laundry. This is worse than St. Urbain Street, he thought. There was a *Room to Let* sign and a bowl of paper flowers in the bay window alongside. He rang three times before the landlady came. "I'm looking for Leonard Kravitz."

"Never heard of him."

"He's my brother. We've got the same mouth."

"Isn't that nice for you?"

Duddy showed her a picture. "I know he's staying here."

"Are you calling me a liar?"

"You're a fine lady. Anybody can see that."

The landlady began to tap her foot. "Have you got a search warrant?"

"Listen. Listen here. I go to the movies too. I'm not a cop. I'm his brother. Lennie! Hey, Lennie! *Lennie!*"

A door opened on the third floor.

"It's me. Duddy!"

"Duddy!"

Duddy pushed the landlady aside and took the stairs two at a time. The whole lousy house was permeated with *goy* smell. Bacon grease. The way they can live, Duddy thought. Jeez.

"How did you find me?"

"Me and Bulldog Drummond went to different schools together. Aw," Duddy said, grabbing his brother, punching and hugging him, "Sandra gave me your address. I had to twist her arm to get it but."

"You went there?" Lennie asked, breaking free.

"Yeah. Come on inside and close the door. I'll bet your landlady's standing down there and listening to every word. Look at you. Wow!"

Lennie needed a shave. He'd lost weight too. "I'm all right," he said. "I can take care of myself."

"Sure. Who said no? Now let's get out of here."

"I'm not going home. I can't. I'm finished at medical school."

"Look, I'm starved. We can't talk in this dump. Is there anywhere near here where we can get a good smoked meat?"

They went to a restaurant on Yonge Street. "Well," Duddy asked, "is it good to see me?"

"Nothing will make me go back."

"What happened?"

"Nothing."

"Why'd you run away then?"

"I felt like it."

"Great! Now that you've brought me up to date I can go home."

"I'm going to get a job here. Tell Daddy I'm O.K."

"You tell him yourself. Daddy wants you to be a doctor. That's his dream of a lifetime."

"Everybody wants me to be a doctor. What about what I want? Look, even if I wanted to I couldn't go back to medical school."

"Why?"

"I can't say. I gave my word."

"No kidding?"

"And if Uncle Benjy doesn't like it he can go to hell."

"I'll tell him that. I'll tell him that Lennie took all that money from you over the years just to prove how much he hated you. What's the diff, I'll say, you've got lots of kids of your own. It isn't as if you put your heart into educating Lennie . . . Daddy is something else. All the other drivers know he's a big liar anyway. They won't be surprised when you don't turn out a doctor."

"Will you leave me alone please?"

"I'll tell Daddy you're getting a job here as a shipper. There's a big future for you. I'll tell him he doesn't have to pimp for Josette any more so that he can give you gifts like Uncle Benjy."

"What?"

"Any more messages for home?"

"I'm getting one of my headaches," Lennie said.

"Tell me why you can't go back to medical school even if you wanted to."

"I've given my word of honor. I'm sworn to silence."

"What are you? A boy scout."

"I'm a gentleman."

"Come again. This ear is blocked."

"You think just because I wasn't born in Westmount I can't be a gentleman?"

"Ah," Duddy said.

"You think just because some of our people made bucket during the war and others, like Uncle Benjy's pals, wouldn't think twice about handing over war secrets to Russia, that still can't be a gentleman?"

"I've got it. You're an anti-Semite."

"O.K. I'm an anti-Semite. I prefer the company of Gentiles."

162

"You don't mind my sitting here, I hope."

"You asked me, I told you."

"I mean you're not scared of being contaminated?"

"No."

"Good. Because I've got a message for you. Sandra says not to worry. Her father doesn't know and Dr. Westcott promised not to tell him."

"That's fine. Thanks."

"But she also told me that Dr. Westcott is going to try his best to find out who did it and that when he does there's going to be a lynching. I'm looking at the leading candidate."

"I see."

"You don't look so good, Lennie. Headache?"

"Lay off."

"What is it her father doesn't know?"

"I can't say."

"You're a gentleman."

"Lay—off—please."

"You're a chicken, that's what you are."

"Sh. People are beginning to look at us."

"You want me to tell you what happened? You performed an abortion on that girl."

"Let's get out of here," Lennie said. "Quick."

They went back to Lennie's room.

"Can we talk tomorrow?" Lennie said. "My head is splitting."

"You're twenty-four years old. Don't you know better than to go bareback?"

"Please," Lennie said.

"We'll start from the beginning. You tell me everything right from the beginning."

"What's the use, Duddy? Nothing can be done."

"That night you came home drunk. When you said, 'It could ruin me for life.' That's when you first found out she was pregnant, isn't it?"

Lennie didn't reply.

"Come on, Lennie, please. I want to help."

Lennie told him about the party where he had quarreled with Riva. "She's no better than a whore," he said. "You should have been there. Boy, did I ever tell her off."

"I heard."

He had run into Irwin Shubert a few days later and they had had a long intimate chat. Irwin, he said, was one of the most intelligent people he had ever met, and he had no use for the Hillel bunch either. "They inhabit a psychological ghetto," he had said, "and dare not step outside of it because they're afraid of being rejected." He had offered to take Lennie to a party the next night and that's where he met Sandra and Andy Simpson.

"This is the man I've been telling you about," Irwin had said.

Sandra had smiled so warmly and Andy had clapped him on the back. "Good to have you with us, kid."

Andy's father, Lennie pointed out, was J. P. Simpson. *The* J. P. Simpson.

"Mazel tov," Duddy said. "Did Irwin seem to be a good friend of his?"

Irwin, it seemed, was very devoted to Andy. He was always fetching him drinks, he went down to watch him at hockey practices, and he was coaching him privately in English and history. Andy had to keep his marks up or he'd have to quit athletics. "Andy liked me," Lennie said, "and so did Sandra. I could tell. I'm sensitive to that kind of thing and anyway Irwin took me aside once and as much as told me that Sandra had a crush on me. He was a bit drunk, you know, and he said he was glad he wasn't Andy. Sandra was supposed to be Andy's girl. Anyway there were lots of parties and after that I was invited to every single one of them. What a swell bunch of characters, honestly, so generous and relaxed and happy. When they have a party or go to a restaurant nobody worries about making too much noise or attracting attention, if you know what I mean. They're just themselves and glad of it. Nothing scares them. They're not always plugging away either, worried about this, worried about that, frightened about the future. They have a good time. *They're young.* That's it. That's what I'm trying to say. I never had such a wonderful time in my life. Honestly, Duddy. If there wasn't a party I'd meet Irwin and Andy and we'd go and drink together in the Maritime Bar in the Ritz. Sometimes we'd pick up Sandra and a couple of other girls and we'd drive all the way out to Ste. Adele to eat. Just like that, Duddy. And Irwin knows so much about food, you know. He knows all the . . . em . . . *exciting* wines too. There were times, it's true, when he and Sandra would bicker about this and that, but—"

"Bicker about what?"

"Oh, you know the kind of thing. Everyone's had too much to drink and Sandra would say something like, I'm seeing Andy tomorrow night, do you mind? It was nothing really. The next day it would be forgotten."

"Yeah? Keep talking."

"They're such a great crowd, Duddy. You must understand that. I never dreamt I'd have such a swell time. They knew I was Jewish too. I told them. *I* wasn't going to hide it. I'm glad I didn't either because it didn't make any difference. Nobody minded."

Then Lennie had noticed that Andy was in bad shape. He drank an awful lot. "Even for him," Lennie said. Irwin took Lennie aside and explained why Andy was drinking so much and how Lennie could help.

"You mean it wasn't even you who knocked her up? Jeez, now I've heard everything."

"Do you want to hear the rest of the story or not?"

"A gentleman. Is that what you said you were? I've got news for you, brother. You're the No. 1 Sucker of All Time."

"You would look at things like that. You have no code of honor, Duddy. That's your trouble."

"Wha'?"

"What's in it for me, that's your philosophy. I knew you'd never understand."

"Tell me the rest, please. Come on."

Irwin had told Lennie that Sandra was pregnant, that much was true, and he had asked Lennie if he would perform the abortion. Andrew, he said, knew nothing about their conversation, he would never ask such a favor of Lennie. "But I know you're not a frightened little Hebe," Irwin had said. "I know you'll come through."

Lennie had said absolutely no. It was too big a risk, he couldn't do it, and that's the night he had come home drunk. "The way he looked at me," Lennie said, "I knew I was through. I'd never see any of them again."

"So what," Duddy said. "A big deal."

"And I was right," Lennie continued, "because after that I began to see less and less of Sandra, Andy, and their crowd." Irwin still drank with him from time to time. Lapsing into that liquid whisper of his, he'd say things like, "I hear there's an Oneg Shabbat at Hillel tonight. Why don't you go?" He told Lennie that he was right not to take the risk. Friendships only went so far, a man had his career to think of.

"Then he'd be off to one of their parties," Lennie said, "and I'd be left sitting there. It was terrible. I never felt so bad in my life. Listen, Duddy, those poeple were my friends. I never really had friends before. She's so pretty, you know. All I could think of was her crying and Andy saying what can you expect, he's a Jew and he's afraid."

"Why couldn't she go to Dr. Westcott for the abortion?"

"Don't be ridiculous, Duddy."

"You want to know something? I know Irwin. I know that bastard inside out and I'll put down a hundred bucks against your ten that before he ever brought you around he told Andy you'd do the abortion."

"There you go again. You suspect everybody. Nobody's decent in your book. They like me, Duddy. They're my friends."

"Don't shout."

"You don't like Irwin because he used psychology to show you up for a money-crazy kid at the hotel. I know all about that."

"I hope you didn't take my side."

"You deserved what you got. You're greedy. I'm saying that to your face."

"O.K. Skip it. Let's get on with the story. The rest, please."

"I phoned Irwin and said I would do it and the arrangements were made. Why he got so jumpy right in the middle of it I'll never know. I could have handled it, I swear it, but Irwin saw the blood and went crazy. Sandra got hysterical. 'Irwin wants to kill me,' she said over and over again. 'He wants to kill me.' And the next thing I knew Irwin had dashed out to call Dr. Westcott."

"I don't get it."

Lennie explained that the phone call had been made anonymously. The three boys had waited in the hall until Dr. Westcott had come and then they had slipped outside. Sandra had naturally refused to tell Dr. Westcott who had started the abortion.

"So what are you doing here?" Duddy asked. "What are you so scared of?"

"He's sure to find out eventually. And when he does it's the end of me. I'll be thrown out of medical school."

"You're goddam right he's sure to find out. Because from what I know about Irwin and from what I hear about this Andy bastard all he has to do is ask."

"They'd never say a word."

"Sure." Duddy rose and cracked his knuckles. "It must be three o'clock," he said. "How's your headache?"

"Right now it's not so bad. Look, Duddy, I'm sorry. I know Daddy will feel terrible. But what can I do?"

"Bernie Altman says you had an excellent chance of winning the medal."

"Lay off. Please, Duddy."

"Let's go to sleep. I've got some business to do here tomorrow." Duddy began to undress. "Look, I want you to think hard. I want you to think hard and tell me the truth. Do you still want to be a doctor?"

"What does it matter what I want?"

"Answer me. Jeez."

"Yes."

"O.K. Which side of the bed do you want? Good Lord! What lumps, old chap. How does that old *fershtunkene tuchus*-head rent these rooms?"

Duddy fell asleep instantly, but not Lennie. Lennie turned on his side and stared at the wall. Duddy huddled close to him, embracing Lennie's waist. Twice Lennie moved away, embarrassed and uncomfortable, but each time Duddy pulled tighter to him again. Duddy snored. His body was seized by sudden jerks in his sleep.

"Lennie?"

It was five A.M. maybe.

"What is it?"

"Talk to me about Maw. Tell me about her."

"In the morning."

"Did she . . . well, like me?"

"You were her kid."

"That's not what I meant."

"Tomorrow. O.K.? And will you stop hugging me, please."

"I'm freezing, you jerk. What are you so scared of? I'm no homo."

Duddy was gone before Lennie woke the next morning. There were several independent film companies in Toronto, outfits that made industrial films, and Duddy, pretending to be a Diamond T Trucks representative, checked them all on prices. He also visited Columbia and Paramount to inquire about the price of films for semi-private distribution and to pick up catalogues. He was exhausted by the time he came round to pick up Lennie.

"Well," he said, "I've got the train tickets. We leave at six."

"What are you going to do?"

"I'm going to see Calder and tell him the whole story."

"Are you crazy?"

"No. But I'm not a gentleman either."

"I won't let you do it."

"I'm not asking your permission."

"It would mean the loss of all my self-respect, Duddy. It's not honorable."

"How would you like to hold this for a while?"

"If you go and tell Calder I did it I'm sure to be kicked out. He could send me to prison."

"We'll have to take that chance. There's no other way of being sure."

"I'm not going there with you."

"I didn't expect you to."

"Don't do it to me, Duddy. Please don't go there and tell them. Sandra would . . ."

"I'll say you don't know I'm doing it."

"When Irwin finds out—Well, there goes my summer in Maine."

"Wha'?"

"Irwin's taking a cottage in Maine this summer with some of the crowd. I was invited."

Uncle Benjy, Duddy remembered, couldn't get into the States. He was a communist. "Listen, Lennie, there's no other way. Calder's sure to find out sometime. I've got to see him first."

"What'll we tell Daddy?"

"You were studying too hard and you went on a fling. That's the story."

"Maybe if I just stayed here for a while Westcott wouldn't find out anything. Maybe it would all blow over."

"Have any other medical students who have been seen at parties with Sandra Calder taken it on the lam at Toronto recently?"

Duddy slept on the train. He didn't wake until they reached the outskirts of the city. "Look," he said as they pulled into Central Station, "snow. The first snow. Aw, come on, Lennie. Buck up."

"Yeah."

"There's Daddy."

"Taxi," Max shouted. "Taxi, sir." He embraced Lennie. "Oh, Duddy, your girl has been calling all day. She says to go right to the office."

"Me and Frank Buck," Duddy said, "we bring 'em back alive," and he punched his father lightly on the shoulder. "See you later, old chap." Duddy ran, he jumped, grabbing for the falling snow, opening his mouth to swallow some.

"Some kid," Max said.

Duddy took a taxi, watching the snow and the rush of light outside, searching for lookers among the window-shoppers gazing at their legs and in his mind's eye stripping the juicier ones down to black lace panties. Boy, he thought impatiently, am I ever in the mood.

Yvette was excited. "Duquette's willing to sell," she said.

Duddy unlocked the desk and got the map out and saw that

Duquette owned a considerable amount of lake frontage on the side opposite Brault.

"The sister in the asylum died. So he's got a clear title now."

"How much?"

"Seventy cents a square foot. Twenty-five hundred dollars." There was no rush this time. The notary said there were no other potential buyers.

"Let's try to knock him down to sixty-five. Tell the notary we'll hand over the works in cash if he'll take sixty."

"Have you got twenty-five hundred dollars?"

"Not quite. But I can get it," he said, picking up the phone. "Oh, I brought Lennie back. He was in Toronto."

"Why did he run away?"

"Aw, he knocked up a *shiksa*. A girl, I mean. Whoops . . . Hello, Mr. Seigal? Kravitz here. Listen, I'm going to need another five hundred in advance on the film—What? Oh, I see. Sure, that's O.K. Good. See you soon. No, don't worry. It'll make *Happy Bar-Mitzvah, Bernie!* look sick. I promise." He hung up. "Seigal says he gave five hundred dollars on account to Mr. Friar this morning. Friar asked him for it. He gave him a receipt. Have you seen Friar today?"

"No."

Duddy looked closely at Yvette. "We need a couch in here," he said hoarsely. "We oughta have a couch." He let Mr. Friar's number ring and ring. There was no answer. "He's probably asleep. Stop looking so worried, please. He needed money for film or something, that's all." Duddy hung up and told Yvette that he wanted her to find him an apartment downtown. "I also want you to get me subscriptions to *Fortune, Time, Life* and—There's another one, but I forget. We also ought to get some stills to hang on the walls. The bigger the better . . . Come here a minute," he said, taking her hand and guiding it. "Some flagpole, eh? A regular Rock of Gibraltar."

Yvette wanted to wait, but Duddy insisted, and they made love on the carpet.

"I don't get it," Duddy said. "Imagine guys getting married and tying themselves down to one single broad for a whole lifetime when there's just so much stuff around."

"People fall in love," Yvette said. "It happens."

"Planes crash too," Duddy said. "Listen, I've got an important letter to write. We'll eat soon. O.K.?"

She didn't answer and Duddy began to type.

To Whom It May Concern:

It has come to my attention that one Irwin Shubert intends to rent a cottage in Maine this summer. It is therefore my painful duty to inform you that the aforementioned Shubert is well known for his communistic beliefs on the McGill campus. He is known far and wide for sticking up for un-Americans like Henry Wallace, Paul Robeson, and Fred Rose, and I hardly think he would be a desirable guest in the fine State of Maine. I don't understand why he is going (unless it is to do some dirty work for the commies) because the aforementioned Shubert is always propagandizing against the United States, saying how it is run by Wall Street and they are fascists and started the Korean War.

PATRIOTIC CITIZEN

PS. It is my firmly held conviction that the above-mentioned Shubert is also a sexual pervert. This is a heartbreak to his family but I thought you ought to know as these are dangerous times.

Duddy handed Yvette the letter. "Check the spelling," he said, "and first thing tomorrow send copies to Senator McCarthy, the FBI, and the principal of McGill. I also want you to take out subscriptions for Irwin to the *Tribune* and any other commie papers you can think of. Pay for them in cash. O.K., let's go eat. I'm starved."

11

Hugh Thomas Calder had not made the family fortune, his father had done that, but he administered it with conservative good sense. His financial operations lacked panache, he avoided the big gamble, but steadily, unobtrusively, he made money with his father's money. *Time* had called him "bland, brilliant Hugh Thomas Calder," but that, he supposed, was because he said very little, and so people, being what they were, put him down for a thinker. That wasn't the case. Most things he had to say were, he felt, rather asinine, usually he was bored, and so he seldom spoke unless he was asked a direct question. Mr. Calder was a widower, and grateful for it. He enjoyed living alone. Well, not quite alone. For there was Sandra. When Sandra had been fourteen he had looked at her and realized that she would grow up to be the true rich bitch, but he didn't care. Why not, he had thought. There's certainly money enough for it, and it's time somebody enjoyed it.

Hugh Thomas Calder did not pine for power, he had had his father's fortune thrust on him. He abhorred the stale atmosphere of board rooms and committees and clubs, but there was nothing else he really wanted to do. He was not a frustrated artist or farmer. Neither did he see himself as a political candidate. A mere fifty and still mildly handsome, Calder was not altogether without enthusiasms. They were short-lived, however. He had collected pictures by young Canadian artists for a time, the non-figurative kind of stuff, and then one day he looked at them all together, gave them away, and never bought another one. He had tried an analyst once, a little German refugee with sour breath, and he had invented the most extravagant dreams for his sake, but the German had been more interested in his opinions on the market and Calder had dropped him. He had once been intrigued with a girl who sang in a night club under the name of Carole—she complained endlessly about the conditions of her work—and one evening he asked her, "I wonder what you would do if you were suddenly given five thousand dollars out of nowhere."

"Oh," was all she said, and he made out a check right there. Carole had seemed such a spirited girl that he had hoped she would do something wild. What she did was quit her job and bring her sister and mother in from the country and open up a hat shop.

There had been other and, when he reflected on it, more shameful little experiments with money. Once, at the Chantecler in Ste. Adele, a hundred-dollar bill had accidentally dropped to the bottom of a urinal when he had hurriedly reached for his handkerchief. Calder hadn't retrieved the soaking note. He had returned to the bar and sat there staring at the toilet door for some time. After four other men, with all of whom he had a nodding acquaintance, had been inside Calder went to the toilet again. The hundred-dollar bill was gone. Back in the bar again, Calder examined each of the four men severely, trying to guess who had stooped for the note. He thought of announcing his loss, he wanted badly to humiliate whoever had done it, and that depressed him. But the shocking part of it—for him anyway—was that following the first accidental loss he had, while staying at smart resorts, two or three times purposely repeated the procedure and then sat where he could keep an eye on the toilet door. Each time he would try to guess the man who had stooped, and shortly afterwards he paid his first visit to the little German analyst.

Hugh Thomas Calder disliked Dr. Westcott intensely, he knew Sandra was not suffering from a mere nervous upset and that Westcott knew more than he was saying and—what's more—was aching to be asked about it. Calder was going to deny him that pleasure. Sandra was, to his mind, a shallow little bitch and unless it was absolutely necessary for him to know he'd much rather not get involved in what was bound to be sordid. So he was displeased and in a most unreceptive mood when Edgar came to tell him that there was a young gentleman who insisted on seeing him alone.

"What does he look like?"

Edgar described him as a thin, shifty boy. He wore pointed patent-leather shoes. "He was here once before, sir. To see Miss Calder."

"I see. Send him in, please."

When Duddy entered the living room, Hugh Thomas Calder rose with studied weariness from his armchair and put on his glasses to have a better look.

"It's about Sandra," Duddy said quickly. "She hasn't got a cold. She was knocked up."

Calder removed his glasses. He stared. "Are you an abortionist?" he asked.

"Me! Are you crazy? Oh, I'm sorry."

"Let me guess, then. You're a blackmailer."

"Hey, one minute. I'm a respectable businessman." He handed Mr. Calder his card. "I'm in the motion picture business."

"I see. Are you sure you wouldn't like to sit down? Now, are you a blackmailer?"

"Jeez. Could I have a drink, please? I mean is that rude for me to ask . . . ?"

Mr. Calder poured two whisky and sodas. "You were saying?"

"Lennie's not going to be the fall guy, see. I've got friends."

"I'm sure you have, but—"

"He's a cinch to win the medal. You're on the board of governors and you can help."

"I'm afraid I don't understand."

"O.K. Sure. But one thing I want to get straight first. Lennie doesn't know I'm here. He'd kill me if he found out."

"Lennie?"

"He's my brother."

Duddy told him about the bungled abortion.

"But they could have killed her," Mr. Calder said. "Why idn't she come to me?"

"They're kids," Duddy said. "I've seen quite a bit of them 1 the last week and if you'll pardon me they don't know from heir ass to their elbow."

"Perhaps you're right. But what do you want from me?"

"This Dr. Westcott can make trouble. He can get Lennie xpelled."

"Don't you think he ought to be expelled?"

"No, sir. I'm speaking candidly."

"Give me one good reason why not."

"Oh, let's not talk like that, please. They took advantage of im like."

"Don't you think he might at least have waited until he got is degree before he started to perform illegal operations?"

"O.K., he made a mistake. Why should he be the fall guy ut? Why should your daughter and Andy Simpson get off and ennie be expelled?"

"I think they all ought to be thrown off the campus."

"Wow."

"I'm trying to be fair."

"Sure. Sure you are. Sandra's expelled and she comes home ɔ this Yankee Stadium here and for all I know she can sleep 1 a different bedroom every night. That Andy Simpson goes ome and sits on his ass until his father croaks and he inherits nough money to choke ten horses. But what about my rother," Duddy shouted, approaching Calder, "what happens ɔ him? He becomes a taxi driver. He gets a job in a candy tore. Do you know what went into getting that guy into medial school?"

"Why didn't he think of that before?"

"Maybe he did. But he's a poor boy and he never met up ith ladies and gentlemen before. Present company excepted."

"That's not a good enough excuse."

"And what happens to my father? He dies of a broken eart. Thank you."

"I'm sorry."

"He's sorry. Hah! Look, it wasn't even Lennie who knoçked er up. He never once touched her. Is that how you people ay off favors?"

Mr. Calder didn't reply.

"All you have to do is tell Westcott to shettup. When he nds out, I mean. Meanwhile he doesn't even know it was ennie."

"Why should I use my influence to conceal a criminal act?"

173

"What are you? A lawyer?"

"Are you very fond of your brother?"

"He's my brother," Duddy said, annoyed. "You know."

"How old are you?"

"Almost nineteen."

"Good God!"

"What's the matter?"

"Couldn't your brother have come here to see me himself?"

"He doesn't know I'm here."

"Nonsense."

"O.K., so he knows. Lennie's very sensitive. He gets head-aches. Coming here was my idea anyway. Be a sport, M Calder. Don't make trouble."

"Why shouldn't I?"

"You'd feel better to see him expelled, ruined for life?"

"No."

"O.K.," Duddy said, "then it's settled. You'll speak to Wescott and—"

"Wait a minute, please."

"I thought you said—"

"Tell me how a boy your age gets into the film business. I'm interested."

Duddy told him about Mr. Friar, Yvette, and *Happy Bar Mitzvah, Bernie!* Each time he made Mr. Calder laugh he fe easier, more hopeful, but it was difficult for him to tell if h was really making progress. Mr. Calder resisted each attempt to bring the conversation back to Lennie's future.

"And what about you," Mr. Calder asked. "Why didn't yo go to the university?"

Duddy guffawed. "I'm not the type, I guess."

"Are you positive?"

"I come from the school of hard knocks."

"And what do you want out of life? Money."

"I want land. A man without land is nothing. Listen, abo Lennie—"

"I still see no reason why he shouldn't be expelled."

"Just this once, Mr. Calder, couldn't you—Well, he's good boy. Really he is. And he's worked so hard like. Studyin and studying . . ."

"If he was such a good boy he wouldn't have allowed you t come here to speak for him. He would have come himself."

"What do you want? Blood. He has to go back to McGill. H has to see Sandra and Andy and all those other rich stinker every day. How could he come here?"

"It would have been awkward. I understand, but—"

"Have a heart."

Mr. Calder smiled.

"Maybe some day I'll be able to return the favor. I've got friends, you know."

"Oh."

"You heard of the Boy Wonder?"

Mr. Calder waited.

"Only the other weekend the Wonder and I went down to New York together for the weekend. Just like that."

"What on earth is the Boy Wonder?"

"Jerry Dingle—*the Boy Wonder*. You mean you never heard of him?" What, Duddy thought, if the truly powerful people in the city knew nothing about the Wonder? Could it be that Dingleman was only famous on St. Urbain Street? "You're sure you never heard of him?"

"Absolutely."

"Jeez. I thought everybody—Look, Mr. Calder, give Lennie a chance and I swear I'll never forget it. I'm only small beans right now, but one day . . . well," Duddy said, "you know the old saying. Mighty oaks from little acorns grow."

Mr. Calder laughed. He refilled his glass. "Very well," he said at last, "I'll speak to Dr. Westcott."

"Shake on it?" Duddy asked, jumping up.

"Is he waiting outside?"

"No. He's at home."

"Well, you can tell him for me that he's lucky to have you for a brother."

"Aw. You'd be surprised at some of the things I've done in my time."

"I wouldn't."

"I'd like to show my appreciation, Mr. Calder. I'd like to send you a gift, but—Jeez, what does a guy like you need?" Usually, Duddy knew, it was safe to send a *goy* booze, but Calder owned a distillery. "I've got it. You name your favorite charity and I'll send them fifty bucks. A token like."

"That won't be necessary, Kravitz, but why don't you come and see me again?"

"Wha'?"

"Phone me," Mr. Calder said. "We could have dinner together."

175

12

"Crook!"

It was Mr. Cohen on the phone.

"Rotten stinker!"

Mr. Cohen had shown *Happy Bar-Mitzvah, Bernie!* to Dave Stewart in Toronto and Dave, who was with Columbia, had walked out in the middle of the first reel. "Amateur night in Dixie," he had said.

But Mr. Cohen was the least of Duddy's worries. Mr. Friar had disappeared. He had not removed his belongings from his apartment, but for three nights running he did not show up there. Duddy and Yvette phoned the police and all the hospitals. They went from night club to night club.

"You'll never see that five hundred dollars again," Yvette said.

"The hell with the money. The day after tomorrow is the Seigal bar-mitzvah. What am I going to do for a cameraman?"

"He's probably back in England by now."

"Do you think," Duddy asked, "if I studied up on it that I could learn how to shoot a film before Saturday morning?"

On Friday afternoon Duddy moved into his apartment on Tupper Street. "This is the berries," he said. There were two rooms, a kitchen, and a tiled bathroom. Duddy tried the shower, he poked his head inside the fridge. "It still stinks of *chazer-fleish* in here," he said.

"Wha'?" Yvette asked.

"*Goy* stink. We oughta rub the walls down with chicken fat before I move in."

Yvette's one-room apartment was in the basement of the same building. "I can come up and cook for you," she said.

"That's my Girl Friday," Duddy said, goosing her.

"Stop that."

"Jeez. Have you got the curse again?"

"Maybe I'm not going to have my period this month. Maybe I'm pregnant."

"Congrats. Come on. We'd better start checking through the bars for Friar again."

"One minute. What would you do if I *was* pregnant?"

"I've got just the guy to fix you. A real pro. My brother Lennie."

They went from bar to bar. They tried the taverns. Duddy showed Mr. Friar's picture to the hat-check girls in at least ten night clubs. The head waiter at Rockhead's had seen him about an hour earlier and Duddy's spirits lifted. "Was he sloshed?" Duddy asked.

"Are you kidding, buster?"

They found him in the Algiers at two in the morning. He was snoozing.

"Ah, Kravitz, come to collect your pound of flesh, I suppose?"

"I'm surprised at you, Friar. We've got to go to a bar-mitzvah tomorrow morning."

Yvette began to go through his pockets.

"Kravitz, I have never in my life held up a production. I always turn up on the floor. Apologize."

"Would it make you feel better if I kissed your ass for you? Come on. Let's go."

Yvette cursed. "A hundred and twenty-two dollars. That's all he's got left."

They took him to Duddy's flat and put him under the shower. Yvette fed him cup after cup of black coffee.

"I've sold my soul to the Hebrews. Shame on me," Mr. Friar said, slapping himself on the cheek. "Shame, shame."

"More coffee, Yvette."

"I was supposed to be a second Eisenstein. What happened?"

"You're a very gifted man. Everybody says so. Isn't that right, Yvette?"

"My essays on the cinema in *Isis* used to be widely quoted. Everyone expected me to . . . I'd like a drink, please."

"Ha-ha."

"Kravitz, you can't treat me like this."

"Listen, Friar, tomorrow night you can have all the booze you want on me. But right now you're going to sleep. We have to be up at eight. That gives you four hours and you're going to need every one of them. Come on."

Duddy led him into the bedroom. Mr. Friar protested feebly, he spluttered, and then he fell asleep.

"You'd better get some sleep too, Yvette. Hey, one minute. You haven't really got one in the oven? You were only kidding me, weren't you?"

"Yes, I was only kidding."

"Good. See you at eight. Eight sharp."

Mr. Friar arrived punctually at the synagogue, but he was in no condition to shoot a movie. He also discovered too soon exactly where the liquor was kept. He was most reassuring, however. "Don't fret, Kravitz. I can shoot this kind of thing with my eyes closed."

"You are, you bastard!"

Duddy, on his side, tried to comfort Seigal. "He's not drunk," he said. "He gets dizzy spells. Malaria."

But during Mr. Friar's four-day absence in Ottawa, Duddy took to biting his fingernails again. "I'll kill him, Yvette. If he ruins this film I'll break every bone in his body."

"I can't stand seeing you like this any more," Yvette said. "You're making a nervous wreck of me too."

"A friend in need," Duddy said. "Aw."

Yvette went to Ste. Agathe for the weekend. Left on his own, Duddy phoned Mr. Calder. What can I lose, he figured. He hangs up, that's all.

"What a pleasant surprise," Mr. Calder said.

They had dinner together at Drury's and Duddy discovered that Mr. Calder had recently bought the controlling shares in a well-known stove and refrigerator factory just outside of Montreal. "I've driven past there many times on my way out to the mountains," Duddy said. "There was sure lots of scrap in the yard."

Mr. Calder said he was going to dismantle the old foundry and put up an enormous new plant. When the bill came Duddy covered it with his hand and said, "Your money's no good here, Mr. Calder."

Duddy phoned Mr. Cohen when he got home. "It's Kravitz," he said.

"Do you know what time it is?"

"Don't hang up. This is important. I've got a deal for you maybe."

"God help me."

"I just got in from dinner. I was out with Hugh Thomas Calder."

"Liar!"

"I'm not lying, Mr. Cohen." He told him about the foundry. "Would you be interested in picking up the scrap there every week?"

"Are you crazy? He'd never give it to a Jew."

"If I can get it for you what's in it for me?"

They finally settled on a twelve and a half per cent commission.

"Listen," Mr. Cohen said, "maybe I ought to go and see him myself. He wouldn't want to deal with a kid like you."

"Oh, no?"

"You really know him?"

"I'll call you next week to say when you can pick up the first load."

"Some kid. Some operator you are."

Yvette returned in the morning. "Now you've gone and done it," she said. "The notary spoke to Duquette and he's accepted our cash offer. Have you got two thousand dollars, please?"

"Don't worry. I'll get it."

"The papers are being drawn up. We've got until next Friday."

Duddy took the map out of the desk and looked at it. He rubbed his hands together. "Next is Cote. He's got a big farm."

"We haven't even got Duquette's land yet."

"Don't worry. Worrying's my department." Duddy grinned. "Give me your hand a minute," he said.

"Oh, go to hell, please. I haven't even had breakfast yet."

Mr. Friar arrived in the afternoon. "It's an unmitigated disaster," he said soberly.

They drove right down to the screening room to look at the movie. Outside it was snowing. Christmas decorations were going up in all the department store windows.

"Oi. *Shicker*-head. *Mamzer*," Duddy shouted. "Did you do this to me on purpose, Friar?"

A headless Bobby Seigal read his *haftorah*, a grotesquely overexposed rabbi delivered his speech cut off at the eyes, and relatives walked down the synagogue steps at a thirty degree angle. "Oh, no. No," Duddy said.

"We'll have to refund Mr. Seigal his money," Yvette said.

"Yeah. Where do I get it?"

"The land will have to wait."

"When do you start on the Farber wedding?" Duddy asked Mr. Friar.

"I was supposed to start yesterday but they won't give me any more film on credit."

"Jeez."

"The chap's going round with the bill tomorrow afternoon. We owe him rather a lot, actually."

"Listen to me, Friar. You've got lots of other footage on Bobby. Can anything be done to save this movie in the editing? I don't care if it only lasts twenty minutes."

"It would take a genius."

"That's the spirit," Duddy said.

"Duddy," Yvette said, "you're going too far this time. You can't show this film. Nobody will ever give you another job."

"*Ver gerharget*. Now you listen to me, Friar. Make me some

179

of those dopy montages. Anything. I don't care if you have to stay up night and day but I want this movie put into shape, you hear. Now when can you have it for me?"

"Two weeks, perhaps."

"Ten days. I'm going to stick with you. I'm not going to let you out of my sight."

Duddy drove back to the office with Yvette.

"The two-fifty advance," he said, "we spent. Friar blew the other five hundred. Where would I get the money to refund Seigal? Let Friar work on it and I'll give the whole thing to Seigal for fifteen hundred. That way we'll get something back at least."

"He'll never make that film any good. You're making a mistake, Duddy."

"Oh, will you shettup, please. You're giving me a headache."

Yvette stopped the car. "I'm getting out right here."

"All right, I'm sorry. I beg your pardon. Tonight I'll buy you some flowers. Come on. Let's get to the office."

They owed the film supply company nine hundred dollars. Another payment was due on the car and there were the office and apartment rentals to be settled. His bank account was overdrawn a hundred and sixty-seven dollars. Duddy seized on the phone bill. "Who," he shouted, "called Ste. Agathe three times last week?"

"My brother's sick. One call was to the notary."

"It's cheaper after six o'clock or didn't you know that?" Duddy sent out for coffee. "When do they start the heating in this building," he shouted, giving the radiator a swift kick, "on January first?"

"What are you going to do?"

"I'm going to get that land, Yvette. I have to take each bit of it as it comes. Do you realize how prices will skyrocket when they find out we're after the whole lake? What are you looking at?"

"You. I'm wondering how long you can keep this up before you fall flat on your face."

"That reminds me." He phoned Lennie. "Hey, you know those pills you told me some of the guys take before exams? Yeah, benzedrine. Can you get me some tonight? I'll pick them up on my way home. Thanks." Next Duddy phoned Mr. Calder.

"He's in Washington," Edgar said. "He won't be back for at least a week."

Duddy hung up. "That's a bad break," he said. He picked up the receiver again and replaced it. No, he thought, Cohen won't give me anything in advance without definite word. "Will you stop staring at me, please."

"Would your Uncle Benjy lend you any money?"

"I'd drop dead before I gave him the pleasure."

The coffee arrived. "Charge it," Duddy said. "Listen, Yvette, when the guy comes about the bill tomorrow I'm in Washington. I'm there with Hugh Thomas Calder. You can't say about what. Hush-hush. But you *can* say I'm thinking of getting my film direct from Toronto. O.K.?"

"I'll try it," she said.

"Forty-five hundred dollars. Jeez. Hey, maybe if I mentioned Calder's name the bank manager . . ."

There was a knock at the door. Duddy leaped out of his seat. "A parking ticket," he shouted. "I knew it. How many times did I tell you not to let me park in a one-hour zone?"

"Take it easy, Duddy. You mustn't get so excited."

Yvette opened the door.

"Hiya."

A skinny young man with a crew cut and a long lopsided face, his hands stuffed into the pockets of an old army windbreaker like a child's into jam jars, smiled ecstatically at Duddy. "Long time no see," he said.

Duddy gave Yvette a baffled look. "Yeah," he said. "Sure."

"Everything's O.K.," the long, loose-boned man said. "Getting 'em over the border was a breeze."

"It was . . . ?"

"You're not happy to see me," the man said and, all at once, his expression was so meloncholy that Duddy feared the flesh would melt and the bones collapse with a rattle to the floor.

"Oh, no! No!" Duddy flung his arms in the air. "It can't be. It's Virgil."

Virgil nodded, he beamed, ducking his head as if to avoid an affectionate slap.

Duddy looked at Yvette and groaned. "How did you ever find me?" he asked.

"You left me your card remember? 'Dial MOVIES.' I thought I'd come straight up, though." He searched Duddy's face for displeasure. "I find telephone conversations highly unsatisfactory."

"Sure thing."

"What's going on, please?"

Duddy explained in a failing voice that he had met Virgil in New York when he had been there with Dingleman. He had told Virgil that he would pay him a hundred dollars each for

181

his pinball machines any time he could get them over the border.

"Em, Virgil, did you bring all ten of them?"

Virgil grinned enthusiastically.

"A thousand dollars," Yvette said.

"They're worth three-fifty each new in the States. More here."

"All you have to do is sell them," Yvette said.

"Sure. That's right," Duddy said, excited. "All I have to do is sell them. Let's say at—Well, we'll discuss that later. Where are they, Virgil?"

They were hidden under a tarpaulin about twenty miles from the border.

"O.K. Let's go. Come on, Yvette."

"At this hour?"

"We'll need two cars. I can pick up my father's taxi."

They picked up the Dodge on St. Urbain Street.

"O.K., Virgil, we'll follow you."

The morning's snow had melted and frozen, the roads were slippery, and there was a big wind. Duddy didn't have any tire chains and his heater didn't work. Yvette did up the top button of his coat and snuggled close to him.

"I couldn't tell you while he was there," Duddy said, "but I think we can get two-fifty apiece for them from the hotels in Ste. Agathe."

Yvette closed her eyes. She shivered. "That boy looks like a lunatic to me," she said.

"I figure if we get them packed in the cars by two-thirty we can be in Ste. Agathe by six-seven o'clock."

"You mean we're going to drive all the way out to Ste. Agathe tonight?"

"Reach into my jacket pocket. Yeah, that one. Lennie got me the pills. Give me one, will you."

Yvette stared at the bottle. There was no label. "I don't want you to take one," she said. "I'm afraid."

"I should fall asleep at the wheel. Is that what you want?"

"Duddy, please, you mustn't . . ."

"Heads up, guys. Here come the waterworks."

"You won't be happy until you kill yourself."

"Gimme the pill, please. O.K., now listen. I'm not going to kill myself. But I'm going to get that land, see. All of it. It's going to be mine."

"Duddy, even if you ever did raise enough money for all the land . . . what then? The price of the land is nothing compared to how much money you'd need to develop it."

"Don't worry. I've thought of that. Just let me buy up all that land first. You wait, Yvette. You wait and see."

"Oh, what's the use?"

"Listen, can we stay at your place tonight? Virgil and I can sleep on the hall floor or something. Wha'?"

"I'd better take you to a hotel."

"O.K. Skip it. You go to sleep."

Yvette took a pill. "I'd better stay up," she said. "Just in case."

13

After covering a hundred and fifty miles, the last forty-five through heavy snow, they finally reached Ste. Agathe. Yvette got Duddy and Virgil a double room at the St. Vincent Hotel and muttered something about sleeping all day. Duddy, too tired to drive any more, put her in a taxi. One of his ears, he was sure, was frozen, and his eyes were bloodshot. There was a ringing inside his head.

"A bed," he said, entering the room. He pulled off his trousers and flopped on it. "Good night, Virgil."

"One minute. There's something I ought to tell you."

Duddy mumbled something inaudible through his pillow. Virgil shook him awake. "Mr. Kravitz," he said.

"Mn?"

"I'm an epileptic."

"Wha'?" Duddy rolled over on the bed and groaned. "Go 'way, Virgil. It's not true."

"I can't help it. That's the way I was born."

Duddy sat up and rubbed his eyes. "You mean you're really an epileptic?"

Virgil nodded. He grinned.

"Jeez." *Ver gerharget* twice, he thought. All the world's banking crap artists, how do they find me? "You got a cigarette? Thanks. What happens . . . em . . . well, if you have a fit like?"

"Oh, don't worry about a thing, Mr. Kravitz. I don't make much noise."

"You don't?"

Virgil grinned.

"Well, there's always a silver lining."

"It's not easy to be an epileptic. You'd be surprised how many people are prejudiced against us."

"Listen, if you have a fit—I mean just in case. No offense, eh? Am I supposed to put a spoon down your mouth or . . . em . . ."

"Naw. Don't worry about a thing. Sometimes I have fits in my sleep and I don't even know about it until I wake up in the morning."

"Oh."

"Yeah, then I can tell by looking in the mirror. My tongue gets cut."

"Do you . . . em . . . have these fits in your sleep very often?"

"A couple of times a week. They're not very severe."

"Is that so?"

"You know, Mr. Kravitz, life is no bowl of cherries for a guy like me."

"You don't say?"

"Who would take a chance on me as a waiter?"

How would you like to kiss my ass, Duddy thought.

"Or a driver?"

Jeez, Duddy thought, I'd better not let him drive the Dodge back to Montreal. A crack-up, that's all I need.

"We're a persecuted minority. Like the Jews and the Negroes."

"Yes, I guess that *is* one way of looking at it." Duddy lit another cigarette off his butt. Who can sleep anyway, he thought, with this one in the room. God help us.

"Only you have B'nai B'rith to fight for you and the Negroes have the NAACP. We have nobody. We're all alone."

"It's a shame, Virgil. A real shame."

"Even the queers are getting organized now. No offense—"

"What do you mean no offense?"

"Well, I don't know you very well, Mr. Kravitz, and you did ask for a double room—"

"Just don't get any stupid ideas," Duddy said, pulling his blankets tighter around him.

"Anyway, like I was saying, even the queers now have organizations to fight for them."

"Is that so?"

"You know, Mr. Kravitz, you're a Jew and wherever you go other Jews will help you. I'm not speaking against that. I think it's swell. Why, you could turn up tomorrow in Kansas City or Rome or—well maybe not Tokyo. But my point is other Jews there will lend a helping hand. You're sort of interna

184

tional. With the fags it's like that too. You know, they have their special little faggoty night clubs in every city. But epileptics? No. Nothing. A lot of them, *plenty*, won't own up to it, that's why. You think there's shame attached to being an epileptic?"

"Certainly not."

"Some of the greatest men in the world were epileptics."

"No kidding?"

"Julius Caesar."

"Yeah?"

"Jesus Christ, even. Dostoievski. Charlie Chaplin."

"Charlie Chaplin is a Jew," Duddy said snidely.

"A guy can be both, you know."

"Jeez."

"That's why I started out in the pinball machine business in the Bronx, you know. Nobody would hire me so I had to go into business for myself."

"Necessity is the mother of all invention," Duddy said.

"Those are true words, but look where it got me. Even with the thousand dollars I'm getting from you I will have lost most all my savings."

"That's show biz," Duddy said. Cuckoo, he thought warmly. I'll call him tomorrow. "Shouldn't we try to get some sleep?" he asked.

"My life ambition, Mr. Kravitz, is to organize the epileptics of the world. I'd like to be their Sister Kenny."

"That would be something, Virgil."

Virgil's voice took on the dimensions of a platform speaker. "Why aren't we covered by the Fair Employment Act?" he demanded.

"Why don't we get some sleep?"

"I like you, Mr. Kravitz. Do you like me?"

"Yeah, sure thing, Virgil."

"Why?"

"Couldn't I tell you in the morning?"

"You're not just saying it, are you? You do like me."

"I think you're a prince of a fella."

"Thanks. So many people are prejudiced against us, you know."

"Good night, Virgie."

"We're going to be buddies. Real buddies. I can tell."

Sure, Duddy thought. You bet. He got up and turned out the light.

"What does Yvette think of me? Be frank."

"Jeez, Virgie. She didn't say."

185

"I like her. She's got qualities."

Duddy pretended to be snoring.

"I've got a theory about women, you know. Mr. Kravitz?"

"Mn?"

"I've got a theory about women. It always works too. There are three types of women. The Berthe type, the Mathilde type, and the—"

"Virgil?"

"Yeah?"

"*I* would like to sleep now. *I* am very tired. *I* must be up in four hours. *I* am saying good night. Good night."

Virgil leaped out of bed. "It's almost light," he said. "It's snowing. I love snow."

Duddy woke with a hacking cough at nine-thirty. The room was freezing. He stumbled over to the sink, splashed cold water on his face, and took another benzedrine pill.

"Good morning," Virgil shouted. "A happy day in store, I hope."

Duddy moaned.

"I want to see all the sights."

Virgil leaned close to the mirror and stuck out his tongue. Duddy stared at him and remembered and suddenly froze.

"Are you O.K.?"

"Not a scratch," Virgil said. "Look, everything's covered with snow outside." He began to dress hastily. "I want to be the first person to walk in it. The first in the world."

"Go ahead and good luck. I'm going to get some coffee downstairs."

It took three days of lies, threats, pandering, cajoling, insult and the ultimate appeal to avarice to sell the pinball machines, but sell them he did. All but one of them. He went to Rubin's first and told him that the Hilltop Lodge had already bought one. "Why," he said to Rubin, "pay rent to some jerk in Montreal—why split the take—on this junky old model when for two hundred and fifty bucks I can supply you with the latest machine?"

"You know how long I can get for receiving stolen goods?"

Duddy assured him that he owned the machines. He had a receipt. "Look," he said, "six months from now you do a switch with the Hilltop Lodge and the Hilltop Lodge changes with the Châlet. I've got ten machines. You keep rotating them."

"I'd like to think about it."

"All right. I'll tell you what. I'll guarantee to buy the ma-

186

chine back from you one year from today for a hundred dollars. Right off you start with a profit. Don't you see?" Duddy put his arm around Virgil. "I brought Mr. Roseboro all the way in from New York special to install and service the machines. He's an expert."

"That's a falsehood," Virgil said.

"Ah-ha-ha," Duddy said. "Would you mind waiting outside in the car, please?"

After he had sold the first four machines Duddy dumped the rest with comparative ease. They went for an average of two hundred and twenty-five dollars and he was paid in cash for all but three of them."

"Well," Duddy said to Yvette, "I've got the money for the notary now."

"What about the bills in Montreal? And you have to give Virgil his thousand dollars."

"Sure. Don't worry."

Yvette took to Virgil and showed him all the sights in and around Ste. Agathe. Once or twice Duddy came out of a hotel after making a sale and found Yvette and Virgil laughing together in the car. "Hey," he asked, "what gives between you two?"

"Virgil wanted to know if you had a wife and children. He thought you were thirty-five at least."

"Very funny."

"*I* thought it was funny."

"You'd make a very good parent, Mr. Kravitz. I observe people and I can tell."

"Let's get moving, please."

Duddy was almost always bad-tempered in Ste. Agathe. Yvette put it down to the benzedrine pills, but she didn't like it. Their second night there she moved out of her house and into a single room in the St. Vincent Hotel.

"Virgil and I are going to the movies tonight. Want to come?"

"No."

"Do you mind if I go?"

"Listen," Duddy said, "I'll tell you what. I'll take over your single room and you can move in with Virgil."

"I don't have to go to the movies. I can stay here with you."

"Go ahead. Enjoy yourself."

Once they had gone Duddy got into the car and drove as near as he could to Lac St. Pierre. He had to walk the last three quarters of a mile through deep snow. The drifts were soft and often, between rocks, he sank in up to his knees. But it gave him quite a lift to see his land in winter. A thin scalp of ice protected the lake and all his fields glittered white and purple and gold under the setting sun. All except the pine trees were bare. It must be pretty in autumn, he thought, when all the leaves are changing colors. Duddy saw where he would put up the hotel and decided that he would not have to clear the wood all in one shot. It's lovely, he thought, and lots of those pine trees I can peddle at Christmastime.

Duddy trudged up and down through the snow with an owner's sharp eye for fire hazards and signs of mischief. He tried the ice on the lake with his foot. It cracked. He urinated into a snowbank, writing his name. It's my land, he thought. But the wind began to cut quicker across the fields, suddenly the sun went out like a light, it was dark, and Duddy began to shiver. Jeez, he thought, why didn't I leave the car lights on? He buttoned up his collar and began to strike matches. Duddy was able to trace his footsteps until the snow began to fall again, and then he was in bad trouble. He circled round and round, his teeth chattered, and twice he began to run. He ran and ran to no purpose until he collapsed panting in the snow. His feet burned from the cold, his eyes felt as if they were stuffed with sand, and he began to think what in the hell am I doing lost in a blizzard, a Jewish boy? Moses, he recalled from *Bible Comics,* died without ever reaching the Promised Land, but *I've* got my future to think of. He tripped, he fell time and again, his nostrils stuck together. If God pulls me through, he thought, I'll give up screwing for two weeks. Smoked meats too. When he finally stumbled on the car, shortly after two, he'd run out of cigarettes and matches. The car wouldn't start. Duddy sat in the back seat and wept, blowing on his hands. Eventually, because it was too cold to sit there any more, he started back into Ste. Agathe. It was nearly four o'clock when he reached the hotel. Yvette and Virgil were waiting up for him in the double room.

"Duddy!" She embraced him. She felt his forehead. "It's a furnace," she said. "I'll call the doctor right away."

"No doctors please. Get me a basin of hot water for my feet. There's a bottle of Scotch in the top drawer. Get me that too."

"I'm calling the doctor."

"Sure. Go ahead. He puts me in bed for a week and I don't sell the rest of the machines." Duddy drank the Scotch neat. He also took three aspirins. "I'll sweat it out tonight," he said. "Tomorrow I'll be good as new."

188

"You're remarkable, Mr. Kravitz. You have a great fighting spirit."

"Will you shut your face, please? Good night."

Each morning at nine o'clock Duddy phoned Mr. Friar. "Well, how goes the battle?"

"I'm working on it, Kravitz. I'm not giving up."

Wherever he went Duddy took the movie catalogues he had picked up in Toronto. He made deals with four hotels to supply them with movies one night a week. Six, he figured, was his break-even point, and anything over a profit. With a run of the resorts between Shawbridge and Ste. Agathe, he hoped to work up to two showings a night, fourteen rentals a week, by summertime. The children's camps could be worked during the afternoons, and that would bring in even more. Duddy didn't forget his soap and toilet supply order book either. He earned enough on this to pay his hotel bill and get his car out of the garage.

When they started back for Montreal on Thursday afternoon Yvette got into the Dodge with Virgil. "Hey," Duddy said. "You come with me."

"I thought I'd keep Virgil company. You're in such a bad mood anyway."

Virgil rubbed the back of his neck. He blushed. "I'd like to assure you, Mr. Kravitz, that I have no carnal designs on Yvette."

"Come on," Duddy said, grabbing Yvette's arm. "Get in the car."

They found Max at Eddy's, and he was furious. "Who do you think you are," he said, "that you can run off with my car for three days? Just like that."

"I phoned you," Duddy said. "I told you it was important."

"I've got a living to earn. Smart guy! Operator!"

"I'll pay you for the use of the car, Daddy."

But Max walked away from Duddy and the proffered fifty dollars. He stood by the window and saw Yvette talking to Virgil outside. "Some kid," he said, turning to Debrofsky, "he's got his own apartment now and a *shiksa* to go with. You dirty dog!"

"Yvette is my Girl Friday."

"I hope you get the clap. That would teach you a lesson," Max shouted.

"He's a healthy kid," Debrofsky said. "A girl's good for him."

"It's all glandular," Eddy said. "At his age—"

"I'm worried about his future," Max said.

"Don't worry. I'm not getting hitched."

Duddy ordered six smoked meats and some pickles to take out. Max sat down at the bar and sucked a sugar cube. "You don't look so hot, Duddy," he said.

"I'm all right, Daddy," he replied, smiling shyly.

"I haven't even seen your apartment yet. I wasn't invited."

"Come tomorrow night with Lennie. We'll all go to dinner."

"Don't try to get around me," Max said. "If there's anything wrong with the Dodge I'm holding you responsible. When you took it there wasn't the smallest rattle."

"He should live so long," Debrofsky said.

"Oh, I want to speak to you." Duddy took Debrofsky aside and they whispered together for a minute.

"What's going on?" Max asked.

"You take it into the garage, Daddy. Send me the bill."

Duddy and Virgil and Yvette went back to the apartment and ate there. Virgil helped Duddy carry the one pinball machine that was left upstairs and they set it up in the living room.

"High score for a dollar," Duddy said.

Mr. Friar came over and Duddy opened a bottle of gin.

"What an intriguing machine," Mr. Friar said.

Duddy, a practiced hand at shaking, coaxing, and pushing won twelve dollars on high score.

After Mr. Friar had gone back to work, Virgil asked, "Can I sleep here tonight, Mr. Kravitz? I've got a sleeping bag."

"Let me refresh your drink, Virgie," Duddy said. "I've got business to talk with you."

"I'm staying," Yvette said.

"Sure."

Virgil grinned. He waited.

"How would you like to stay here and go to work for me, Virgie?"

"Duddy," Yvette said, "that would be wonderful!"

"Well, Virgie?"

"You mean you'd give a guy like me a job, I mean knowing—" He noticed Yvette watching him and averted his eye. "Well, you know . . ."

"I could trust you. That's the most important thing with me."

"What do you want him to do?" Yvette asked.

Duddy explained that he was expanding into the distribution side of the movie business. Yvette could book the rentals. But he needed a man on the road to show the movies, some

190

ody trustworthy and presentable: Virgil. In summer, prob-
bly, he would have an assistant.

"But I don't know how to work a projector," Virgil said.

"That's something a four-year-old kid could learn in a week.
Don't worry."

Yvette kissed Duddy on the cheek. "I'm sorry if I was sharp
with you in Ste. Agathe," she said.

"You'll never regret this, Mr. Kravitz. I'll work so hard."

"There's only one thing. I need a man with a truck."

"Oh."

"You know. A small panel job."

"I see."

"What's the matter with you two? That's no problem. Look,
Virgie, I owe you a thousand bucks. Right? Right."

"Duddy," Yvette began apprehensively. But he looked at
her sharply and she sat down again.

"What would you say if for that thousand bucks I could put
my hands on just the truck for you?"

"Could you, Mr. Kravitz?"

"I spoke to Debrofsky at Eddy's. His brother-in-law has a
used-car lot and there he's got a '42 Chevvie. A half-ton job.
It's in beautiful shape and he wants twelve-fifty for it. But if
you were interested, Virgie, and willing to pay cash, I think
I could swing it for a thousand."

Virgil's eyes filled with excitement. "When could you know
definitely?" he asked, his fists clenched.

Yvette started for the door.

"What's wrong?"

"Go to hell," she said, and she slammed the door after her.

"Maybe you ought to sleep on it, Virgie. I don't want to
push you."

"Imagine. You'd give a guy like me a job. You'd trust me."

"I'll give you sixty bucks a week to start, Virgie, and of
course I'll handle all the gas bills and stuff. You'd have to put
the company name on the truck, though."

"Dial MOVIES?"

"Yeah."

"It would be a genuine honor, Mr. Kravitz."

"O.K., Virgie, I'll see about the truck first thing tomorrow
morning. Now if you'll excuse me for a minute . . . I want
to see Yvette."

Duddy poured himself another drink and took it with him
to Yvette's apartment. She sat on the sofa in her nightgown.

"O.K., what's got into you?"

191

"I've seen you do lots of dishonest things, Duddy, but never in my life did I expect you to cheat a boy like Virgil."

"Cheat. I'm a cheater? Wow!"

"How much are you paying for the truck?"

"It's a gift. From Debrofsky's son-in-law to me. I'm getting it for nothing."

"You are getting it for nothing. The company is, anyway."

"I'm smart. Can I help it?"

"You can't do this to Virgil."

"What am I doing? Twisting his arms. I take a boy in off the streets and give him a job and—"

"Please, Duddy, I'm not Mr. Cohen."

Duddy sat down beside her on the sofa and tried to kiss her. "I'm in the mood," he said.

"I never thought you were such a bastard," she said, moving away.

"Hey, one minute. What's with you and this Virgil?"

"I like him. I think he's sweet."

"Is that all? Are you sure?"

Yvette laughed. "Is that why you wouldn't let me drive back to Montreal with him?"

"He's an epileptic. I wouldn't let you drive with him because I was afraid of an accident. I think of your welfare, you know. You'd be surprised. What's wrong now?"

"You're not lying to me, Duddy? He is an . . . an epileptic?"

Duddy told her how Virgil had kept him up all night at the hotel. "There, aren't you sorry now? You thought I was trying to swindle him when all the time I was being a big help to him. I'm taking a chance on the boy. I like him."

"I ought to slap your face."

"What did I do now?"

"Do you mean to say that knowing how grateful he'd be for a job—any job—you managed to swindle him out of his thousand dollars? Oh, Duddy."

"Swindle. The truck will be registered under his name. I'm paying him sixty-five bucks a week too. *While I train him.* Where could he earn that kind of dough?"

"How much are you paying for the truck? Tell me the truth."

"I'm a humanitarian. I took such a chance on a boy like that and this is the thank you I get."

"Chance? Do you think he could have a fit while he was driving the truck?"

"Why not?"

"You mustn't let him do it, Duddy. You have to stop him."

"I'm exaggerating," Duddy said, sighing. "He can tell when they're coming on. All he has to do is pull over to the curb."

"Are you sure?"

"Yeah," he said wearily.

"I'll never forgive you if anything happens to him. I swear it."

"What's so special about Virgie?"

"I told you. I like him."

"Is that way you moved into the hotel the second night when," he began to shout, "you could have stayed at your place for nothing?"

"I had a fight with my family."

"Oh. About what?"

"Never mind."

"About what, please?"

"My brother found out I'm living with you."

"Which brother? Jean-Paul? That anti-Semite! That *shicker!*"

"I won't be able to see my parents again."

"Oh, gee. I'm sorry." He took her hand. "Really, Yvette."

"Duddy, I'm very tired. I want to go to sleep. I know that truck isn't costing you more than five or six hundred dollars. I want you to return the rest of the money to Virgil."

"Listen, listen, the cat's pissin'."

"I'm not coming into the office until you do that."

"That does it," Duddy said. "I was just on the verge of giving him a couple of hundred dollars . . . just to make you feel good. But I won't be threatened, you hear?"

"Do as you like. But just remember what I said."

Duddy leaped up. "You're fired," he said, "and that's final."

He took the steps back to his own apartment two at a time and poured himself another drink. Virgil was laying out his sleeping bag on the floor. "Listen," Duddy said, "I'm giving you sixty-five bucks a week. Not sixty."

"Gee."

"He hasn't even worked for me one day and he's got a raise. Oh, that bitch." Duddy picked up an enormous book. "What in the hell is this?"

"A rhyming dictionary, Mr. Kravitz. I'm a poet."

"He's a poet."

"I wrote two sonnets for Yvette in Ste. Agathe."

Duddy put down his drink. "I'd like to see them, please," he said.

"She has them. She wanted to keep them."

"Turn your back for one minute. That's all you need."

"I beg your pardon, Mr. Kravitz?"

"You want to play high score again?"

"Whatever you say."

"We'll play for five dollars this time."

"Gee whiz, that's a lot of money."

Duddy was ahead on the fifth ball when he shook the machine too avidly and tilted it. "Here," he said, handing Virgil the five dollars.

"Oh, I couldn't take it, Mr. Kravitz. I'd feel so guilty."

"For Christ's sake!"

"You work so hard for your money."

"A gambling debt is a gambling debt. Tomorrow you'd better find yourself a room."

"Are you angry with me, Mr. Kravitz?"

"No. I'm not angry." He picked up the dictionary again. "A poet, eh?"

"I've got a very good name for a poet. Virgil was the most famous poet of olden times. He wrote in Latin."

"You read a lot?"

"Whenever I can."

"Well, I read a lot too. I'm no dope. You ever read *God's Little Acre?*"

"No."

"You get a copy. I recommend it highly." Duddy began to pace. Twice he ran to the door and opened it. "I thought I heard somebody." That bitch, he thought. "Well, let's see a sample of your work."

Virgil jumped up, dug into his kitbag, and handed Duddy a page. Duddy read the poem and handed it back to Virgil, smiling broadly. "It doesn't even rhyme," he said. "A poet."

"Modern poetry isn't supposed to. This is a blank verse."

"Wha'?"

"I'm a follower of Kenneth Patchen."

Virgil told him about Patchen. He said he was great.

"Get me a copy of his book. I'd like to read it. Excuse me a minute."

Duddy ran downstairs and listened at the door. He heard Yvette in the kitchen. "Can I come in?" he shouted.

The kitchen light went out.

"Try to be ready at eight-thirty. I want to get down to the office early tomorrow."

Again there was no reply and Duddy went upstairs to sleep. Yvette did not come into the office the next morning or the morning after. Duddy sent flowers, but they came back; so did the chocolates. Meanwhile he discovered that Yvette was seeing Virgil every evening. Duddy worked late with Mr. Friar every night and helped to get the Seigal movie into presentable shape. When he got in early one morning he told Virgil, "Tell Yvette I'm drinking too much. Say I look terrible."

"I don't mean to intrude, Mr. Kravitz, but I understand the two of you have had a disagreement. I put in a good word for you whenever I can."

A week went by. Ten days. Duddy called Virgil into the office. "Look," he said, "a funny thing happened. Debrofsky's brother-in-law made a mistake. The truck only cost seven-fifty." He handed Virgil a check for the difference. "I'm afraid it's postdated," he said. "But if you wait a couple of weeks . . ."

Yvette returned to work the next morning.

"I want you to go to Ste. Agathe," Duddy said. "I've got the money for Duquette."

She put out her hand for the keys.

"I've got nothing to do this afternoon. Maybe I'll tag along for the drive."

"If you like."

Back in Montreal again they drove straight to the office. Duddy had lots of letters to dictate. But first he took out the map and red crayon and colored in the land that used to belong to Duquette.

"I own nearly half of it now. Well, more than a third anyway. Six months it took me. That's all. Well, what do you say? What's your opinion of Duddy Kravitz now?"

Three

Duddy's winter was exceptionally properous, and happy too. Mr. Friar had succeeded in making something of the Seigal bar-mitzvah movie and Duddy had picked up a small profit, although he let it go at a reduced price. He did extremely well, too, with his third bar-mitzvah movie and two of weddings. He hired a girl to help Yvette. Making commercial films for television, it seemed to Duddy, might turn out to be even more profitable than—as he called them—his "social featurettes." He began to think in terms of larger offices with a studio of his own and he made several trips to Toronto to find out what he could about industrial films and the profits to be made there. Meanwhile, on the distribution side, he was breaking even, better sometimes, and building up lots of goodwill. Whenever it was possible he showed films free of charge at, for instance, a Knights of Pythias evening for underprivileged kids or any charity event in Ste. Agathe. He was determined to make friends with the mayor there and he succeeded. He rented his films by the week and Virgil's salary had to be paid anyway. Lots of his free showings got him mentions in *Mel West's What's What* and once he got a whole paragraph to himself. It read:

ADD MONTREALERS WITH A HEART: Up-and-coming cineman Duddy Kravitz informs me he's rarin' to show movies free any time, anywhere, if the cause is worthy . . . Kravitz, soon to celebrate his first year in show biz, has three original productions under his belt already, and his plans for the future include a feature-length comedy production with Ourtown's Cuckoo Kaplan . . . *Howdy dood it?* "I work eighteen hours a day," he says, "and if I drive my staff hard they know I've always got my schonzola to the grindstone too." How old is he? Nineteen! *So don't let any socialist sad sacks tell you it's no longer possible to go from rags to riches in this country* . . . Born and bred on St. Urbain Street, Duddy was working as waiter not many moons ago . . . REMINDER: For those free films DIAL MOVIES.

Virgil never found a room. He stayed on in the apartment—he was on the road three or four days a week anyway—and Duddy got to enjoy having him there. With his second week's salary Virgil bought Duddy a record player and he never returned from a trip to the Laurentians without flowers or a box of chocolates for Yvette and a trick cigarette lighter or maybe a book for Duddy. Only twice during the first month did he waken with a bruised and bloody mouth.

One of Virgil's poems was published in *Attack!*, a mimeographed magazine published by some fighting young followers of Ezra Pound. It was called "Himmler Has Only Got One Ball."

"At least this one rhymes," Duddy said, "but why don't you try something longer. You know, with a story."

Virgil had met the editor of *Attack!*, a fierce little man with a broken nose, at Duddy's apartment soon after it had become a gathering place for bohemians. That came about through Duddy's acquisition of the record player and his discovery that he was a music lover. Duddy bought Beethoven's nine symphonies on long-playing records and listened to them in order. He kept a date stamp and ink pad next to his records and each time he listened to one of them he stamped the date on the album. He also began to collect Schubert and Mozart and Brahms and that's how he ran into Hersh, his old F.F.H.S. schoolmate. Hersh had come into the record store to collect an extremely rare African war chant record he had ordered some months before.

"For Christ's sake," Duddy shouted. "Hersh, of all people."

Hersh wore his hair long. He had grown a beard.

"Hey," Duddy said, punching him lightly on the shoulder, "where's your violin and the cup, eh?"

But Hersh made a sour face.

"I was only kidding," Duddy said.

Hersh, who had campaigned against the 7¢ chocolate bar and come second in the province and won a scholarship to McGill, had quit the university. Duddy was astonished. "Jeez," he said.

Hersh was no longer short, he'd lost his squint, but he was still somewhat pimply. He had grown up to be a big, chunky man with a long severe head and enormous black eyes. "There was no sense in staying on," he said. "I had no intention of becoming the apogee of the Jewish bourgeois dream. Namely a doctor or a lawyer."

"Aha," Duddy said.

"I think I've succeeded in purging myself of the ghetto mentality."

Duddy took Hersh to his apartment for a drink.

"A writer," Duddy said. "Can you beat that? How are you doing?"

"Writing isn't a career. It's a vocation. I'm not in it for the money."

"No offense. Publish anything?"

Hersh quickly told him what he thought about editors. He said his writing wasn't commercial. He pointed out that he didn't get the usual printed rejection slips, but personal notes from editors, always asking if they could see more of his work.

"Sure," Duddy said, "but have you published anything?"

"No."

"Well, some people hit it off right away. Others struggle for years. I'm sure you'll be famous. I'll bet you'll be another Ellery Queen."

"I don't write detective stories."

Hersh told him that he was going to Paris in the autumn.

"A St. Urbain Street boy. Isn't that something. Boy, I understand that the dames there . . ."

"That's a cliché. It isn't true."

Duddy grinned. "Hoohaw," he said, and he poured Hersh another drink. "It's so good to see you. We ought to have reunions like. When I think of all the swell characters I used to know at F.F.H.S. Hey, remember the time that lush-head MacPherson accused me of killing his wife?"

"He's in an asylum."

"Wha'?"

"He's in Verdun. I think I'd better be off. Thanks for the drink."

"Aw, come on. Sit down."

"Why pretend we're friends, Duddy? We hated each other at school."

Virgil arrived and Duddy sent him out for some smoked meat and more liquor. "Virgie's a poet. He writes blank verse. Like Patchen."

"Do you read Patchen?"

"Sure."

"He's a minor talent."

"No kidding?"

Yvette came and Hersh decided to stay. He had a date, though.

"Tell the broad to come here," Duddy said.

The girl came and brought two others with her. Mr. Friar arrived. One of Hersh's friends got on the phone and by ten-thirty there were twelve people in the apartment, including the fierce editor of *Attack!* Duddy sent Virgil out for more booze and began a high score competition on the pinball machine. When the party finally broke up at two A.M. or thereabouts he shouted, "Come again. Come any time."

They did, too, and they brought still more friends. Yvette was amused. "I never thought I'd see the day when you were played for a sucker. Maybe there's still hope for you."

"Hersh is going to be another Tolstoi. Boy, are you ever a killjoy."

"All right," Yvette said, "but if you think I'm going to clean up this mess every night . . ."

"Intellectual stimulation is good for you," Duddy said. "I read in *Fortune* where nowadays many executives go to the university in the summer to read up on philosophy and shit like that. It broadens you."

Virgil showed Yvette a book of poems by the editor of *Attack!* "He signed it for me," he said.

"He tried to sell me a copy too."

"Jeez, Yvette, a poet's gotta live too. Have a heart."

"Don't tell me you bought one off him?"

"What if I did?"

One or another of Hersh's crowd dropped in every night. Keiley was the noisiest and the most troublesome. He left burning cigarettes everywhere and when Yvette got angry with him he said, "A man shouldn't be dominated by his possessions." The hardest to get rid of, however, was the fierce editor of *Attack!* Blum never left until the last bottle was empty. Virgil adored him. After the others had gone he would sit on the floor and Blum would recite his latest poems to him in a booming voice. "I can't understand it," Blum said, "when you think how well known the other poets of my generation are . . . Spender and Dylan and George Barker . . . I can't understand it . . ."

When he had too much to drink and began to cry Blum reminded Duddy of Cuckoo Kaplan. Hersh didn't like Blum. "An unsigned copy of his poems," he said, "is a collector's item."

But Hersh was hard and cynical only when the others were around. Alone with Duddy he was a different sort of person. "Watch out for some of the others," he once warned Duddy. "They don't understand your kind of generosity. They poke fun at you behind your back."

Yvette agreed. "They're taking advantage of you," she said.

"Gwan. The trouble with you, Yvette, is you just can't understand people who are interested in the higher things."

"Like what?"

"Man does not live by bread alone," Duddy said.

It was a rare night when Duddy came home from the office and found nobody sitting in the apartment. He ran up enormous food and liquor bills but Hersh's crowd gave him more pleasure than he had ever had before. There were other guests too. Max and Lennie came occasionally and Bernie Altman was invited to dinner at least once a week. Duddy, taking him into his confidence one night, told him about Lac St. Pierre, and with Yvette's help the two boys constructed a relief model of the area. That took them weeks of painstaking work on the floor with balsam wood, flour, paints and airplane glue while Yvette fed them sandwiches and coffee and outside the snow fell. There were fierce arguments too over the site of the camp dining room and whether or not it was in good taste to have the boys' and girls' bunkhouses laid out to spell D.K. Bernie lent Duddy books by Mumford and spoke passionately to him about Le Corbusier, but though Duddy swore he would have no other architect design Lac St. Pierre, he still felt that some of Bernie's designs were a little too unusual.

"You're being too arty-farty. Buck Rogers won't be sending his kids to my camp but Mr. Cohen might, if you get what I mean?"

During the winter Duddy purchased two more small lots on the lake. Yvette enjoyed the evenings with Bernie enormously —it was good to have Duddy home and happy for a change instead of pursuing deals—but she was also frightened. More and more it began to look as if one day he would actually own all the land surrounding Lac St. Pierre and what then, she thought. How in the world would he ever raise the thousands and thousands of dollars needed to develop the area? Impossible, she thought, and the day he discovered it would be dreadful.

Virgil didn't agree. "Duddy can do anything," he said.

"You think so?"

"I love him."

Duddy saw other friends too. He was careful to keep up his contact with Hugh Thomas Calder and he had reason to believe he was making a hit there until the evening he brought up the scrap deal with Cohen. This seemed to displease Mr.

Calder even though Duddy, speaking on Cohen's behalf, offered him two-fifty more a ton than he had been getting up to now.

"I suppose," Mr. Calder had said, pushing his plate away, "that I should have expected something like this from you. I had hoped we were friends."

"Sure we are," Duddy had replied, flushing. "But friends help each other."

"Certainly."

"Aren't you getting more for the scrap than you got before? Mr. Cohen will do nicely too; that's true. This deal is to your mutual advantage."

"I expect," Mr. Calder had said, "that you're earning a good commission on this?"

Something had risen in Duddy's stomach. His eyes filled. "I look after myself," he had said. "Why not?"

"Why not, indeed?"

"Listen, Mr. Calder, the truth of the matter is it's not the money. The commission I get from Cohen is more trouble than it's worth. My plate is full, as they say. But I'm in your debt because of what you did for Lennie. Speaking frankly, I also happen to know that your reputation in the Jewish community is nothing to shout about. There are even some people who say you're a lousy anti-Semite. That's crazy, I know. But public opinion counts for plenty in this day and age, a man like you needs the goodwill of all sectors of the community, and that's why I put myself out to push through the Cohen deal. It's a good thing for word to get out that you're not against doing business with people of my faith."

The deal had gone through, but a month had passed before Duddy had seen Mr. Calder again and this time he was much cooler.

White men, Duddy thought. *Ver gerharget*. With them you just didn't make deals. You had to diddle. They were like those girls you had to discuss God or the Book-of-the-Month with so all the time they could pretend not to know you had a hand up their skirt, but just try to take it away. Just try, buster. He's offended, Duddy thought, but he made the deal all the same. Two-fifty more a ton, sure. I suppose he wanted me to play golf with him for eighteen years first or something. I haven't got that much time to waste, he thought.

Time became an obsession with him and he was soon trying to do two and even three things at once. He kept self-improvement books beside him in the car to glance at when he stopped for a red light. He did exercises while he listened to his records and in bed with Yvette he memorized stuff from *How to Increase Your Word Power* while she went on and on about a scary but horny dream she had had or some dumb story about her childhood. After his anger against Mr. Calder had cooled he bought a set of golf clubs and an instruction book by Ben Hogan and practiced whenever he could. One weekend when Yvette had gone to Ste. Agathe to stay with a old friend and Mr. Friar was out of town somewhere, he invited Bernie round to teach him how to play bridge. That, he felt, was important too.

"Listen," he said, "what kind of a friend are you? You must know lots of nice Jewish girls in Outremont. Why don't you ever fix me up?"

"What about Yvette?" Bernie asked, embarrassed.

"Yvette? I could never marry her. She's my Girl Friday."

"Does she know that?"

"It's one of the first things I ever told her."

So Bernie arranged a double date.

"Tell me something about this Marlene kid first," Duddy asked.

She was pretty, a sweet girl, and studying sociology at McGill. Bernie pleaded with Duddy to take it easy, though. She might neck a little, but no more.

"A bang I can get any time, Bernie. What's her father in?" Mr. Cooper owned Cooper Knitting. He had no sons. "That's for me," Duddy said.

But he had a lousy time, so did Marlene, and for Bernie it was an awful evening. Duddy behaved in a stiff, unnatural way, and he was embarrassingly aggressive about paying all the bills wherever they went. He insisted on discussing Shakespeare and Patchen with Marlene and whether or not Canada would be wise to pull out of the UN. "She's a very refined girl," Duddy whispered to Bernie at one point. "I think she goes for me too. But help me, for Christ's sake. I'll dance the next one with Charlotte and you build me up to her while I'm gone. O.K.?"

But while Duddy was gone Bernie had to pacify Marlene. "I'm sorry," he said. "I don't understand what's got into him tonight."

"What a drip! He told me Cooper Knitting turned out some of the finest sweaters on the market. He wanted me to tell my father that."

Marlene wouldn't go out with him again. There were other girls, but few of them would see him twice.

"Do you think I'm ugly?" Duddy asked Virgil once. "Be objective."

"There's so much character in your face."

"I think so too, you know. I just can't understand . . ."

He couldn't understand, but he was relieved too. I've got plenty of time to find myself a rich wife, he thought. Meanwhile, with Yvette, he could be himself. She came from a poor family too and she knew that a guy's underwear got dirty sometimes and didn't look disgusted if you scratched your balls absently while you read *Life* on the living room floor. It was true that she didn't have class like Marlene or some of those other Outremont broads but he didn't have to watch himself with her every minute, just in case he did something vulgar. With those rich girls probably a guy couldn't even read in the toilet. He didn't know, not for sure, but that's how it looked to him anyway. She'll have to have *lots* of money, he thought.

During that winter when Duddy prospered and made so many new friends he did not have much time for his family. He kept his eye on Lennie, however, and whenever he was in the vicinity of Eddy's he dropped in to see if his father was there.

"Look who's here," Eddy would say. "Montreal's own Cecil B. DeMille-nik."

Eddy's hair was beginning to fall out.

"Where's Debrofsky?"

"Retired to the pastures. Like Whirlaway."

Max was depressed. "It's not like it used to be," he said.

"Don't worry, Daddy. You'll be able to retire soon too. Lennie and me will look after you."

"I don't like the way you're living. I don't approve. I'm beginning to see I should have given you more of a religious upbringing."

Then one day Duddy ran into Uncle Benjy on the street. "Jeez," he said, "I hardly recognized you. Have you ever lost weight."

"An operation. Luckily it was only an ulcer. Well, Duddel, how are you?"

"Can't complain."

"And your grandfather?"

"I haven't seen him in weeks. But I'm going to visit him tomorrow afternoon, that's definite."

But first Duddy phoned Lennie. "Listen," he said, "what's with Uncle Benjy? He looks terrible."

"Auntie Ida left him for good."

"Wha'?"

"She wants a divorce. There's another man. Somebody she met in Miami."

What a family, Duddy thought, what a bunch we are.

"I guess it should have been expected," Lennie said. "You know."

"Is that how come he's so skinny all of a sudden?"

Lennie hesitated.

"Tell me," Duddy shouted.

"Daddy's here," Lennie whispered. "I can't talk."

Duddy found his grandfather seated next to the Quebec heater in the shoe repair shop. "I won't beat around the bush," Duddy said.

"Good."

"Maybe it's not in my place, *Zeyda*, but don't you think whatever it is you have against Uncle Benjy it's time to forgive and forget?"

"How can I go and see him now?"

"But you used to be so close. Can't you let bygones be bygones?"

"Your Uncle Benjy is no idiot and he knows me very well. If I went to see him all of a sudden he'd understand right away why." Simcha put the kettle on top of the Quebec heater and brought the bottle out. "All I'd have to do is ring his bell and he'd know it was no ulcer."

"Does Auntie Ida know?"

"She's in New York."

"With the other man?"

Simcha nodded. "Somebody should tell her. She has a right to know."

"Yeah."

"Benjy can't even get into the States any more. They say he's a communist."

"Guess who goes? Shit."

Simcha served him tea and brandy. "You have to be very, very careful because if she does come back with you he mustn't suspect why. Your Uncle Benjy is a proud man."

"There's no love lost between us. You know that, I hope."

"You don't understand each other."

"I worked for him once," Duddy said.

"We're a small family, Duddele."

"I didn't say I wasn't going, did I? It's just that he'd do anything for Lennie and he's always made fun of me and my ambitions. I'm living with a *shiksa*," Duddy said.

"I know."

Duddy rose. "There are lots of scientists working on it," he said. "Maybe they'll find a cure for it before . . ."

"Maybe."

Outside, the spring thaw had begun. Driving past the mountain, Duddy saw clumps of dirty yellow grass thrusting through the snow. There were no more skiers and the streets were black with slush. Stopping for a red light, Duddy was taken aback to see Linda Rubin seated with Jerry Dingleman in the back of his Cadillac. Duddy averted his eyes, hoping Linda wouldn't see him. He felt like sleeping, that's what, and for the first time in weeks he hoped there would be nobody in the apartment when he got there.

"Hullo?"

No answer. But Duddy had no sooner stripped down to his shorts than the doorbell rang.

"It's Yvette. Let me in, Duddy."

He opened the door. "Listen," he said, "I'm getting into the bath. Mix a couple of drinks and come in."

Yvette brought one of the kitchen chairs with her. "Here," she said, "take a long sip and prepare yourself for a shock. Friar's run off."

"Are you sure he's not off on a drunk somewhere?"

"He's gone for good this time. He took the cameras with him."

"Jeez. I thought he was so happy working for me."

Yvette laughed.

"A big joke. We've got the Hershorn wedding coming up in two weeks."

"We'll have to hire Reyburn full time, that's all."

Reyburn had worked on the last two films. Duddy didn't like him. "Let's try to find somebody else," he said.

"There isn't enough time."

"Did you say he took the cameras?"

"The insurance will cover that."

"What a bastard. He didn't even say good-by to me."

"He left because he was in love with me."

"Look," Duddy said, "it floats."

"He asked me to marry him."

"Are you kidding? He was my friend. I liked him."

"What's that got to do with it?"

"Aw, you're crazy. He wasn't in love with you."

Yvette threw her drink in Duddy's face.

"What in the hell's going on here?" he asked. But Yvette

rushed out of the bathroom and by the time Duddy had wrapped a towel around himself he heard the outside door of the apartment slam. Virgil had arrived, he was typing at the table by the window. "When are you going to find yourself a room?" Duddy shouted.

Virgil flushed.

"Oh, what's the use? Were you writing a poem? I mean I hope I'm not disturbing you or something."

"I was writing a letter to my father. You know what I said, Mr. Kravitz?"

"No, I don't know what you said, Mr. Kravitz, and I don't give a shit either."

"I wrote him that one day you'd be as big a hero to epileptics as Branch Rickey is to the Negroes."

"Come again, please?"

"Look at it this way, Mr. Kravitz. Before Branch Rickey hired Jackie Robinson—"

"Come here, Virgie. We're going to play high score. For twenty dollars but."

"Gee whiz, Mr. Kravitz, I couldn't take any more of your money. I'd feel—"

"For Christ's sake!"

"You're upset. Is it something Yvette said?"

"Why don't you just kiss my ass and die!"

Duddy gulped down his drink, secured the towel round his waist, and ran down to Yvette's apartment. She was lying on the bed with a book.

"Are we not having dinner tonight?" he asked.

No answer.

"We're not speaking, I see."

Yvette turned her back to him and Duddy stuck out his tongue and made an obscene gesture. Turning around, she almost caught him. Duddy lifted his hand quickly to his mouth and coughed twice delicately.

"Did it ever occur to you," Yvette asked, "that you're still under age and all the deeds are made out in my name?"

"What is this? Traitor's night on Tupper Street? I'm hungry. Make dinner."

"Go to hell."

"Now, is that a way to talk?"

"Are *you* going to teach *me* manners?"

"Listen, I just got an idea. Why don't you move upstairs and Virgil move down here? Living this way is crazy."

"Are you trying to cut expenses?"

"Are you ever in a mood. Boy! Did Friar write you little poemsy-woemsies?"

"As a matter of fact, yes."

"You're a real poet's delight, aren't you?"

"You don't know how to treat a woman. That's your trouble."

"Aw, let's eat, eh? I'm starved."

"He was in love with me, you know. It was nice."

"I'm tickled for you."

"Wouldn't you ever be surprised if I did get married one of these days?"

"Guys stop you on the street to propose left, right, and center. Oh Christ, I almost forgot. Get me a sleeper on the train to New York tomorrow night."

"Why are you going to New York?"

Duddy told her about Uncle Benjy.

"Does it always have to be you?" she asked.

"That's show biz, I guess." Duddy stopped, his face went white. "He's going to die, Yvette. Isn't that terrible?"

2

His memories of Auntie Ida were jumbled. He recalled his lips touching one of the curly red locks when she held him tight for one of so many good-bys. Her ear had seemed enormous, with waxy hairs inside. But she had the whitest, most delicate skin, and the only time she had taken him down the street for an ice cream, men had stopped to smile. He remembered the dizzying smell of violets that lingered in his grandfather's house after she'd gone. Taken to his uncle's house once, he had stumbled on her in the soft pink bedroom. Ida had just emerged from her bath and she sat in a powder blue nothing before a mirror at a little table crammed with jars. The mirror had an elaborate white frame with armed cupids carved into each corner. The cupids, cheeks puffed, blew at Aunt Ida's reflection. Humming a tune, Aunt Ida picked up a tiny bottle, spilt something on the palm of her hand, and rubbed it into her calves and wrists and neck. There were two packed suitcases on her bed and a trunk on the floor. The sticker on the trunk read NOT WANTED ON VOYAGE.

That, Duddy figured, must have been twelve years ago, and he had not seen her since. There had been rumors and reports, however. "She's here again," Max would say, sitting stiffly in his best dark suit. "I just come from there." And turning to Lennie, he'd add, "Is-payed again, the two of them."

But there were always gifts delivered via Max. Crazy ones, too. A seashell, perhaps, or an elaborately tooled leather book cover. For his bar-mitzvah she had sent Duddy a small hand-woven carpet from Algiers. Rolling his eyes, he had said, "Come with me to the Casbah, Pepele."

Duddy couldn't remember what had happened to the carpet but he had made good use of another one of her gifts. This one had actually been sent to Lennie for his twenty-first birth-day. It was an enormous scroll with lots of Chinese writing running down it and a faded drawing of a man and a house and a lake and some trees.

"You can hardly make it out any more," Max had said. "She probably got it reduced."

A certificate signed by somebody from the Louvre had come with the scroll. Lennie and Duddy, somewhat baffled, had taken the scroll to How Lee, the laundry man. "It's an old 'prayer," he told them. "It is a blessing on your house and everyone who visits there."

Soon after he had moved into his own apartment Duddy had given Lennie twenty-five dollars for the scroll and had it cut up into place mats with bamboo frames.

She won't even recognize me after all these years, Duddy thought. This is crazy.

Her hotel was a small junky-looking place not so far from where Dingleman had taken him to that party on his last trip to New York. Duddy was surprised, he had thought Uncle Benjy gave her a whopping allowance. A slender young man opened the door. He wore a T shirt and blue jeans that seemed too small for him.

"I beg your pardon," Duddy said. "I'm looking for a Mrs. Ida Kravitz."

The man turned to a woman seated on a large sofa. "There you are," he said. "I told you they'd send a boy over before three."

Duddy looked at the woman and groped anxiously for a cigarette. There must be some mistake, he thought. He looked at the room number again.

"Ida thought you'd never get here," the young man said.

The heavily made-up woman on the sofa was small and round and fat. She wore what he guessed from his experience of MGM musicals was a Mexican costume. A white embroi-dered blouse and a wide skirt of many colors. Beads dripped endlessly from her neck and when she rose with a small apprehensive smile there was a clack of bracelets. Her toenails were painted silver and the ring on her proffered hand swelled like a green sore. Her hair had been dyed black. Her eyebrows had been plucked and heightened, the eyes were smaller than he had remembered them, but he was sure now that it was she. There was the thick smell of roses and the luggage on the bed. A crust of torn labels obliterated the original NOT WANTED ON VOYAGE, but it was the same trunk.

"Auntie Ida?"

She held a hand to her throat.

"I'm Duddy. Your nephew like."

The young man threw his hands up in the air. *"Ça, alors,"* he said.

"Uncle Benjy has cancer of the stomach. He's going to die."

* * *

There was a lot to do. Ship reservations to Cannes had to be canceled and sleepers reserved to Montreal. There were disputes over luggage and many anguished telephone calls and puzzling telegrams, deliveries from the cleaners were late, pills and creams not available in Montreal had to be procured quickly and in large quantities, and only an hour before train time Aunt Ida collapsed on the sofa and said she couldn't go.

"Isn't it just like Benjy," she said, "to get cancer just after I've finally made the break. Don't look so shocked. Psychology has proven that people can bring such diseases on themselves."

"You mean he wants a cancer? That's crazy but."

"Benjy has suffered from an overpowering death wish all his life. He wants his death to be my fault though. That's part of it."

"Oh. Oh, I see."

"But I'm no longer the guilt-ridden girl he used to know. If I go to him now I don't want there to be any hypocrisy about it. I want to be clear in my mind about motives."

"He's your husband and he's dying. So?"

"I try to look at all my relationships honestly. I'm not going to him because I'm afraid he'd cut me off without a penny. He's too subtle a sadist for that. He'd want me to suffer."

"You mean if he left you his money it would only be to make it harder for you?"

"That's right."

"Jeez."

"Your Uncle Benjy and I . . . Well, we never had a satisfactory horizontal relationship. I guess you know that?"

212

"Come again, please?"

"Our sex life was never satisfactory to either partner."

"Listen, we don't want to miss the train, do we?"

"Did you think he was impotent?"

"Well, I heard stories. You know how it is?"

"He was as capable as the next man. I can't have children."

"Wha'?"

"I used to think there was something noble about Benjy. That he told his father he was impotent because he loved and wanted to protect me."

"You mean Uncle Benjy can have babies?"

"But his relationship with his father was never what it appeared to be. The father figure has dominated Benjy since he was a child. He was always afraid that if he did something wrong the old man's love would be withdrawn and he grew to hate him for it. So he hurt him the worst way he could. He told him he was impotent."

"Maybe I'm stupid, but—"

"At the same time," Aunt Ida continued, "he was protecting himself. As long as he stayed with me there would be no children. Benjy never wanted a child. He wanted to be the child. (He always slept in the fetal position, you know.) He was scared stiff that if he had a child your grandfather's love would be projected onto it and he would be forced to cope for himself. Benjy has a castration complex."

"Listen, he's got cancer. I don't know what complications there are, but—Please let's go. Auntie Ida?"

"I bet you think he's a socialist?"

"Who cares?"

"That's his technique of winning attention. He doesn't believe in it for a minute, but he's always wanted to shine and that's his way—If only he'd go to an analyst. I'd be so pleased if he'd learn to live with himself."

"He's dying," Duddy said, "so what's the point?"

"Are you sure? He could have all the symptoms of cancer and not have it, you know. It could be psychosomatic. There are lots of case histories . . ."

"Do you really think so? I mean there's a chance he hasn't got it?"

"It wouldn't surprise me."

Pretending to be fascinated by what she had to say and all the while coaxing her with drinks, Duddy somehow managed to get her downstairs and into a taxi and onto the train.

"The human personality is like an iceberg," Aunt Ida said. "Nine tenths of it remains submerged."

Ver gerharget, Duddy thought, slumping beside her on the train at last, and ordering more drinks.

"You think he's been wonderful, don't you, when all these years have really been a torture to me. Doctor after doctor after doctor he sent me to, and afterwards he'd always say it's all right, dear, never mind, it's not your fault. Why wouldn't he leave me if he wanted a child so badly? He hasn't got a mistress either. He never had one. He couldn't do that to me, he said, and then he'd forgive me all my little affairs. I understand, he'd say, it's all right, darling, and he'd send me to still another doctor . . . *He was trying to murder me with guilt.* Your Uncle Benjy is the next thing to a psychopath."

Duddy patted her hand. "Aw, you're only saying that," he said. "Deep down you love him. In your heart of hearts I'm sure—"

"We could have adopted a child and been happy together. But no, he wouldn't have it. He knew of another doctor." She began to weep. "He won't be happy until I'm a raving lunatic and he'll make me one yet."

"Look," Duddy said, "we're passing the Hudson River!"

"The few times I came home and tried to make a fresh start he wouldn't let me do a thing around the house. At first," she said, blowing her nose, "when we were still happy together, I thought it was because he was so kind. He used to kiss my hands and tell me how pretty and white they were and how he didn't want them soiled."

"No kidding," Duddy said, grinning. "Uncle Benjy said that?"

"While all the time he was already plotting my mental destruction."

"Oh. Oh, I see."

"He wouldn't let me cook or wash the floors or do the laundry because he wanted me to feel inadequate. He succeeded too."

"Hey," Duddy asked, "did you see *Gaslight?*"

"The more he martyred himself the happier he was."

"Joseph Cotten was in it. I forget who played the wife."

"What?"

"Skip it. Never mind."

Nothing surprised him, so that when after a few more drinks the conversation turned dirty he was not shocked. Aunt Ida confessed that if their horizontal relationship had been a failure then she was not blameless. There had been her own problem of penis envy, for instance, and this she illustrated

214

with some smutty stories about her childhood. Uncle Benjy, he said, was an oral fetishist, and when she explained that for him he blushed and quickly ordered another drink. Then she turned her attentions on Duddy and, hoping to distract her, he talked bout Yvette.

"The Oedipus," Aunt Ida said.

"Wha'?"

"Your mother was taken from you when you were young and all your life you will be searching for a woman to replace her. All boys want to have sexual relations with their mothers," she said.

"Hey," Duddy said, "enough's enough."

"Don't tell me you're a prude."

"My mother's been dead for years. I don't want her talked bout like that."

"You see. I hit a vulnerable spot. That's why you lost your temper."

"Oh for Christ's sake!"

Eventually she fell asleep and began to snore. Tears had wrecked her makeup. Duddy lifted her glass gently out of her hand and stared at her and thought, what can Uncle Benjy see in her? But the more he reflected on it the smaller was his comprehension. Imagine, he thought, she's the one who can't have kids and now he's dying.

Breakfast together was trying. Her hands shook, she looked very old—silly, even, with all the fresh makeup—and Duddy understood that she was afraid. "Listen," he said, "there's one thing. Uncle Benjy doesn't know he's got cancer. He's got to think you came back because you wanted to."

"Come with me to the house."

"Are you crazy? He doesn't even know I went to New York to get you."

"I can't go. He knows about Larry and he'll make fun of me. An old woman with a gigolo."

"You're not old. Why, one man on the train asked me if you were my sister."

"I'm afraid of him. I'm afraid of how he'll look at me. You have no idea how pretty I used to be."

"He's dying, Auntie Ida. Please . . ."

Uncle Benjy summoned Duddy to his house three days later. He lived on Mount Royal Boulevard, above Park Avenue and overlooking the mountain. The house, built according to Uncle Benjy's specifications, represented his idea of how an English gentleman lived. The dominant room, *his* room, was the library and this was severely furnished. There was also an enormous glassed-in sunporch looking out on the garden and the central feature of the living room was a fireplace of immense proportions. His basement was "unfinished," and here he kept his stores of hard liquor and wines. There were four bedrooms and a nursery. On the living room walls Uncle Benjy had hung prints and engravings and maps of nineteenth-century England. His collected edition of Dickens he had had bound in morocco leather and kept on a special shelf handy to his bed.

Uncle Benjy wore his ornate silk dressing gown and smoked a cigar. "Sit down and don't stare, please. I know I'm getting thinner. I suppose you expect me to thank you for bringing her back?"

"Will you leave me alone, please?"

"I know what I've got so we won't pretend. I knew before she came back. The day they let me out of the hospital I knew."

"I'm sorry, Uncle Benjy. But—well, where there's life there's—"

"Oh, shettup! Did she fill your head with foolish talk on the train?"

Duddy shrugged.

"Don't let me ever catch you making fun of her. I'm warning you. Now there are some favors I have to ask. Why are you smiling?"

"Don't you find it funny?"

"I have lots of money."

"I know," Duddy said.

"If you'll give up those vulgar movies you're making and take over the factory you can have fifty per cent. The rest is hers."

"I've got other ambitions."

"You can make more running my factory and you like money so much."

"Why can't Manny run it for her?"

"Manny's a fool."

"You mean I'm not a fool? Thank you, Uncle Benjy. Thank a lot. I thought you were the only one in the world with brains."

"Why do you hate me so much?"

"I worked for you once. Remember?"

"How long will you hold a grudge, Duddel?" he asked smiling.

"You think it's funny. Everything about me's funny. I'm regular laughingstock. You know as a kid I always like
216

Auntie Ida. But I remember when you used to come to the house you always brought a surprise for Lennie. I could have been born dead as much as you cared."

"Let's not pretend. Everybody has his favorites. There was always the *zeyda* to bring you surprises. He'd never hear a bad word said against you."

"Why," Duddy asked, "did you try?"

"You've developed quite a *chuzpah* since I last saw you. You have money in the bank, I suppose."

"Why did you send for me?"

"A man should arrange his affairs."

"Well, if you can't trust Manny to run the factory you'd better sell out. I'm not interested."

"What is it about us, Duddel, that we can't sit together for five minutes without a quarrel? I really brought you here to say thanks. I'm grateful for what you've done. Aw, what's the use? We bring out the worst in each other."

"We don't pretend but."

"That's true. I wonder what will become of you, Duddel. Well . . ."

"I'll never be a doctor, that's for sure."

"Now why did you say that?"

"Because Lennie never wanted to be a doctor either. You forced him."

"I did my best for that boy."

"You sure did, Uncle Benjy."

"If I'd left it to your father to bring him up he'd be driving a taxi today."

"I don't like the way you talk about my father. I never have."

"I'll be generous. Max is not very bright. I can't change that with my talk one way or another."

"You're very bright and nobody likes you. I'm sorry, Uncle Benjy. I say things I don't mean. It's just that you make me so sore sometimes . . ."

"We eat each other up, Duddel. That's life. Take Ida. I know what you think of her. I know what everyone thinks . . But she wasn't always such a foolish woman. She was once so lovely that—I'm not apologizing for her to you. You understand that? It's just—Well, I won't be sorry to die. I'm leaving lots of money. There's some for you too."

"Jeez."

"I thought we didn't pretend?"

"Why didn't you ever have time for me?"

217

"Because you're a *pusherke*. A little Jew-boy on the make. Guys like you make me sick and ashamed."

"You lousy, intelligent people! You lying sons of bitches with your books and your socialism and your sneers. You give me one long pain in the ass. You think I never read a book? I've read books. I've got friends now who read them by the ton. A big deal. What's so special in them? They all make fun of guys like me. *Pusherkes*. What a bunch you are! What a pack of crap artists! Writing and reading books that make fun of people like me. Guys who want to get somewhere. If you're so concerned how come in real life you never have time for me? It's easy for you to sit here and ridicule and make superior little jokes because you know more than me, but what about a helping hand? When did you ever put yourself out one inch for me? Never. It's the same with all you intelligent people. Except Hersh maybe. He's different. You never take your hand out of your pockets to a guy like me except when it's got a knife in it. You think I should be running after something else besides money? Good. Tell me what. Tell me, you bastard. I want some land, Uncle Benjy. I'm going to own my own place one day. King of the castle, that's me. And there won't be any superior *drecks* there to laugh at me or run me off. That's just about the size of it."

"You're such a nervy kid. My God, Duddel, you're even touchier than Lennie and I never realized it. Take care. Take my advice and take care."

"I don't want your advice."

"You don't want anything from me. Come to think of it, you're the only one in the family who never came here to ask for something. My God, it never occurred to me before. You're the only one. Duddel, I've been unfair to you."

"I can never tell if you're joking. There's such a tricky business in your voice, if you know what I mean?"

"I'm not joking. Lennie, your father, all of Ida's family, nobody has ever come to visit me without the hand outstretched. Except you. Now isn't that something?"

"There were lots of times I needed help."

Uncle Benjy waited.

"No sir. I wouldn't come to you."

"You're hurting me. You know that?"

"I'm sorry."

There was a knock at the door. "That's for me. It's the doctor."

Duddy rose.

"Would you come again?" Uncle Benjy asked.

Duddy rubbed the back of his head.

"Sometimes. When you're free."

"Sure."

But Uncle Benjy knew he wouldn't come. "Was I that bad to you when you worked for me?" he asked.

"You were my uncle," Duddy shouted, "and I thought it was the right thing to tell you the *goy* was stealing from you. I'm no squealer. I wanted you to like me. You treated me like dirt."

The doctor knocked again.

"You always looked for the bad side with me," Duddy said.

"I wish I'd made more time for you. God help me but I wish I'd seen what your *zeyda* saw."

The door opened. "May I come in, please?" the doctor said.

Without thinking, Duddy seized the doctor. "Don't let him die," he shouted. "He's my uncle." And then, embarrassed, he fled the house.

"I'm sorry," the doctor said, "I didn't realize I was interrupting."

Uncle Benjy went to the window and watched Duddy leap into his car and drive off. Run, run, always running, he thought, he can't even walk to his car. "What kind of pills did you bring me today?"

"You mustn't be so cynical, Benjy."

"I can't stand pain, Harry. As soon as it starts for real I want the morphine. Lot's of it."

He won't come again, Uncle Benjy thought. I don't deserve it either.

"Benjy, please. What did the boy say to you? You're so excited."

"We're a very emotional family. Come back later, please."

"Is there anything I can do?"

"Yes. Go away, please," Uncle Benjy said, turning his face away quickly.

3

Yvette brought him the news.

"Virgil's been in a accident. The truck went into a tree outside St. Jerome. They had to use blow torches to get him out."

219

Just when everything seemed to be going right, Duddy thought. Son of a bitch.

With the coming of summer there was the promise of two wedding movies and the camp featurette to be made for Grossman. The distribution side of Dudley Kane Enterprises had begun to show a nice profit too. Duddy had just been considering making a bid for more land at Lac St. Pierre when Yvette came into his office.

"Where is he?"

"At the Neuro. They brought him in at one last night."

It had taken them nearly ninety minutes to free Virgil from the cab of the Chevvie. Luckily he had been unconscious most of the time. But his injuries had been so severe, he had lost so much blood, that the ambulance driver had taken his time driving back to Montreal. "This guy's had it anyway," he said.

Five ribs were broken, his skull had been fractured in two places, and his spine had been severed near the base, but Virgil survived the crucial first night. Duddy and Yvette found him in the public ward. He was only semiconscious. His head had been shaved and bandaged, both eyes were blackened, and he was held in a huge plaster cast. Virgil's face was gray. A tube coming from an overturned bottle ran into an arm that was yellowish and twitching. He's going to die, Duddy thought, and, his stomach rising, he took out a handkerchief and wiped his mouth.

Virgil's eyelids flickered, he smiled faintly. He had recognized them. Yvette began to sob quietly.

"I think we'd better go," Duddy said, taking her arm.

"Don't touch me."

"You can stay longer tomorrow," the doctor said.

Who are you trying to kid, Duddy thought, and outside the ward he excused himself. He swayed dizzily over a washbowl for a while, but he wasn't sick. Duddy splashed cold water on his face, wiped his eyes, and went to look for the doctor and Yvette. The doctor was gone.

"He says Virgil will never walk again. His spine was smashed."

"Let's get out of here, please."

"It has something to do with torn nerves and the spinal fluids. I couldn't understand everything he said."

He led her outside. They sat in the car together and smoked

"I'll take care of him for the rest of his life," Duddy said "He'll never want for anything. I swear it."

"It'll be months and months before he gets out of bed

220

Then it's a wheelchair for the rest of his life. If he pulls through, that is."

"All right, Yvette. O.K. He's my friend too."

"They lose all sense of feel below the hips. They can't control their bowels and they don't know when they're urinating."

Duddy slumped forward with his forehead pressed against the wheel. He stared at the clutch.

"I want you to know all the details. You're not going to get off easy."

I wish I'd never met him, Duddy thought. I hope he dies and I never have to see him again. "You're taking a lot for granted," he said. "How do you know he had a fit? Accidents happen every day."

"Their legs get thinner and thinner. Like dry sticks. They would break them twenty times and they wouldn't know and it wouldn't heal. The circulation is practically dead."

"He was happy to get the job. I didn't force it on him."

"You knew it was dangerous. I warned you."

"Crossing the street is dangerous. You've got to live. A guy takes chances."

"There's no getting around it. You're to blame."

Only a week before, what with the summer season coming on, Duddy had considered hiring a man to work with Virgil. But after so many months the distribution side was just beginning to show a profit and Duddy had decided to hold back on the assistant until July first, when things would really be moving up north.

"I'll take care of him. Anything he wants."

But he knew what Yvette was thinking. Virgil's fits had begun again when Duddy had asked him to move downstairs into Yvette's apartment. He had understood, he said, that Duddy and Yvette wanted to be together, but he no longer ate with them every night he was in town and Duddy and Yvette sometimes went off to dinner or to the movies without him. He understood, he had said, but the fits began again.

"We were entitled to some privacy," Duddy said, "weren't we?"

"You always treated him like your personal message boy."

"Look, I happen to like Virgie."

"You like me and that doesn't stop you from behaving like . . well, like you owned me."

"Oh," he said, relieved, "we're going to start on that, are we?"

"No, Duddy. We're not."

But when they got back to the apartment she gathered

her bedclothes together. "I'd rather sleep downstairs," she said.

"Would you like to marry me?" Duddy asked.

Yvette smiled.

"We could get married," he said. "You know."

"Are you beginning to worry that the deeds are in my name?"

Duddy slapped her hard across the face. "Get out of here!" he shouted.

Yvette didn't come into the office the next morning or the morning after. She sat by Virgil's bedside. Duddy drove out to St. Jerome to take a look at the truck. It was a complete loss and—according to the lawyer—once the insurance company established that Virgil was an epileptic he wouldn't collect a cent. The projector, miraculously, was not badly damaged and the sound equipment could be easily repaired. Duddy had dug the playing schedule out of the battered glove compartment, ripped off the bloody cover, and shoved it into his pocket.

The lawyer told him. "He can sue you, you know. He's got a case."

"Aw."

"He can sue you for everything you've got."

"He's a friend."

"Get him to sign a release. I'll make up a letter for you."

"You must be crazy! I can hardly bring myself to go to the hospital."

"Don't look at me like that. You hired me to protect you and that's what I'm doing."

"I can't do it. Let him sue me, better."

Duddy began to interview replacements for Virgil but he didn't like anyone he saw and finally decided to rent a truck and do the job himself in the meantime. He was short of cash and in no mood to chase around after deals or sit in the office. Reyburn was hired full time to work on the Hershorn wedding. He was competent, and not really such a bad guy, but Duddy was forever finding fault with him. "That's not how Friar would have done it," he'd say. Without Yvette the office was a bore. Going out on the road, doing Virgil's job, was the only peace he knew those days, and heading back for Montreal at two in the morning he always drove as fast as he could, sure that Yvette would be home when he got there. He never left the apartment for even a package of cigarettes without leaving a *Back in 5 Min* note tacked on the door. Often he woke in the middle of the night, thinking he had heard her on the stairs, but he did not go down to her apartment, and he waited for more than two weeks before he phoned her. "As long as you're still drawing a salary," he said, "you might show up in the office once in a blue moon," and he hung up.

Yvette came upstairs. "You might go and see him," she said.

"I phone the hospital every morning. They tell me he's doing fine."

"He's not out of the woods yet. They're worried about the fracture. There's a sliver of bone that—"

"Awright."

"He asks about you every day. He thinks you're angry he smashed up the truck and that's why you won't come."

"Let's not waste time," Duddy said. "Here's a box of matches. You poke them under my fingernails and light them one at a time. Go ahead."

"I don't feel sorry for you."

Duddy poured himself a drink. "Did he have a—"

"He had a fit. Yes. It was brought on by fatigue."

Duddy began to play the pinball machine. He won three free games.

"I want you to go to the hospital tomorrow."

"When can I expect you back at the office?"

"I'm not coming back. You can stop my salary right away. I'll consider the last two weeks as my notice."

"What are you going to do?"

"As soon as possible I'm going to take Virgil to Ste. Agathe. I'll get a job there and I'll take care of him."

"You make me laugh. Have you any idea how much money it's going to take to look after him? The doctors' bills alone—"

"I'll manage."

"How? On a chambermaid's salary? *I'm* looking after Virgie. He's going to have the best care. Anything he wants."

"It's all settled. I'm sorry, Duddy."

"What about me? You said you loved me."

"Looking after Virgil will be a full-time job."

"Couldn't we look after him together?"

"I don't think so."

"You've got a martyr complex. Do you know that?"

"If you start shouting I'm going to leave."

"I'm a realist but. I know you inside out. You're gonna look after a cripple for the rest of your life? You're no nun, let's face it. You like it as much as I do."

"There are times when I wonder what I ever saw in you."

"You do, eh? Well, I'll tell you. You know what you saw in me? You saw a young guy who was going to make it. You saw a pretty good life ahead. Don't look at me like that either. Let's be frank. If not for me you might have been a lousy chambermaid for the rest of your life. Don't! You try to slap me and I'll kick your teeth in. 'Sometimes I wonder what I saw in you.' Don't make me laugh."

"We had some good times together, Duddy. Don't spoil it. I prefer to remember that."

"You want my handkerchief?"

"I'll speak to the notary. The deeds can be transferred to your father's name until you come of age."

"You think the business is going to fall apart without you?"

"I never said that."

"Well, there were lots of things you did pretty bad in that office. You couldn't add your way out of a paper bag and it takes a magician to read your handwriting. You know what? I'll tell you what. I'm going to get myself a real experienced secretary. *A girl who can spell.* Somebody real pretty. Boy, am I ever going to start having a good time."

"Are you finished?"

"Shettup!"

"I want you to go and see Virgil tomorrow. I won't be there. You won't have to see me."

"I wish Virgie was dead. Get out," he hollered. "Get out, please."

4

Duddy didn't go to see Virgil the next morning. He put an advertisement in the *Star* and began to interview girls to fill Yvette's job. He hired the cutest one, but she left after a week because she couldn't abide his language. He hired another one, a kid just out of school, began a desultory affair, and fired her when her period started eight days later. The third girl was highly experienced. She wanted desperately to put the office in order and went in for bullshit like interoffice memos (rockets, she called them) and asked Duddy so many questions he couldn't answer that he fired her too. Four days of the week he was on the road, showing movies. He was not getting much sleep again and Lennie got him more benzedrine pills. Every Friday he sent Virgil his check and every Monday morning it was back on his desk, the envelope unopened

We'll see, he thought. She's proud, but they can't hold out forever.

By the end of June the hotels had filled for the summer and Duddy's playing schedule required him to be on the road all week. He kept Virgil's sleeping bag in the back of the truck and slept in the fields and on the beaches to save money and hoping to catch pneumonia or be bitten by a snake. He'd go for days without shaving and was seldom seen in a clean shirt. If anyone remarked on his appearance he'd smirk and say something rude. He looked for fights everywhere and by mid-June he had already lost three clients. Even so his schedule was a grueling one, enough to keep two men busy, and there were times when he forgot to take a pill and fell asleep at the wheel. He drove recklessly too. The hell with it, he thought.

"You look like a bum," Max said to him one day at Eddy's.

"A big deal."

"Business isn't so hot? I knew you'd get your fingers burnt one day. I warned you."

Reyburn did a surprisingly good job on the Hershorn wedding. His film was straightforward, exactly the sort of thing Duddy had wanted and never had from Friar. But now he found it boring. He missed the crazy angle shots and montages and outlandish commentary.

"What's wrong?" Reyburn asked.

"Nothing."

"Mr. Hershorn is delighted."

"Mr. Hershorn doesn't know his ass from his elbow."

"Look here, Kravitz, I don't think you're happy with me. I've been offered something in Toronto, but—"

"Take it. Good-by."

"You're a funny kid. I don't understand you."

"I'm a comedian."

It was crazy, he had the Camp Forest Land film coming up and he'd never find another cameraman in time. Duddy phoned Grossman and offered to return his advance.

"We've got a contract," Grossman said. "I promised all the parents that the kids would be in the movies . . ."

"My heart bleeds, Grossman."

"A contract is a contract."

"Sue me," he said, hanging up.

He refused to show movies at Rubin's because he was afraid to see Linda again, but one night in Ste. Agathe he ran into Cuckoo.

"Hey," Cuckoo said, "remember the old days, before you were a movie mogul? No time for your old pals now, eh?"

"I'm working day and night."

"All work and no play. You know what they say? Hey, how would you like to see one of my new routines?"

Duddy went to Cuckoo's room. He couldn't get out of it.

"The band's playing Yiddish music, but eerie. There's a scream offstage. I come on in this leather jacket, see. I'm on a tricycle. I'm slouching. Did you see *The Wild Ones*?"

Duddy nodded.

"I'm on a tricycle, see. I've got a lollypop in my mouth and the number's called 'The Return of Moivyn Brandovitch or Mumbles the Macher.' Wait till you hear the lyrics . . . 'I'm a vild von from vay'—What'sa matter? You dead?"

"Cuckoo, you're never going to make it. You're not good enough."

Cuckoo staggered. He freed an imaginary dagger from his chest. *"Et tu, Brute."*

"You're going to be playing this lousy hotel for the rest of your life."

"Boy, have you ever changed. I've heard stories, but—"

"What kind of stories?"

"Stories."

Duddy grabbed him. "What kind of stories?"

"Yvette's back in town, living with some guy in a wheel chair. They say you took them both for every cent they had."

"You little bastard."

"Irwin's graduated, you know. He's got his law degree and he's been speaking to Yvette. It seems the guy never should have been allowed—"

Duddy shoved Cuckoo across the room. He collapsed on the floor there, shielding his face. "Don't hit me on the nose," he shrieked. "Whatever you do don't touch my nose! The operation cost me—"

Duddy fled. That makes the second time this week I hit a guy, he thought, and he drove to Montreal that night, even though he had to be back in the mountains to show his first movie at two the next afternoon. Duddy got out his typewriter and made a pot of coffee. He wrote a long intricate letter to Hersh, saying how much he loved and missed Yvette, how Virgil's accident was destroying him and the business was in ruins, and ending with how he saw no reason why he shouldn't commit suicide. It was dawn by the time he finished. Duddy put the letter into an envelope addressed to Yvette and wrote another letter to her, this one shorter.

DEAR MISS DURELLE,

IT APPEARS MY SECRETARY SENT A LETTER FOR YOU TO MR. HERSH. SINCE I WROTE YOU BOTH AT THE SAME TIME MR. HERSH'S LETTER MUST HAVE GONE INTO YOUR ENVELOPE BY MISTAKE. PLEASE DON'T OPEN IT. THE LETTER TO MR. HERSH IS PERSONAL & CONFIDENTIAL. I WOULD APPRECIATE IT IF YOU WOULD RETURN IT TO MY OFFICE AT YOUR CONVENIENCE. I HOPE YOU ARE WELL. I'M KEEPING VERY BUSY.

SINCERELY,
DUDDY

He mailed the long letter in the morning and held the shorter one back for a day, but both of them were returned to his office unopened.

At ten-thirty Monday morning the phone rang. It was Max. "Your Uncle Benjy died at three o'clock this morning," he said. "He passed away in his sleep. He didn't suffer."

Everyone from the factory came to the funeral and so did lots of buyers and competitors and old comrades. Duddy drove in the car that followed immediately behind the hearse with his grandfather, his father, his brother, and Auntie Ida.

"We're a small family," Lennie said.

"But we stick together," Max said. "We're loyal."

Duddy took his grandfather's hand and held it between his own.

"He couldn't have weighed more than a hundred pounds," Simcha said.

Ida looked out of the window. Duddy could make out the stays beneath her black silk dress and he imagined the raw marked flesh underneath.

"It's about time either you or Lennie got hitched," Max said. "Paw here would like to see some grandchildren . . ."

"Shettup," Duddy said.

"He waited by the window for you day after day," Ida said.

"I came whenever I could," Lennie said.

"She means Duddel," Simcha said.

"Gwan," Max said. "He never had time for Duddy. Lennie was his favorite."

"There's a letter he left for you," Ida said. "I've got it at home."

"Sure thing," Duddy said.

They drove in silence.

"He had his faults," Max said.

227

Nobody answered.

"A better brother I couldn't have had. I'm just saying he had his faults."

They finally turned onto the gravel road leading to the cemetery.

"I've got faults too," Max said. "I recognize it."

Simcha watched without tears when they lowered the coffin into the earth. But when Duddy freed his hand from his grandfather's he saw that the palm was cut and bleeding and he wrapped a handkerchief round it. *"Zeyda?"*

The old man was muttering something in Hebrew. A prayer.

"Where's my mother's stone?"

He pointed it out. Lennie was already standing there.

"He did so much for me, you know," Lennie said. "But I was always frightened of Uncle Benjy. There was something about him . . ."

"Easy. Take it easy, Lennie."

"Towards the end, you know, I had a feeling he was making fun of me."

"He loved you like a son. Everybody knows that. Let's go, eh?" But Duddy lingered to take a last look at his mother's stone. "We're supposed to come here once a year, aren't we? This year let's try. We could come together."

Duddy went home. They had heard about his uncle's death in the mountains so they didn't expect him with the movies, but his clients were annoyed because he didn't even bother to phone.

I'll get into bed, he thought, and never get out, not unless somebody comes for me. But nobody came and the heat made his head ache. He dreamt again about somebody else's bulldozers clearing his land. He saw himself horribly mutilated in a road accident. Yvette came to the hospital, but it was too late. The doctors led her away. "He kept calling for someone," they said. "A girl named Yvette. He's left everything he owned in her name." *Go ahead, cry your heart out, you lousy bitch.* In another dream he was an old man of forty, toothless, bald, a drunk, and he stopped at a big rich house to ask for a cup of coffee. Yvete answered the door wearing a mink coat. She recognized him and sank to her knees, but Duddy wouldn't stay; he freed himself from her embrace and limped away. "I've got the mark of Cain on me," he told her. He woke with a cry of anguish. His bed floated like a raft amid a wash of orange peels last week's newspapers, cigarette butts, sticky glasses, and watery ice cube trays. As the piercing sun sought him through a haze and a vulture circled predatorily, the sea

228

lifted him onto an island. "Where does the white man come from?" a girl asked. "I think he's dying," her brother observed. "Bring me to your head man," Duddy said. *"Capishe?"* Old, handsome, a scornful multimillionaire presiding over a banquet table, he heard whispering in the background.

"But why didn't he ever marry?"

"They say that when he was very young . . ."

Sometimes the phone rang and twice the door.

"Yvette?"

Anxiously she ripped open the telegram.

> THE WAR DEPARTMENT REGRETS TO INFORM YOU THAT DUDLEY KRAVITZ FELL WHILE LEADING HIS MEN OUT OF A TRAP IN KOREA. STOP. HE HAS BEEN AWARDED THE VICTORIA CROSS. STOP. HE ASKED THAT THE MEDAL BE SENT TO YOU. STOP.
> THE PRIME MINISTER

There were broads, an endless spill of beauty queens for him and Friar, the merry movie-makers, as they wandered from country to country, but at the Academy Award dinner there were those who saw through his mask of forced gaiety.

"He hates all women so, poor devil."

"But what an appetite! The comings and going from his house in one night. Jeez."

A crowd gathered round the grizzled old lush who had expired on the Bowery pavement. Flies filled his battered face.

"Any identification?"

"Nothing in his pockets, except this."

A faded photograph of Yvette.

"Let's get him down to the morgue quick. He's beginning to stink."

On Fifth Avenue the hearse passed a Rolls-Royce going in the opposite direction. Inside, Hugh Thomas Calder pressed a french-kiss on Yvette.

"Why are you crying, my sweet?"

"I don't know. I felt a chill just now."

Aunt Ida's face loomed so large he had to avoid the hairy ear again. "It's psychosomatic," she said. "He's no cripple. It's he only way he could get Yvette from you."

"Wha'?"

"He's got a whang that makes yours look like a mosquito bite. She's crazy about him."

A leering Mr. MacPherson waited round every corner.

"You'll go far, Kravitz. I told you you'd go far." He tried to run, he wept for trying so hard, but his legs wouldn't work.

At home Irwin waited with a briefcase on his lap. "We'll expect you in court first thing tomorrow morning."

"But—"

Even a white wig failed to disguise the judge's red fussy face. Mr. MacPherson's laughter squirted across the court room.

"Please!"

Duddy woke with a shriek. He staggered out of bed, tripping over a pitcher and spilling stale orange juice on the floor. He sat down at the kitchen table and filled a bowl with corn flakes. He poured the milk without looking and realized too late that it had curdled. Duddy knocked over the bowl with his fist and started for the bedroom again. He stepped into the spilt orange juice and for hours afterwards in bed he couldn't get his toes unstuck. He wept bitterly before he sank into a stupor again. I ought to get up, he thought, but he kept putting it off. I'd do it, he thought, if I could just get up and get out of here. But he'd have to brush his teeth, wash, wipe up the orange juice, clean out the fridge, do the dishes, shop —*shave, don't forget shave*—phone the office, and all for what? He fell asleep again and dreamt he saw Yvette in bed with another man. It could have been Bernie Altman, he wasn't sure, but she was certainly enjoying it. Duddy woke with a bone and pulled the sheet over his head. His toes were stuck together again. He sat up in bed, rummaged around for some empty cigarette boxes, and stuffed silver paper between his toes. I'd still get up, he thought, and do everything, but there's no toilet paper. Next time he woke the room was dark and outside it was raining hard. The thunder and lightning excited him, but after the storm the heat seemed more oppressive. I'll wait here, he thought, until somebody comes with good news. But nobody came and when he woke again it was dawn. There was a mosquito in the room. Sliding his arm stealthily under the sheet, he reached down for a newspaper, but orange juice had seeped through all the papers within reach. They were stuck to the floor. Duddy pulled his pillow over his head and began to concoct a delightful dream about Linda and himself going out horseback riding and getting caught in a storm. He got to the part where they take refuge in the barn quickly enough—and he was interrupted by the discovery that now his fingers were sticking together. Duddy tried wiping them on the sheets, he licked one finger dry with infinite care, but afterwards his fingers still tended to stick to gether. His feet had begun to ache too. The silver paper had formed into hard balls and was cutting into the tender flesh. His mouth tasted stickily of stale orange juice. I was just going to get out of bed too, he thought, but I'm not going to get up just because of the orange juice. If I get up it will be because I want to get up. He fell asleep again, but he couldn't wangle his way back into the barn with Linda. That dream was lost. He lived through what he could remember of *The Maltese Falcon*, taking the part of Bogart. But when he got to the point where the police come to wake him up he could no longer remember the name of the actor who played the nasty cop. Regis Toomey was one, but the other . . . Duddy could see his face so clearly and he could remember him from *She Wore a Yellow Ribbon* and umpteen other movies, *but he couldn't remember his name* and that prevented him from continuing with the Falcon story. Five times he got to the point where the cops come to wake him up, once he almost had the name, and three times he tried to substitute other actors for whosits, but it didn't work. He woke again around noon, freed the silver paper pellets from his aching toes, and dozed off and dreamt that he had brushed his teeth, washed, wiped up the orange juice, cleaned the fridge, done the dishes —and woke to discover that he was still in bed and had to go to the toilet something terrible. He slept only fitfully now— two, three minutes at a time—and woke again from a dream that he had, indeed, gone to the toilet. He had a headache. He leaped out of bed and ran to the toilet. Quickly he urinated, soaked a towel in warm water, grabbed it, and got back into bed. He washed his sticky hand and both feet and triumphantly pulled the sheet over his head again when there came a pounding at the door. Go away, he thought. F—— off. But the pounding persisted and he got out of bed to answer the door, stepping into the orange juice again. It was a registered letter for him. A large, serious-looking envelope.

"They're suing me," he said.

"I beg your pardon?"

"What time is it, kid?"

"One-thirty-two approximately."

"Tuesday?"

"Thursday, buster. Where have you been?"

The letter was from his Aunt Ida. Inside, in another large envelope, was the letter from his Uncle Benjy. Duddy laid it in the palm of his hand, trying it for weight. It's not a letter, he thought, it's a goddam book. He flung it onto the pinball machine and turned on the shower. He drank cup after cup of black coffee and finally he went to the office. "Any calls, doll?"

Creditors, canceled orders, indignant clients. Hugh Thomas Calder had called twice.

"Get him on the line for me, please."

Mr. Calder wanted to know why Duddy hadn't called in such a long time. He suggested that they have dinner together that night. "Can do," Duddy said. He went to Mr. Calder's house and they dined alone there.

"You're not in a very talkative mood tonight," Mr. Calder said.

"What do you want from me, Mr. Calder?"

"I enjoy your company."

"Come off it. I amuse you. That's what you mean."

"You're a friend of mine. I take a fatherly interest in you."

"Yeah," Duddy said, "then how come you never introduce me to any of your other friends?"

"They might not understand you."

"You mean I might try to make a deal with them like I did with you over the scrap and that would embarrass you. I'm a little Jewish *pusherke*. Right?"

Mr. Calder didn't answer.

"If I was a white man I wouldn't say that. You guys never say what's on your mind. It's not—well, polite. Right?"

"You're acting like a young man on the verge of a nervous breakdown."

"Bullshit."

"Is there anything I can do?"

"Would you excuse me if I went home? I don't feel well."

But Duddy couldn't sit at home. The apartment was too depressing and he did not feel up to reading Uncle Benjy's letter. He went to the office and looked at his bills. The sum they added up to was terrifying. Duddy unlocked the desk and took out the map of Lac St. Pierre. He found Yvette's first letter and the photographs of the lake. I'd like to see the day she ever got a job as a photographer, he thought. Boy. He sat there chewing on a pencil and trying to think of somebody he'd like to see. Bernie Altman was out of town, Hersh wasn't home. Duddy went to a bar around the corner. I wonder, he thought, if—objectively speaking—I could be blamed for the death of MacPherson's wife? I never even met her. He drove down to Waverly Street and parked outside Hersh's house. An hour, two hours, passed before he showed up.

"Hersh!"

"Hi, Duddy, how are you?"

Duddy began to cry.

"Hey, what's wrong?"

"Nothing. Get in, please."

They drove to the nearest bar.

"How's Yvette these days?" Hersh asked.

"Aw. We're through, you know. We've had it."

"That's too bad. I'm sorry to hear it."

"They're a dime a dozen. Don't you get involved. Take my advice."

"I'm sailing for Europe next Wednesday."

Duddy's eyes filled. He had to blow his nose. "I must be becoming an old lady," he said. "This afternoon I heard somebody say that the Dodgers' lead had been cut to half a game and I burst into tears. Hey, did you ever see *The Maltese Falcon?*"

"Yeah."

Duddy asked him if he could remember the name of the guy who had played the other cop. Regis Toomey was one.

"Ward Bond."

"Ward Bond! That's it. *Ward Bond.*"

"Are you going to cry again?"

"Naw. I'm awright. Honest. Listen, there's something I want to ask you. I—About MacPherson. It's true, I made the phone call. His wife died, you know."

"Look, we were kids then. How were you to know—"

"We used to phone them all the time, didn't we? All the guys did. *You never phoned.*"

"I was something of a sissy in those days."

"Next Wednesday. Jeez. Will you write me, Hersh?"

"Sure."

"Aw, you'll never write me."

"Sure I will. I promise."

"You're my only friend."

"You don't look so hot, Duddy. Maybe you ought to see a doctor."

"How was I to know that his wife would answer the phone?" he asked, his voice breaking.

"Let's go for a walk."

"You'll never write me," Duddy said. "You'll forget all about me."

"Come on, Duddy. Let's get out of here."

"If I had known that his wife was going to get out of bed to answer the phone," Duddy said, "I never would have—Let me send you money when you're in Paris. Let me help you."

"I'm your friend, Duddy. You don't have to give me money."

"I'm going to write you every week. Even if you don't answer my letters."

"You've got to calm down, Duddy. You've been working too hard."

He gave Hersh a lift home. "I'm going to come and see you there," Duddy said. "I can go to Paris too."

"Sure. Why not?"

"You'd be embarrassed to see me there. All your friends in Paris will be intelligent. Artists like."

"Duddy. Listen, Duddy—"

But Duddy stepped on the gas and drove off.

"Duddy!"

Hersh pursued him for thirty or forty feet before he gave up. Duddy skidded around the corner, turned into St. Urbain Street and parked the car. He rested with his forehead pressed against the steering wheel and stared at the clutch.

5

Lots of painful facts came to his attention the next morning at the office. He had ruined himself up north, nobody wanted him to show movies any more.

"You're not reliable."

"Sure you say you'll come. That's what you said last time."

His bills, long overlooked, had reached insupportable proportions. There were enough lawyers' letters around for him to paper the walls with. There was no money coming in either. He had no prospects.

"There's only one thing to do," his lawyer told him. "Declare bankruptcy."

"Wha'?"

"Have you any other assets?"

Duddy thought of the deeds Yvette held. "No," he said.

"You go bankrupt, that's all."

"Listen, I'm not a failure. I don't want people—"

"People! Failure! Everyone's gone bankrupt at least twice. Think of it like a Purple Heart, that's all. There's no disgrace."

"But—"

"Next year you go into business again. It's simple."

"After all that work."

But it was the only solution. So Duddy drove back to his office, gave the girl two weeks' notice, and cleared out his desk.

Clearing out required several trips. For now that he was broke he did not omit to take the typewriter, all the office supplies, including a dozen boxes of paper clips and the wastepaper basket, and, naturally, his map of Lac St. Pierre.

Twice during the week he picked up Uncle Benjy's letter, but he could not bring himself to read it. He began to sleep until noon and go from one downtown movie to another. At night he usually hung around Eddy's.

"Here it comes," Eddy would say. "St. Urbain Street's Nine-Day Wonder." But he let Duddy have anything he wanted on credit. "Until your ship comes in," he'd say.

"I think you've got the sleeping sickness," Max said. "Listen, why don't you go to New York for a week. A vacation. Poppa pays."

"Aw."

"Go see the Wonder again. Maybe he'll put something your way?"

"On Schnorrer's Day?" Duddy asked.

"A word from the wise. Before, a swelled head was bad enough, but now when you couldn't rub two cents together to save your life and you bum around like a haunted house—"

"Lay off, Max," Eddy said.

Whenever one of the men wanted to knock off for an hour Duddy took over the taxi. That kept him in spending money. That, too, was how he happened to run into Mr. Cohen one night.

"Duddy, it's you!"

"A big deal."

"What are you doing driving a taxi? Look at you."

"Where do you want to go, please?"

Mr. Cohen got in beside him in the front seat. "Look at you. Oi."

"Is there a law against driving a taxi?"

"But you, Duddy. You? No, it can't be."

"I went into bankruptcy."

"Gangster. What did you clear on it?"

"I'm broke. Honest."

Mr. Cohen clacked his tongue. "Come to the house," he said. "I want to speak to you."

"I'll take you there, but I'm not going in."

"You can't have a drink with me? The family's up north. I'm all alone."

Once settled in the furnished basement, Mr. Cohen removed his shirt, pulled off his shoes, and started all the fans going. He stood behind the bar, looking at Duddy and clacking his tongue. "Here," he said, handing him a drink. "Now tell me about it."

"There's nothing to tell."

"Are you going to start lying again? Don't you ever tell the truth?"

"I had some bad luck."

"Who hasn't had some bad luck? Tell me what happened."

"I'd rather not talk about it. O.K.?"

"You know what you look like in those old clothes? A communist. A potential menace."

"Thanks."

"I had such hopes for you, Duddy. I thought you'd go so far and look at you. A boy with your get-up-and-go."

"Money isn't everything, Mr. Cohen."

"A real communist. Oi-oi. Gimme your glass."

"I really should be going. I—"

"Gimme your glass I said. That's a good boy. Sure, money isn't everything. Who in the hell ever said it was? Duddy, I like you. Tell me what happened. Maybe I can help?"

"I don't think so."

"Any time you want to come and work for me you name the salary. How's that? A girl. Is that the trouble?"

"Jeez."

"Duddy, I've got a soft spot for you. You know the way I feel about you? If you told me right now that you wanted to shave and start out again in another business I'd finance you. That's the kind of confidence I have in you."

"My driver was in an accident."

"I heard."

"He's crippled for life. It's my fault."

"The hell it is!"

Duddy told him haltingly about Virgil.

"Duddy, it's not easy to earn a living. If you went out in the trade and asked about me there are lots of men who would tell you Cohen is a lousy son of a bitch. You think I've never had troubles? You think you run a scrap yard for twenty-five years next September without accidents or lawsuits or under the table pay-offs or lies? There's not one successful business man I know, Duddy, who hasn't got something locked in the closet. A fire, maybe. A quick bankruptcy, the swindling of a widow . . . funny business with a mortgage . . . a diddle with an insurance agent. It's either that or you go under, so decide right now. You're going to drive a taxi all your life or build a house like this and spend the winters in Miami.

"You know I once nearly went to jail, Duddy? I came this

close," he said, "but I had a partner and he wasn't as smart as me so he went to jail instead. He did two years for receiving stolen goods and all that time I took care of his wife. When he got out he yelled his head off at me. He picked up a knife to me, even. But I didn't feel bad because I know that if he'd been smarter than me I would have been the one to go to jail. Listen, Duddy, it's not all wine and honey in this world, but I've got a family and I take damned good care of them. My Bernie won't have to send his partner to jail. But he didn't land in this country with three words of English and fifty cents in his pocket, either, and there you are."

"But he's crippled for life, Mr. Cohen."

"It's not your fault. Goddam it, I never thought you were such a softie."

"It was dangerous to let him drive the truck."

"Duddy, in my yard once there was an accident with the derrick and a *goy* got killed. The derrick was on its last legs and I got it cheap. So? I was working night and day then like you. It was the best derrick I could afford. I'm no monster. I had bad dreams. I'll tell you this and I never said it not even to my wife before. I cried too. But you know what I thought to myself? Moishe—I thought to myself—your wife's got one in the oven. A boy maybe. When that boy grows up do you want him to have to stand under faulty derricks for a lousy thirty-five bucks a week? No. Then pull yourself together, Moishe, and stop being a woman. Make yourself hard."

Mr. Cohen told Duddy more stories that reflected badly on himself, he even exaggerated some, but Duddy didn't respond as he had hoped.

"Listen here, my young Mr. Kravitz, you want to be a saint? Go to Israel and plant oranges on a *kibbutz*. I'll give you the fare with pleasure. Only I know you and I know two weeks after you landed you'd be scheming to corner the schmaltz herring market or something. We're two of a kind, you know. Listen, listen here. My attitude even to my oldest and dearest customer is this," he said, making a throat-cutting gesture. "If I thought he'd be good for half a cent more a ton I'd squeeze it out of him. A plague on all the *goyim*, that's my motto. The more money I make the better care I take of my own, the more I'm able to contribute to our hospital, the building of Israel, and other worthy causes. So a *goy* is crippled and you think you're to blame. Given the chance he would have crippled you," he shouted, "or thrown you into a furnace like six million others. You think I didn't lose relatives? I lost relatives."

"Jeez," Duddy said. "Wait a minute. Virgie is no nazi."

"You're sure?"

"He's my friend."

"They're all nazis. You scrape down deep enough and you'll see. Up to here, Duddy," he said, repeating his throat-cutting gesture. "That's how I like to get them. Have another."

"Cheers."

"You want a helping hand? A loan until you get on your feet again?"

"No. But thanks just the same."

"Duddy," Mr. Cohen said sternly, "you won't find me plastered like this again in another five years. Take while I'm in an offering mood. I'm not the Red Cross that you can call at any emergency."

"But I'm not sure what I want to do any more."

"Well, whatever you want to do, don't stand under any faulty derricks for thirty-five bucks a week. That's how people get killed. Good night and good luck."

After Duddy had gone Mr. Cohen took his drink into the kitchen and got some more ice.

The *goy* had hollered, he had rolled his eyes, and it had taken him longer than an hour to die. The health inspector had cost him five hundred dollars, but the case had never come to court. Death by misadventure was how the coroner put it. And five weeks later the coroner had sent Mr. Cohen a Christmas card and, terrified, Mr. Cohen had phoned his lawyer.

"Don't lose sleep," the lawyer had said. "Send him a case of Scotch. The best there is."

Mr. Cohen still had the card. It was one of those religious ones, *Joyeux Noël* and a *Yoshka* on the cross. Some sense of humor they have, he thought.

It's a battlefield, he thought, it sure is. But you and I, Duddy, we're officers, and that makes it even harder. (Remember how Gregory Peck had to send his fliers out to die in *Twelve O'clock High?*) We're captains of our souls, so to speak, and they're the cabin boys. Cabin boys, poor kids, often get left standing on the burning deck, just like in that poem Bernie read me. It's a battlefield. I didn't make it (I wasn't asked). I've got to live, that's all.

Mr. Cohen poured himself another drink. It had cost him fifty thousand dollars to build the house, his wife's dream, and the only room he could tolerate was the kitchen. Mr. Cohen got up and looked in the fridge. With his wife up north for the summer he had a rest from that stinky new-style Chinese

238

food, all those nuts and pineapple and not a chunk of meat anywhere as big as your toenail. With his wife away he was even able to keep a smoked meat in the fridge. There was nobody to lecture him about calories and stomach linings and fatty tissue around the heart. He made himself an enormous sandwich, leaned back, and let out a resounding burp.

It's my house, he thought, and I can do what I want here.

Duddy started to take his father's taxi out on a full shift. He usually started at six and drove until four in the morning. Most days he slept until noon, went out for a bite, and came back to sit by the window in his apartment until it was time to work again. He still couldn't bring himself to read Uncle Benjy's letter and he avoided any place where he might run into old friends. The heat wave worsened and Duddy began to make do on one meal a day. He lost lots of weight. Nights when he couldn't sleep or woke from a dream of Virgil he played his pinball machine endlessly. He invented a league with eight teams and, playing for each one of them in turn, he kept track of the results and standings on a specially designed chart. He knew the machine extremely well, it would have been possible to cheat for his favorite team, but he was scrupulous about giving his best to each one. The machine had other uses too. If he wanted to go out for a drink, for instance, when he should have been trying to get some sleep, he would make an agreement with himself that if he hit five million on the machine—not an easy mark—he could go. Here he cheated sometimes. If he wanted to go out badly enough and the score on three balls was unpromising he'd tilt the machine accidentally, which entitled him to another game.

He played other games too. In one he was a blind man and had to find his way round the apartment with his eyes shut. He lost if he bumped into anything. There were penalties to be paid too, like sleeping without a pillow or cutting out smoked meat for two days at a time. The apartment was gradually filled with crossword puzzle magazines and he worked out a method for playing two-handed Scrabble. He could roll dice for hour after hour and kept elaborate graphs to illustrate his imaginary winnings set against time invested, physical depreciation, and some even more esoteric data. The bookcase was soon crammed with the cheaper kind of paperbacks and in each one he marked how many manpower hours it had taken him to read it. The results of his overall paperback chart were gratifying. His reading speed per manpower hour showed a consistent tendency to improve.

One night, bored with his other games, he got out the model of Lac St. Pierre and started a fire at the hotel. It was brought under control quickly, however, with a minimum loss of life, and he estimated the damage at approximately twenty thousand dollars. Luckily, he was covered with a good insurance policy.

Duddy discovered that he was broke four days before his rent came due. He didn't want to borrow from his father again, so he arranged to drive Miller's taxi during the day. Working day and night for seventy hours, catching a half hour's sleep here and there, he took in the necessary seventy-five dollars, staggered back into his apartment and collapsed on the bed. There was a letter for him from Ste. Agathe. It wasn't from her, though. It was from Virgil.

DEAR DUDDY,

I hope this letter finds you in the best of health. I know that you are still angry at me or you would have come to see me by now. I am also aware of the fact that you've had a quarrel with Yvette. She didn't tell me about what but it would be tragic if the two of you severed relations. She doesn't know that I'm writing you. I must make that clear. But you must come to see her. I've never seen somebody so depressed. Come out soon, Duddy, *please*.

Sincerely yours,
VIRGIL

P.S. Enclosed are two copies of my magazine. I'm looking forward to your frank opinion of same.
PPS. I miss you too.

Duddy picked up one of the magazines. It was mimeographed.

THE CRUSADER

The Only Magazine in the World Published by Epileptics for Epileptics

Vol. 1. No. 2   September

Famous Health Handicappers Through History No. 2

A BIOGRAPHY OF JULIUS CAESAR

Julius Caesar was born in 102 B.C. and died of twenty-three dagger thrusts on March 15, 44 B.C. But between those dates he won world-wide fame as a soldier, administrator, author, and emperor, in spite of his health handicap. He was the author of several Latin books, including *The Conquest of Gaul,* still a good seller in the English translation. He is also the hero of a famous play by Shakespeare, part fact and part fiction. This play was recently made into a movie with Marlon Brando heading the all-star cast.

Life was no breeze for the young Julius, but from the day of his birth until the day he met his untimely end he never once let his health handicap stand in his way. *Julius had been born an epileptic and he was not ashamed of it.* He had guts a-plenty.

Like Abe Lincoln, another great man, his beginnings were humble. There was no silver spoon in his mouth at birth. He came up the hard way. First as a soldier and then as a politician. He served in Spain, Germany, and other lands, making him very well traveled before the air age, broadening his mind, and therefore making him fitter to rule. But his fantastic success story, his amazing popularity with ordinary joes, naturally made smaller men jealous and when he returned triumphant from Gaul they began to plot against him. This plot, in fact, led to a civil war, and the death of Caesar's old comrade, Pompey. It also resulted in Caesar's being appointed Dictator for life of the Holy Roman Empire, quite a big honor. Unfortunately, only a month later—after one of the dirtiest double-crosses of all time—he was stabbed twenty-three times on the steps of the senate. One of the murderers was his best friend, Brutus, and that's how the expression *Et tu, Brute* [1] (meaning double-cross) has come into the English language.

Caesar, though always at odds with the senate, was not the Hitler type Shakespeare (also an anti-Semite) made him out to be. He was always good to his mother and a faithful husband. He was also very good to his troops and centuries ahead of his time he introduced something like our own GI Bill. His books, according to scholars, were models of their kind, and the word "honor" was often on his lips. Among other accomplishments he did lots for economic reconstruction and aggrarian reform in old Italy. It's a dirty lie to say he was a tyrant. We have every reason to be proud.

[1] You too, Brutus.

Next Issue: A Biography of Jos. V. Stalin

A SPECTER IS HAUNTING EUROPE

THE CRUSADER

Editor & Publisher   *Business Manager*
          Virgil Roseboro   Yvette Durelle

THE CRUSADER is a nonsectarian magazine with no political bias. Yearly Subscription: $2.00. No part of this periodical may be reproduced without consent of the publishers. All mms. should be addressed to 8 Rue St. Paul, Ste. Agathe des Monts, Que., Canada. A self-addressed envelope should be enclosed.

YE OLDE EDITOR'S CORNER
United We Stand
Divided We Fall

IT'S time to get in there and start pitching, comrades. We've got to organize. We've got to take a leaf from the book of the Negroes, Jews, and the homosexuals. Let's not be too proud to learn from other minority groups.

LET'S NOT BE SLOUCHES.

If a Jew gets kicked out of a hotel the B'nai B'rith hollers. If a Negro is refused a job the NAACP goes to court. In Scandinavia the homosexuals were brave enough to organize and now they have laws to protect them. I'm not saying that, like the Jews, we need our own homeland or, like the queers, we want our own night clubs. WE'RE BETTER MIXERS THAN ANY OF THEM. But look at what the Harlem Globe Trotters have done for their race. Everybody knows that Einstein was a Jew, F.D.R. a polio victim, and Marcel Proust a homosexual, but how many folks know that Mackenzie King, record-holding prime minister for the whole

Empire, was born with a Health Handicap?

(cont. p. 3)

OUR READERS WRITE
Sweet (and Sour) Notes

Sir:

Congratulations and good luck! Your first issue was great. Let's have more of those fighting editorials! Enclosed, please find two dollars for my subscription.

Sincerely,
Harvey S. Pignatano
Houston, Texas

Thanks, Harv. We'll try to keep up the good work—ED.

Sir:

Until you started your moronic magazine the best thing about sufferers from epilepsy is they didn't band together against the world. Your sectarian rag is just about the biggest step backwards we can take. Next thing you'll want to elect an epileptic pope, so people can say we have dual loyalties too. If you mail me another copy it goes right into the ash can, like the last one.

U.S. MARINE
CAPTAIN, Retd.

Check your history book, Captain. We've had a pope with a health handicap. Leo IX.

Sir:

Everyone in the asylum thinks your mag is the mostest.

ouple of suggestions, however. Iow about a special supplement for paraplegics? What about some pin-ups?

THE GUYS OF WARD SIX

Watch for news of our Miss Health Handicap competition —ED.

ir:

I have been going steady with . boy for six years. He is very ice. All my friends like him. love him and want to marry im. But last Saturday eve at he church dance he had a fit n the middle of the dance loor and I'd be less than honest f I didn't admit I was *very* mbarrassed. I had no idea before the dance that he had a ealth handicap. What should do? I'd still like to marry him, ut I'm very fond of dancing oo.

What about our kids, if we ave any?

VERY UPSET

urn to Verne Delaney's moving story on page 4—ED.

OOKS

LOOMY IS THE NIGHT by Derek Marler. Stubbs. $3.50.

ou said it, buster. The night read this novel was the gloomest I've spent in years.

Here we go again, boys. We're ack in Paris, on the left bank, ith those crazy mixed-up kids. Ias Marler's hero got problems? ure. His next check from home nay be overdue and meanwhile

the world's going to pot. He hates everybody and he's just too, too sensitive to live. But Marler can write. Some of his dialogue just leaps off the page.

A word of advice, Marler. How about giving us a novel about real people with real problems next time out. Hemingway was there before you, remember, and his hero had a bigger problem than mere *Weltschmertz*. Jake had a real health handicap.

When oh when will somebody give us a novel about epileptics? Not since *The Idiot* has anyone made a real stab at it and there's a subject big enough for any artist.

Rating: One Star.

EDITORIAL *(cont)*

They all use publicity. *We don't.* And why not? Because we're not organized yet. We don't meet and form pressure groups. If the communists can have an international SO CAN WE. The Senator from New York is a Jew and he speaks up for his people. According to Senator McCarthy there are plenty of commies and homos in the state department. There must be some epileptics too. WHY DON'T THEY SPEAK UP FOR US? Are they ashamed? The hell with them, then. We health handicappers want legislation to protect us.

PEN-PALS CORNER, PERSONALS, CLASSIFIED ADS Health Handicapper, 38, female, Witness of Jehovah, interests: musical appreciation, reading, theater, walks, swimming, would like to meet another H.H., male, early forties, over 5ft 5in and with similar interests. Box 2213

Rm to LET in quiet, socialist atmosphere, 18 Brewer St., Montreal. No color bar. Health Handicappers welcome. Box 5528

For Rubber products, free book on Family Planning, Surgical Belts, Etc., write Box 8211

WHEN IN BUFFALO GET YOUR EYES EXAMINED BY DR. ERNEST BELAIR, 22 Argos Blvd., Special discount for fellow Health Handicappers.

IN EVERLASTING MEMORY OF MRS. EDNA PLUNKETT

Break, break, break, at the foot of thy crags, oh sea,
But I would that my tongue could utter the thought that arise
IN YOUR FAMILY AND FRIENDS

DR. SABLE can cure you with herbs. Profit from the wisdom of the ages. Hundreds of testimonials. Write or visit 112 St Andre Blvd., Montreal, P.Q.

BEST WISHES FOR
YOUR
CONTINUED SUCCESS
Anonymous

CRUSADER readers in Toronto Let's meet. Refreshments. Ring MO 4-2122

POLIO VICTIMS HAVE THE MARCH OF DIMES (AND WE DON'T BEGRUDGE 'EM IT)
BUT WHAT IN THE HELL IS BEING DONE FOR US???????

A Short Story with a Moral

A CHANGE OF HEART by Verne Delaney

"It's terrible," Mr. Dermott exclaimed, "I just don't know what to do."

Big, kindly old Jim Brody stuffed his pipe slowly. "Nothing can be that bad," he laughed. "Come closer to the fire. Tell us about it."

There were three of them seated round the fire in the old homestead. Outside the moon smiled down on the river. Clouds sailed to and fro, blotting out the stars. The fish were jumping.

There was the visitor, Hugo Dermott, a fat fellow with beetle brows. He was 52. There was old Jim Brody, who everyone in town came to for advice. He was 60 maybe, but still straight as a ramrod. He looked so kind you'd think he couldn't harm a fly, but he had a list of war decorations as long as your arm. The third man, Rock Holmes, was Jim's son-in-law. He was tall, dark, and handsome.

"Anything I can do?" Rocky grinned.

"Thanks, Rocky, but I don't think so," Mr. Dermott answered, returning the young man's smile. What a fine lad, he thought.

"Darn it all," Jim said, "will you tell us what's ailing you?"

"It's about Lindy Lou."

Lindy Lou was Mr. Dermott's only daughter, his pride and joy. She was gorgeous with blonde hair and pear-shaped breasts and firm thighs.

"She wants to marry Bill Handy and nothing I can say will stop her."

"Ah, that would be Jake Handy's boy," Jim said. "They're good folks. Why are you agin the match?"

"Bill's a fine fellow," Rocky said, his teeth set grimly.

"Sure," Mr. Dermott snarled. "Oh, sure. But you know how fond I am of Lindy Lou?"

"Bet your life I do," Jim smiled.

"Well," Mr. Dermott said, gritting his teeth, "Bill Handy's an epileptic."

The silence that fell was so thick you could cut it with a knife, but Mr. Dermott didn't notice that Rocky turned pale as a sheet.

"I'm not having my girl marry one of those shakers," Mr. Dermott exclaimed. "I'd always hoped she'd hook a fine feller. Somebody like Rocky here."

Rocky rose to interrupt, but Jim stopped him. "Quiet, son. Easy does it." Turning to Mr. Dermott he asked, "Why are you agin epileptics?"

"I've got nothing against them personally. I even like Bill. He's a quiet, hard-working lad, but Lindy Lou is my only daughter," he said, reddening. "I want grandchildren and—Look here, Jim, how'd you feel? I mean would you have let your girl marry an epileptic?"

Jim poked his pipe some before replying. "She did," he said with a twinkle in his eye.

"You mean—"

"That's right," Rocky said.

"For Pete's sake!"

Just then Jim's daughter Mary brought in handsome little Harold, hers and Rocky's 2 year old boy, for a good-night kiss from gramps.

"And the boy," Mr. Dermott inquired nervously, "is he—"

"Right as rain," Jim replied.

Mr. Dermott bust out in a big smile. "I want to invite you all to a wedding," he laughed. "I've just had a change of heart."

THE END

6

"You see," Virgil said, "it was a blessing in disguise. I'm glad you're not angry though. I mean, well, remember I said you'd be remembered as the Branch Rickey like of the Health Handicappers? Well, what if Jackie Robinson had turned out to be a two hundred hitter? That's what I turned out to be, you know. A prize flop. But if not for the accident there'd be no *Crusader*. It might have taken me years and years to get going. See my point."

"Sure, Virgie. Sure thing."

There was a kind of flask attachment under the mattress of Virgil's bed and it was gradually filling with urine.

"You know what," Virgil said. "You get a life's subscription and a monthly 'Dial MOVIES' ad free. How's that?"

"Oh, fine. Fine, Virgie."

Yvette sat in a chair by the window. "How are things at the office?"

"Oh, *comme-ci, comme-ça*."

"Not that I care," she said, "but how's the new girl making out?"

"Can't complain."

"I hope she can add and has a better handwriting than I had."

"Jeez."

"The *Crusader* doesn't look like much yet," Virgil said. "But it's a start."

"It looks just swell to me, Virgie."

"We've got eighty-five subscriptions all paid up. In a year maybe, I'll be able to have it printed."

"I sure hope so. Yvette?"

"Yes?"

"Well, why don't you say anything?"

She didn't answer.

"Are you all right?"

"That's a new dress she's wearing," Virgil said. "She made it herself."

"It's very elegant," Duddy said stiffly. "Stylish."

Yvette got up and left the room.

"Shit," Duddy said, "I'm always putting my foot in it."

"Why didn't you bring some flowers?"

"Aw."

"It's so good to see you. You're my buddy."

Ver gerharget, Duddy thought. "Listen," he asked, lowering his voice, "what does she do at night?"

"What do you mean?"

"You know."

"I don't understand."

"What's there to understand? It's a simple question."

"Well, she goes out for walks . . ."

"Alone?"

"With her brother sometimes."

"The little Hitler one?"

"Jean-Paul."

"That's the one. What else?"

"She goes to the movies."

"Has she ever been out all night? Quick, she's coming back."

Yvette came in. "Would you boys like some coffee?" she asked.

Duddy looked at his watch. "Well," he said, looking hopefully at Yvette, "I guess I'd better be moving along . . ."

"Aw, stay some more."

"I'd like to, Virgie, but it's getting on dinnertime and . . . well . . ."

"Isn't he staying for dinner, Yvette?"

"If he wants to."

After dinner Duddy and Yvette sat together on the porch steps.

"He looks well," Duddy said.

"He's been through a hard time." She explained how after such an accident the focal point of the body's balance alters. Virgil had suffered severe headaches and dizzy spells. "But starting next week he'll be able to spend all his afternoons in the wheelchair."

"Isn't that something?" Duddy said.

Yvette sighed.

"You must be proud. I think you've worked miracles with him."

"Please." There was an edge to Yvette's voice.

"Well, *I'm* proud of you, that's all."

Yvette rose abruptly.

"What have I done now?" Duddy asked.

"You look awful."

"Thanks. It's getting late, you know."

"A bag of bones."

"That's me."

"What's happened to your car? How come you drove up here in the taxi?"

"My car's in the garage."

"You've stopped showing movies at the hotels. This is the best part of the season. Why?"

"I was spreading myself too thin. There are more lucrat—"

"Is that why your ads have stopped too?"

"Listen," Duddy said, getting up, "how would you like to kiss my ass?"

"Is business that bad?"

"I've gone into bankruptcy. I hope that makes you happy."

"Oh, Duddy, I'm sorry. Really I—"

"Stop being so sorry. I didn't die. There's not a businessman in town who hasn't at least one bankruptcy in his pocket I've got plans, you know."

"Like what?"

"There are possibilities. Never mind. It's getting late, you know."

"Are you driving the taxi again?"

"For two cents I'd wring your neck. One cent."

"Have you missed me?"

"What do you care? You're having a pretty good time here."

"Oh."

"I hear things, you know."

"Is that so?"

Duddy shrugged.

"I asked you a question. Have you missed me?"

"What's the diff, eh?"

"I missed you."

"Oh, here come the waterworks. Boy. It's late, you know."

"I missed you so much."

"This is an age of scientific wonders. You miss somebody so you pick up the phone to say hello. Three minutes for sixty-five cents. Nobody goes broke."

Yvette laughed.

"It's getting late," Duddy said.

"You've said that three times already."

"Have I?"

"Why don't you just come out with it and ask me if you can stay?"

Duddy drove to Montreal the next morning, picked up his stuff, and returned to Ste. Agathe by bus the same evening Yvette met him at the station. "Hey," he said, "did you see the paper? They raided Dingleman's joint For real, though There's going to be a trial."

The house Yvette had rented for Virgil and herself was near the tracks, some distance from the lake. But there was a fine back yard and Duddy used to take out a blanket and lie in the sun there. Yvette had a good job, she was a lawyer's private secretary, and every day at five-thirty Duddy would wheel Virgil out to meet her. Duddy was thin and, it seemed to her nervously spent. But in a week's time he was tanned, he had stopped biting his nails and he ate with appetite again H was gradually losing his fear of Virgil too. At first Duddy had treated him cautiously, stiffly, like a bachelor with a newborn baby, but now he was beginning to joke with him. He no longer stared morosely at the urinal attached to the bed. Neither did Duddy moan or twitch in his sleep any more. But he avoided the lakeshore, the hotels or, indeed, any place where he might run into old friends or business associates. She knew that he had the map of Lac St. Pierre locked in his suitcase and that occasionally he took it out to study, but he would not discuss it. Neither would he go swimming there with her. She had, at first, been pleased when he slept late every morning; he needed the rest. But when she discovered that he was sleeping until noon and taking a nap before dinner she began to worry. She tried to joke about it. But he misunderstood. He snapped at her. "O.K.," he said, "so you're the breadwinner. You work hard."

That made it awkward to ask him about his plans for the future. He was evasive. He'd say no more than, "I've got plans. I'm just letting them jell, that's all."

But what he thought was, Maybe I can just stay here, maybe everyone will forget me. He enjoyed it most when it rained and he could sit on the screened porch playing Scrabble with Virgil or, still better, just staring glumly. Then one afternoon when he was going through his papers he stumbled on Uncle Benjy's letter. This time he read it.

The date doesn't matter

DEAR DUDDEL,

I've lived fifty-four years and lots of terrible things have happened to me, but I didn't want to die. That's the kind of malarky you can hear on the radio any Sunday morning. But I didn't want to die and I'd like you to know that.

I wish there were some advice, even one lousy little pearl of wisdom, that I could hand down to you, but— It's not for lack of trying, Duddel. I have notebooks full of my clever sayings: don't worry.

Experience doesn't teach: it deforms.

Some Oscar Wilde I would have made, eh? Anyway, I've burnt the notebooks. I have no advice for you.

Wear rubbers in winter and don't go bareheaded in the sun. It's a good idea to brush your teeth twice a day. That, Duddel, is the sum of my knowledge, so this letter isn't to teach you how to live. It's a warning, Duddel. You're the head of the Kravitz family now whether you like it or not. It took me by surprise, you know. I thought it would be Lennie. He was the bright one, I thought. O.K. I was wrong. Your *zeyda*, bless him, was too proud and I was too impatient. I hope you'll make less mistakes than we did. There's your father and Lennie and Ida and soon, I hope, there will be more. You've got to love them, Duddel. You've got to take them to your heart no matter what. They're the family, remember, and to see only their faults (like I did) is to look at them like a stranger.

You lousy, intelligent people, that's what you said to me, and I haven't forgotten. I wasn't good to you, it's true. I never took time. I think I didn't like you because you're a throwback, Duddel. I'd look at you and remember my own days as a hungry salesman in the mountains and how I struggled for my first little factory. I'd look at you and see a busy, conniving little Yid, and I was wrong because there was more, much more. But there's something you ought to know about me. Every year of my life I have looked back on the man I was the year before—the things I did and said—and I was ashamed. All my life I've ridiculed others, it's true, but I was the most ridiculous figure of all, wasn't I?

NOTE: Before you go any further you might as well know that I haven't left you a cent. Not a bean. The estate will be administered by Rosenblatt and there's money for Ida, a regular income, and enough to set Lennie up in practice. I've also left something for student scholarships (I haven't got a son, and my name has to live on somehow). What I have left you is my house on Mount Royal with the library and everything else in it. But that bequest is conditional, Duddel. You are not allowed to sell it. If you don't want to live in it with your family when you have one then it reverts to the estate and Rosenblatt will sell it.

Anyway, now that you know where you stand with the inheritance you can read on or not read on, just as you please.

There's more to you than mere money-lust, Duddy, but I'm afraid for you. You're two people, that's why. The scheming little bastard I saw so easily and the fine, intelligent boy underneath that your grandfather, bless him, saw. But you're coming of age soon and you'll have to choose. A boy can be two, three, four potential people, but a man is only one. He murders the others.

There's a brute inside you, Duddel—a regular behemoth—and this being such a hard world it would be the easiest thing for you to let it overpower you. Don't, Duddel. Be a gentleman. A *mensh.*

Take care and God bless,

UNCLE BENJY

PS. I built the house on Mount Royal for my son and his sons. That was the original intention.

Duddy folded up the letter, replaced it in the envelope, and locked it in his suitcase.

"Hey," Virgil said, "where are you going?"

"Out."

"It'll soon be time to pick up Yvette."

"Tell her I might be late for dinner."

The lake, as he suspected, looked splendid even in autumn. Some of the trees were going yellow, others burned a brilliant red. Duddy crouched by the shore. He searched for flat pebbles and made them bounce two-three times across the water before they sunk. It's mine, he thought. This is my land and my water, and he looked around hoping for an interloper so that he could say, "I'm sorry, there's no trespassing allowed here." But all he could find were footprints, reasonably fresh, a man's and woman's. The man had used a cane. Maybe two canes. The cane or crunch points dug deep near the water.

Duddy walked the length of the land he owned, tapping a tree here, picking up a piece of paper there. Lying on the grass, he chewed on a weed and considered the topmost pine trees in the surrounding hills. The frogs began to croak. I could have salted the lake with trout, he thought. That would have been a fine attraction. He entered the cool damp woods and climbed to the top of the highest hill overlooking the lake and that land was his too. A natural ski run, he thought. Around and around he could see all the land he owned and the rest, a third maybe, that was still in other hands. Beyond the woods he could make out the highway and Ste. Agathe. Wheat, potatoes and barley were being grown on some of the fields between and here and there wretched, skinny cows wandered, but already ranch-style houses were encroaching on the countryside, drawing nearer. I was right, he thought. I knew what I was doing. Five years from now this land will be worth a fortune.

There could have been a real snazzy hotel and a camp, the finest ski tow money could buy, canoes, cottages, dancing on the lake, bonfires, a movie, a skating rink, fireworks on Israeli

Independence Day, a synagogue, a Western-style saloon, and people saying, "Good morning, sir," adding in a whisper after he'd passed, "That was Kravitz. He built the whole shebang. They used to say he was a dreamer and he'd never make it.'

There could have been his father, sitting on the porch and sucking sugar cubes maybe. "My boy was broke," he'd say. "He hadn't made his name yet. He was just another kid at the time and he got this job as a waiter at Rubin's. But he wasn't going to be a waiter for long, you bet. All the while he's serving those *chazers* ideas are ticking over like bombs in his head. Ticktock, ticktock . . . He sets up a roulette game, can you imagine? There he is not even eighteen yet, a St. Urbain Street punk, and he takes on all the B.T.O.'s at the hotel in a roulette game. On this side Fort Knox, so to speak, and on the other my kid, the house. And what does he say, 'The sky's the limit, gentlemen,' and he doesn't blink an eyelash. The money goes down one-two-three on the table, fives and tens and twenties, and the wheel begins to spin. Round and round she goes where she stops nobody knows. It's up to fate. Kismet, as they say. Outside, the stars don't care. They shine on and on. Midnight, the monkey-business hour. Bears prowl the woods, a wolf howls for its mate. Somewhere a wee babe is screaming for its mommy . . . The waiters and office girls are banging away for dear life on the beach: nature. *Plunk!* The wheel stops. *Zero.* My kid rakes the table clean . . ."

There could have been his grandfather on the farm and everybody saying how Duddy was the easiest touch in town, allowing ten St. Urbain Street boys into the camp free each season, helping out Rubin with his mortgage after the fire there, paying a head-shrinker fortunes to make a man out of Irwin Shubert, his enemy of old ("Throwing good money after bad," people said), building a special house for the epileptic who had been hurt working for him in those bygone days of his struggles, and giving so many benefit nights for worthy causes. They would have said that he was cultured too. "A patron of Hersh in the early days. The great man's best friend."

Duddy started back through the woods as the sun began to sink and he stopped twice to rest and reflect on the long walk home. Yvette was waiting for him on the porch steps.

"Are you all right?" she asked.

"I went for a walk."

"You've been crying."

"Don't be crazy. Where's our fighting editor?"

"Duddy! Asleep. Listen, I've got some news for you."

252

"Bad?"

"The notary phoned me at the office. The rest of the land as gone up for sale. There are two different owners and—"

"I'm not interested. Save your breath."

"*What?*"

"Where could I raise any money now?"

"You'd need forty-five hundred dollars."

"You might as well say a million. You mean for forty-five undred I could have complete control?"

"Yes. But—well, other people are beginning to show an iterest. Everybody's beginning to buy land around here. The otary says there's a boom. Since the Korean War he says—"

"I'm not interested. No more."

"If you really mean that I'm glad. You almost killed your-elf running after that land, Duddy. And how would you have ver raised the money to develop it?"

"Sure."

"We don't need to be rich."

"Let's not rub it in, please."

"We can do anything you want."

"I own a house," he said. "A big one." He told her about ncle Benjy's letter. " I think we should move in next week, efore the winter. It's time I got started again."

"What are you going to do?"

"I'm going to be a gentleman. Ha, ha, ha."

"What?"

"How do I know what I'm going to do? We'll make out."

"I've got faith in you. I'm worried."

"Good for you."

"But I don't want you to start running again. I couldn't and it."

"Maybe Virgie will give me a job as a reporter?"

"Are you depressed?"

"Smiling Jack, that's me. Laugh-a-minute Kravitz from way ack."

"What's wrong?"

"Forty-five hundred bucks. How soon?"

"I thought you said—"

"Look doll, with my name I'd be lucky if I could raise five. m just asking. You can't shoot a man for being curious."

"Three weeks. Duddy, if you start running again I'll leave u. You'll ruin your health."

"Running doesn't give you cancer."

"What?"

"Skip it. I'm going for a walk."

"Again?"

"Come with me. I'll buy you a smoked meat."

It was the first time he had taken her near the lakeshore where the Outremont people, and tourists from the States strolled arm in arm.

"The house will be a big help," she said, taking his arm. "There'll be no rent to pay. There's no point in killing your self, is there?"

"I'm not exactly the kind of shmo who opens a candy store you know. A paper route I'm not looking for."

"There are lots of things you could do."

"I could be a fireman."

Yvette kissed him on the cheek. "If you want to," she said.

"I'm thinking of going to night school."

"Oh, that would be wonderful. I can get work as a private secretary and—"

"—and *The Crusader* brings in about eighty-two cents month. Listen, my little *katchka,* I'm not going to live off you any more."

"Duddy, you have to take it easy for a while. A little while anyway. Do you realize that you had a nervous breakdown?"

"Don't be ridiculous."

"I'm just repeating what the doctor told me."

"That's crazy. I didn't have a breakdown."

"You had a nervous collapse. What do you want to study?"

"Things."

"Like what?"

"I came so close too. Forty-five hundred fish." They entered the restaurant together. "One minute, I want to get paper." There had been a rush on the *Gazette* and there was only one copy left. Duddy took a look at the headline and whistled.

DINGLEMAN LINKED WITH DOPE SMUGGLING
Cote Alleges New York Tie-up

He was out on bail, the bastard.

"Oh boy," Duddy said. "Jeez."

"What is it?"

"Shettup. I'm reading."

Cote had charged that Dingleman was connected with an international smuggling organization with an Italian tie-up. He was vague about proof, however. He wanted permission to bring in some American witnesses and to use testimony that had come up during Senator Kefauver's investigations he United States. Dingleman, questioned at his apartment, ad denied everything. The only comment he'd make on his requent trips to New York was that they were "of a highly ersonal nature." He had, it seemed, been removed from the Montreal—New York train twice, but nothing had been found n his luggage. The rest of the story was a recapitulation of he gambling house and police bribery charges.

"Zowie!"

"Duddy, what is it?"

"I've got to make a phone call. I'll be right back."

Luckily, Lennie was home. "Listen," Duddy said, "is heroin vhite and does it smell like cinnamon?"

"Yes, but—"

"That's all, brother. I'll see you tomorrow morning. One ninute. Could you make a lab test on some stuff for me and ell me for sure if it was heroin?"

"Duddy, you're not taking drugs?"

"Once a day and twice on Sunday. Don't—"

"Don't worry, Duddy. It's tough, but cures are possible. here are new techniques. I—"

"Don't be a jerk all your life. I'm no addict. Are you going o be in tomorrow morning?"

"Yes, but—"

"Good. Wait for me. And not a word about this to Daddy. Understand?"

"You're a dope-runner. Duddy, I'm warning—"

"The chief rabbi of the underworld, that's me. See you to-norrow. Good-by, Lefty."

He came running out of the phone booth, rubbing his hands ogether and grinning. "I'll bet the last train has gone," he aid.

"What?"

"I've got to get to Montreal tonight. Kid Kravitz rides again. oy!"

"Duddy, what's going on?"

"Aw, there's a bus at six in the morning. I'll take that. Lis-en, my little *chazer*-eater, tell the notary we're going to buy. ell him not to advertise the land or even mention it out ud. I'll have the forty-five hundred in no time. Jeez, am I ver hungry."

"Will you please tell me—"

"My luck's changed, that's all. Give me that paper again."

Four

"O.K.," Duddy said, "I'm here."

Dingleman smiled. He wiped his neck with a handkerchief. "Obviously you're here," he said.

"You know why I'm here?"

"Certainly. You read I was in trouble and you owe me five hundred dollars."

"Oh, a big joke. A *very* big joke."

"You mean that's. not why you're here?"

"No such luck. I'm here about New York."

"Aha."

"I need some money."

"Yes?"

"A loan."

"I see." Dingleman burst out laughing. He slapped his desk. "Aren't you afraid that a gangster with my reputation might take you for a ride?"

"Listen, Jerry, one thing let's get straight from the start. I'm tired of people making fun of me. That includes you. O.K.?"

"O.K."

"I need forty-five hundred dollars."

"Really?"

"Yeah."

"Do you really think I'm going to give you forty-five hundred dollars? *Loan you*, that is?"

"I opened the suitcase in the toilet. I took some of the heroin out. I've still got it."

"You're sweating. Are you frightened, Duddy?"

"This isn't blackmail. I'll pay you back. Honest, I will."

"What if I told you I didn't have that much money?"

"The world is flat. Somebody once tried to tell me that too."

"When the trial begins next Wednesday the lawyers will be costing me fifteen hundred dollars a day."

"I feel for you. How much do your night clubs bring in a week?"

"The night clubs are finished. They cost me money these days. I'm selling out all over before television really gets going here."

"Oh, yeah."

"What I'm really interested in these days is real estate. Take my advice, Duddy. Buy land."

"What do you mean by that? Why should I buy land?" Duddy shouted. "Go ahead. Tell me."

"What's wrong with you?"

"Look, let's not quarrel. I'll sign a note for the money. I'll pay you back at the rate of a hundred bucks a month."

"I haven't got that much cash to spare."

"Would you sign for me at the bank if they'd give it to me?"

"I'm not exactly what you call a good credit reference. Besides, any securities I own are tied up in bail money. Sorry Duddy." Dingleman looked at his watch. "Come around again some time."

"You must think I'm kidding. I could go to Cote. If I testified at the trial—"

But Dingleman began to laugh again.

"What's the big joke?" Duddy asked.

"You carried the suitcase across the border, sonny, not me. They took me off the train, remember? I was stripped. They searched me from top to bottom. I mean that literally."

"I didn't know what was in the suitcase."

"Duddy," Dingleman said reproachfully, "I don't pay three lawyers fifteen hundred dollars a day to let that kind of story stand up."

"It's the truth but."

Dingleman didn't reply.

"It *is* the truth."

"You must need that money very badly."

"Oh, I'm the dirty guy, eh? I'm the squealer. What do you call a guy who gets an innocent minor to smuggle dope across the border for him?"

"You got five hundred and fifty dollars for it."

"I thought the five was a loan."

"If I had given it to you just like that you would have suspected something. I never expected to get the money back."

"Please lend me the money. I'll pay it back. I promise."

"What do you need it for?"

"Some land."

"Where?"

"In Southern Siberia. What's your business? I'm sorry. can't tell you."

"Am I being asked to invest or—"

"You're definitely not being asked to invest."

Dingleman looked at his watch again. "I'm late," he said. "Aren't you worried I might go to Cote?"

"Go ahead."

Duddy hesitated. "I'm not scared. Give me the money or I go to Cote."

"You're beginning to sweat again. Look at you."

"You really think they wouldn't believe me?"

"Duddy, you sold some pinball machines up north. I saw one of them at Rubin's this summer. How'd you get them into Canada?"

"I imported them."

"Not in somebody else's suitcase, I hope."

"Jeez, I've got to get that money somewhere."

"I wish I could help."

Duddy walked to the door. "I hope they put you away for life," he said.

"Maybe they will. Good-by now."

"How'd you find out about the pinball machines?"

"Good-by, Duddy."

"Boy, when I was a kid I used to think you were some guy. My father used to—What a dirty son of a bitch you are!"

"Mickey!"

"O.K. I'm going. I'm going."

"One minute."

"I thought you were in such a goddam hurry?"

"I'm interested in real estate. I wasn't kidding about that. If you're broke and have something you want to part with, or if you know of anything that might—"

"Hanging's too good for you," Duddy said, slamming the door.

He knows, Duddy thought. He found out. Oh, Christ. Duddy began to bite his fingernails, he ordered another cup of coffee. Dingleman had said he'd seen the pinball machine at Rubin's. Twice at least in the last six months Duddy had seen him with Linda. Oh, the dirty dogs. Those odd marks on the lakeshore. Canes my ass—crutches had made them. Choke to death on razor blades, Dingleman. Let them bury you on a Wednesday night with an onion in your stomach. Now I'm in for it, he thought. Jeez. Duddy hurried home and phoned Yvette.

"I've been trying to get you all day," Yvette said. "Have you got the money?"

"Not yet. Christ almighty."

"Somebody else is after the land. A Mr. Dingleman."

261

Duddy sighed. "What do you mean after it? He's got the money. Why doesn't he just buy it?"

"You know Dingleman?"

"It's Jerry Dingleman. The Boy Wonder."

"Didn't you go to New York with him once?"

"Listen, this is long distance. Why doesn't he just buy?"

"Because our notary found out about the land going up for sale first. He put in a first offer and he's got an acceptance on paper. There's something else . . ."

"Wha'?"

"It's not important. Skip it."

"Oh, come on. What else?"

"One of the farmers . . . well, he hates Jews. He'd prefer to sell to me."

"God bless him. Listen you get a hold of that farmer and tell him Dingleman is the biggest, fattest, dirtiest, goddam Jew who ever lived. If he gets hold of that land he's going to build a synagogue on it. You tell him that."

"Are you coming back tonight?"

"No. Not tonight."

"Dingleman's offering more money than we are. Our option's only good for twenty-one days."

"I'll get the money. Don't worry."

"There's something else. According to the agreement I signed we have to put up three hundred dollars option money tomorrow morning. Have you got it?"

"Oh, shit."

"All right. I'll get it here."

"Can you?"

"Yes."

"Listen, tomorrow I'm going to see about the house. Maybe you and Virgie can move in by the weekend."

Duddy went to see Mr. Cohen at his office He'd only just sat down when he realized it was a mistake. I should have waited until tonight, he thought, and seen him at home.

"Look," Mr. Cohen said. "He's shaved. *Gottze dank.*"

"I'd like to take you up on your offer."

"He hasn't even sat down yet. What offer?"

"I'd like to borrow some money."

"I beg your pardon," Mr. Cohen said.

"You offered to lend me some."

"Stop shouting. What do you want it for?"

"I've got my eye on some land."

"Where?"

"No, sir."

262

"You mean I should trust you and you won't even tell me—"

"You said you had a soft spot for me. You said—"

"A soft spot, Duddy, but not a hole in the head. You want to come to work for me?"

"No. I want forty-five hundred dollars."

"*Azoi.*"

"I'll pay interest."

"Duddy, if you're on to something good and it's too big for you to handle tell me about it. I might be interested. But to lend money at interest—phooey."

Boil in acid, Duddy thought. I hope all your teeth fall out. All except one. And the one that's left should give you a toothache for life.

"You're still a minor. Your signature is worth *kaduchus* to me."

"You said you'd help me. That's why I'm here, Mr. Cohen."

"Don't cry, please. I told you that night that I don't offer loans every day of the week. I'm not the Marshall Plan. Unfortunately, I've had a very bad month. Believe me, Duddy, a terrible month."

"A loan until you get on your feet again. Those were your exact words."

"But forty-five hundred dollars? Some feet."

"Lend me what you can."

"Duddy, I've been speculating. Take a look out in the yard and see how high the steel is piled. It's not moving, Duddy. The bank's on my neck too. Where's the land?"

"It's a good investment. I swear."

"I'm sure it is. Tell me about it."

"I'm not looking for a partner. I want a loan. Can you lend me three thousand?"

"Listen, to change the subject for a minute. Your friend Hugh Thomas Calder has got lots of other interests nearby besides the foundry. Who gets the scrap?"

"Funny you should bring that up," Duddy said, lighting a cigarette. "Hugh and I are having dinner again tonight."

"He wants your advice on the market maybe?"

"I'll get you the rest of the scrap. But I want an advance against commission right now."

"Why don't you come to work for me? Name the salary."

"I want three thousand dollars."

"What guarantee have I got that you can get me the contract? I'll give you five hundred."

"You must have got up very late this morning. There—"

263

"I know. There are other scrap dealers in town—and they'd trust you about as far as they can throw you. Duddy, I'm going to take a gamble. I'll lend you a thousand dollars. You can give me a postdated check for eleven hundred, just in case. But if you don't get me the rest of that scrap . . ."

Duddy picked up a couple of smoked meat sandwiches, hurried back to the house on St.Urbain Street, and tried to locate Aunt Ida. Rosenblatt, the lawyer, thought she was at a hotel in Saratoga Springs. He phoned there, but she was gone. They said she and her son were at the Savoy Hotel in London. Duddy rang up London. Mrs. Kravitz and her nephew had left four days ago. They were staying at the Ruhl Hotel in Nice. He phoned the Ruhl, and Mr. and Mrs. Kravitz were registered there, but they were out. Duddy put in another call for midnight, French time.

"Auntie Ida? Hullo. *Hullo!* It's Duddy."

"Duddy, what are you doing in Nice? Come on right up here and we'll have a drink together. You *must* meet Gino. Gino, it's my nephew."

"I'm not in Nice. I'm in Montreal."

"Montreal? Then this is long distance."

"Yeah. Listen, Auntie Ida—"

"Isn't that sweet! Gino. *Gino.* It's my nephew phoning me from Montreal. Isn't that sweet? Duddy, can you hear me?"

"Yes," he said, sighing. "I can hear you."

"What's the weather like there?"

"Warmish. Listen, Auntie Ida I need—"

"We've just come from the Casino. I lost two hundred thousand francs, Duddy, isn't that just terrible? You must do me a favor. The minute you hang up I want you to call Mr. Rosenblatt to tell him I simply must have my next check right away. I haven't a penny. Wha—Excuse me a minute, Duddy." There was a pause. "Gino says he can cable it care of the American Express."

"Sure thing."

"You sound so clear. Just like you were around the corner."

"You don't say?"

"Are you sure you're not in the lobby and playing a trick on me?"

"No," Duddy said, "it's *long* distance."

"Isn't that sweet! Gino, don't you think he's sweet? Duddy, you must—"

"I think I'd better hang up, Auntie Ida. It's—"

"Quick. Give me a lucky number for tomorrow night."

"Ten. Good—"

"You'll call Rosenblatt?"

"Right away. Good-by, Auntie Ida."

"*Au revoir*. Call again sometimes."

Lennie had come in. He was sitting in the bedroom. "It's nice to have you back, Duddy," he said. "Just like old times."

"Yeah." Duddy slumped back on the bed and groaned.

"Duddy?"

"Mn?"

"Riva and I are going to be engaged."

"Isn't that sweet?"

"What?"

"It's very nice. I'm happy for you."

"You're the first person I've told. I owe you a lot, you know."

"Skip it."

"We're going to go to Israel together."

No reply.

"I wish you'd come. I think any Jew worth his salt ought to go. What is there for us here?"

"Balls all squared."

"I've given a lot of thought to what happened to me, you know. To Sandra and Andy . . . I've come to realize that they're all anti-Semites and out to use you. Every single one of them. They were never my friends. From the very first minute they were out to exploit my racial inferiority complex. They could have ruined me for life."

"It's hard to be a gentleman—a Jew, I mean—it's hard to be. Period."

"That's O.K. You have every right to tease me. Don't think I don't remember all those foolish things I said in Toronto. You're some brother, Duddy. Without you—"

"Listen, Lennie, how much did Uncle Benjy leave you?"

"It's all in trust. I don't get a penny until I graduate."

"I see."

"You need money?"

"Something terrible. And quick, too."

"I've got eighty-five dollars in the bank. It's yours."

"Come on," Duddy said, "I'll make us an omelet."

"Like old times."

Max arrived shortly after Duddy got to work in the kitchen. "Have you seen the paper?" he said. "Boy, the Wonder's lined up the sharpest battery of legal-eagles in the country. He's playing it smart too. He's got Shubert—that's the brains of the outfit, I figure—and two bigshot *goys* for display. Aw, they'll wipe the floor with Cote."

Duddy stared at his father. He won't lend me any money, he thought, but if I got Lennie to ask him for a loan, pretending he needed it himself, then maybe, just maybe—

"You know what they say about Cote closing down all the whorehouses in town? He's a sadist. He hates dames."

"I hope they put Dingleman away for life," Duddy said. "But they should burn his crutches first."

"I oughta wash your mouth out with soap. What's the matter with you these days?" Max asked. "That's what I'd like to know. You're not happy."

"Jeez."

"No. Don't turn your back on me like that. I can sense these things. Why, I haven't seen a smile cross your face ever since you moved back in here. Right, Lennie?"

Duddy forced himself to smile. It was hideous. "There," he said.

"Oi. Lennie, you're a doctor. Almost, anyway. Diagnose. What's ailing the kid here?"

"He needs some money, Daddy. He—"

"Lennie, for Christ's sake—"

"No, Duddy. Daddy ought to know. Maybe he can help."

That does it, Duddy thought. No chance of getting any money out of him any more.

"Duddy would like to borrow some money, Daddy."

"Who wouldn't?" Max reached into the kitchen drawer for his backscratcher. "Money," he said, "is the root of all evil. In olden times they used the barter system. I favor it."

Duddy grinned in spite of himself. Standing behind his father, he reached out to touch him. Gently, however, almost surreptitiously, just in case he moved away.

"For instance," Max said, "I would drive a guy from Windsor Station to . . . let's say the town of Mount Royal, and if he was, let's say, a baker he would give me six loaves of bread, or maybe three loaves and a tasty cake. You think that's so bad?"

"Will you lend him the money, Daddy?"

"How much?"

Duddy gaped. "Are you kidding?"

"*Combien?*"

"Well, I've got to raise thirty-five hundred dollars," he began, "but—"

"Whew! Water, please. My heart."

"Listen, Daddy, it's for something good. It's for land. If it works—"

"Your last brain wave ended in bankruptcy."

"This is land, Daddy. Valuable land. I already own plenty of it and in the eighteen months since I bought it its value has doubled. Daddy, it's a lake. A whole lake. It's gonna be ours— it's gonna belong to all of us—and you'll be able to retire. We'll be rich."

"What's under the lake? Oil."

"Jeez."

"Talk to him, Duddy. You mustn't get impatient."

"Yeah," Max said, "and you could smile. It wouldn't hurt you."

"All right. Let me put it this—"

"A smile, please. Just a little one."

"*There*. O.K.?"

"So, did it hurt you? What did it cost you that smile?"

"Let me put it this way, Daddy. Dingleman is fighting me for the land. He's dying to have it."

"You mean to say you're competing with the B.W.?"

"Right."

"I can smell the burning fingers. I'm sitting right here waiting for my omelet and—"

"It's coming," Lennie said.

"—and what do I smell? *Burning fingers*."

"His you smell. Not mine. Help me, Daddy. Please help me."

"You know," Max said, "I've seen plenty in my time. I have eyes and I see. Every day they come into Eddy's with sure winners, but—"

"This is not a horse, Daddy. It's land."

"—but do I ever bet? Ixnay. That's how come I've got money in the bank."

"How much?" Duddy asked, grabbing him by the arm.

"I've worked hard, you know. There's my old age to think about. If you think I'd risk my whole roll—"

"How much can you let me have?"

"He's never asked you for anything before," Lennie said. "Come on, Daddy. Be a pal."

Duddy began to bite his fingernails.

"You're ganging up on me," Max said.

"Jeez."

"You've put me in a position where if I don't lend you any money I'm suddenly an s.o.b. Who put you through school?

Do you know that when you had the mumps I stayed up with you three nights running? (At a great personal risk, brother, because I never had them, and you know about what the mumps can do to a grown man, I suppose?) I missed Lux Theater and the last game of the Little World Series when you had the chickenpox. Some fathers, you know—"

"I give up," Duddy said.

"He never told you the whole story, Daddy. He came to get me in Toronto. If not for Duddy I would have been expelled from medical school."

"Aw."

"One minute," Max said, "I'm not paying Duddy a reward for helping you. He did that because you're his brother. Not for money. We're one family and we should stick together, just like the Rockefellers. In our own small way, I mean."

"All right. You said it. Help him then."

"He won't help me. Not in a million years. He's pulling my leg."

"Would you help a boy who talked to his old man like that?"

"Wow!"

"If I was John D. Rockefeller would he talk to me like that?"

"He's nervous, Daddy. He's excited."

"I was just on the verge of offering him—"

"I'm going out for a walk before I go nuts," Duddy said.

"Wait," Lennie said. He took a deep breath. "Daddy, how much can you lend him?"

"A thousand dollars."

Duddy stopped. "Are you kidding?" he asked.

"I'm not kidding but, frankly speaking, I feel I've just kissed a grand good-by."

"You see, Duddy, I told you he'd help you."

"I can see it," Max said, "right before my eyes. A bill with one thousand printed on it. It has wings this bill and it's flying away from me. Flap, flap, flap go the wings. Wham! There she goes through the ceiling. Good-by grand."

Duddy began to scratch his head.

"It'll be interesting to see what happens," Max said, "When I come to you for help in my declining years. Well, couldn't you give us a smile? It's cost me enough."

Duddy sent Yvette a certified check and told her not to worry, he'd raise the rest of the money in time. Meanwhile he urged her to quit her job and come into town with Virgil. But twenty-two hundred dollars, he thought, where am I going to get it? The bank, of course, was out of the question after he'd already gone bankrupt once. He went to see Rosenblatt, picked up the keys and the deed to the house on Mount Royal, and hurried over to see his lawyer.

"I'm sorry," the lawyer said, "but it's airtight. You can't sell, you can't take out a mortgage, and you can't even rent."

"Some gentleman. Some son of a bitch. Listen, what about the stuff inside the house? The furniture, the books—He's got a fortune in liquor stashed away in the basement."

"I don't advise it. You'd never get even a third of what it was worth."

But when Yvette arrived with Virgil the following afternoon there was an enormous moving van parked outside and the men were busy inside.

"What on earth's going on here?" she asked.

"Aw, I'm getting rid of some of the old furniture."

"Duddy, those are antiques. What are—They're not taking the books too? You haven't sold your uncle's library?"

"Quack-quack-quack. Can't you keep your face shut once in a blue moon?"

"Duddy, you can't do this. You've got to stop them. Your uncle left you this house as a trust."

"My uncle's dead. I've got to go on living. When I've got the money we'll furnish the house according to our own tastes."

"Oh, Duddy, this is terrible."

"Terrible? It's robbery. Seven hundred and fifty bucks I got for the works."

"You ought to be ashamed of yourself."

"Listen, my little *katchka*, I'm not a British lord and this isn't the old ancestral home. Lots of that furniture was stinky and uncomfortable anyway."

"If your uncle knew . . ."

"Awright, he's spinning in his grave. If he'd set it up so that I could take out a mortgage on this place everything would be fine. I wouldn't have had to sell the furniture to a robber and I wouldn't be in such a spot either. Under normal circumstances I could raise at least ten thousand on a first mortgage on this house."

"There's not a decent sentiment in your body."

"I eat babies too, you know. Come around tomorrow morning at eight and you'll see. Listen, do you mind sleeping on a mattress on the floor? It's only for a couple of weeks."

"Couldn't you sell the mattress?"

"Where's Virgie?"

"In the taxi. Is there a bed for him at least?"

"Oh, you're smart. You're so smart."

Duddy couldn't sleep that night. Long after Yvette had scrubbed the floors and done her best to make a huge empty house seem hospitable, even as she slept exhausted on the mattress beside him, he scratched his head, bit his fingernails, and lit one cigarette after another. Fifteen hundred dollars, he thought, it might as well be fifteen thousand. Blood, he heard, sold for twenty-five dollars a quart. McGill paid something like ninety-eight cents for a man's body. Was there anything valuable he could steal? His stamp collection, that ought to be worth fifty dollars. Jeez, he thought, if one thousand people would lent me two dollars each or two thousand people one dollar each . . . This is crazy, he thought. It's not that much money, speaking objectively. I can raise it.

When Yvette rose at seven Duddy was in the kitchen, preparing an enormous omelet. He was singing. "I'm going to call Hugh Thomas Calder," he said.

"Don't count on anything."

"He likes me. He takes a fatherly interest."

"Just don't count on anything."

"What's fifteen hundred dollars to him? Beer money."

"Are you going to eat all those eggs?"

"They're for the three of us. Hey, we could rent rooms here. There's nothing in the will that says I can't have friends staying with me."

"What would your tenants do for furniture?"

"Sometimes I wonder what I'd do without you. Really, you know. You're wrong about Calder. I'm his pal. Maybe I ought to ask him for more than fifteen hundred. A round figure, you know. Not too little, either. Those guys are never impressed if all you need is pin money. You've got to use psychology."

Yvette went to wake Virgil.

"Well there, Mr. Roseboro, how do you like your new abode?" Duddy asked.

"He's in a good mood," Virgil said.

"Yes," Yvette said. "Take care."

"I'll ask him for five thousand," Duddy said. "Excuse me." And he went to phone.

"Does Duddy need more money?" Virgil asked.

"Don't you say a word," Yvette said.

"But—"

"You heard me, Virgil."

"That son of a bitch," Duddy said, re-entering the room

"that king among anti-Semites, I'll see him strung from a lamppost yet."

"What happened?"

"Coffee, please," Duddy shouted.

"You were in such a good mood," Virgil said, grinning.

"You know, Virgil, sometimes you just give me one long pain in the—"

"Duddy!"

"Coffee, please."

"All right. Here you are. Now what did he say?"

"If I have to make it my life's work I'm going to see that Calder *dreck* busted. Anti-Semitism's gone out of style. He doesn't know that yet but. I'm going to spread the word around about him. Hitler, that's what he is. Worse, maybe."

"What did he say, Duddy?"

"He won't lend me the money. He had hoped we were friends. What in the hell's a friend for it you can't borrow money from him when you need it? He—he's hurt. Can you imagine? I've hurt the bastard's feelings. Oh, those white men. He ought to swallow a golf ball, that's what. The core of the ball should be stuffed with cancers and it should take years melting in his stomach," he said, getting up.

"Aren't you going to drink your coffee?"

"Aw, stuff it. I'm going out for a walk."

Duddy walked down to Park Avenue with his head lowered and his hands stuffed belligerently into his pockets. Guys rob banks every day, he thought, they rake in fortunes on the ponies, and me? Aw. Maybe, he thought, I should try Dingleman again? But he decided there was no point. A rich wife, he thought, that's what I need, but that kind of a deal takes time. You just can't find and pursue and bleed one in a week. All that work, he thought, so much struggle, heartache, nights without sleep, scheming, lying, sweats, fevers, and for what? *Bubkas.* I'm a failure. All I needed was to be born rich. All I needed was money in the crib and I would have grown up such a fine, lovable guy. A kidder. A regular prince among men. God damn it to hell, he thought, why was I born the son of a dope? Why couldn't my old man have been Hugh Thomas Calder or Rubin, even? What's fifteen hundred bucks anyway? A piss in the ocean, that's what. But I haven't got it.

Duddy thought of forging Mr. Cohen's signature on a check, depositing it to his own account, and writing another check against it, but dismissed the idea as unsound. There was a black market in babies, he'd read that in *Time*, but it was just his luck not even to have one of those. Maybe, he thought,

271

if I got a passport, mailed it to Hersh, and asked him to sell it for me in Paris . . . He'd never do it. (There's not enough time, either.) The stock market, he thought, guys with no brains are shoveling it in like snow, but you've got to have a stake to start with. Suicide? Boy, would they ever be sorry to see me go. Virgil would—*Virgil!*

Wow, he thought suddenly, smacking the side of his face, why didn't I ever think of that before?"

"Jesus Christ almighty!"

Yvette was waxing the dining room floor when Duddy returned from his walk. He came with a bouquet of flowers for her, a book of poems for Virgil, and a bottle of whisky.

"You got the money?" she said.

"No."

"You're sick?"

"Wrong again."

Duddy waited restlessly, answering questions with curt nods, until Yvette went out to do the shopping. Then, turning his most expansive smile on Virgil, he asked, "Join me in a drink, kid?"

"A small one."

"You know something, Virgie, the two of us just don't sit around and chew the fat enough any more. We don't know each other as well as we could."

Virgil ducked his head. He grinned.

"Once," Duddy began, "when we had the apartment on Tupper Street, I interrupted you while you were writing a letter to your father."

"That's right. I remember."

"Now you're obviously one of my most treasured friends, but—"

"Gee whiz, Duddy."

"—but what do I know about your father? Nothing. Maybe—"

"I'll tell you all about him," Virgil began enthusiastically. "My father's name is John. He was born on January 18, 1901. He's five foot ten with graying hair and lovely blue eyes and—"

"*Maybe* . . . I mean for all I know he's . . ." Duddy hesitated. He jumped up and began to chew his nails again. ". . . well, a man of means, as they say."

Virgil looked grave.

"Virgie?"

He averted his eyes.

"I'm talking to you, Virgie."

"Well, he's not exactly broke."

"Here, old chap, let me refresh your drink."

"No thanks. I think I've had enough."

"Aw, Gwan." Duddy poured him a stiff one. "Cheers."

Virgil hesitated.

"Cheers, Virgie."

"Cheers."

"You know, Virgie, we're buddies. Real buddies. Isn't that ue?"

"Sure, Duddy."

"And a friend in need, as they say, is a friend indeed. ight?"

Virgil, looking somewhat bewildered, a little oppressed, said, Yvette ought to be back soon, huh?"

"Sure. How's your poetry coming along?"

"All right, I guess. No, as a matter of fact, my muse hasn't xactly been—"

"Jeez, I wish I had your talent."

"Do you mean that, Duddy?"

"Why, I'll bet E. E. Cummings would give his left ball for me of the stuff you've written. You make that Patchen look ck. Someday, boy, I'm going to be proud to have known u when."

"Would you like me to read you some of my more recent forts?" Virgil asked, and he began to wheel his chair to-ards the door.

"Later. Here, let me refresh your drink."

"But I haven't even finished this one."

"Aw. Gwan. Cheers."

"Cheers."

Duddy sat down, rose quickly, and began to pace. He acked his knuckles. "You know what I've been asking my-lf, Virgie? Where did you and Yvette get all the money to ver your hospital bills? How come Yvette was able to put r hands on three hundred bucks for the notary? Questions e that. That's what I've been asking myself."

Virgil's head began to droop.

"How much have you got, Virgie," Duddy asked, kneeling side his wheelchair, "and where did you get it?"

"I'm not supposed to say. I promised Yvette."

"Aha."

"She made me swear I wouldn't lend you one cent. She says an't afford to gamble."

"She's right too, you know," Duddy said, rising. "That

273

girl's certainly got her head screwed on right." The bitch, h
thought.

Virgil smiled, relieved.

"But I'd never dream of asking you for a loan, Virgie. I'r
only inquiring because I want to help you to invest you
money wisely. Let's say you had as much as five thousand,
Duddy said tentatively, never taking his eyes off Virgil, "o
maybe ten . . . Ten, Virgie?"

"Well, I . . ." Virgil looked away. "Yvette's taking a lon
time," he said feebly.

"Where'd you get it?"

"My grandfather left me some. Well, in his will he lef
me . . . some, you know . . ."

"No kidding?"

"You mustn't tell Yvette I told you."

"Of course I won't. But you know what, Vergie? Tha
money's rotting in the bank like a lousy old apple left in th
sun. Every day you leave it there it's worth less and less. I
depreciates. You know what the real value of the dollar is to
day? Forty-five cents. Tomorrow it'll be forty-four and nex
year, wham, forty maybe . . . A guy's got to invest his mone
and invest it wisely. Where is it, Virgie?"

"What?" he asked, lifting his head heavily.

"Where do you keep the money? In a Montreal bank."

"The Bank of Nova Scotia on Park Avenue," he said, h
voice beginning to wobble.

"You don't say?"

Virgil bit his lip. He nodded.

"Are you O.K., Virgie?" Duddy asked, kneeling beside hi
again.

Virgil nodded again. "A headache," he said.

"I'm only asking you all these questions because I want t
help. You know what, Virgie? Real estate, that's the thing. A
the wise money's going into real estate today."

It seemed to Duddy that Virgil's eyes were glassy, but h
didn't feel so hot himself, his own hands were clammy. It's n
like *I'm* enjoying this, he thought.

"I'll tell you something, Virgie," Duddy said, pouring him
self another drink, "I close my eyes and before me I see
lovely spread of land before a lake, the land is all yours, an
on it is a pretty white house and in the basement is a printin
press . . . Health Handicappers. needy ones, come an
go . . . I see you in the picture . . . Happy? *Happy*."

"I can't," Virgil screamed so sudden and loud that Dudd
started.

"Wha'?"

Virgil gripped the arms of his wheelchair. His eyes were bloodshot. "I promised Yvette. I can't."

"Virgie, what are you yelling about? You can't what?"

"Yes," Yvette said, entering the room. "You can't what, Virgil?"

"Oh, for Christ's sake. Here comes the United States Cavalry. Right on the dot too."

"What were you doing to him, Duddy?"

"Breaking his arms. Trying out the Chinese water torture. Geez."

"I can't," Virgil muttered. His head fell, bobbed between his shoulders, and he began to sob brokenly.

Yvette set down her parcels with a bang and wheeled Virgil out of the dining room. "I'll speak to you later," she said to Duddy.

Duddy poured himself a stiff drink. Speak your heart out, you lousy, *chazer*-eating Florence Nightingale, he thought. A lot I care. I'm going to get that land no matter what, see? I'm not giving up now, he thought, taking a big gulp of his drink. Duddy sat down on the mattress and began to drink even more quickly. An hour passed before Yvette returned.

"He's sleeping," Yvette said. "What did you do to upset him?"

"I bopped him one. Wham! Right on the spine."

"You're drunk."

"A big deal."

"Pour me one."

"You've got hands. Pour yourself one. I'm going out," he said. "I require some ozone."

Duddy didn't return for dinner. He stayed away for hours. He walked all the way downtown, played the pinball machines, drank some, chatted with whores in chromium-plated bars, stared into department store windows, weaving, his nose pressed against the refreshingly cold plate glass, drank some more, walked his feet sore, rested, was told to move on twice, and finally staggered into a taxi.

Yvette had waited up for him. "Did you try to get any money out of Virgil this afternoon?" she asked.

"F—— Virgil," he said. "You don't even ask how I am? Maybe—"

"How are you?" she asked.

"Drunk and sad."

"Now then, did you try to get any money out of—"

275

"You've got a voice like a knife being sharpened," he said. He began to giggle.

"*Answer me.*"

"Has he got any?"

Yvette hesitated.

"Jeez. Has he?"

"No," she said.

"Listen," he said, "you're beginning to remind me of my family. That's a fact. I'm always in the wrong. *Why?*"

Yvette's face flushed.

"W," he said, plucking one finger, "H," he said plucking another. "Y. Cue-wesh-tion mark."

"I'll help you undress," she said.

"You can look," Duddy said in a falsetto voice, "but don't touch." And in a moment he was snoring.

He was surly at breakfast and Virgil, embarrassed, did not say much either.

"What are your plans for today?" Yvette asked.

"I'm just going to hang around my house for a bit," he said, "if you and Virgil don't mind."

"We're going out for a walk," Yvette said quickly.

After they'd gone Duddy began to chain-smoke. It's their fault, he thought, they wouldn't help me, they're forcing me into it. Pushing me, he thought, and he went into Virgil's room. The checkbook wasn't even hidden. Jeez, he thought. It was on top of the dresser with the passbook. Duddy took a quick look at Virgil's bank balance, whistled, noted his account number and ripped out two checks. He forged the signature by holding the check and a letter Virgil had signed up to the window and tracing slowly. This is a breeze, he thought. But the signed check frightened him. He concealed it in his back pocket. I'll wait an hour, he thought, well, three quarters anyway, and if they show up before then I'll tear up the check. If not—Well, they shouldn't leave me alone for that long. Not in my desperate condition.

Duddy waited an hour and a half before he attempted to make the phone call. Even then he hung up three times (See, he thought) before he lit another cigarette off his butt and actually put the call through. Disguising his voice, he told the bank manager, "This is Mr. Roseboro speaking." He gave the address. "I'm sending Mr. Kravitz down to have a check certified for me, please."

Duddy hung up and waited. Just as he expected, the bank manager called back to check. "Yes," Duddy said, "Mr. Kravitz just left. Thanks a lot, sir."

Duddy's heart began to bang as soon as he entered the bank, ut nobody questioned the signature on the check, and so he ushed down to his own bank with it and deposited it there. owie, he thought. Rushing into the house, he announced, I've got the money."

"Really," Yvette said.

"Duddy can do anything," Virgil said.

"You said a mouthful, kid."

But when the phone rang Duddy started. "I'll take it," he aid swiftly. It wasn't the bank. "All right," Duddy said, we're all going out to dinner. Uncle Duddy pays."

He got them out of the house as quickly as he could. Each ime Yvette asked him where he had got the money Duddy vinked and said, "I found it under my pillow."

"He can do anything he puts his mind to," Virgil said. Duddy's going to be a tycoon."

Early the next morning Yvette left for Ste. Agathe to see he notary. Duddy met her at the station when she returned he same evening. He took her to a bar nearby. "Everything o O.K.?" he asked.

"The land's all yours now," she said.

"At last," he said. "Jeez."

"Are you happy?"

"Boy, would I ever like to see Dingleman's face now. The oy Wonder? They'll soon be calling him the One-Day Won-er. You wait." Duddy had some papers with him. He tried o produce them casually. "Oh, you'd better sign these," he aid.

Yvette looked puzzled.

"It's about the land. You sign over all the deeds to my ather. Just a formality, you know."

She hesitated.

"What'sa matter? Your feelings hurt?"

"Give me a pen," she said sharply.

"Listen, it's just a legal formality. My lawyer insisted. In ase you were in an accident like. Aw, you know."

"What if your father's in an accident?"

"Will you just sign, please?"

Yvette signed.

"Well," Duddy said. "Cheers."

But she didn't lift her glass.

"Listen, if my father's in an accident the land automatically oes to me. But if you were—"

"Let's talk about something else."

"Oh, boy. This is going to be a night. A real night."

"I'd like you to take me home, please."

All the lights were on downstairs.

"Virgil," Yvette called.

There was no answer.

"Maybe he went out dancing," Duddy said.

Yvette walked ahead into the living room. "Oh," she said, holding a hand to her cheek. "Oh, no."

Virgil lay twisted on the floor beside his overturned wheelchair. His face was thin and white and drying blood dribbled down his chin.

"He's had a fit. Duddy. Oh, Duddy."

Above him the telephone receiver dangled loosely.

"Get me some hot water, Duddy. Quick!"

But Duddy had gone. Yvette reached the window just in time to see him pass outside.

Duddy ran, he ran, he ran.

2

They took the taxi to go out to see the land, Duddy drove, his grandfather sat in front with him, and Max and Lennie sat in the back. "Like customers," Max said.

"Will we tip him, Daddy?"

"Into the lake. That's where we'll tip him."

"Wait till you see that lake, *Zeyda*. Even where the water is twenty feet deep it's so clean and clear that you can see the bottom."

"What about mermaids?" Max said. "Have you got any of those?"

"You've got to see the sun set. You've just got to see the sun set over my land."

"Did you buy the sun too?" Lennie asked.

"And *Zeyda*," Duddy said, "you just take your time and look around and pick a farm, any farm, and that's where I'll put up your private house."

But Simcha seemed preoccupied. He merely nodded.

"Wait till you see the trees I've got there."

"You're beginning to sound like a real dumb farmer," Max said. "What's so special about trees?"

"Aw, you'll love it, Daddy. It's so restful by the lake."

"Oh, sure. I know all about the country. Ants and mosquito

278

and skunks and—if you've got the appetite—bull-pies all over. You can have it, buster."

"I'll tell you something," Lennie said, "I wouldn't want a lake here if they gave it to me on a silver platter. Why develop things for them? Now Israel, that's something else. There—"

"All right, Ben-Gurion. Keep the commercials to yourself."

"Oh, it's easy to laugh," Lennie said. "I'll bet in Germany in 1930 they laughed too."

"Lennie's got a point," Max said.

"Jeez."

"I'm only joking. He said that in Germany in 1930 they laughed too. I said he's got a point. *A point*. Get it? Lennie's got a point."

Duddy groaned.

"Nobody in this family's got a sense of humor."

"You've got enough for all of us," Duddy said.

"Life should be approached with a smile. If you can't get laughs out—"

"That's enough," Simcha said.

"We're almost there." Duddy turned off on a dirt road. "A couple of more miles and then we start walking."

"Alaska, here we come," Max said.

They got out of the car and began to walk.

"Over there. Over the next hill. It's all mine. Everything."

Duddy was always ahead of them, running, walking backwards, jumping, hurrying them, leaping to reach for a tree branch.

"That field," he said, "it's mine," and he watched to see their expressions. Simcha, he noticed, remained grim.

"All you can see to the right, Lennie. Everything to the left. All mine."

Lennie smiled encouragingly. But Max seemed let down. "Just a bunch of crappy, godforsaken fields. What do you want them for?"

"Now close your eyes," Duddy said. "Close them until you reach the top of the hill . . . Keep them closed," he said, taking Simcha's hand. "Don't cheat . . . O.K. Look!"

Autumn leaves floated on the still surface of the lake.

"Injun territory," Max said.

"Christ almighty!"

"A wilderness," Max said.

"Sure," Duddy said, jumping up and down, "a goddam wilderness, and remember it, goddam it, take a good look, goddam everything to hell and heaven and kingdom come, because a whole town is going up here. A camp and a hotel

279

and cottages and stores and a synagogue—yes, *Zeyda*, a rea *shul*—and a movie and . . . well everything you can think of.'

"Dream," Max sang, "when you're feeling blue. Dream, le the smoke rings rise in the air—Hey, look over there!"

Mounting slowly and cumbersome, puffing and pausing to wipe his forehead, came a man on crutches, with a young girl

"It's the Boy Wonder," Max said. "Hey, here. Over here Jerry."

Duddy lit a cigarette and waited. "Well," he said as Dingle man approached, "aren't you in jail yet?"

"Jesus," Max said, smacking the side of his face.

"Hello, Linda," Duddy said.

Max pulled Lennie over. "This is my boy Lennie," he tol Dingleman. "He's going to be a doctor. A specialist."

"That's grand," Dingleman said. "Hullo, Duddy." He ex tended his hand, but Duddy didn't take it. "I came to con gratulate you," he said.

"Shake with him," Max said.

Duddy shook hands with him.

"There. Isn't that how sports should behave? Jerry's a goo loser," Max said.

"This is a fine property your son's got here, Max."

"Well, you know. He's a shrewd cookie. A chip off the ol block."

"Yeah," Duddy said, "and I'll tell you something funn about this land, Dingleman. No trespassing."

"It's a joke," Max said quickly. "Duddy's a kidder. Natura born."

"The sign goes up tomorrow. It reads. 'Trespassers will b prosecuted.'"

"Ah ha ha," Max said, poking Duddy.

"You're a big boy now," Linda said, "aren't you?"

"I'm not a waiter any more, if that's what you mean?"

"It's going to cost you a fortune to develop this land, Jerry said.

"So?"

"Who's the old man?" Jerry asked suddenly.

"He's not an old man, he's my grandfather. This is m property, sonny. Watch how you talk."

"You're going to need lots of money, Duddy. A fortune."

"A million," Duddy began, "maybe more. Because there going to be a children's camp and a hotel and—What's th matter, *Zeyda*, where are you going?"

"Back to the car."

"Have you picked your farm yet?"

"I don't feel well. I'm going to sit in the car."

"But you haven't chosen your farm yet. *Zeyda,* wait."

Dingleman stopped Duddy. "Let him go," he said.

Duddy watched the old man retire slowly down the slope. All his life he told me a man should have land. He said he wanted a farm. I don't . . ."

Dingleman laughed. "Maybe he never expected you to get him one?"

"Wha'?"

"Have you ever read any Yiddish poetry?"

"*Zeyda,* come back. *Zeyda!*"

But the old man continued towards the car.

"Certainly not," Dingleman continued. "But if you had you'd know about those old men. Sitting in their dark cramped ghetto corners, they wrote the most mawkish, schoolgirlish stuff about green fields and sky. Terrible poetry, but touching when you consider the circumstances under which it was written. Your grandfather doesn't want any land. He wouldn't know what to do with it."

"Will you shettup, please?"

"Duddy, don't talk like that. He's excited, Jerry. He—"

"He said a man without land was nobody."

"He never thought you'd make it," Dingleman said. "Now you've frightened him. They want to die in the same suffocating way they lived, bent over a last or a cutting table or a freezing junk yard shack."

"He can have any lot he chooses. Any one."

"Duddy, listen to me."

"He's listening, Jerry. *Listen,* Duddy."

"I'm interested in this land. I'm interested in you too. I can raise the money for development. You can't."

"Last time I saw you," Duddy said, "you couldn't even raise forty-five hundred. Remember, sonny?"

"We could be partners."

Duddy watched his grandfather getting smaller and smaller. He disappeared behind a clump of trees.

"Alone, you'll never raise the money you need. With my help we could turn this into a model resort town in five years."

Duddy began to laugh. "You heard him, Daddy. You heard the man."

"Imagine," Max said, "my boy and Dingleman. Partners."

Duddy laughed some more. "Listen, Dingleman," he shouted, "get off my land. Beat it."

"Duddy," Max began, "what's got into you?"

"Take off, sonny."

Max began to shake Duddy.

"You'll never do it alone," Dingleman said.

Duddy broke free. "I'm giving you five minutes to get the hell off my land. I'm the king of the castle here, sonny."

"He's gone crazy," Max said to Lennie.

"Duddy," Lennie said. "Why don't you listen to Mr. Dingleman? He makes sense."

Duddy picked up a stone. "I'm giving you exactly five minutes to take Linda and get the hell out of here."

Linda made as if to slap Duddy's face, but he caught her hand and held it. "I remember you," he said. "You slap me and I'll kick your ass so hard you won't sit down for a week."

Linda spit.

"It's good for my grass," Duddy said.

Dingleman turned and began the long, difficult descent. Max pursued him. "Listen he's only a kid. You talk to me, Jerry."

"You two-bit, dope-smuggling cripple!"

"Stop it," Lennie said, alarmed.

But Duddy cupped his hands and hollered. "On my land," he shouted, "no trespassers and no cripples. Except on Schnorrer's Day."

"Duddy, please."

Duddy jumped up and down, he laughed, he grabbed Lennie round the waist and forced him to dance round and round. "Don't you understand?" he asked. "Don't you realize that you're standing smack in the middle of Kravitz Town? This is a goldmine, don't you realize—He came all this way to see me for an in. *Faster, you bastard. Run, Dingleman. Let's see you run on those sticks.*"

"Take it easy, Duddy. Please try to calm down."

Duddy whirled around and heaved the stone he still held into the lake.

"Boy," Lennie said, "are you ever the manic-depressive type."

"Come on. Let's go see what's ailing the *zeyda.*"

Max caught up with his boys halfway down the hill. "You're my son, Duddy, but I'm going to be frank. You're in the wrong."

"You don't so-say," Duddy said.

"He's angry at you, Duddy, and when the Boy Wonder gets—"

"I know. He eats bread and it comes out toasted. I'm angrier but."

Simcha sat silent and severe in the front of the car.

"Why didn't you pick a farm for yourself?" Duddy asked.

"I don't want a farm here."

"Why?"

"The girl came to see me last week."

"What girl?"

"Your girl."

"I haven't got a girl."

"Yvette came to see me."

"You don't have to worry," Max said. "He's all washed up
with her. A good thing too. Mixed—"

"Will you not interrupt, please?"

"She told me what you did," Simcha said. "And I don't want
farm here."

"So you couldn't even wait to hear my side of the story? Is
that right?"

"I can see what you have planned for me, Duddel. You'll be
good to me. You'd give me everything I wanted. And that
would settle your conscience when you went out to swindle
others."

"Will you all get into the car, please?" Duddy slammed
the door. "Nobody's ever interested in my side of the story.
I'm all alone," he said, pulling savagely at the gearshift.

"The boy's fits are getting worse and worse."

"I didn't give him epilepsy."

"What's going on?" Max asked.

"Would you have rather I married a *shiksa*, Zeyda?"

"Don't twist. Not with me."

"You don't twist either. You don't want a farm. You never
have. You're scared stiff of the country and you want to die
that stinky old shoe repair shop."

Simcha took a deep breath.

"A man without land is nothing. That's what you always
told me. Well, I'm somebody. A real somebody."

"Why do we have to quarrel," Max said. "We're one family."

"You couldn't even go to see Uncle Benjy before he died.
Naw, not you. You're just too goddam proud to live. You—"

Simcha looked resolutely out of the window.

"I'm sorry," Duddy said.

"You see, Paw. He's sorry. Kiss and make up," Max said.

Eventually they reached the highway.

"I'm sorry, *Zeyda*. I . . . Please?"

But Simcha still stared out of the window. Duddy parked
front of Lou's Bagel & Lox Bar. And Simcha wouldn't get
out of the car.

283

"We won't be long," Duddy said. But inside he couldn't eat. "Here, Lennie," he said. "Take him a coffee."

"Forget it," Max said. "He gets like that. I know from long experience."

"Shettup, please."

"Time heals," Max said.

"Will you shettup, please."

Lennie returned with the coffee. "Would you believe it," he said. "He's crying. I thought I'd never live to see the day . . ."

Duddy bolted out of the store. He did not pause to look into the car, but hurried past it and around the block. He began to run. The land is yours, he thought, and nothing they do or say or feel can take it away from you. You pay a price.

Yvette wasn't at the house. Neither was Virgil. He found them in the park. Yvette saw him coming and motioned him back, behind a tree, before Virgil could see him. Then, after she'd whispered something to Virgil, she came to join him.

"Seeing you again," she said, "might be enough to bring on another fit."

Duddy swallowed, he wiped his hand through his hair, he didn't speak. He looked exasperated.

"Now tell me quickly what you want," she said. "I've got nothing to say to you."

"Maybe. Maybe that's so. But I've got plenty to say to you, sister. Why for two cents I'd wring your goddam neck. Wh did you go to my grandfather? Of all the people in the worl he's the only one—"

"That's exactly why I went."

Duddy made a fist. He shook it.

"I told him about the check. I told him everything. I wante to hurt you as badly as I could."

"Gee, thanks. Thanks a lot."

"Please go."

"Look, I did it all for us. Do you think I enjoyed forgin the check? Am I a thief?"

"I don't know what you are any more. I don't care, either.

"I had to act quickly, Yvette. I had to think for all of u What I did was . . . well, unorthodox. That's the word I' looking for. But you know, like they say, he who hesitates— Don't you understand? It's mine now. At last the land is min Yvette. All of it."

She tried to walk away. He stopped her.

"I'm going to pay him back. I swear it, Yvette."

"We don't want your money. If we wanted it we could su

ou. All we want from you is to be left alone. Can you under-
tand that?"

"He'll get every last cent of his money back whether he
kes it or not. And that's not all, either. I'm going to build
im a pretty white house. Just like I said. So help me God
will."

"We don't want to see you again, Duddy. Ever, I mean."

"Oh, where do you get this 'we' crap suddenly? We-we-we.
isten—"

"Are you finished?"

"—you listen, Yvette. You are looking at the man who is
oing to build a town where only bugs and bullshit was be-
re. I'm going to create jobs. Jeez, I'm a public benefactor.
ut you've got to have faith in me, Yvette. You've got to help.
ive me time."

"You can have all the time in the world, Duddy. But I don't
ver want to see you again."

"I don't ever want to see you again," he said, mimicking her
oice. "Quack-quack-quack. What do you think this is? Some
umb movie?"

"I'm serious, Duddy."

He gave her an anguished look, started to say something,
eld back, swallowed, shook his fist, and said, his voice filled
ith wrath, "I have to do everything alone. I can see that now.
can trust nobody."

"We betrayed you, I suppose."

"Yes. You did."

He had spoken with such quiet and certainty that she began
doubt herself.

"You'll come crawling," he said.

"I want you to know something. I'd sue you. I'd even get
win Shubert to take the case. But Virgil won't let me. He
oesn't even want to hear about it any more."

"You hate me," Duddy said. "Is that possible?"

"I think you're rotten. I wish you were dead."

"You don't understand, Yvette. Why can't I make you un-
erstand? Listen, Yvette, I—"

But she turned away from him.

"You'll come crawling," he shouted after her, "crawling on
ur hands and knees," and he walked off.

When Duddy finally returned to the store his father's back
as to him. Max sat at a table piled high with sandwiches and
rrounded by strangers. "Even as a kid," he said, sucking a
gar cube, "way back there before he had begun to make his

mark, my boy was a troublemaker. He was born on the wrong side of the tracks with a rusty spoon in his mouth, so to speak and the spark of rebellion in him. A motherless boy," he said pounding the table, "but one who thrived on adversity, lik Maxim Gorki or Eddie Cantor, if you're familiar with thei histories. You could see from the day of his birth that he wa slated for fame and fortune. A comer. Why I remember whe he was still at F.F.H.S. they had a teacher there, an anti-Semit of the anti-Semites, a lush-head, and my boy was the one wh led the fight against him and drove him out of the school. Jus a skinny little fart he was at the time, a St. Urbain Street boy and he led a fearless campaign against this bastard Mac Pherson . . ."

The strangers looked up at Duddy and smiled.

"That's him," Max said.

Duddy retreated. He raised his hands in protest.

"My brother," Lennie said. "Hey, what's wrong?"

"Nothing," Duddy said. "I'm fine."

"Can't you ever smile?" Max said, turning to the stranger with a chuckle. "Would it cost you something to give us little smile?"

"I'm not driving back with you," Duddy said gruffly. "Yo take the *Zeyda* home. I'm going by bus."

"Why?"

"Never mind why. Christ almighty. Just give me the mone for my fare. I'm flat broke."

"That's a laugh," Max said, turning to the others agai "Isn't that a laugh. He's broke."

Duddy's cheeks burned red.

"Are you O.K.?" Lennie asked. "You look sick, Duddy."

"I'm fine. Just give me the money, please."

"Aw, I know what it is. You can't hide anything from th old man. I'll bring in the *Zeyda* and you'll kiss and make up.

"In a minute," Duddy said, "I'm going to explode. I'm g ing to hit somebody so hard—"

"Easy," Lennie said.

Max smiled at the strangers. "It's been a big day for hin Red letter stuff. And you've never seen a nervier kid."

Duddy started for his father, but the waiter got in his way "Mr. Kravitz?" He smiled shyly at Duddy, holding out th bill. "Are you the Mr. Kravitz who just bought all that lan round Lac St. Pierre?"

"Yeah. Em, I haven't any cash on me. Daddy, can you . . .

"That's all right, sir. We'll mark it."